LOVE'S LAST REFRAIN

SUNSET *West*

SUZANNE CATALANO

Dedication

Skeleton in the closet: Idiom or phrase referring to an undisclosed fact that when revealed could hurt and harm others.

This book is dedicated to all those who have collected a closetful.

Contents

Part Three
Letting Go

ACKNOWLEDGEMENTS

First, I'd like to thank my editor, Sandi Wissinger, for her knowledge and skill in keeping my ideas and characters real. Dedicating her time grinding over first the developmental edit followed by line and proof-editing gives my work the credibility I want to present as an author and the quality my readers deserve.

Next, I'd like to acknowledge my children; the inspirations in the creation of the young characters in this story.

Finally, I'd like to thank 100Covers for the delightful cover design and the formatting that makes this book a piece of creativity I can truly be proud of.

PART ONE
Undisclosed Truth

CHAPTER 1

Armstrong Woods

"C'mon, Mom! We're late! I'll have to check in at the office. Mrs. Saunders will stare at me from over the top of her glasses and it gives me the creeps. She hates to correct the numbers after she's done the attendance."

A young girl stood in the doorway of a cottage behind a house on Bodega Ave in the small town of Sebastopol and yelled into the interior. With a pack on her back as big as she was, the ten-year-old stomped her foot.

"Sorry, Jesse! I'm coming!" Ainsley Tobin, a young woman of average height, in good physical shape, with a thick head of curly, reddish brown hair and deep green eyes, hustled out and the two people climbed into their Jeep.

"So, what are you going to do today?" the pixie asked her mom who was now concentrating on backing out of the long driveway past the main dwelling.

"Well, first I will play with my Barbies and when I get hungry, I'll make brownies in my easy bake oven. Then I'll have a tea party with Barbie and Ken," her mother answered sarcastically.

"I was just curious. You don't need to get smart," the child scolded.

"Sorry, Jesse," Ainsley smirked as she pushed in the clutch, gunned the engine, and switched gears when they got to the street. "Do your friends know what their mothers do all day?"

"Maybe they do, or maybe they don't care, but I do."

"I love that you care." Ainsley softened. "I plan to go for a hike. After that I'll do the grocery shopping, then it's back home for a fun-filled day of housecleaning."

"Other than the hike, I like your first plans with Barbie dolls better," Jesse teased.

"Me too, actually." Ainsley gave her daughter a warm glance and smiled.

The challenges of juggling her dual-role as mother and father to her pre teen-age daughter was one she cherished. Though her life could be hectic, she wouldn't have it any other way.

Speeding down the road, Ainsley held her hand on her head in an attempt to capture her unruly hair that was moving about in the breeze with a mind of its own. She focused her eyes on the left shoulder looking for the white sign with red and black letters that said Apple Blossom Elementary School.

"Oh, yeah," Jesse gave her mother a stern look as she gathered her backpack. "Don't forget to get dish liquid and paper towels. And we're running low on shampoo." Jesse paused, then added with an impish grin, "and can I have some of those juices that come in the little squeezy bottles?"

"We'll see," Ainsley said with maternal authority, "And thank you for the reminder." Ainsley chuckled at her daughter's way of never missing a beat. "Now go on. You're already late!"

"Have a wonderful time on your hike, Mom, and don't use your earbuds. You won't hear the rattler snakes."

Ainsley smiled as she watched Jesse hurry down the breezeway to catch up with a group of friends. The backpack made Jesse move with a wobble as she joined the herd of wobbling children. Jesse acted once again the same age as her peers which gave Ainsley a sense of relief.

Ainsley drove her car north to Armstrong Woods, an ancient stand of redwoods in reserve near the town of Guerneville, along the Russian river. It was a short drive from Sebastopol through Forestville, then along Mirabelle Road to River Road. She rounded the signature half-circle curve on the highway just before Korbel Estate's winery. Its familiar sign projected her back in time.

"We can't buy alcohol," Ainsley pleaded as her friend Patti tried to angle the old Ford Aerostar van between the lines of a spot in front of the Korbel Winery's tasting room. "We're only seventeen years old!"

"Just go in and act like you belong. You're the one who looks older! And the picture on this fake ID looks way more like you. I'll get caught if I try."

Ainsley remained in the car.

"C'mon, Ains. I thought you were my ride or die." Patti tried one more time. When Ainsley folded her arms across her chest, Patti stormed off into the brick building. After several minutes of waiting, Ainsley wondered if Patti was expecting her to follow. Five more minutes passed before Patti came running out with three uncorked bottles in her arms, one only a bit more than half full.

"What did you do?" Ainsley grabbed the sloshing bottles from her crazed friend and realized she was now an accomplice.

"I couldn't get away with buying the wine, so I took these when the bartenders weren't watching," Patti squealed and started up the van.

"Are you serious? If they catch us," Ainsley turned to look over her shoulder expecting to see someone running from the building, "They will kick us out of school."

"Stop being such a prude." Patti sped out of the Korbel parking lot. "Engine, don't fail us now!" was her battle cry.

"I may be a prude, but what you did is lame," Ainsley let out as her heart rate and the speed of the vehicle began to slow.

"Calm down, Ains." Patti glanced over at her friend. "I expected the van to blow a gasket, not you!" Then she softened. "We need this wine for tonight. I don't want to show up empty-handed. These guys are older, and I want to seem…more mature."

"And you think showing up at their party with uncorked and partially consumed bottles of wine says maturity?" Ainsley shook her head hearing herself saying something her mother would say.

"Fine then." Patti hit the steering wheel with her hand. "You can stay home tonight and miss out."

"Maybe I will," Ainsley proclaimed.

Later that night, the pebbles in Patti's hand flew into a moonless sky, making a plink-plink sound against the glass window of Ainsley's bedroom.

"I knew she'd come for me," Ainsley said to herself with a smile. Though Ainsley would just as soon have stayed home, Patti wanted her to go to the party. She needed a side-kick and Ainsley, with her fictile personality, was perfect for the role.

Ainsley's tires hit the wheel stop of the spot right by her usual trailhead, which jerked her out of the memory completely. She looked around and smiled in gratitude at the beauty of this place, her sanctuary.

The first ten minutes of the trail were steep and Ainsley concentrated on breathing as she climbed. She felt lugged down by the thoughts of whether she was a cool parent to Jesse. Or at least cooler than her own mom was to her.

As the trail opened up above the forest floor, so opened the veils of responsibility hanging over her. With so many complexities that come with being a parent, Ainsley sought this time in nature to replenish her energy.

Listening to the birds sing, enjoying the blooming wildflowers, covering the distance with a lightening of spirit, Ainsley left behind her insecurities with each step. Stopping at the edge of the meadow to observe quietly, Ainsley found comfort in how nature works. There was no judgment. Everything took its course, with no mistakes.

After an exhilarating hike to Bull Frog Pond, Ainsley climbed into her Jeep with more energy than when she had started. On the route home from the reserve, more out of habit, she turned left just before the city limit sign. It took great effort on her part to visit her mother. A spontaneous drop-in might show the respect Rose thought Ainsley never gave her. As she steered the car down the narrow, tree-lined driveway, the home complex appeared, and she fought the urge to turn around. Gone was the enthusiasm she had felt coming off the mountain, to be replaced by instant anxiety.

"Good morning, Mother. I thought I'd stop by on the way through town."

"On your way through? Unannounced? Nice of you to squeeze us in," Rose grumbled, then wrinkled her nose.

A shining example of aging gracefully was Ainsley's mother, Rose. With a rounder figure and some stray gray hairs sprinkled in, Rose Tobin was a mirrored image of her daughter, from her rich, auburn hair to her green eyes. Rose stood in the doorway as Ainsley approached to give her a kiss on the cheek.

Grabbing her daughter's arm to pull her inside, Rose asked. "Are you not concerned about being seen in such dreadful attire? Or is this behavior reserved only to embarrass your parents?"

"It's good to see you, too, mother." Ainsley ignored the criticism.

"Come in, come in." Rose grabbed her daughter by the arm and pulled her inside. "What on earth are you wearing?"

"What I have on is appropriate for hiking."

Rose looked at Ainsley's khaki cargo shorts, light green v-neck tee and dusty hiking boots as if she might scold her again. "Thank goodness your grandfather isn't here to see you. He never let me leave the house without his strict approval."

Sebastopol was a redneck town. Despite Ainsley's shabby attire, Rose acknowledged she was better dressed than some people in their community. Still, she hoped Ainsley would aim for more. Rose kept her comments to a minimum and turned towards the kitchen. "We can have tea. In here."

Rose's dictatorial invitation tempted Ainsley to put up a mock fuss. Playing devil's advocate, she asked, "Am I not good enough to be served in the formal room?"

"With the way you're dressed, no." Rose called her daughter's bluff.

The house Ainsley grew up in was pleasant no matter where you were inside, and despite all the memories of the painful childhood, Ainsley still loved it.

At nineteen, William Tobin, Ainsley's father, brought his young bride, Rose, to live in his folks' home until they had enough money for a place of their own. With only William's father living there, there was plenty of room. William's mother had died when he was fifteen.

When William's father had a stroke, their temporary arrangement became permanent. The young couple stayed on to take care of the old man. In the quick turn of events, Rose's plans to attend college to study anthropology and travel the world ended. She was married, became a wife and a care-giver for his invalid father, and had a newborn baby all in her eighteenth year.

"I just came down from Armstrong Woods. It was beautiful up there." Ainsley joined Rose in the kitchen and launched on a neutral subject. Maybe she could regain the airy feeling she had carried with her from her exercise high. If only Ainsley could share with Rose the beauty she found so rewarding when she hiked.

If Rose were to accompany her, she and Ainsley could walk across a green meadow with wildflowers ablaze and capture the essence of nature. Together, they would observe how the flowers grew thicker on the parts of the meadow that got the most daily sunshine. Ainsley wanted to show Rose how she sat quietly, waiting for even the tiniest of critters to pop up from the ground. From their holes, the squirrels would scamper behind a rock or scatter off in search of some life-sustaining morsel to feed their brood.

Ainsley had stopped inviting Rose to come on hikes after Rose declined too many times.

"So, you've been traipsing about on a hike? That explains the apparel." Rose lifted her head with antipathy.

"You guessed it. I am presentably dressed, Mom. In fact, over-dressed for a hike."

Ainsley draped the pull-over, which she had removed when she warmed up from the exerting hike, across the back of the kitchen chair. Everything she had on was spotless and with no visible wear and tear. Even her hiking boots were clean compared to what they should look like after a five-mile trek across all terrain. Rose had taught her child to never get dirty. Ainsley was thankful for the comfortable, colorful clothes she got to wear on her days off from work. The fact that it bothered her mother was a bonus.

"Most young ladies work out in a gym or exercise in the privacy of their own homes. You would never catch them in public looking like that," Rose lectured with an upturned nose.

"There are no rules against exercising in public," Ainsley heard herself snap back.

Silence fell in the chasm between mother and daughter. Each suppressed their respective emotions, but Rose was unable to let the tension ease. "You're being ridiculous. I'm saying that outfit is very unbecoming."

"So is being fat and unhealthy, which is why I exercise. And these clothes are what hikers wear."

"Why do you have to be so dramatic? Did you stop by solely to antagonize me?" Rose tried a different tactic: blame.

Ainsley let it go, knowing the conversation wasn't about clothing or exercise. Arguing and disagreeing is what they did.

"It's that post office. You're surrounded by all those foul-mouthed letter carriers." Rose pointed out. "When can you get a position as a clerk? You'd be in an environment more suited for a lady. Or maybe you could be a secretary. Does the postmaster need one?"

"Such high expectations you have of me, Mother. You're giving me a lot to aspire to."

Rose often expressed embarrassment when her friends would announce they had seen Ainsley out and about on her route. Ainsley remembered when Rose introduced her to a couple who had recently moved to Sebastopol and joined St. Sebastian's church.

"Remember when Mr. and Mrs. Douglas asked what I did for work and I answered, 'I'm a streetwalker.'" Ainsley laughed as she spoke.

"It wasn't funny then, it isn't funny now." The slight lift at the corner of Rose's mouth suggested she found a touch of humor in remembering the shocked look on the faces of her new friends.

"I just don't understand your sense of humor, Ainsley." Rose stifled her smile. "If you could ever learn to hold your tongue and not say the first things that come into your head, your prospects of finding a man would increase."

"Mother, like I've said many times, I'm surrounded by men, half of them single. If I were looking for one, I would have to look no farther. Give me a net and I could catch a dozen." Ainsley smirked at the image of herself skipping about a garden surrounded by manlike butterflies and catching them with a big net.

"You need a partner, someone to grow old with, or else your life will be very lonely. Jesse needs a father, and none of those men you work with would be suitable."

"Jesse is fine. She has her grandfather. He is the best father figure a girl could ever want." The entertainment value of mincing words with Rose dropped when she brought up Jesse.

"I'm tired of worrying about you." Rose's energy to fight was subsiding, too. As she placed on the table two full cups of steaming herbal liquid, the lavender-chamomile aroma filled the silent space between the two women.

"You remember Mrs. Winslow from church? You'll never guess what she told me last night. We had them over for dinner after choir and..."

Ainsley relaxed as the herbal elixir did the trick and the conversation had changed direction. She prepared herself to listen to her mother tell the stories that she had already heard at the post office. The same rumors the "foul-mouthed carriers" had spread.

Ainsley was content to be a letter carrier for the Post Office for over ten years. She would spend the first part of her day conversing with some of the funniest, best-tempered people she knew. The camaraderie was intense, and the fun was positive and wholesome. Once in a while, the guys got rowdy, but Ainsley and the few other women carriers in the office could all hold their ground.

Rose went into yet another story about the widow, Mrs. Dixon, Ainsley's landlady. Rose's grapevine of friends enjoyed talking about others, and Mrs. Dixon was often a target.

"... and Mrs. Michaels saw her in San Francisco coming out of the cannabis club."

Ainsley noticed Rose's exaggerated expression and knew she wanted a certain reaction.

Rose recognized the gossiping protocol was lost on Ainsley, so with a heavy sigh, she announced, "I'm making your father some lunch. He just pulled in. Can I make you a sandwich, too?"

"Hi, Daddy!" Ainsley jumped from her chair to greet her dad, William, who, as if on cue, entered from the side door.

Dressed in stained and worn out coveralls that were none the less clean and well-fitting, William's attire offered the image of a hard-working man. William Tobin was a successful, self-employed plumber, to be exact.

"Hello, darlin'. To what do we owe the pleasure?" The handsome, salt-and-pepper-haired man squeezed his offspring tight.

"I was coming from Armstrong and stopped by after my hike." Ainsley's anxious energy toggled over to joy. "How are you, Dad?"

"Oh, good! I'm great. Business is good. I found a place for you to ride bikes." William was glad to share some information. "I was called to a work site out on Burnside Road, and it turns out the man owns about 250 acres of rolling hills with forested areas. There are many fire trails back and forth across his land. He runs cattle out there, but said you and Belle and Jesse are welcome to ride up there anytime."

"Don't sit down," Rose instructed when she saw William reaching to pull out a chair. "You shall eat in the other room after you remove those dreadful coveralls." Rose couldn't ignore her two shabbily dressed family members.

But Ainsley could ignore her mom, as she often did when Rose got like this. "What brought you out to the place on Burnside?" she asked her dad.

"Oh, the usual thing that brings me out that far." William pulled a kitchen chair out from under the table to sit. "A septic system not properly cared for. Nothing a pumping won't cure. The homeowner is a fella from the city. He had no clue how to maintain a septic system. He believes the back-up is because of old pipes. The pipes were junked up, but it's nothing a system-wide pipe cleaning wouldn't fix. I was, however, instructed to replace as much pipe as I felt was necessary to bring the place up to standards."

"William," Rose protested, "Why do you insist on working in the trenches when you have employees for that?"

"I wasn't in the trenches, as you say. I was out helping Ken oversee the recently hired apprentice," William said to his wife. Then, returning to the topic with Ainsley, who was all ears, he said, "We have an apprentice. Jason is his name. Ken is training Jason. This work on Burnside is a straightforward process and a chance for the youngster to learn a lot."

"Ken is a nice guy," Rose interrupted. "You should go out with him, Ainsley."

Ainsley paid no attention to her mother's offer to arrange a blind date and gave her attention to William. "You were saying..."

"Ken is engaged, Rose," William acknowledged his wife's comment. "Anyway, about Jason. So, Ken is giving him a chance to determine if he wants to do this kind of work."

William's business was small, but successful. He had built it from the ground up himself. There were two other plumbers and a receptionist on the payroll. Adding a newbie was a big deal considering it was a 25% increase in personnel.

"Septic systems. What a charming topic for an afternoon conversation," Rose said. Leaving no room for disobedience, she ordered, "Go to the family room, William. You may eat while watching the news. I'll bring your lunch in."

After dismissing him, Rose asked Ainsley, "Will you stay for lunch?"

"Only if we may talk about septic systems," Ainsley teased and winked at her dad.

"Don't get smart with me," Rose flashed angry eyes, her Irish temper reaching its threshold. "William!" she ordered, then exited through the swinging door into the adjoining room with her husband's meal.

Seeing her mother's temper spill over onto William more than usual left questions. Ainsley turned to ask, but William's pursed lips, wide eyes, and head-shake warned her not to.

"Might be menopause," William whispered, making light of his wife's mood. Then he stood up and headed for the door that was still rocking back and forth on its hinges. "See you later, Ains."

"Why does your father have to talk about plumbing? And why does he insist on wearing those awful coveralls? He shouldn't need to protect his clothing. He doesn't have to do the dirty work anymore." Rose blew back through the swinging doors to see Ainsley had no reaction to her questions. She rolled her eyes. "Did you say you will stay for lunch?"

But Ainsley didn't hear the last question. The scene with her parents had sparked a childhood memory, fuzzy around the edges. Ainsley was six or seven years old.

"Television is toxic," Rose warned her husband when he bought a brand new, big screen color T.V. to replace the tube set.

"The screen is bigger and get a load of the picture. It's called HD for 'high-definition' and it makes everything on the screen come to life." William had been so excited. He had been wanting to upgrade their tv set for some time.

"I won't have that in my house." Rose had made no secret of how she felt about television. To her, it was the devil's way of sucking the time away from life.

The quarrel between her parents about the television lasted a few days. Eventually, they agreed the television would stay in the family room, but Rose was in charge of what, when and how the television was to be used. There were many ball games they had all watched together without volume.

"There's no need to hear the game. You can see what's happening without the sound." Rose's words were final and everyone had to obey.

"Still controlling the television, huh, Mom? Tell me, does Daddy still have to watch T.V. without audio, too?" The memory had stirred up some buried energy. "And while we're on the subject, do you decide who Daddy can and cannot be friends with, like you used to do to me?"

"Ainsley! Where are you coming up with this hostility? It must be the stress from work."

Ainsley's last button was pushed.

"Stress? My job is not as stressful as the anxiety I feel when I try to talk to you."

"I don't understand you at all, Ainsley. There are no victims here. You are all over the board. Is this some kind of game you are playing with me?"

"You dismissed your husband as if he were a dog put on a down-stay." Ainsley scooted back her chair and leaned forward.

"Honestly, Ainsley. Calm down. You're hysterical. Thank goodness we are not in public. These outbursts are unacceptable."

And so it was, unchanging.

"Now, answer the question, Ainsley. Will you be staying for lunch?"

"Seriously?" In total exasperation, Ainsley stood and raised her arms up in the air.

"You are leaving? You are just going to walk away?"

"Yes, I am leaving. You are impossible, Mother."

"That is enough, Ainsley. Get back here."

William arrived just as Ainsley was rushing out. "What's going on?" William had heard the familiar escalation of conversation between his daughter and his wife.

"I'm leaving, Daddy." Ainsley's anger was replaced with sorrow when she addressed her father. "You know how it is. I'm sorry."

"Never mind, William. This doesn't concern you. Go back in and watch the news."

William remained in place.

"Stay out of it, William," was Rose's final warning, which blanketed the disturbances in her realm.

Before Rose could say another word, she and William heard the sound of tires grinding with increased acceleration and a spray of gravel.

"'Tis a funny thing," William remarked, "She often goes faster on her way out of here than she ever does when she arrives."

CHAPTER 2

Post Office

"There you are. Why didn't you return my calls? Is everything okay?" Belladonna Carrano, who was at her desk sorting mail, pounced on Ainsley when she arrived at work the next morning.

"I went for a hike early yesterday." Ainsley knew she hadn't exactly answered the question. Belle's concern was legitimate. The two friends got together nearly every day for a run or bike ride.

"You ghosted me, though." Belle didn't hide her feelings.

"Yes, I ghosted you," Ainsley confessed. Interactions with Rose often left Ainsley in isolation mode. "I should have at least let you know."

"I understand if you didn't wanna exercise, but to leave me hanging? Not cool. *Davvero scorretto.*"

"*Mi dispiace.* It was Rose."

Belle nodded knowingly and turned away. "Oh."

"Anyway, how was your date with the pilot? What was his name?" Ainsley waited respectfully for Belle to recover before changing the subject.

"Scott is his name. He is really cool, but a little too military, if you know what I mean. You know, *my honor, my country.* Blah-blah."

Ainsley didn't understand what Belle meant, but she let her friend chatter on about all the reasons the man she had been out with wasn't a suitable mate.

The letter carriers in the central processing facility sorted and cased their mail to prepare for delivery. As they worked, conversations naturally shifted between one-on-one and group chats.

"We are going out again this weekend," Belle confessed about her date. "I'm gonna give him a second chance."

"You pointed out all the things that bothered you about the guy," Ainsley teased Belle through the space between their letter cases. "Don't tell me you're going to lower your standards. You can't give in yet. There are still so many other men out there dying to be put to the test."

"Why shouldn't I settle?" Belle missed the irony. "Dating is so tiring and there is always something with each guy. There is no Mr. Right. Nobody is perfect. I'm not gonna wait for my knight in shining armor. Romance is for schoolgirls."

"Ah, the schoolgirls. Young and romantic," Howard interrupted.

"You leave those schoolgirls out of it, you perv." Another voice chimed in.

"Hey, Howard, you out there again trolling for a date in front of the junior high school?"

"I heard the cops are watching out for you, Howard," yet another co-worker added. Everyone in the room burst out laughing.

Ainsley's hands mechanically sorted the row of letters into her case, but her mind was a million miles away. The vibe of the room brought her back to being in the Girl Scouts as a teen. They'd had a meeting on how to spot predatory male behavior and stay safe from it.

"Let's cross the street." Ainsley had suggested when she and Patti were walking home from school one day. "That guy walking towards us might be predatory."

"What?" Patti asked, looking around for the threat. "That guy?"

"We learned in Girl Scouts how to stay safe."

"You still go to Girl Scouts?" Patti said when she found out Ainsley hadn't quit. "I thought we agreed when we started high school. No more scouts."

"Well, you quit. I didn't." Ainsley asserted.

"It's so juvenile. It just ain't cool." Patti had no better reason.

"The Scouts do good things for the community. I know it's a little corny, but the things we stand for are ethical, admirable, important." Ainsley heard herself parrot her mother's words.

"Well, go on then. Be a girl scout. Just don't spread it around."

Ainsley cringed at this suggestion. Of course she wasn't going to advertise her participation. She didn't need to be told it would be social suicide.

But that day, Patti got her thinking.

"You can't quit. The Scouts are depending on you. And participation looks good on college applications," Rose advised when the question came up.

"I've already quit." Ainsley confessed.

Ainsley had caved to the social pressure from her friend and, unbeknownst to Rose, had been blowing off the Girl Scout meetings to hang out with friends.

"If you are not going to the Girls Scouts, where have you been all these Wednesday afternoons?" Rose had caught Ainsley playing frisbee in the park and hanging out with a group of kids.

Though spending time with kids her age was a normal teenage activity, Rose had made it seem ominous. Ainsley could never explain to her mom why she had quit the Scouts, so she kept it a secret. When Rose found out, she was determined to get her daughter back into the Scouts, but before she had made the arrangements, there came up a much bigger issue to tackle in Ainsley's young life.

"Shall we meet up later for exercise?"

Belle's voice sounded far away and out of context.

"Hello? Earth to Ainsley."

Belle's urgent tone snapped Ainsley back into the present. Ainsley looked around and realized she was ready to load her cart and hit the street. The whole time she was daydreaming, she had been correlating flats and magazines in route order without thinking.

"Sorry." Ainsley shook her head to clear the residue of the painful memory. "What?"

"Exercise. Do you want to meet up?" Belle asked again.

"Of course," Ainsley forced a response.

"What time?"

"We can meet up…later. The days are getting longer."

"Okay, let's go later. You're the one with a child to worry about. Four-thirty, then?" Belle left it up to Ainsley.

"Four-thirty it is." Ainsley affirmed. "See you then." Ainsley waved.

With their afternoon jog planned, Ainsley and Belle separated as they rolled their way into the parking lot to ready their vehicles for delivery.

At the end of a smooth day, Ainsley was eager to pick up her daughter. It brightened her spirits the closer she got to the school.

"Hey, Mom," Jesse greeted her mother as she fastened her seat belt, "Are we going to the stable right away? We gotta see Casey. And Pete said I can take a lesson with the big kids if I want. And you can ride after my lesson…"

Ainsley enjoyed the sweet sound of Jesse's monologue.

"…and Pete said Casey and I are becoming quite the team." Jesse finished her story.

"I had a great day. Thanks for asking." Ainsley spoke when Jesse finally stopped chattering about horses.

"Sorry, Mom." Jesse laughed, not really apologetic for having been impolite. "I forgot to ask you. I can't focus when I am thinking about riding Casey."

"Do you have homework? That should be first on your mind."

"Yeah, right." Jesse laughed. "Me and my friends all think about homework first. We can't wait to get home so we can do our homework."

"My friends and I," Ainsley corrected. "Homework may not be a priority on your list, but it is a responsibility and it will get done."

Ainsley hated when she sounded like Rose but could never stop herself before it happened.

"I always do my homework. I'm the only one in Mr. Cary's class that has turned in everything when it's due since day one."

Ainsley noticed her words had taken a little wind out of Jesse's joyful sails. She never intended to break her daughter's spirit that way. She remembered how badly she herself had wanted a pony when she was Jesse's age.

"We have plenty of room for a horse," William advocated on behalf of his daughter. "She has her heart set on having a pony."

"The answer is 'no.' Case closed." Rose had laid down the law, and once she did, there was usually no going back.

"She worked so hard to save her money. Why did you let her believe it was a possibility?" William's pleading only seemed to make Rose angrier.

"Ainsley. Wash up and set the table for dinner."

"You are breaking her spirit," Ainsley heard her father say as she left the room with a broken heart.

"Homework and horses. We will find time for both." Slipping out of the memory, Ainsley reassured Jesse there was a way to balance the two. She never wanted her daughter to feel the way she had felt as a child.

She turned the Jeep into the driveway, proceeded past the main house and parked in front of their cozy split-level, two-bedroom studio that used to be the garage.

Ainsley and Jesse simultaneously waved to Mrs. Dixon, who was relaxing on her front porch swing, grooming her cat, Tiger.

"Quiet down, Brooke." Ainsley murmured when she heard her border collie, Brooke barking in the yard. She knew the dog wouldn't hear her but felt the need to call out.

"Can I throw the Frisbee with her?" Jesse asked on her way out of the vehicle.

"Yes, but don't...." Ainsley began as Jesse opened the gate to the yard, "... let the dog out." She finished her sentence as the Border Collie flashed past her on the way to the front porch where Mrs. Dixon and her cat were.

"Brooke, come!" Ainsley yelled, but Brooke was focused on the tiger-striped feline.

Ainsley saw the cat spring from the porch rail as Brooke leapt the distance from the driveway up and cleared the spot the cat had occupied only moments ago. Mrs. Dixon squealed and Tiger was an orange streak disappearing into the house through his private kitty door. Ainsley started after her dog and got to the porch as a black and white blur disappeared through Mrs. Dixon's front screen door.

Opening the door, Ainsley let out a whistle with all her breath, and the ruckus inside the house came to an immediate halt. Brooke came slinking from behind the couch and Tiger, instinctively knowing the danger had passed, sauntered out from under the bookcase.

"Hi, dear." Mrs. Dixon greeted her tenant. "Is that a new dog collar you have for Brooke?" Mrs. Dixon pointed towards her former cat door that was mangled and twisted and dangling from the now obedient canine's neck.

"Sorry about the redecorations." Ainsley looked inside at the overturned dining chair and throw-rugs all askew.

"No worries, dear." Mrs. Dixon continued. "That is the work of a great remodeling team called Tiger and Brooke. I can give you their contact info if you are thinking of hiring interior designers."

"I believe this belongs to you." Ainsley reached for the aluminum-framed swinging door that the cat had gone through but that had been too small to accommodate the 45-pound dog.

Mrs. Dixon patted the naughty dog's head, reached for the cat door, and said, "Thanks, I will need this. I have one on the back door. They're a matched pair and we wouldn't want to be breaking up the set."

"I will pay for the repairs. I really am sorry."

"Nonsense, dear. It was an accident. It's part of the routine." Mrs. Dixon scooped up the orange cat who now had no interest in the predator he had run from moments ago.

"I guess Brooke didn't want to play Frisbee after all." Jesse walked beside her mother and the dog past Mrs. Dixon's house to their cottage.

Ainsley laughed and reached down to pet Brooke behind her ears, where she loved to be scratched. "Thank goodness Mrs. Dixon is so good-natured about you!"

Ainsley enjoyed being home, and the cottage suited her and Jesse. William joked that the place was taller than it was wide. The bedrooms and bath were above the first floor, which had the kitchen and living area. Ainsley went up to change clothes while Jesse set herself up to do her homework at the dining table.

"Emily is taking me to the barn. She has a lesson today, too." Jesse informed Ainsley when she finished dressing and came downstairs.

"So, Emily is driving now?" Ainsley returned to the kitchen with the now empty glass of water she had taken upstairs.

"No, silly. Her dad is driving us."

"Oh, good. I didn't think it was okay for ten-year-olds to drive a car."

"It's probably fine in some countries where children can drive farm equipment."

"Well, that is a different story. Wait…" Ainsley faked a horrified expression. "Emily is coming in a tractor? They should never let a four-foot tall person pilot a huge 40-foot combine."

"Mom, you are so silly." Jesse closed the subject and opened her history book.

The smile on her daughter's face warmed Ainsley's heart. In contrast, she remembered how cold her relationship with her own mother had been.

"Girls, this is my daughter, Ainsley." Rose had introduced Ainsley at age ten to a gathering of teenage girls at a counseling session at the community center.

"Pleased to meet you." Ainsley had practically given a curtsy. She grimaced at the memory now.

Sitting on chairs in a circle, the meeting continued as Rose engaged with each of the participating young ladies in turn. From where Ainsley sat, off to the side, she could hear a conversation between two girls who were not paying attention.

"Look at that child." The girl with straggly blond hair whispered to her friend and pointed at Ainsley. "She's the reason Ol'lady Tobin is trying to help us. 'Do as I say not as I do?'" The teenage girls began to giggle.

"Story is the old bag got herself knocked up and had to get married." The whispering continued as Rose pontificated, oblivious to the sidebar.

"Ya, mean she's sittin' there tellin' us not to do what she done?"

Ainsley had sat in the chair and felt embarrassed, even though she didn't fully understand the conversation.

"Mom, what does 'knocked up' mean?" Ainsley had asked her mother after the counseling session finished.

Rose had bristled, then lectured Ainsley on how that was not a proper subject for a young girl but she never answered the question. When Ainsley had then posed the question to her father, he was forthright with an answer, then asked where she had heard such a term.

"You might rethink bringing Ainsley to those counseling meetings," William had told his wife after talking to Ainsley.

"I'm trying to help those girls," Ainsley had heard Rose's reply. "If I can help even one of them make better choices, then it is all worth it."

"Your intentions are good, your heart is in the right place, but why does it have to include our daughter? Have you thought about how it might make Ainsley feel?"

Rose ranted, "Those young ladies need guidance. The church is telling them to keep their babies. I'm telling them how bad the consequences of their choices are. They need to know keeping their babies is not the only option. I'm advising them to consider putting them up for adoption."

At a tender age, Ainsley had made no full connections, but she had gleaned enough to form the sentiments. She understood Rose wasn't happy about being a mom, and she knew it hurt her father's feelings.

"Mom, they're here!" Jesse shouted and ran upstairs. The announcement broke through Ainsley's thought barrier.

From the front window of the living room, she had a straight view up the driveway, where she saw her daughter's friend's car pulling up.

"Hello, Auntie Ainsley." Ainsley answered the door to see Jesse's classmate and best friend, Emily's smiling face.

"Jesse went to her room to get ready. Go on up."

As the youngster scurried up the stairs, Ainsley almost closed the door on Emily's father, Phillip. "Oh, goodness, I didn't see you."

"Hello, Ainsley."

"Thanks for swinging by for Jesse."

"You are quite welcome. It is my pleasure." Phillip Martin, who usually waited in the car, stood awkwardly, half in and half out. "I can bring them home, too, since I am staying to watch the lesson. I was hoping you'd be coming along with us to the stable."

It was obvious to Ainsley whenever she interacted with Phillip that he was hoping for something. He was hoping for a date—or more. Before he could bring the conversation around to the part where he would ask her out, Ainsley intercepted with, "If you will excuse me, I have to go, too. I'm going for a run while Jesse's at her lesson."

"Maybe we can have dinner, the girls and you and I?"

Ainsley ignored the question by focusing on tying the laces on her running shoes. She audibly let out a sigh of relief when the girls came downstairs and slipped through the door past the adults.

"It's nearly four-thirty. Y'all better git moving," Ainsley said.

"One day you will answer my question." Phillip threw the comment over his shoulder.

Ainsley's fists tightened at the warning in Phillip's words. She bent forward to snap the leash on Brooke's collar and pretended not to hear. She couldn't see his face, nor could he see hers. She and the dog were off and running before they were all even in Phillip's car.

"You're late." Belle was running in place when Ainsley finally crossed the street.

"I am not. You were just coming down the street yourself. I saw you, so don't pretend like you've been waiting."

Belle giggled, and they headed to the paved trail by the highway that connected Sebastopol to Santa Rosa.

"So, is Jesse at the stable?" Belle asked when they had found their running rhythm. "When can I come watch my goddaughter ride again? It's been a while, and I promised Jesse I would."

"Jesse would love that. She loves an audience."

"Maybe this weekend? And by the way, what are you doing this weekend?"

"Well, until a moment ago, I had no plans, but now it seems I am meeting you at the ranch."

"Great, because after we watch Jesse's lesson, let's go out. I'm sure Jesse can stay with Phillip and Emily or Mrs. Dixon."

"No, no. Not another blind date." Ainsley looked at her friend suspiciously. "After that last double date, I warned you never again."

"Please don't say no yet. It'll be different this time." Belle pleaded, wishing she could erase the disastrous blind date to which Ainsley referred. "Remember the Air Force pilot, Scott? He has a friend..."

"Humph!" Ainsley responded. "Have you forgotten the last time? You set me up with that guy who left me stranded in the city as soon as he realized I wouldn't put out."

"C'mon, Ainsley. You said you forgave me."

"Forgive is not the same as forget, Belle." Ainsley relived the humiliation. "He left me at the bar and took off with that bleached-blond floozy because she was a sure thing!"

"Please, Ainsley. I have met this guy. His name is Dale. He really is nice, good-looking, and a civilian employed at the Air Force base in Arizona. He is responsible, respectful and funny. I hate for you to miss out on a nice guy because of one unpleasant experience." Belle could see Ainsley's resolve weakening. She pleaded in Italian. "Solo di sì. I am not against begging. Ti prego! Pretty please."

Even when she begged in Italian for more impact, Ainsley left Belle's pleas unanswered. Belle's behavior reminded her of how, with unwavering persistence, her childhood friend Patti had set her up with a boy from school. In her own experiences, blind dates and set-ups seemed to end badly.

"We can tell your parents you're staying at my house." Patti had wanted Ainsley to join her at a party thrown by a classmate. A cheerleader, Rachelle, from school.

"Rachelle and I are not friends, and those kids don't even know I exist," Ainsley had protested. "Besides, I wasn't invited and I don't want to go."

"You will know them when you meet them and Rachelle's boyfriend told me about the party, so that's as good as an invitation."

"If I tell my parents I'm at your house, they will call. They will be suspicious after the last time." Ainsley had reminded Patti about the time she was supposed to be at a slumber party at Patti's, but they had gone bowling with Patti's boyfriend and his buddies. They got caught in the ruse when Rose and William had showed up at the bowling alley. Rose had grounded Ainsley for weeks after.

"Here's what we do." Patti had had a plan. "You'll call home from my house around nine o'clock and tell your mom my parents are going to bed. Your mom won't wanna call and wake them. Tell her we are going to bed, too, and voilà, we go to the party."

That party led to more sneaking out when Ainsley met Rick Johnson, a senior from school. Ainsley had started down a path that would change her life in ways she couldn't have imagined.

"Focus, please. What do you say? Saturday night? Is it a date?" Belle's persistence brought Ainsley back from her thoughtful wanderings.

"I was thinking about when I was a kid." Ainsley avoided the questions.

Belle changed her tactic to positive affirmations. "Saturday night. Me and Scott, you and Dale. We'll meet for dinner. No strings attached. Just dinner."

"Dale? Sounds like a girl's name."

"You are pathetic, Ainsley." Her purposeful avoidance frustrated Belle, but no matter. She hadn't said no, so Belle took it as a yes.

CHAPTER 3

Double Date

"You're going out? On a double date?"

Ainsley sensed Phillip's annoyance on Saturday when she tried to arrange Jesse's care. She hadn't wanted to ask Phillip to babysit.

"Never mind. I know. It's a last-minute request. I shouldn't have asked."

When Belle made the plans for their double date, Ainsley expected to be able to leave Jesse with her grandparents, but she couldn't call on them this time. Rose was imposing the silent treatment after their fight.

"I didn't say we couldn't have Jesse over. I'm just surprised you are going out. You said you weren't dating right now." Phillip's annoyance now made sense. Ainsley had used that excuse to get out of accepting Phillip's invitations to dinner or a movie in the past.

"It was a last-minute plan. Belle set me up with her friend's friend." Ainsley cringed. She didn't feel she should have to explain her actions to Phillip.

"Jesse can come stay the night while you go out on your date. We always welcome Jesse. And you are always welcomed, too, Ains."

Ainsley was glad Phillip couldn't see the look on her face. It was the snarky tone he added to the word "date," followed by the use of her nickname, that made her skin crawl.

"What time will you be coming by to drop off Jesse?"

"If this is a problem, Phillip…"

"It's fine. The girls will have a blast. What time?"

"I'll drop Jesse by your house at 6:30, if that will work?"

"So, tonight at 6:30."

"Yes, see you in a while. Thanks."

Ainsley was just finishing her call with Phillip when Jesse came bounding down the stairs.

"Do I get to stay at Emily's?"

"Yes, you do. So, pack for an overnighter."

"Yay! I'll need my sleeping bag and we'll watch movies, maybe go see the horses tomorrow…"

Ainsley listened as they climbed the stairs together. Jesse had been at home all day with no one to talk to and now her chatter seemed to make up for lost time. It was not the best choice leaving Jesse home alone while she worked. Normally the child spent the day at her grandparents'. Other than having no one to talk to, Jesse seemed to take the novel arrangement in stride.

"Never mind Rose," Ainsley thought as she got ready for her date. Focusing on her closet, she was relieved to find a suitable outfit; a stylish pleated kona blue skirt and a loose-fitting peasant blouse that gathered at the waistline. Balancing between dressy and casual, her outfit, like the evening, could go either way. Feeling confident, Ainsley remembered her first one-on-one date as a young teen. Confidence was not the word to describe her back then.

"I'm not kidding, Ains." She remembered Patti had been so excited their sophomore year after a party the previous weekend. "Rick Johnson told Rachelle's boyfriend he thinks you're cool. He wants to go out."

"Rose will never let me date."

"You're almost an adult. You gotta start dating sometime. There's nothing to be afraid of."

Excited nerves had replaced Ainsley's anxiety. Rose had instilled such fear in her, constantly cautioning about the perils of teenage love. Years of no terrible experiences had weakened the force of Rose's warning messages. "I can't believe he wants to ask me out."

"He totally does! I can see it now. You getting a ride to school every day for the rest of the year in the coolest car. He can take you to ball games and dances. You'll be at the prom with Rick Johnson!"

"You're getting a little carried away, Patti…"

"Oh, Ains. You are going to be Rick Johnson's girlfriend!"

With a unified squeal, both teenagers had jumped up and down, then hushed each other as some of the other kids in the crowded school food court had noticed.

In a much quieter voice, Ainsley asked. "What do you think I should wear? Where will he take me? Out to dinner? I don't know how to act."

"Just be yourself." Patti's advice had been of no use at all. What did that mean, *be yourself*? Ainsley didn't understand who she even was.

"Wow, Mom. You look great." Jesse came in to see what her mother was up to for so long and interrupted the memory.

Ainsley styled her tightly curled and sometimes frizzy hair with a flat iron, then used a heat styling wand to create wavy curls. She had put on makeup, modest eyeliner and shadow with mascara. She was standing before the mirror in her satin slip putting on earrings when Jesse came in and complimented her mother's appearance.

"I'm not dressed yet. This is my slip." Ainsley wondered if her daughter thought she'd wear something so skimpy.

"Hilarious, Mom. I was referring to your makeup. You look pretty even in a slip." It seemed Jesse's modesty was still intact. "But that slip would make a cute dress, too."

"Come here, you little smarty-pants," Ainsley grabbed Jesse in a bear hug. Though they often acted like roommates, tonight there was a clear mother-daughter bond. "Now, help me get dressed, please."

While putting a finishing touch on her hair and face, Ainsley remembered when she had been at Patti's house getting ready for her date with Rick Johnson.

There had been no dinner that night. After picking Ainsley up at Patti's, Rick Johnson had driven them straight to the coast to a turnout and parked. The popular way to spend a date in those days was to watch the sun set over the Pacific and make out.

Ainsley hadn't even ever had a first kiss, but Rick had been oblivious. He leaned in without any prelude. Their kiss had been awkward. Ainsley was nervous and hadn't known which way to turn her head. They had bumped noses, then their lips met clumsily. She remembered still how it was all rather slimy and unhygienic. Rick had seemed to notice her repulsion and retreated. Ainsley had scooted up against the door of the '67 Mustang, feeling grateful for the center console as a convenient barrier.

A few minutes later, Rick moved toward her as Ainsley stayed put. "Relax," Rick had said as he had moved in for the next kiss. The noses had been in the right place this time, but it had shocked Ainsley to find too many tongues in her mouth. She had gagged, turned her head, and wiped the saliva from her lips.

"Jeez. It's just kissing."

There had been no more kissing that evening. Frustrated with her, Rick drove Ainsley home.

"All you did was talk? The cutest boy in school and you didn't even make out with him?" Patti was unimpressed when Ainsley had phoned later that night after the date.

"It was nice." Ainsley had defended herself. "He started out a little forward, but acted like a gentleman after that. We watched the sunset."

"Acted like a gentleman? What does that even mean? Why don't you join us in the current century?"

"I shouldn't have to apologize or explain my sensibilities." Patti's judgmental assessment was hurtful.

"Did he ask you out again?"

"No, but I'm sure he will. You said he likes me."

"Don't get your hopes up," Patti had warned.

The next day, Patti told Ainsley she had seen Rick the night before. After he had dropped Ainsley at home, he showed up and hung out with the rest of the gang. He had told Patti he was disappointed to find out Ainsley was, in his opinion, a goody two-shoes.

Studying her reflection in the mirror, adult Ainsley still felt the sting of the name-calling.

"C'mon, Mom! We're gonna be late!" Jesse had her backpack and pillow in her arms and was sitting on the bottom stair waiting to go to Emily's.

"It's just six-thirty now." Ainsley grabbed the keys, and they flew out the door.

"I should meet the guys you date." Jesse slipped the seat belt around and latched it.

"If I ever meet a guy that is worthy, I will introduce you."

"Sara's mom lets her meet, like, all her dates."

"What Sara does is, *like*, up to Sara's mom. And it's, *like*, nothing little girls should be, *like*, thinking about." Ainsley copied Jesse, purposely misusing the word "like."

Jesse shrugged and said, "Whatever."

The conversation ended there, and the three-minute drive to Phillip and Emily's was quiet. Up Bodega Ave and then a right turn into the subdivision. The house was a cookie-cutter floor plan on a postage-stamp sized lot, but Phillip and his late wife, Désirée, had created a pleasant home. Just before Ainsley stopped in front of the blue house that could only be told apart from the rest by its color, she reached for Jesse's hand.

"Some rules may seem silly, but I'm only trying to do my job as the parent and give you as normal a life as I can. I don't want you to go through anything out of the ordinary because of our unusual situation."

"Don't you always say, 'Why be normal?'" Jesse kissed her mom on the cheek and said, "I love you, Mom. Have a good time. See you in the morning."

Ainsley smiled and blew a kiss as her daughter approached the house. Before Jesse could knock, Phillip came out waving, and Emily squeezed past him to greet her friend.

"I'll pick Jesse up tomorrow morning." Ainsley engaged the clutch, and the Jeep rolled as she spoke through the open window.

Phillip looked disappointed, knowing there would be no conversation between them. Ainsley made the short trip back to the cottage and when she got there, Belle had arrived with their dates.

"How do you do?" Ainsley shook hands with the strangers. "Would you like to come in?"

The introductions gave Brooke enough time to realize there were unfamiliar voices, and the dog barked a warning. "That'll do, Brooke."

"We don't have time," Scott reminded the group. "We have a seven-thirty reservation.

"Let me just secure Brooke inside."

Before opening the door to leave, out of habit, Ainsley glanced at the old answering machine and saw the blinking red light. Rose had finally called, she thought. Leaving her date waiting, Ainsley pressed play.

"I don't know if I have the right number," the machine began. It was not Rose, "but I am trying to reach Ainsley Tobin. This is—" Ainsley nearly knocked the machine off the corner table in her haste to stop the voice she thought sounded familiar. She steadied the table and hit *delete*.

"Who was that?" Belle was standing in the doorway.

"Wrong number."

"He asked for Ainsley Tobin."

"Must be some other Ainsley Tobin."

"Let's go, ladies."

Ainsley closed her front door and Scott held the driver's side back door for Belle.

As Ainsley slid into the back of the sedan on the other side, she prepared herself for more questions from Belle regarding the phone message.

"That wasn't the wrong number, Ains. Do you know who it was?"

"It's probably a telemarketer or the firefighters asking for donations again. Don't make a mountain out of a molehill."

To Ainsley's surprise, Belle let the subject go and began sponsoring the get-to-know-you conversation. Ainsley learned Dale was an aeronautical engineer working as a civilian at the Travis Air Force Base where Scott was an enlisted officer.

Upon arriving in downtown Santa Rosa, Scott chose a parking spot in the commuter lot under the freeway. They would walk a couple blocks to the recently renovated section of the city, Old Railroad Square. The area had degenerated after the freeway was built in the 1960s, but it was restored. It was now a vibrant section with touristy stores and restaurants.

"Right on time," Scott announced. "Good job, crew."

Ainsley giggled, and Belle whispered, "I told you how they are. So militant."

"They're from the military. Punctuality is very important to them." The conversation ended when the men led the way to Fleur de Pommier, a small restaurant with a big reputation.

"Fleur de Pommier is rated the best in its class in not only the food, but as an entire experience." Taking credit for choosing the location, Scott boldly led them to the table. "No need for menus. I've already placed our order with the chef. Prepare for a traditional seven course meal."

With a sideways glance, Ainsley saw Belle rolling her eyes. Was she frustrated with Scott's take-charge attitude? Ainsley pondered.

"Perhaps the ladies wanted to choose their own meals?" Dale informed his bloviating buddy.

"It's okay, Dale," Ainsley cut in. "Let's try it since Scott already ordered." Ainsley didn't take offense to having her meal ordered for her. It wasn't very often she had the chance to enjoy a well-prepared meal at a five-star restaurant. She kicked back to enjoy the experience. While le garçon de café served the apéritif, Ainsley observed her date.

Dale was easy to look at, handsome even. He carried himself proudly and his manners were impeccable. Maybe this blind date would not be a bust after all.

"Ainsley," Belle noticed her friend hadn't been talking. "I was telling the story about us hiking in the Desolation Wilderness. Tell them about how we had been hiking for years up to a lake we thought was Lake Aloha."

"We hiked up to the wrong lake," Ainsley summed up.

"Tell them how we found out we had been mistaken."

"You were the one who discovered the error. You tell the story."

Scott and Dale looked from Ainsley to Belle, hoping one of them would tell the tale. Dale made eye contact again, and Ainsley felt compelled to speak.

"As Belle said, we had followed this one trail that skirted two small lakes on the way to one big lake."

Ainsley paused as Belle encouraged her to continue.

"The maps are not that great. We did the best we could, but our interpretation was wrong. We had been passing what we thought must be the lakes we saw on the map and when we came to the third one, we assumed it was Aloha Lake. After four hours of hiking, we were content with what we had achieved. It wasn't until Belle went hiking with..."

"A friend who knew the trails," Belle interrupted, not wanting Ainsley to mention one of her previous boyfriends.

"Belle's friend brought it to our attention that the first two bodies of water we passed were unnamed puddles of run-off and not the lakes we had assumed they were."

"It embarrassed us and we planned our next hike so we could see the real lakes," Belle added.

"The beauty of the actual lakes is breathtaking and worth the extra couple hours of hiking. When you get to the real Lake Aloha, you feel you are on top of the world and nestled in this bowl-shaped valley in between the peaks is this gorgeous lake."

"The second lake is called Heather." Belle picked up the thread. "Jutting peaks of granite surround the lake from all sides, and the water is crystal-blue. It's so clear you can see these enormous fish swimming along the granite banks, but don't take your eyes off the trail for too long. The way around the lake is slippery and etched into the very rock that contains it."

"The Sierra is the place to go." Ainsley felt spiritual just thinking about it. "There is nowhere on Earth I feel closer to God."

Ainsley stopped then as she realized she might have gotten too personal, but as she looked around, it appeared the others were right there with her. For the second time tonight, Dale's eyes locked with hers. His smile was genuine and understanding. She felt she could trust him and smiled back.

After dinner, they all agreed to visit El Infierno, a Latin night club close to Fleur de Pommier. They found a table, and the guys went to the bar to get some drinks.

"I told you these guys were nice." Belle began the conversation.

"Shhh, they'll hear us." Ainsley knew the music was too loud for Belle to hear her, let alone their dates who were now standing twenty-something feet away at the bar.

"You like him, don't you?" Belle teased.

"It's rude to talk about them."

"They can't hear us from there, and they won't be back in a hurry. It's what we are supposed to do. They aren't talking about the weather. They're talking about us, so we're gonna talk about them."

"Maybe they can read lips?" Ainsley responded with a hint of coyness when she thought about Dale's lips. The truth is what she saw she liked, a handsome man with kind eyes and a quiet disposition.

"You do like him. I can tell by that smile."

"Talk about something else. They are coming back."

"...with the ponytail. That guy worked at the mall before the Post Office." Belle pretended to be in mid-sentence on a different subject.

"Oh, yeah." Ainsley was not as good at improvisation.

The men returned, and when everyone had a drink in hand, they all raised their glasses. Scott clinked Belle's glass and said, "Another day, another bender. No retreat, no surrender."

"Cheers!" the other three chimed in.

Wondering about the words in Scott's toast, Ainsley thought it might be military themed, but she could only speculate. She glanced at Dale, who gave her a wink. It would be up to Ainsley to delve into the emotions behind the wink.

"It's too loud to talk. Would you like to dance?"

Ainsley nodded at Dale's question, and they moved through the crowd. Taking Ainsley by the hand, Dale danced with enough confidence for the both of them. Hoping she'd remember the steps to the salsa dances she learned in school, she found it easy to follow Dale and they moved about the room in sync to the rhythm of the Latin band.

"Shall we take a break?" Dale asked when the band slowed to a softer beat. Ainsley nodded, thinking it was polite that Dale hadn't assumed she'd want to continue with a slow dance.

Back at the table, Dale spoke, no longer competing with the blasting music. "I'm having a really good time, Ainsley."

"I am, too."

"May I ask you out again?"

"I'd like that."

"Good." Dale's head bobbed up and down. "Good." His kind smile and gentle eyes had no agenda behind them. Ainsley's shoulders loosened some more.

On the drive back to Sebastopol, Belle sat in front with Scott, and Ainsley and Dale sat together in the back seat.

"How long are you here in California?" Ainsley asked Dale, wondering when he had to return to his work in Arizona.

"I have another couple months of work to do here before I go back." Dale explained about what he did for the military in their aeronautic development department. They sent him from Davis-Monthan to help Travis Air Base with new technology and training.

Ainsley listened with interest and tried to quiet her mind from thinking about their next date. When Dale walked her to her door, he leaned forward, chin first.

To Ainsley's relief, Dale was a capable kisser and it was a nice first kiss. Dale then took her hand and gently turned it palm down before placing a second kiss there.

"Now we have a few kisses on record." Dale spoke an octave below his normal voice.

Smiling up to her eyes, Ainsley liked the kiss on her hand, and Dale's gravelly voice. She'd always thought under general circumstances a gallant, gentlemanly kiss on the back of the hand was a bit much. But with the humbleness of the delivery, Dale had pulled it off.

"I'll call you."

"You have my number."

Dale's smooth moves were apparently not just for the dance floor.

With a wave to the departing car, she reached for the door and braced herself for the exuberant greeting from Brooke.

"I'll take you for a quick potty-walk," she said to the dog. Leashing her up, Ainsley took a deep breath and opened the door. "Oh, Brooke," she said as they walked out together. "I'm gonna have to watch out. I could like that guy."

CHAPTER 4

Annadel State Park

"Good morning." Belle was the first to speak when she and Ainsley met at the state park for an early morning run.

"Yes, it is a good morning." Ainsley greeted her friend who was leaning against her car stretching.

"Did you have sweet dreams?"

"I slept well, thank you. And you?"

"How are you feeling this morning?" Belle emphasized the word "feeling," knowing Ainsley was missing what Belle was asking on purpose.

"I FEEL fine, Belle." Ainsley was eager to share about Dale but enjoyed forcing Belle to ask.

"I'm done playing your game, Ainsley," Belle said. "Don't tell me."

"I'm teasing," Ainsley added when she saw the exasperation on Belle's face. "I feel the same this morning as I did last night."

"So?" Belle stretched the two-letter word into multiple syllables. She waved her hand, expecting Ainsley to elaborate.

"Well, you know I don't date much and have strict rules about bringing strangers into Jesse's world…"

"Yes, everyone knows, you live like a nun, but…" Belle raised her arms and clenched her fists as if punching the air. "Are you two going out again or not?"

"He said he'd call me."

"I see."

"What do you mean, 'I see.'? You say it like there's something wrong. He was into me, wasn't he?"

"Of course he'll call. I'm just messing with you."

Belle had triggered a forgotten insecurity of Ainsley's. Her hard yank on Ainsley's chain caused her friend to fall deep into another memory.

"Did Rick call yet?" Patti had asked Ainsley a week after their date.

"No, not yet."

"I'm sure he'll call any day now." Patti had said it, but wasn't as sure. "How 'bout you come to Rachelle's cousin's party tonight? Maybe you'll see Rick."

Excited to see Rick, Ainsley had agreed to go.

The girls had gone through the now well-rehearsed ritual of tricking their parents: the fake sleepover.

Ainsley had followed Patti around at the party like a puppy that night. With no sign of Rick, Ainsley decided she should leave. "Rick's not here. I'm going home. I'll see you tomorrow."

"C'mon, Ains. Stay. There are plenty of other fish in the sea. I say forget about Rick."

Patti's request hadn't been enough to change Ainsley's mind. As she had turned to go, she felt a hand on her arm. Ainsley had stopped and looked at the person keeping her from leaving, hoping it was Rick, but it hadn't been his face she saw.

"Stay, Ainsley." The face she hadn't recognized had a jeering grin.

"Let go of me." Ainsley had smelled the alcohol on the breath of the nameless face.

"Whoa, take it easy, bitch." The drunk boy hadn't let go, but pulled Ainsley closer. "Let's dance."

"What are you doing? Leave me alone."

"C'mon, baby. Give me a little kiss." The foul-breathed boy had puckered up.

"That's enough, Todd!" Patti defended her friend when she saw what was going on.

"Rick said she was spunky, but that makes it even more fun." The kid leaned in for an uninvited kiss.

"I said that is enough, Todd!" Patti had yelled, but before she finished the sentence, Ainsley's fist contacted Todd's face with substantial force. She hit him so hard it had given him a bloody nose.

The drunken teen seemed to have sobered up after Ainsley clobbered him. Rick materialized as the misbehaving boy drew back his arm and made a fist, angry at having been decked by a girl.

"Leave it alone, Todd." Rick had warned, taking hold of the drunk boy's arm.

"Who's side you on, Rick? She broke my nose." The bloody-faced boy had jerked free of Rick's grip. With his hand now clutching his dripping nose, he said, "Fine. You can have her. She's not worth it." He muttered as he disappeared into the crowd that had gathered around the disturbance.

"What's going on?!" Rachelle had joined the scene and screamed when she saw blood on the floor from across the room. "My parents are going to kill me!"

"I'm so sorry." Ainsley apologized, wishing she could have been the one who disappeared into the crowd.

"This is your fault?" Rachelle had turned her attention to the blood drops on the cream-colored carpet. "I should have known. Little Miss Goody-two shoes."

The faces in the crowd had then started laughing and Ainsley looked for her friends to help set straight the record but neither Rick nor Patti spoke up to explain the broken nose hadn't started the fight but ended it.

"I better go," Ainsley had almost whispered. She had left the party and walked home alone, blaming herself for the incident and nursing a throbbing hand that would need icing.

"Do you wanna take Stevenson's Trail? Earth to Ainsley!" Belle reached over, waving her hand in Ainsley's face.

"Sorry. Daydreaming, I guess." Ainsley realized she had been running in silence and now they were at the fork in the trail which required a decision.

"Do you want to do the full loop today?"

Ainsley gathered her thoughts. "Let's stay on the main path."

"A wise decision. You are so distracted you'd probably fall off the bank into the lake or twist your ankle on that trail."

"No, I wouldn't." Ainsley never considered herself clumsy and took offense.

"Regardless, I agree we should go up to where we can sit on the shore while you daydream. We both know what you're dreaming about. Must be love."

"I'm not in love with Rick. We've only just met. I don't even care if he calls back or not."

"Who's Rick?"

"Nothing," Ainsley sprinted ahead. It embarrassed her she used the name from the past in place of Dale's. Belle matched Ainsley's pace.

Ainsley didn't want Belle to catch up. Discussing Dale with her had prompted the memory she'd rather have forgotten. That experience when she was a young girl, and the aftermath, was still so painful, she was reluctant to share it with her friend. But not talking about it didn't mean she wasn't thinking about it.

"I can't go to school. It's just too embarrassing." Ainsley had talked to Patti on the phone a few days after the party.

"I'm sorry I didn't have your back that night, Ains, but staying away is only making things worse."

Todd had had his revenge by telling everyone his version of how he got the shiner. He claimed Ainsley was a tease and that she sleeps around. He added that she and Rick had been intimate and that she was so wild in bed she had accidentally broken his nose. The other kids repeated the lies, which spread farther and farther from the truth.

"You can't keep pretending you're sick. How much longer do you think your mother will believe you?" Patti had asked after school.

"I'm sure the rumors have already made it to Rose's ears through that stupid counseling thing she does for those troubled girls." Ainsley saw no alternative. "Just bring me my homework assignments. Will you please?" She was determined not to fall behind in class.

"I can't believe what everyone is saying about you. If they knew you, they'd know it's not true."

"Then why can't you tell them?" Ainsley knew Patti was wholly focused on her own status but hoped she'd get some support. "Can't you set the record straight?"

Ainsley got no help from Patti when the rumors spread that far.

"How could you do this to me?" Rose had been furious. "I've lost all credibility with my girls. I can't expect them to listen to me when I tell them not to do what my daughter is out there doing."

"That's all you care about? You care more about those girls than me."

It had hurt that Rose hadn't even given Ainsley a chance to explain. Her mother didn't know her at all. If she had, she wouldn't have ever believed the rumors. Ainsley hit her thighs with her fists in frustration as her tears spilt.

"Don't worry, mother. You can turn this around. You can use me as a poor example. Why not put me on display again like you did when I was little and show the girls what not to do? This way, you don't have to worry about the example that is your own past!"

Ainsley shuddered at the thought of how angry Rose had been.

"Let's take a break." Belle broke into Ainsley's thoughts when she noticed Ainsley appeared to be upset. "You're not much fun today, Ains." Belle leaned up to a tree to stretch her hamstrings. "You were in a great mood when we started. What happened?"

"Nothing. I'm just not like you. You meet a guy, get all goofy with infatuation, say you're in love, then in a few weeks, sometimes days, you break up. It's a roller coaster and you love it. I choose to stay on an even keel."

"You sure have me all figured out. I guess you're the expert." Insulted by her friend's true but hurtful assessment, Belle sprinted up the next rise. Ainsley caught up when Belle stopped at the crest, taken by the view of the lake.

"Most folks miss out on sights like this 'cause they don't get up early enough in the morning to see it," Belle whispered, gazing down at the meadow. A deer stopped grazing and lifted her head, still chewing a mouthful of meadow grass.

"Lucky we are early risers." Ainsley was about to apologize to Belle, but before she could say another word, Belle took off again towards the lake.

"C'mon, slow-poke. Let's be the first to get there."

They jogged to the lake, but discovered they were not the firsts. A couple of boys had hiked in to do some fishing. Ainsley and Belle waved a greeting, and the boys giggled and waved back.

"Let's walk around the lake before we head back." Ainsley began chatting about any pleasant subject she could think of, leaving the mood created by the memories to fade away among the trees. Belle didn't deserve to be treated badly because Ainsley was in a foul mood. Belle held her end of the conversation to the light subjects, too, and soon the girls completed the lake loop and were running back to the trailhead.

"See you in the morning," Ainsley said when they returned to their cars.

"Ugh! Don't remind me." Tomorrow was Monday, a workday. "I must object to this ridiculous work schedule. *Un giorno libero non basta!*"

"Bye." Ainsley got into her Jeep with a mock salute to her friend.

On the way home, Ainsley picked Jesse up from Emily's.

"Did you three have a fun time?" she asked Phillip.

"Yes." Phillip didn't elaborate. She was relieved that Phillip seemed in a less chatty mood.

"Did you behave in church?" Ainsley asked her daughter.

"Of course," Jesse answered, then to Phillip she said, "Thank you for letting me stay the night."

"Any time, Jess." Phillip had a smile for Jesse.

"Next time you need a sitter, I'm here." Ainsley tried again for conversation, to no avail. Phillip nodded an acknowledgement. That was all.

Ainsley pinched her eyebrows together and contemplated Phillip's mood as she and Jesse drove away. She knew he wasn't happy she was dating. Part of her didn't care. She hoped the message she wasn't interested in dating him had been received. The time for contemplating Phillip was brief, as Jesse fired off more questions than Ainsley could answer.

"Did you have an enjoyable time on your date? Is he cute? Was he polite? Are you going to see each other again?"

"Whoa, whoa, whoa! One question at a time." Ainsley smiled. "Yes, I had a suitable time. He is nice and good-looking, and I think it would be nice to date Dale again. We'll see."

"You should see him again."

"Maybe, maybe not." Ainsley hesitated to come across as too excited.

"Oh, here we go again. 'I don't need a man. I'm content raising my daughter.' The 'I'm not looking for a boyfriend' speech."

"You think you know me so well?"

"That is what you were going to say, isn't it?"

"No." Ainsley hoped she wouldn't get struck by lightning for lying. "Dale is very busy with his job. He has many responsibilities and may not have much free time either. We may get together, we may not. Either way, it is none of your concern."

"My teacher says when a person is about to tell a lie, they begin a sentence with, 'The truth is' or 'To be honest.'"

"Your teacher is not wrong about that. There are many ways to read a person's body language to tell if they are speaking the truth or lying."

"You changed the subject, Mom. That is a sign of avoidance."

"Look, Jesse. I am telling the truth. Dale is a busy guy. I like him and he likes me, but that doesn't mean as much for adults as it does for kids."

"So, that's it? No romantic eye contact from across the table? No shooting stars or fireworks?"

Shocked by her daughter's questions, Ainsley took her eyes off the road. "Where do you get these ideas?"

"Health class. We are learning about human behavior. It's the part about hormones and where babies come from. I was just wondering about love. They don't teach us about that part in class. I just wonder how it feels to be in love."

"Why are you asking?" Ainsley needed more context. "You are much too young to be thinking about a boy."

"Not for me, Mom." Jesse giggled. "For you. The teacher said when two people are in love, they can have babies. How do adults know when they are in love?"

"It's hard to explain. Love feels different for each person and there are many kinds of love."

This was a loaded subject for Ainsley, who had never spoken in depth about Jesse's dad. She knew how important it would be for Jesse to know that her mother and father had created a child out of love.

"What were things like with my dad?"

And just like that, they were in the thick of it. Ainsley thought she had prepared for this discussion, but found no words.

"You loved my dad, didn't you?"

"Of course. Yes. I did." Ainsley was going to pay more attention to her own body language after her daughter's newfound ability to read nonverbal cues.

Ainsley longed to tell her daughter the complete story, but she was waiting for the right time. She needed to be sure her daughter was old enough to understand. Ainsley wished to spare Jesse any undue pain.

Luckily, the child seemed satisfied at the moment. Perhaps there were no follow-up questions because Jesse believed her mother. It was what any kid would want to hear.

When Ainsley and Jesse got home, Brooke pushed past the opening door. After spending the morning inside, the dog was eager to be out. She circled twice then laid down in her favorite spot of sunshine by the roses.

"Since I am all done with homework, can I watch a movie?" Jesse had stepped aside to let the dog pass.

"First, unpack and get your school work in order for tomorrow. Do you need any laundry done?"

Jesse went to get her clothes from the hamper. Looking up from the laundry, Ainsley noticed the red blinking light on her answering machine. She pressed the play button and listened as she readied the ironing board to press some work shirts. "Beep." Then, "Hi, Ains." It was William. "Just checking to see how you and Jesse are getting along. Will we see you at church?" The first call must have come in earlier that morning.

"Beep." The next message played. "Hey, where are you?" It was Belle's voice. She must have called from the trailhead using her cell phone.

"Beep." The third message. "Hi, Ainsley. We need to talk." Here it was—Rose's voice. But it seemed void of criticism or judgment. Instead, there was a sense of warning.

With another "beep" came the fourth message, adding clarity to Rose's warning voice. "Well, hello there, Ainsley. I have been trying to contact you. I saw your folks at church…"

Ainsley's heart felt like it had stopped beating. Tom West. This time she identified the same voice she had heard and erased the night before. Jesse's father. The voice continued, "… and your mom gave me permission to call you. It's been a long time. I'd like to see you. Call me."

"Beep." Then, the last message. It was Belle. "Call me when you get this message. Scott and Dale invited us to the air show at Travis Air Force Base on Thursday. I told them we'd go."

Ainsley pressed delete. She erased all the messages and called no one back. The message in the middle, a ghost from her past, was paralyzing. This couldn't be happening. Ainsley had left this part of her life behind a long time ago. She had shut away a lot of pain and heartache and had no plans to reopen those wounds.

"I'm gonna play outside with Brooke." Jesse came down the stairs and startled her mother, who had been ironing her uniforms.

"Oh!" Ainsley exclaimed.

"Sorry to scare you. Are you seeing ghosts?" Jesse giggled.

Ainsley brushed off Jesse's observation and smiled. Inside, her heart still raced and she thought, "Not seeing ghosts, but hearing them."

Jesse went outside, and Ainsley pondered the order of the messages on her answering machine.

Rose must have spoken with Tom West at church. What had Rose told him? Why did he want to talk to Ainsley after all these years?

"RRRing!" The phone made Ainsley jump, and for the second time, she felt her heart rate quicken. She hurried to answer it.

"Ainsley, don't hang up. It's about Jesse..." The caller was Rose.

"What did you tell him?" Ainsley skirted the subject Rose offered and went to a point of her own.

"I told him nothing..." Rose answered knowingly. "You know how I've felt about keeping this a secret."

"It was your idea! You convinced me to make that decision. You will not convince me now to change course. All the reasons you used to encourage me to keep Jesse's father a secret still exist, don't they? Why are you thinking of changing your mind now?"

"Back then, we both felt differently. There were reasons for keeping this secret. You were my child, and I was protecting you, Ainsley. Whether it was right or wrong makes no difference now."

"The hell it doesn't." Ainsley quieted her voice when she saw Jesse and the dog coming back inside.

"We must come clean, Ainsley." Rose begged.

Rose's declaration surprised Ainsley. Why the sudden change in Rose's position on the matter? "You already told him, didn't you?!"

"No, I..."

"You feel guilty enough about carrying this lie around and now you intend to make it right with God. Well, the time for that was right away." Ainsley paused when Jesse walked by and then turned on the TV. Ainsley continued.

"I begged you, 'Let's tell him.' He deserved to know, even if he couldn't stay and be a father." Ainsley struggled to keep her voice low. "You didn't care back then about what I wanted. You still don't. Nothing has changed. It's too late to cry over spilt milk and we all have to live with our actions." Ainsley slammed the phone down in its cradle with satisfaction. Land lines could still come in handy for something.

"That was grandma, wasn't it?" Jesse had heard her the hiss in her mother's voice and paused her show when she heard her mother's conversation ended. "You must be extra mad at each other this time."

Ainsley needed to think about the discussion she had just had with Rose, but there wasn't time. Instead, she squashed down the jumble of feelings ricochetting inside to tend to her daughter.

"It's fine, Jesse. It was nothing. Me and your grandma. We always fight. Then we get over it."

Ainsley forced back the emotion and joined Jesse on the couch.

"It's 'Grandma and I' and I just wish you and gramma didn't fight at all."

"I'll try harder not to, sweetie." Ainsley put her arms around her child, and Jesse squirmed.

"I'm missing my show!" Jesse pretended to protest her mother's affections.

"Okay. I can see where I fall in order of importance." Ainsley faked a hurt expression. "I have some book work to do. I'll be upstairs."

"Mom?" Jesse called out when Ainsley was halfway up the stairs.

"What is it?" Ainsley didn't turn around.

"You left the iron plugged in."

"Would you please unplug it?"

Jesse gave a small sigh and did as she was asked. "Good thing I am here to take care of you."

Ainsley let Jesse's last comment go without a response. It was not safe to prolong the conversation when she was on the edge of her emotions. Retreating to the privacy of her room, she sat down at the desk, but she didn't do any bookkeeping. The bills were all up to date. It had been a decent excuse for some alone time.

CHAPTER 5

Music Store Fans

"I'm not calling to chat. Will you pick up Jesse from school on Thursday?" Ainsley called Rose on Monday after work when she and Jesse came home. For her second date with Dale, Ainsley needed to make additional arrangements for Jesse. She was still in turmoil on the inside from the events on Sunday and hadn't spoken to her mother since the conversation cut short when Ainsley hung up on Rose.

"Well, at least you're honest. Is that the only virtue you have left?" Rose's response was oh-so predictable.

"Should I make other arrangements? Or are you interested in seeing your granddaughter?" Ainsley spoke slowly.

"Is that how you see me? Are your father and I merely people with whom to arrange childcare?"

Ainsley and Rose had been doing this dance with each other for decades. The steps were so familiar. It was a game where the players had to answer a question with another question. The loser was the one who couldn't come up with another question, forcing them to give an answer. Most of the time, it was Ainsley who gave in. But not today.

"Are you saying you don't want to see Jesse, Mother?"

"Of course we do. But I am insulted. You take for granted our availability to babysit." Rose had broken the sequence. Ainsley explained briefly why she needed a sitter.

"We'll get her from school." Rose took back control as she laid out a plan. "Have her pack for overnight and we'll bring her to school the next day, too."

"Thank you, Mother."

"You have a lot going on, Ainsley. Is it wise to pursue romantic interests when you have important issues to address?" Rose attempted to restore the game's tempo, but Ainsley had already taken off her dancing shoes.

"Thanks for taking Jesse Thursday, Mother."

Though the conversation ended with a positive outcome, Ainsley took no comfort. She wished she and Rose had a better rapport. There had been many times in her life she could have used the support, someone on her side. Someone in which to confide.

She remembered the painful days following the breakout of rumors after the bad date with Rick Johnson and the disastrous events at Rachelle's party. Most of all, she remembered the day she realized who her mother truly was. Ainsley remained silent for days, afraid to say a word because Rose's fuse was short and her anger lingered.

That Wednesday, after a long day at school, Ainsley had come home to find Rose behind a fortress of boxes stacked on the floor. Ainsley recognized the signs of Rose's obsessive compulsion to purge. She cleaned out all the closets and cabinets and got rid of clutter.

Ainsley knew Rose's binge cleaning often culminated with her concocting a plan to solve some problem. With trepidation, Ainsley stepped inside, and when Rose saw her, she squealed with delight.

"Good, you are home. Help me load this into your father's truck. We can drop off these boxes at the Church Mouse thrift store."

Suspicious of her mother's perky attitude, Ainsley obliged. On the way to the donation center, Rose's intentions became known.

"Do you know about a presentation happening at school?" Rose waited for an answer. When she got no response, she continued. "It's called 'Teenage Parents: Getting comfortable talking about an uncomfortable subject.' It's designed to help parents talk with their kids about the dangers and consequences of promiscuous teenage behavior."

The patronizing bounce in Rose's tone was the opposite one would expect when discussing such a serious topic. It was as if she was trying to convince Ainsley it would be fun.

"I want you to come tonight, Ainsley. It'll be good for you. You may hear some encouraging words." Ainsley had agreed mostly out of fear of what her mother would do if she didn't go. But nothing would ever be worse than what Rose did when Ainsley *did* go.

Sponsored by the Gold Ridge High School booster's club, of which her parents were active members, the presentation was the second in a series that addressed current issues teenagers are facing. That night's meeting was on the subject of rising teenage pregnancy rates. Led by a school board member, Linda, who, like Rose, took a personal approach, the presentation was indicative of the school board's fixation on controlling the kids and treating them as if they were all culpable. In anticipation of a substantial turnout, the plan was to hold the meeting in the high school theater.

"Are we late?" Rose hurried Ainsley across the empty parking lot.

Inside the auditorium Ainsley noticed the seats were barely half full. Hoping they'd sit in the back, she intended to humor her mother, but was disappointed when Rose chose to sit near the stage, front and center. Leery of Rose's choice of seats, Ainsley sensed more deception in Rose's overly exuberant smile that did not match the place nor the subject matter.

The meeting began with a recounting of an incident that involved a class that graduated five years before. It was the same story cited every time parents and teachers were discussing with the kids, teenage drinking, drunk driving, drug use, and underaged sex. Designed to instill fear into the kids so they would practice abstinence from every harmful behavior, the retelling of the incident time after time undermined its impact. Most of the kids doubted the facts, and some believed it was a lie altogether.

The story went that what had started as a graduation party had turned into a massive, out-of-control bash. The police were called and an ambulance came to treat a student for alcohol poisoning.

After the bogus story of a party gone awry, Ainsley had zoned out during the remainder of the presentation. The meeting then went into the part where the audience, both students and adults, were allowed to share their thoughts and experiences and discuss any subject. Suddenly, Ainsley felt a hand grip her biceps.

Dragging Ainsley to her feet, Rose asked permission from the presenters, "Would you like to hear from my daughter Ainsley? She will share with you her negative experiences. She has gone against my wisdom and advice and followed a path of promiscuity."

The betrayal hit her like a punch to the stomach. Ainsley froze when it dawned on her that her mother had chosen to retaliate publicly against her, based on nothing but lies. She knew she had broken some rules, but she didn't deserve this. Realizing Rose wouldn't stop until Ainsley wore the Scarlet Letter "A" on her chest, she felt something inside shut off to be replaced by a welling of adrenaline that flowed through her body.

Ainsley stood up as ordered but didn't start to speak. Rose was looking at her with expectation. The silence in the room pounded her ears and in order to stop the ringing, she heard herself saying, "My name is Ainsley and I am a sexaholic."

The statement left the room buzzing. The teenagers started laughing, and the parents gasped for air.

Rose stood there with her mouth open, then sank into her chair without saying another word after Ainsley had blurted her announcement.

One woman who had brought her girl to the assembly had spoken up. "We're leaving. This is not the kind of help my daughter and I need."

Another mother stood up with her teen and walked out. Others who had appeared befuddled followed, while a few stayed until the assembly session was adjourned.

The dreaded car ride home had begun—and so had the belittlement. "What are you thinking? Why did you say that?" The questions had kept coming, despite Ainsley's silence. "Don't you have anything to say?"

"What did you expect me to say?" Ainsley had found her voice.

"You were supposed to tell the other girls about how your reputation has been marred by shameful rumors. How promiscuity can ruin your life in many ways. They need to hear the truth, Ainsley."

"The truth? You never asked me for my side, Mom. You heard the rumors and believed them. I simply told them what I thought you wanted."

"This is not a game. Do you understand what you have done? Some of these parents won't trust me enough now to bring their daughters to my group."

"What do you want me to do? I didn't know what to say. You wouldn't listen to me before. All you care about is your reputation with your stupid group. You care more about them than you do me."

"So you ruined it for me? All I want is to guide you and teach you about the dangers you and other young girls face. And that's the thanks I get?"

"Thanks?" Ainsley hadn't backed down as she had done in the past when their fights became too intense. Feeling the power in her voice rise, she continued, "You want me to thank you for putting me on the spot like that?"

"Yes, thanks, Ainsley. Thanks for my efforts to keep you from making the same mistakes I made." Rose's words cut straight to Ainsley's heart.

So I am a mistake? Ainsley had thought. This underlying truth had been a stabbing pain inflicted upon her many times before.

Ainsley needed no more confirmation of what she believed in the depths of her heart. She struck back.

"I'm sorry, mother." Ainsley smirked in the darkened interior of the vehicle. "I apologize for spoiling your treasured group. But no matter how much you punish me, I am not guilty of your sins. I am not a pregnant teenager like you were."

Ainsley had run from the car when they arrived at the farm and locked herself in her room.

"Open the door this instant." Rose had knocked outside Ainsley's bedroom for twenty minutes.

There was no response from Ainsley.

"You're grounded until further notice."

Ainsley had recognized her mother's anger. She had seen it many times before when Rose conflated her past onto Ainsley. But that night after the disastrous meeting, something had shifted in Ainsley. She realized no matter how hard Rose tried, she didn't have to carry Rose's baggage any longer.

"You have the power to ground me. Punish me all you want. And as long as you do, I might as well commit the crimes."

That had been the last time Ainsley had trusted Rose, and she remembered the pain of the aftermath. Shrugging off the memory, she pushed away the emotions.

"I'm meeting Belle at the corner and we are going to run up the bike path." Ainsley called to Jesse as she came down the stairs.

"How long will you be?" Jesse had set up her schoolbooks on the kitchen table.

"Same as always. An hour or so." Ainsley felt comfortable leaving Jesse alone for a brief period in the afternoons. "Go to Mrs. Dixon's in case of an emergency, and you know the number for nine-one-one, right?" Ainsley headed out.

"Yes," Jesse sighed, showing she was tiring of the old joke. "It's '9-1-1,'" she recited.

"Be back soon."

Ainsley swung her arms and kicked out her legs to warm up, then slowly picked up the pace. Down the street she ran past historic buildings, some remodeled and restored, that embodied the small town charm that was Sebastopol. Once a vibrant agricultural hub of the apple growing industry, there were few reminders left of the long forgotten days.

"Let's do the other half of the path today." Belle suggested when they met up at the intersection.

"Then we'll have to run on the sidewalk longer." The afternoon traffic was heavy, both on foot and in cars.

"We can handle it." Belle took off, heading north on Main, and Ainsley followed. The pair of runners didn't get far before a throng of people gathering impeded their progress.

"What is happening here?" Ainsley was about to take a sharp right into the oncoming traffic lane, but Belle had stopped to find out what was the commotion.

"They seem to gather in front of the music store." Belle stood on her tippy-toes to look beyond the crowd. "Oh, my gosh!" Belle exclaimed.

Ainsley's jaw dropped, but no sound came out when she saw what Belle had seen.

"It's Tom West! He's signing autographs! Let's get one for Jesse. She loves his music." Belle pushed through the throng.

"No, Belle." Ainsley gripped Belle's arm, glancing toward the fans gathered around their idol.

"It's no big deal. This won't take but a minute. Jesse will be thrilled."

"Jesse doesn't need an autograph. Let's not bother. These big celebrities don't have time for kids." Ainsley pulled Belle in the other direction.

"But..." Belle protested, surprised at her friend's intensity to flee, "... this is Tom West! He's a local legend. I hear he has family here in Sebastopol."

"I'm serious, Belle. Please..."

"Ainsley?" A voice rose above the gatherers. "Is that you?" The voice cut through the crowd. "You haven't changed a bit. You are a sight for sore eyes." Tom West emerged from the swarm to stand before the only person who seemed intent on getting away.

Belle turned to face him. "You know her?"

"He knows you?" Belle refocused on her speechless friend.

"It's been a few years, but yes, you could say that," Tom answered, then spoke to Ainsley. "I'm so thrilled to see you."

Flustered, not ready to speak, Ainsley squeaked, "Good to see you, Tom." Then, to Belle, "C'mon, we better be leaving."

"Wait! I want an autograph!"

The singer held several CDs in his hand and opened one. "Who do I make it out to?"

"Jesse," Belle spoke with dreamy eyes, "with an 'e.'"

"Here you are, Jesse with an 'e.' No charge." Tom closed the CD case and handed it to Belle. "Any friend of Ainsley's is a friend of mine."

"I'm not Jesse," Belle kept talking as the gatherers begged for autographs. "My name is Belle. Jesse is Ainsley's daughter."

Tom West stopped dead and turned as the mob closed in.

"Ainsley's daughter? I see." Tom broke free a second time and gave Belle his full attention. "Well, Belle, can I sign one for you, too?"

"Yes, please." Belle gushed. "That's Belle with an 'e.'"

Tom chuckled as he scribbled on another CD. "Here you go, Belle, with an 'e.' And for you, mother of Jesse with an 'e'? Miss Ainsley Tobin? Or do you have a married name?"

"No, thanks." Ainsley backed away from the scene.

"She's not married." Belle threw the words over her shoulder, as Ainsley, with strength anew, dragged off her friend.

"Let's get going," Ainsley said through gritted teeth.

"You know Tom West? How come you never told me?" Belle pounced on Ainsley after they cleared the crowd.

"He's just a guy who grew up here and went to high school here, but graduated before me."

Belle noted Ainsley's tense expression, and the reaction confused her. "Just a guy?"

"Yes." Ainsley held almost no hope her friend would drop the subject.

"Tom West is not just a guy. He is the most popular country singer in the country. Multi-platinum hits on the charts for close to a decade. He does tours all across the nation."

"You're the expert. There's nothing else to say."

Free at last from the busy sidewalks, Ainsley took off.

The paved multi-use trail built on the old railway tracks ran along the highway that connected Santa Rosa to Sebastopol. From Sebastopol heading northwest, the trail twisted through houses until it reached orchards.

When Ainsley came to the most western point where the trail crossed the highway, she didn't continue on the path. Making the uni-lateral decision to run a loop and circle home, Ainsley had no inten-tion of going through town again.

"Gonna keep running, huh?" Belle asked rhetorically.

Ainsley kept pushing her feet at a much faster pace than usual. At least if they were out of breath, Belle couldn't ask any more questions.

"Please, Ainsley!" Belle gasped. "Slow down!" Gasp. "I need to breathe!"

Ainsley obliged.

"You can... tell me... when you... are ready." Belle spoke in huffs as she exhaled and inhaled the precious, life-sustaining oxygen her deprived muscles were screaming for. "But one way or another, you gotta tell me..."

"I knew Tom West before he was a superstar. He was an aspiring artist. A garage-band singer/songwriter hoping to make it big."

"Why were you so reluctant to talk to him? He remembered you and seemed happy. You ran off like a flushed rabbit. What are you not telling me?"

"I didn't know him as much as I knew of him." Ainsley resorted to semantics. She had no interest in conversing about Tom West.

"He sure knows you, Ainsley." Belle implied, sensing Ainsley was minimizing. "Are you sure there isn't more to it?"

"I knew him in high school. End of story."

"Okay." Belle let the subject die, but for Ainsley, the wounds were just opening. Tom West's return released a rush of memories. She remembered when she first met Tom.

"What's there to hurry back to? We just got our diplomas. We can do what we want!" Patti had protested when Ainsley mentioned she was leaving the graduation party. "Please stay until the band gets here."

Ainsley's last year of high school had been lonely, but she hadn't minded. Keeping to herself, she focused on her education and graduated with honors. Though she had agreed to come to the school-sponsored graduation night party, she hadn't promised she would stay. She wanted to get home and start making plans. Now that she was almost 18, figuring out how she could leave town was the priority.

"There's gonna be live music?" Ainsley's interest was piqued. Most of the teen dances had a DJ. The high school board members were not in favor of spending the money on live music. It turned out they had invited musicians to play for their hometown, as three of the members were Gold Ridge High alumni, and they agreed to play for free.

"It's the group my cousin plays in. They are only getting started, but I think they are gonna be huge. They call themselves Sunset West. And wait till you see the lead singer." Patti had revealed. "He is so cute." Patti's excitement had inspired curiosity, so Ainsley stayed.

"So, you're a roadie," Ainsley chatted with Patti's cousin, Paul, while the auditorium full of teeny boppers continued to celebrate.

The lead singer noticed his bandmate talking with Ainsley and left the groupies to come over. "And who have we here?" he asked.

Paul introduced Ainsley.

"Nice to meet you, I'm Tom. Tom West."

Ainsley shook his outstretched hand. His grip was strong but not crushing. There was a soft warmth that made her want to hold on. It seemed he wanted to stay and chat, but his bandmates beckoned him to return to the stage.

Ainsley changed her mind about leaving and decided to see if she could get more time to talk with Tom West. She wanted to find out about this intriguing singer. Tom's music had a deep and passionate quality, and she admired his commitment to playing with professionalism at a non-paying high school gig.

Though they had only met, Tom showed interest in Ainsley, too. Through the overnight event, Sunset West played, and when they took breaks Tom spent the time with Ainsley.

"Where's mother?" Ainsley had asked when William arrived at dawn to take her home at the end of the party.

"Your Aunt Ruthie needed emergency surgery. Your mother went to stay with her."

"Is Aunt Ruthie alright?" The news shocked Ainsley.

"She is fine. Cut her hand while repairing an easel for a student. Your mom will stay with her until she can provide for herself again."

Ainsley heard her father, but it wasn't easy to not worry.

"Appears as if you enjoyed yourself. Are you smiling?" William had altered the conversation as he evaluated his daughter's mood. "Now that you've pulled your first all-nighter," William had said, referring to the graduation event, "what's next?"

"It's too early for breakfast, but too late to go to bed." Ainsley didn't wish to disappoint her dad, but she wanted to plan for her solo phase of life and had lots to do. Lying on her bed, Ainsley thought about getting out of this town. Her last thoughts before she drifted off to sleep were of the only thing painful about her plans; leaving William.

Ainsley hadn't slept long when William woke her. Tom West was at the door.

"Daddy, this is Tom. He is in the band with Patti's cousin, Paul." Ainsley made introductions as William scrutinized the young man at his door.

"I'd like permission to ask Ainsley out." Tom had said.

Though Tom was older, William had agreed to allow her to go on an afternoon coffee date.

"Tom is not a boy, Ainsley. He's a grown man," William had warned.

"Daddy, I'll be fine. It's only a cup of coffee. And he's not that much older."

Jolted from her reverie, Ainsley heard Belle proclaim, "Well, here's to another interesting run. Another one of your 'lost-in-your-own-mind' times. I may as well exercise alone."

Ainsley stopped running when she realized where they were. They had run for several miles from the outskirts of town along the converted railway tracks. She had gone the entire way deep in thought.

"Look, I understand these moods, but what's really happening?" Belle questioned her friend's recent distractions with suspicion.

Belle was familiar with most things about Ainsley, including her strong desire for privacy, but their friendship was too close for many secrets. She also knew there were deep parts of her best friend that must be too dark to visit. These spells of silence, while in deep concentration, were not anything new. Belle would wait for it to pass.

"I am here if you need to talk."

"Thanks, Belle."

Ainsley was sorry to be such a poor exercise companion to Belle, and she appreciated Belle's supportive indulgence. She realized her friend had questions and deserved an explanation.

"See you at work. Neither snow nor rain nor gloom of night..." Ainsley made a weak attempt at lightening the mood with a bit of post office humor.

"... shall stay these couriers... blah... blah. However the rest goes." Belle responded playfully and smiled in an effort to show forgiveness. "See you tomorrow."

Walking alone now the rest of the way home, Ainsley breathed the late spring air as her body cooled. Wisteria, gardenia and honeysuckle mixed together and took her back in time. Dating Tom West had given Ainsley a sense of power and had brought her a happiness she hadn't felt in a long time. She remembered their first date.

"From the moment Paul introduced us," Tom had said, "you intrigued me."

They had sat at the local coffee house. Ainsley tried to appear comfortable at the quirky hometown hangout but felt intimidated by Tom's intensity and was tongue-tied. She focused on carefully sipping her mocha so as not to be further embarrassed by giving herself a foam mustache.

"You looked so deep and contemplative at the grad party while the other kids were enjoying themselves." Tom continued, "You are so out of place among all those teenagers." Tom held Ainsley with his eyes, then mindfully glanced at his cup and sipped his slightly sweetened plain black coffee.

"They're my friends." Ainsley hadn't understood Tom's observation and didn't know if it was complimentary or critical. Ainsley thought it strange that Tom was claiming she didn't fit in when it was him, a man in his twenties, who stood out at the high school event.

"Would you like to walk around town after coffee?" Tom had offered when he and Ainsley were nearing the bottom of their cups.

"That would be nice."

They had walked up to and across the main street and ended up at Yves Park.

"I haven't been here since I was a kid," Ainsley announced as they walked towards a footbridge across a dry creek bed. "We did the bridging ceremony from Brownies to Girls Scouts here at this bridge."

Ainsley had heard herself talking and quickly stopped. It embarrassed her, and she thought, *I'm such a dork. Why am I talking about Girl Scouts?*

"I should have known you were a Girl Scout." Tom had teased without ill intention.

Tom's statement embarrassed Ainsley. "There is nothing wrong with being a Scout." Then she had been even more embarrassed, and was mad at herself for having gotten defensive.

"I meant nothing by it, Ainsley." Tom had clarified as he reached out and turned her towards him. He had held onto her, not too close, but in a more romantic way than she was accustomed to.

She was on the verge of ending the date with a thank you for coffee, but she didn't get the chance. Her thoughts never became words when Tom captured her lips with his. It had been a soft kiss with a touch of intensity. Relaxing into it, relieved he was a good kisser, she forgot what she had intended to say.

"How does it feel to be a rock star?" she blurted out. This had been worse than the previous statement regarding her participation in the Scouts.

"Well, for starters," Tom chuckled. "We are not a rock band, and I am not a star, but I will be some day." He had sparkled with energy when he explained how his music career was about to take off.

"You seem determined," Ainsley had observed.

"I am very determined. Nothing will stop me. Nothing." Tom repeated. Ainsley had been convinced.

Shaking her head at the thought of Tom's declaration all those years ago, Ainsley was reminded of why things had turned out the way they did.

The lights were on in the cottage when Ainsley got there. Brooke barked when she heard Ainsley's footsteps approaching. "Hey, girl! It's me! It's your momma," she assured the dog, who was jumping and wagging her tail. "You're such a good watchdog, aren'tcha."

"You're back!" Jesse heard her mother but continued watching TV.

"We ran a bit longer than I thought we would."

"Some man called. He said he'd call again and left me his number. I wrote it down."

Ainsley saw the notepad by the phone with some scribbles and, with trepidation, picked it up. Had Tom West called again? She stared at the lines Jesse had squiggled out in her ten-year-old style script. "I can't read this. What does this note say?"

"I think the name started with an 'A' or an 'S.' I don't remember."

"Was it Dale?" Ainsley imagined it might have been the aircraft engineer.

"Maybe, yah," Jesse answered without losing focus on the screen. "He was hard to understand."

"Dale doesn't know our home phone. He would have called on my cell."

"He asked for you to please call him."

"It makes no sense..." Ainsley began, but the action on the television screen already transfixed Jesse. The conversation was clearly over for the child.

"With this writing," Ainsley said to herself, "she could be a doctor. No one can read their writing either."

Staring at the scribbled note, Ainsley's stomach tightened and her breath shortened. She realized the caller could have been Tom West. Jesse may have spoken to him. She felt the need to rid them of the evidence.

"It must be a mistake." Ainsley crumpled the note and tossed but missed the receptacle. "Probably the wrong number again."

Hearing Ainsley talking to herself, Jesse refocused on her mother with questioning eyes.

Ainsley felt the scrutiny as she stooped to retrieve the note. "I have Dale's contact info. I'll call him."

With more precise aim, Ainsley tossed the paper into the trash receptacle. "Or he'll call me."

Jesse rolled her eyes and watched her movie. Luckily, the child was used to her mother's spastic behavior.

CHAPTER 6

Misdeliveries

Ainsley hoped Belle would keep quiet about their encounter with Tom West, but the next day at work she realized that wouldn't be the case. The news was too tempting. Meeting a big country music star was a juicy bit of gossip. Belle shared the story with her co-workers of her encounter with the famous singer while keeping Ainsley's name out of the tale.

"I know it's hard to believe." Belle supported her story as each postal worker listened on from their respective cases, "but it's true. We were jogging along when we passed this crowd of people on the sidewalk."

"I saw the crowd," said Darrel from Route 201. "It was in front of the music store, right?"

"Yes," Belle confirmed.

"Must be some musicians drumming up publicity for a concert." A voice came from the case behind Ainsley's.

"It was the lead singer of the band Sunset West," Belle confirmed. "He was signing CDs."

"Yeah, that country music singer, Tom West," came a voice from Route 110 across the floor. "He grew up here, graduated, then went off to become a star. There is going to be a concert at Luther Burbank Center for the Arts. I saw the flyers."

Ainsley tried to check out of the conversation as she tended to the row of letters she was sorting. She loaded the cart with her sorted mail. Before Ainsley could wheel away out to her vehicle, Belle stepped around her case and whispered, "Sorry, Ains. I couldn't help myself. Meeting Tom West was a big deal for me."

"No sweat. They have to talk about something," Ainsley said nervously. "Look, Belle, I know you think it's cool that Tom West knows me, but please keep that part to yourself. Things are not always as they appear."

"Of course, Ains." Belle said. "My lips are sealed. And what am I gonna say, anyway? You haven't told me a thing."

"Trust me, Belle. I will tell you everything I can when I can." Pushing her loaded cart outside, Ainsley knew she couldn't hold Belle off forever. In contemplating how to tell Belle about her past, Ainsley was thrown back to those uncertain and dramatic times.

"Ainsley, don't you leave this house. You have no business going out with that man." Rose had been unhappy that Ainsley was dating Tom West, an older man in his early twenties.

Tom and Ainsley had grown closer following the intimate conversations they had had. Tom was a good listener and Ainsley shared with him things no one else knew. Ainsley was mutually supportive of Tom and his dreams.

"Who's going to stop me? I'm almost an adult." Ainsley had gotten good at ignoring her mother during the short time she and Tom had been together that summer after graduation. But that hadn't stopped Rose from trying to intervene.

"Don't continue on this path…" Rose spoke to Ainsley's retreating backside.

Ainsley had gone that day on foot to check if Tom was at his cousin's house, but he was out. She walked home to an empty house feeling lonely. She found a note on the table in Rose's handwriting instructing her there were leftovers for dinner. Ignoring the instructions, she took out the box of macaroni and cheese she kept hidden in the pantry.

The doorbell had rung as Ainsley was about to assemble the milk, butter and a pot. Tom had swept in without waiting to be invited when Ainsley opened the front door.

"My cousin said you stopped by. I must have come home right after that." Tom had kissed Ainsley with familiarity as she wrapped her arms around him in greeting.

"Come in," Ainsley had motioned towards the kitchen. "Can I offer you something to drink?"

"You got a beer?"

Ainsley had turned to retrieve the beverage from the refrigerator. She hid her initial expression when he had asked for a beer. She had often forgotten Tom was twenty-three and well above the legal age to drink alcohol. She knew how William liked his beer, served in a mug kept cold in the freezer. "Do you want it in a mug?" she offered.

"Sure, I'll take the mug." Tom had taken the beer and frosty mug from Ainsley. "Where are your folks?"

"Rose is at the teen center at church."

"And William?" Tom had leaned forward to glance into the family room where it was customary for Ainsley's dad to be, but the recliner chair had been empty.

"Dad is at a Plumbing-Heating-Cooling Contractors Association meeting."

"It's not appropriate for me to be here. In the house. Alone... with you." Tom had known how volatile things were between Ainsley and her mother and had been knowing how Rose would not approve.

"You don't want to be alone with me?" Ainsley had then looked at Tom, hoping she was being coy.

"You're teasing me." Tom had fallen into Ainsley's game. "You're playing with fire."

"I?" Ainsley had placed her hand, palm down on her chest, channeling Scarlet O'Hara in her favorite movie, *Gone with the Wind*.

"Stop it, woman." Tom had warned. "Are you sure you know what you are doing?"

He and Ainsley had spent time together, either at the garage where Tom's band rehearsed or the park nearby. Sometimes Ainsley could get away with a longer trip to the beach without Rose's knowledge, but that time never resulted in intimacy beyond kissing, talking and sharing with each other their deepest thoughts and feelings.

Ainsley had continued to look Tom in the eyes with intention.

"Come here." Tom had risen from the chair and locked Ainsley in a kiss in one move. The fire smoldering beneath the surface for weeks leapt over the confines of restraint.

Ainsley allowed what happened next to come naturally. Tom took her participation as consent.

As it had been her first time with a man, she was surprised when the lovemaking was over in less than ten minutes. She spent more time than that brushing and flossing her teeth.

Once she was dressed and in the kitchen making tea, Ainsley noticed the sunset and stood looking out the window. A clothed Tom came in and wrapped his arms around her from behind, extending the intimacy of the moment with the woman he was holding in his arms. He gave her a long, lingering kiss on the cheek.

Ainsley sank into his embrace and let out a peaceful sigh.

Then she became self-conscious. Her naivety had crept back into her mind, leaving her feeling awkward. She wondered if there was more she should have done.

Ainsley pivoted away from Tom and finished steeping tea for both of them. Careful to keep the steaming mugs steady, she walked toward the dining room, set down the tea on the table, and took a seat. Tom followed.

"So, *that* happened," Ainsley blurted, "It wasn't at all what I was expecting."

Tom had stopped mid-sip, not sure how to interpret Ainsley's comment. Ainsley saw his reaction.

"Oh," Ainsley blushed. "It was fine, I guess. I mean…" Ainsley paused. She wasn't sure how to say she had nothing to compare it to. "Just not how I thought it would be."

"Are you telling me this was your first time?" Tom had set his teacup on its saucer, un-sipped.

"Did I do it wrong?" Ainsley's heart began to beat faster. The peaceful feeling she had was evaporating.

"I wish I'd known. You should've told me." Tom had then seemed angry.

"Sorry. I…" Tom's response confused Ainsley. From her perspective, their lovemaking had been okay. Now she wasn't sure.

Ainsley hadn't had time or experience to understand the significance to a man when it was the first time for his partner. Ainsley hadn't known the burden of responsibility for making her first time a positive experience was the man's.

"No, no. I am sorry. I should have asked. If I had known it was your first, I would have… Well, I could have done things differently."

Ainsley didn't understand what Tom meant by doing things differently, but the tenderness in his expression, his considerate words, touched her heart. She had smiled then and Tom had reached across to take her hand.

"What is going on here?" Ainsley heard from the back side of the house. Rose had flung open the side door so fast it took a moment for the air in the room to stabilize. It had taken a moment for Ainsley and Tom to adjust, too. They had been holding each other's hand resting on the table top but quickly let go.

"Mother."

"Mrs. Tobin, hello…" Tom rose abruptly, almost tipping over his chair. This was not the way to leave a good impression. Holding out his hand, he offered, "Nice to see you." His outstretched hand remained empty as Rose glared across the room.

"I think it's time for you to leave, Mr. West." Tom's last name, when spoken by Rose, came with an added hiss. "You have no business being in this house alone with my daughter." Rose had descended upon Tom like a snarling, rabid dog.

"Mom!" Ainsley's mother's venomous reaction had surprised and embarrassed her. Then Ainsley had thought of the couch, and wished she'd inspected it to make sure she and Tom had left no trace of their intimacy. Tom had seen Ainsley's nervous expression.

"I'll go. It's probably best if I do. I'll see you later, Ainsley…" Tom glanced at Rose, then softly said to Ainsley, "I'll call. I promise."

Catching her daughter in an open display of tenderness with a man had driven Rose to the edge. For two days straight, whenever Ainsley came into a room, Rose made some reference to that afternoon.

"You know a man his age wants one thing only."

"He showed no respect. A complete lack of decorum."

"You think you should trust a guy like that?"

With each passing moment, Ainsley could feel Rose's wrath. Scared her mother would find out what she and Tom had done, Ainsley remembered how terrifying it was having no way to measure how much her mother already knew.

"Ainsley, dear." Pulling her out of her daydream, a white-haired lady in a housecoat came running up the sidewalk behind Ainsley as she delivered the mail. It was Mrs. Stevens waving a handful of mail. "You gave me the wrong mail. These letters are for the Trumans."

"I can't believe I did this." Ainsley looked at the mail in her hand and realized she was off by one house. She had put Mrs. Stevens's mail in the empty house on the corner. "I am so sorry, Mrs Stevens."

"Don't worry, dear. This sort of thing happens."

"I will call my supervisor and we'll figure out how to get your mail."

"No worries. I'll call the realtor who's selling that vacant house. She came out last time this happened. I had my mail within an hour, and everyone else exchanged their mail later that day."

"This happened before?" The thought of making this mistake more than once mortified Ainsley.

"It wasn't you the first time it happened, dear. It was the tall, good-looking man who does the route on your days off. Is he your husband?"

"Kevin has a wife and kids. Why would you think he's my husband?" The little old lady's assumption amused Ainsley.

"You would make a handsome couple, that's all." Mrs. Stevens gave a wink, then looked off into the distance at nothing. "That young man reminds me of my Harry, rest his soul."

Ainsley felt the loneliness displayed on the old woman's face. "Would you like me to call the real estate agent?"

"No, dear. You best be on your way. Your other customers will be mad if you are late. But pay attention now and be careful as you go to Old Man Cutler's house. He is a dirty old coot. Comes out just to watch you walking away after you deliver the mail. Then he pretends to be tending his flowers. That garden gets more attention since you began bringing our mail than it ever did before."

Ainsley laughed as she continued delivering the mail. Mr. Cutler's behavior cracked Ainsley up, and Mrs. Stevens' characterization was funny, too. She stepped lighter and the rest of the mail practically delivered itself. At the end of the day, Ainsley gave a sigh of relief and slid into her Jeep having made no additional mistakes.

"Mom, can we swing by the house and get my breeches? I forgot to grab them on the way out this morning." Jesse admitted her oversight when Ainsley picked her and Emily up from school after work. She was driving them straight to the barn for their lessons.

"We don't have any wiggle room on time today," Ainsley reminded Jesse. "I'm meeting Belle. We planned a relaxing bike ride while you two are riding horses. You'll have to ride in your jeans and use your chaps. And next time, you'll be more likely to remember everything."

"It'll only take a second to stop at home. Please?" Jesse was persistent.

"Is there a reason you can't use your chaps?" Ainsley wanted to use this as a teachable moment.

"The thing is," Jesse explained, "the chaps make me sweat and I get hot during the lesson. Then I need to drink lots of water and that makes me have to pee. Do you see where I'm going with this?"

Getting the chaps on and off was no easy task. With a full bladder, that long zipper down the sides of the legs could be troublesome when delaying the process. Emily giggled at her friend's antics.

"I believe I see."

Ainsley let the girls have their laugh and Jesse resigned to riding in her jeans and chaps.

"Thanks for the ride, Ainsley," Emily said, and the young equestrians exited the car and trotted off to the barn. Ainsley was still smiling at their silliness all the way home.

"Need some help?"

Back at the cottage, bending over her bike as she filled the tire with air, Ainsley looked up when she heard the question. Brooke barked at the man standing outside the gate.

"Brooke!" Ainsley called the dog to her side, then turned to the intruder. Thinking it was Phillip, she said, "I dropped off the girls..." her words trailed off as recognition set in.

There before Ainsley stood the man she had been trying for over ten years to forget. In his mid-thirties now, Tom West seemed in fine physical health. The color of his eyes was as blue and piercing as Ainsley remembered, and the intensity of his stare challenged her convictions to keep him in her past.

"I was in the neighborhood." Tom's hand reached for the gate latch. "May I come in?"

Tom's reaching to unlock the gate caused the dog to react with a low growl and a step forward.

"Wait, Brooke," Ainsley commanded. The dog then licked her nose but never took her eyes off the man. Ainsley and the dog both stared at the visitor.

"Sorry to come over unannounced," Tom said as he reached once more for the gate. "I won't keep you from your plans, but I hadn't heard from you. I was wondering if you got the message from my associate about the concert tickets?"

"Your associate?" Ainsley suppressed the effect of Tom's physical presence and concentrated on being mad that he had someone to call her on his behalf. Tom was one of those people who had people to do everything for him. "Is that who talked to Jesse? Your associate?"

"So, can you make it to the concert?" Tom noticed the way Ainsley repeated the word *associate*.

"I know nothing about a concert." It wasn't a complete lie. "I never spoke to any of your people."

"Oh, I'm sorry," Tom sensed her animosity and took a step back. "I'd like to invite you to a complimentary concert here in Santa Rosa."

"Thank you, but no. I'm busy." Ainsley was as polite as a lioness stalking a gazelle.

"I didn't even tell you what day. It's Thursday evening." Tom escaped the lioness's initial attack and fought back. "I'd like to meet your daughter. I heard she is a fan."

Ainsley bristled when Tom mentioned Jesse. The lioness crouched, ready to spring.

"Like I said, I am busy." Ainsley pounced on her prey.

This time Ainsley wasn't lying. She had a date with Dale on Thursday. *Yes, Dale*, she told herself. *Safe to focus on Dale.*

"I understand. I'm sorry to bother you." Tom took another step back. The lioness's hostility hit the weakening gazelle as she continued to attack.

The celebrity gets turned down, Ainsley thought. The lioness smugly moved in for the kill. It was a matter of survival.

"Well, how-dee-do." Belle came rolling down the driveway on her bike. Why couldn't she have been running late? "Tom West. We meet again."

"Hello, Belle, with an 'e.'"

"Che sorprese verderti chi. And you remember me, too?" Belle was grinning at Tom, then at Ainsley.

"How could I forget such a memorable gal?" The twinkle in Tom's eyes returned. Belle's timely appearance brought the gazelle a glimmer of life. "I was just inviting Ainsley and her daughter to a concert this Thursday but they are busy. Perhaps you might like the tickets?"

"One of your concerts? I'd love to. I've heard your concerts are *uno spasso.*"

"She can't go either." Ainsley interjected, disappointed that Belle was so excited she had relapsed into speaking Italian. "We both have a date that evening."

"We had dates, but now we are both free on Thursday. The double date got canceled."

Ainsley glared at her friend. *You're not helping*, she thought, gritting her teeth so hard it made her gums hurt. "I haven't heard anything about a cancellation."

"Then you are free after all." Tom announced after a pause. He glanced from Belle to Ainsley and back, then asked, "How many tickets will you need in total?"

"Just the three." Belle accepted the invitation. "It's a date. A ladies' night. I'll handle the details."

"Wait, what's going on?" Ainsley tried to stop it, but the gazelle had found an ally.

"Good. It's settled. I'll let you girls get to your bike riding then. I'll arrange for your tickets."

And with a wave, Tom was gone. The lioness watched as her catch bounded away.

CHAPTER 7

In Concert

"It's nearing bedtime, Jesse," Ainsley announced after they had finished dinner.

"She might be going to bed, but I bet she won't sleep," Belle teased. Jesse nodded with a teeth-clenched-together grin.

Belle had stayed after the bike ride to tell her goddaughter the news about the tickets to the Sunset West concert. All through dinner, Jesse and Belle giggled and squealed about Tom West and counted how many songs each of them knew by heart.

After saying good night, Jesse sang as she climbed the stairs, "Hoping for your love so true, I'm forever waiting for you."

Ainsley had heard Jesse singing along to a Tom West song on the radio and her iPod many times, but her rendition of the country music song tonight held significantly more impact.

"And I know deep in my soul, love will find its way home" Belle joined Jesse in singing the final line of the song. Ainsley tried to let go of the implications and smiled at Belle's joy. Seeing Belle interact with Jesse this way, she imagined what Belle might have been like as a teen.

"I best be on my way, too," said Belle. "Thanks for dinner."

"We always welcome you." Ainsley replied. "I'm grateful you and Jesse could chat about your favorite group."

It warmed her heart to see the excitement in her daughter and her friend, but this particular subject threatened to stir up the deep emotions that had remained unaddressed within her for over a decade. The mere thought of it tightened her shoulders. Ainsley took a deep, quiet breath in, then out, and rolled her shoulders in an attempt to rid herself of the tension. It was imperative she keep the past buried. Jesse was only a child. It wasn't necessary for her to suffer from baggage in the adult world.

"I realize you don't share the same enthusiasm for music as us. Sorry the subject doesn't interest you," Belle prodded, as she was certain there was much more to the story than Ainsley was telling.

"It's not that I don't like country music. I am just not as passionate as you and Jesse. That's all."

The day prior to the concert had arrived, and the buildup of worry in Ainsley about her daughter seeing the famous singer had steadily risen. To offset the rise of inner tension, though it wasn't part of the normal routine, Ainsley found release from the pressure by adding to her exercise regime. Along with her regular meet-ups with Belle for a run or bike ride, Ainsley did calisthenics, pilates, and yoga stretching at home.

"Can you take a day off, Mom? We only have one day left to prepare. We need to go shopping. You can't wear regular clothes to a country music show." Jesse stood over her mother who lay supine on the floor, holding her legs just above the mat.

"You mean there's a uniform?" Drawing her knees to her chest in rhythmic succession, Ainsley teased through puffing breaths. "I have to wear a uniform at work and now for fun? What does one wear to a country music concert?"

Jesse pondered thoughtfully. It was becoming easier for Ainsley to forget her discomfort about their invitation when she saw how happy it was making her daughter.

"Cowboy boots, Wrangler jeans, cowboy hat. You know, Western wear."

"You said, 'no regular clothes.' Aren't boots, jeans and a hat regular clothes for a cowboy?"

"Mom, you know what I mean."

"Of course I do. But we won't be taking a day off for clothes shopping." Ainsley flipped over onto her stomach to work her back muscles. Jesse's downcast face and drooping bottom lip caught her eye.

"After school," Ainsley quickly added, "we can go to Santa Rosa Saddlery. They should have everything we need. I'm trusting you, Jesse. You are the expert on concert attire!"

"YES!" Jesse jumped up and down on her tiptoes with her fists above her head. "They have the best stuff. We want to look proper!"

"The best stuff." Her daughter's enthusiasm amused Ainsley. "Then that is where we must shop."

"I gotta call Emily to tell her we are shopping for clothes. That should prove it to her. She still doesn't believe I'm going to see Sunset West!" Jesse trotted off to tell her friend the news.

When Ainsley tucked her into bed that night, the child was still abuzz. Ainsley's first instinct had been to downplay the concert, but she hadn't anticipated Jesse's extreme level of excitement.

"I knew you liked country music bands, but I didn't know you were so into Sunset West specifically. Don't they just sound like any other band?" Ainsley's breath caught on her words as she realized she almost revealed her familiarity with their songs.

"This is my first concert! And Sunset West is not just any band, Momma! I *love* Sunset West. And the lead vocalist, Tom West—he's only the greatest singer of all time!"

Hearing Jesse say the name Tom West was like the blast of a fog horn on her ears—over and over.

"And Sunset West has the record for most consecutive concert dates performed without cancellations, too," Jesse went on. "Tom West hasn't missed a show since, like, ever."

"Since…like…ever?" Ainsley exaggerated her daughter's vernacular.

Ainsley wouldn't admit she knew these statistics. Stories of the band were in the hometown newspapers often. Ainsley would have had to be living under a rock to not be aware.

"So you knew Tom West when you were kids?" Darrel, from his case, was the first to jump in with the questions at work the day of the concert. "What was he like back then?"

"Ooooo, this conversation just got interesting," Joe from Route 202 chimed in. "Yes, Ainsley. Do tell."

Ainsley had avoided her co-workers after Belle let it slip that they had tickets to the Sunset West concert, and that Ainsley had connections to the lead singer. Ainsley refused to join the conversation; she wanted to let Belle handle what she started. The curious carriers continued.

"How old were you?" "Did you date?" The questions filtered in.

"Maybe Ainsley has had this clandestine relationship all along and has been slipping off to meet up with him after concerts." Howard shared his speculations.

"Okay, that's enough. Less talking, more work." Bob, the floor supervisor, put an end to the chit-chat after he could no longer focus on his own work.

"Really? You guys!" Belle was sorry she had brought up the subject when she saw how uncomfortable Ainsley was. "I step away to get my parcel tub and you attack. *Quando è troppo è troppo.* You never grasp when to quit!"

Ainsley made haste to get out the door with her mail and get away from all the chatter.

"Will you please forgive me?" Belle caught up to Ainsley as she and a herd of carriers were leaving the mail facility at day's end.

Ainsley kept walking with no intention of answering. She had ignored Belle's repeated emails and texts earlier. It had been a long day; the guys' teasing words had hit a serious note for Ainsley and it was all she could do to stay out of her mind full of memories.

"I get it—the silent treatment." Belle responded to Ainsley's silence. They walked side by side to the employee parking lot a few blocks away. "You are acting like Rose."

"I am nothing like Rose, and I may never talk to you again."

"Ah-ha! I convinced you to talk to me. Silent treatment broken," Belle said childishly.

"ERRRRR!" Ainsley growled. "Why did you have to tell them?"

"It slipped out."

"Why do you have to say anything? Why do you need so much attention?" Ainsley felt her energy and anger wax.

"It's not my fault you have stuff, and this thing called life is happening to you! Don't take it out on me."

"It's not your fault? I have a life fraught with issues, but you don't have to tell everyone. How can I tell you anything in confidence when you can't control yourself?"

"Now you are being hurtful. I would never tell them anything that's personal. The stuff they know they would have found out anyway. Small-town people talk. And the stuff they were saying to tease you? It was just that—teasing."

Ainsley knew all too well about small-town talk. She remembered vividly having been among the victims of the rumormongers in her teens. The townsfolk could find out anything, and if it wasn't juicy enough, they would embellish so they had something to use against others.

Well, let the vicious gossip mongers talk, Ainsley thought. She wouldn't give them any of her energy, either denying or affirming. They would have to make stuff up and believe what they wanted to believe. The genuine truth would remain locked inside along with the thoughts and feelings. Ainsley had fallen victim to gossip in the past, but she had learned. She would never be vulnerable again.

"I might talk to you, but that doesn't mean I forgive you." Ainsley stood beside her car.

"Fine. Mad or not, are you and Jesse coming tonight?" Belle asked.

Ainsley gave a huff and shuffled through her backpack for her keys. It wasn't as if there was a choice. Jesse had been so looking forward to the concert, there was no way out of it.

"We can travel together. Tom's agent is sending a private car to pick us all up."

"His agent?" Ainsley delivered an eye roll using her entire head with a slow and deliberate motion. To top it off, Belle addressed Tom by his first name. Upon hearing the singer's name again, Ainsley gave a final growl before climbing into her vehicle. Leaving Belle to wonder, she gunned the engine as she drove.

"The limo will be here any minute!" Jesse had dressed and was ready for over an hour wearing the clothes she had chosen during the shopping spree at the Western saddlery and apparel store. With an unusual sense for fashion, Jesse had chosen cute outfits for the both of them.

"You have like twenty minutes, Mom," the anxious 'tween-ager warned.

"Have you seen my hat?" Ainsley asked.

Ainsley had already dressed but was putting on some finishing touches to the makeup on her face. Last thing before heading down, she put on the boots Jesse had convinced her to buy. They were as dressy as they were functional—red with fancy white stitching on their eighteen-inch shafts, with pointed toes and authentic heels with ledges to support spurs.

"You have to wear nice boots!" Jesse had pleaded. "It's like a requirement." Ainsley had given in to Jesse's whim even though the boots were out of the price range she would normally spend given she'd probably never wear the boots again.

Jesse's chin dropped when she saw her mother come down the stairs. "You look perfect!"

"I thought I set out my hat."

Jesse smirked.

Ainsley watched Jesse's face drop when she opened the hall closet. "How did it get here?" She winked at her mischievous child and grabbed her costume cowboy hat and announced, "Now, to complete the outfit..."

Jesse glared at the wide-weaved, straw monstrosity she had hidden on the top shelf. It's woven-in beadwork around the crown and long, dangling, beaded tassels morphed her expression into disapproval.

"Now I'm perfect. Didn't you say the hat completes the outfit?"

Jesse gave a girlish, mini-groan of vexation and face-planted into her open palm. "Not *that* hat!"

Catching her image in the hall mirror, Ainsley turned to observe herself fully. As she studied the reflection, she decided she looked decent. She quickly adjusted the ruffle in the back of the cute sleeveless, floral print V-neck dress with a draw-string waist. Then, she and Jesse headed out to wait on Mrs. Dixon's front porch for the limousine that would soon arrive.

"I can't believe you girls are off to see the Sunset West concert," Mrs. Dixon said. She and Tiger had come out to wait for the limo with Ainsley and Jesse. "For weeks the community gossipers have been vibrating about the hometown boys coming back for the first time to play here."

"And we are going in a limo!" Jesse couldn't contain her enthusiasm.

Had she been given the choice, Ainsley would have preferred they drive themselves. She didn't like giving up control, and cruising in a private vehicle seemed so indulgent. Placing such a high value on it might give Jesse the wrong idea about what is normal.

"Are you serious?" Belle had shaken her head in disbelief as she and Ainsley discussed the prospective drive. "Only you would be against riding in a limousine. You must hate having fun."

Belle's proclamation had hurt Ainsley's sensibilities. She wasn't a fun-hater at all. It was her job to protect her daughter. Ainsley wanted to honor her responsibility to keep Jesse grounded, but she also wanted them to enjoy themselves.

Jesse was excited about the travel arrangements, and Ainsley wanted to prove to Belle she was not a party pooper.

"Mom, the limo is here. Where is Belle? Isn't she riding with us? We can't leave without Belle." Jesse said, without breathing.

"Relax, Jesse." Ainsley soothed, "The car service will wait. It's not on a schedule. He doesn't have any other stops to make."

"Thank goodness." Jesse's relief was quick to replace the angst. "Oh, there's Belle! She's already in the car."

"Goodbye, Mrs. Dixon," Ainsley said to their landlady.

"You have fun, dear," Mrs. Dixon replied. "You deserve it."

The driver approached to introduce himself. "My name is Ed and I'll be your driver."

Ed held the door as Jesse jumped up and down beside the car. "Nice to meet you, Ed. I'm Jesse." In a single motion, Jesse was in the vehicle.

The black stretch limousine was only a six-seater, but it was plenty big. The vehicle was stocked with adult beverages and sodas for kids, and it blew Jesse's mind. She only got to drink sodas on special occasions and never in their car.

"Hey, Jesse!" Belle greeted her goddaughter. "Come on in. Let's get the party started." Then she glanced at Ainsley and patted the seat. "Hey," she offered somewhat leery.

"There are no seatbelts!" Jesse exclaimed.

Ainsley sat down beside Belle and fought the urge to discuss how the lack of seatbelts made it unsafe. Unconcerned, Jesse continued bouncing from seat to seat.

"Sit back, Jesse." Ainsley forced herself to smile while the vehicle moved. "We don't want to get carsick."

Ainsley took her own advice and sat back to enjoy the scenery, not something she could often do.

The ride to Santa Rosa was smooth and luxurious. On the surface, getting chauffeured around appeared to be an acceptable arrangement, but Ainsley decided, based on nothing more than conjecture, that it was not the life for her.

The driver took a left when they reached the Luther Burbank Center. Using the lane reserved for limos, charter buses, and dignitaries, they passed all the cars waiting in line to find a place to park.

"Jesse. Let's make weird faces at them. The people can't see us through the windows." Belle stuck out her tongue and crossed her eyes at the dark tinted glass.

Jesse laughed and joined in on the game.

Ainsley would have scolded Jesse but remembered her promise to be fun. Instead, she glared at Belle and said, "Thanks for showing Jesse that fancy trick."

"Lighten up."

Instead of speaking, Ainsley mused, *You have no idea how hard I'm trying!*

Jesse detected the tension, though she didn't understand it. She studied her mother for clues and looked at Belle, too.

"They'll drop us off at the front door." Belle leaned forward and held the button to roll down the window so Jesse could poke through.

This concert was supposed to be fun, but Ainsley couldn't shake the intensity she felt thinking about how many things could go wrong.

She was glad Belle was there to deflect Jesse's attention.

The driver stopped at the main grand entrance and pointed out the Will Call window. There was no line at the window and once Belle gave the attendant their names, an usher appeared and led them to their seats, front row center. Jesse and Belle scanned their surroundings looking back at all the seats behind them and giggled. The proximity to the stage bothered Ainsley.

Belle and Jesse struck up a conversation with two teenagers sitting behind them. The girls had won tickets to the sold-out concert and had taken a bus from Sacramento to get there.

"Wow!" Jesse said. "You went through a lot to get here. You're so brave!"

"Are you using public transportation to return home?" Belle considered the dangers the young teens would face traveling by public bus at night.

The conversation ended as the house lights flickered and the opening act walked onstage. The up-and-coming artist who went by the name Libby Wexford sang a set of folksy acoustic versions of 80s hits Ainsley remembered listening to with her dad. Her tight smile turned into a more natural expression as she enjoyed the music. As abruptly as she started singing, Libby Wexford was finished, and once the applause died down, she bowed and exited.

The theater stayed dark and after a brief pause, three musicians walked on, fiddled with their instruments, and began to play. By comparison, their confidence in playing revealed how inexperienced the musicians were in the opening act. These musicians weren't overdressed, nor did they overplay. The tightness of their sound said it all. These were without a doubt main act musicians.

Ainsley felt her shoulders rise and her teeth clench as the tempo picked up, and a strolling and singing guitar player joined them. The crowd cheered wildly. It was Tom West.

Jesse and Belle joined in as the audience continued to scream their appreciation. Ainsley thought it was silly the way they carried on. To her, Tom West was just a guy she knew. She didn't even think of him as Jesse's father. It all seemed surreal.

After forty minutes of continuous upbeat country songs, the band changed up the vibe. They counted off at a noticeably slower tempo with the bass guitarist leading. Ainsley thought it was interesting that they had chosen a reggae aesthetic for this one, which was recognizable once the drums came in. Once the lead guitarist joined, the fans, most of them on their feet, spilled into the aisles, swinging and swaying with island energy. Building up the rhythm perfectly and complimenting the drummer, a percussionist walked onstage alternating shakers and bongos to complete the sound. Tom sang:

> "Sittin' on the sandy beach, my toes in the sand
> Palm trees swaying to the reggae band."

The song's climactic finish seemed to satisfy the fans. When the last note drifted up to the rafters, the audience showed their appreciation with generous applause for the musicians who gave it their all.

"Now we're gonna take a moment to catch our breath," Tom spoke with ease to the full auditorium, "We're gonna give the guys a break."

Tom turned to his bandmates, who stood on cue. "Y'all can give them another round of applause and they promise to come right back."

The fans cheered, whooped, and whistled.

"And I'm not going anywhere," Tom said when the applause died down.

Tom reached for his acoustic guitar he had earlier placed on its stand during the first set, and a stagehand brought out a backless stool.

Tom repositioned the stool closer to the edge of center stage, which bought him a moment for a long drink from the bottle of water he had set down near an amplifier.

"And now, if you'll indulge me, I want to bring y'all in a little closer." Everyone responded with delight. "This might get intimate."

Ainsley felt something flicker inside. Tom had such a presence as he performed. His charisma captivated the entire audience. They became mesmerized by his charms. Ainsley extinguished the flicker. *He is quite the showman. Don't get sucked in*, she warned herself.

Tom plucked his strings as everyone in the theater waited to hear the notes about to be played. The crowd erupted with pleasure when they recognized the song before Tom began the lyrics to his most recent hit love song. When the clapping died down, the hush seemed louder. No one wanted to miss a single note played. Ainsley thought, *This all seems so scripted.* She fought to remain in the logical realm, as the music slowly moved her.

> "In a small town where the wildflowers grow,
> We danced under the moonlight, love began to flow,
> But like a cruel summer storm, you left me on my own,
> Left me with a shattered heart, and a love that's now
> unknown."

As the words flowed, Ainsley could feel Tom's eyes on her. They lingered a little longer each time his gaze made its way around the faces in the rows and rows of seats. Tom sang the chorus:

"Oh, summer hearts and broken dreams,
I thought our love was stronger.
With memories of what could have been,
I feel your love no longer."

Halfway through, Tom stopped looking at anyone else but Ainsley. His piercing eyes bore through, reigniting her flickering response.

"The sun it shines so brightly, but I feel so cold,
A summer love so fleeting that left me alone,
You were my sunshine, my only light,
But now I'm lost in darkness. Can't find my way tonight."

The song had taken things to an intimate level. The feelings it evoked were unsettling, yet Ainsley wished the song would never end..

"Help me, Lord, to dry these tears, find a brand new start,
Though the scars may still linger, I'll trust God to mend my heart,
Through the music and the sunshine, a new love I will find,
Leaving these summer hearts and broken dreams behind."

Tom brought the attendees to the finish line as they savored the music till its finish. Through the last phrase, Tom remained focused on Ainsley. The song ended, but the audience for the first time that evening was confused. They held their applause while the artist remained locked in on only one person.

"Oh, my gosh." Ainsley gave herself a quick shake.

As if thrown back into reality, Tom looked up towards the theater full of fans. With relief, the applause ensued. Returning to character, Tom stood up and broke into a lively song on his guitar. The other musicians returned with their instruments and joined their leader.

The second half of the show went by quickly, and the flicker of emotion she had experienced during Tom's performance of the love song faded away. After two encores, and a final bow, all the musicians, including Tom, went behind the curtains and the house lights shone.

"That was so great!" Jesse exclaimed.

"Outstanding!" agreed the teenagers behind them. "So worth it."

"So glad it was a great concert. You guys came a long way to see Sunset West." Jesse reiterated her admiration for their dedication.

Conversations hummed as individuals moved through the four open double doors to exit the auditorium. The initial progress of movement into the lobby slowed as the lobby filled. Belle caught Ainsley's arm and looked her in the eyes, as if seeing her friend anew.

"What the hell, Ainsley? There is so much more to this. You have got to reveal to me your connection with this man. We shall not be friends anymore if you hide something this major from me."

Belle's directness took Ainsley aback. She could sense the seriousness of the threat and knew she owed Belle more pieces to the puzzle. She nodded, affirming Belle's request, then nodded towards Jesse.

Jesse was chatting with the Sacramento teens when a familiar face approached. Jesse waved. "Hi, Ed."

The driver approached and turned to the two teenagers. "Tiffany and Linda?"

The Sacramento girls giggled as Jesse introduced them to Ed. "Ed will take you home. My Aunt Belle hired him."

"Your trip will be safer." Belle confirmed the validity of the arrangement.

"Are you serious?" The girls looked at each other with wide mouths. "Thank you so much."

Belle wasn't about to claim credit. "Thank the guy who is footing the bill."

"What did you do?" Ainsley's brow furrowed in confusion.

"During the concert I texted Tom and told him about the girls. He took it upon himself to see to their trip home."

"You texted Tom?"

Only Belladonna Carrano had the moxy to text a famous musician during a performance to ask a favor.

"Someone say my name?"

Ainsley caught sight of the performer, who was coming out from a door behind the side stairway. Her face was on fire, there were no more words on her tongue.

"That's right, Tom West," Belle confirmed to the teenagers. "The responsible party behind this arrangement."

As if still performing on stage, Tom approached the group and gave his attention to Jesse and the Sacramento teens, who were ecstatic to meet the star in person.

Ainsley couldn't help but appreciate how much Tom's generosity meant to them.

"I want to ensure these two girls are safely on their way. If you three will please wait here. I'll be right back. I want to introduce you to the band," Tom requested.

Tom, Ed, and the girls climbed the side stairs on the left and headed across the stage to the exit doors on the right. They weren't going into the lobby and out the main entrance. They were heading for the security area reserved for the performers, to avoid the public.

"Mom, can you believe it?! Now we can meet all the musicians, too!" Jesse hopped up on the stage and sat on the edge with her back towards the curtains, her legs dangling down.

Ainsley leaned up against the raised wall and put her hands on the stage behind her as the three waited. "Well, what choice do we have? Tom West gave away our ride."

"Are you okay?" Belle interpreted Ainsley's frustration but didn't know the depths.

"I'm not happy, Belle."

"Jesse can miss a day of school for this. This here is huge." Belle wagged her finger, pointing from Ainsley to the curtain from which Tom had emerged a short while ago, "This... whatever it is you have happening... Well, *this* is way more important."

From behind the curtain appeared a man strolling towards Jesse. "Hi. You must be Jesse."

Jesse turned and with caution answered, but with a question, "Yes?"

"I'm Charlie." the man introduced himself as he continued to approach them from behind. "I play the drums with Tom." The musician hopped down to the auditorium floor and stood in front of Jesse. "And you must be the lovely Ainsley."

The drummer had a glimmer of familiarity in his eyes that made Ainsley curious. "I am Ainsley. Ainsley Tobin. Have we met?"

"No, ma'am, but I feel as though we have. Tom has talked a lot about you over the years. You are even prettier than he describes." For a man with a ring on his finger, Charlie was flirty.

"A-hum." Belle cleared her throat, giving Ainsley an even more threatening look. "Tom has talked about you?"

And to Charlie, Belle held out her hand. "Pleased to meet you, Charlie. My name is Belladonna Corrano."

"Ah-ha, Miss Belle. Lovely to meet you, too. I believe we have you to thank in part for this evening's plans. And on that note," Charlie clapped his hands together. "If y'all can follow me…" He reached for Jesse, who dropped to the floor and let him lead her to the far side of the theater towards the side doors. "We can all proceed to Tom's rig."

Belle put on her flirty face, linked her arm with Charlie's, and was ready to go wherever the musician led them. Reluctantly, Ainsley followed.

Inside the tour bus were a gang of people Charlie introduced them to: the musicians, some sound technicians and the band's agent/publicist. They greeted the guests, then went back to discussing the evening's performance.

Not long after, Tom entered the vehicle. "Hi, guys. Sorry to keep you waiting." Tom addressed them all, then his attention went to Jesse. "Jesse, at long last, we meet! Thank you for waiting. Did you enjoy the show?"

"Oh, yes. It was awesome. Just awesome," Jesse oozed.

Ainsley's senses were on heightened alert as she listened. When he said 'at long last,' she felt a sharp pain poking out from her stomach. When he quickly followed it with, 'thanks for waiting,' the pain subsided. Ainsley continued to watch for any signs the conversation between them would drift into undesirable territory—anything regarding the past, or Jesse personally.

"Great! I was hoping you'd enjoy the show."

Tom turned to Ainsley and may have been about to ask how she liked the show. He studied her as if he were savoring the sight. Then, before he could speak, Ainsley beat him to the line.

"We all had a fantastic experience. You've all been most gracious and we appreciate your generosity. We need to be getting home. And how might that be happening?"

"You just got here. Why the hurry?" Charlie responded to Ainsley, though he was looking at Belle.

"Ainsley, you're being rude." Belle agreed with Charlie.

"Excuse me if I seem impolite, but to the point, it is a school night for Jesse."

"Of course." Tom sided with Ainsley. "The company is sending another car. It'll be here shortly." Then Tom turned again to Jesse. "Would you like to play this guitar while we wait?"

"Yes, please!" Jesse took hold of the instrument, and Tom showed her how to hold her hands and strum.

Suppressing the urge to flee, Ainsley was stunned at how everyone acted like this was normal. The musicians were chatting with the sound man. The agent was on the phone. Brian, the bass player, had joined Charlie and Belle, and they were having a conversation about Lord knows what. It was only Ainsley who was out of place.

Ainsley jumped when a loud knock echoed up the boarding stairway, followed by an announcement, "Pearl Lustre Transportation."

"We'll be right out." Ainsley took it upon herself to confirm with the transportation service. "C'mon Jesse. We best be leaving. Belle?"

Jesse stood and handed over the guitar. "Thank you so much, Mr. West. This has been the best night of my life."

"You are quite welcome, Lil' Beans. It's been my pleasure."

"G'night, everyone! It was nice meeting you." Jesse turned to the greater group, then to Tom, who seemed surprised as the young fan hugged him tight.

Recovering from the surprise, Tom gently hugged the child. "Good night, Jesse. Sweet dreams."

On the ride home, Jesse's heavy lids dropped before the vehicle cleared the parking lot. Belle was quiet, too. Ainsley rested her head on the seat and contemplated the events of the evening. She remembered the touching moment when Jesse and Tom had said good night. There was a sadness in Tom's eyes after that hug.

Ainsley wondered if he was lonely despite his bus being full of people. She felt a twinge of guilt that she had never told Jesse about her father, nor him about her. Jesse was so happy to meet Tom, and the two had an instant connection. It was no accident they seemed like two peas in a pod after only having just met.

In the darkness of her room, safe under the covers of her bed, the guilt that started as a twinge turned into the burden of secrets kept. Sleep would not come while Ainsley cried.

CHAPTER 8

Unexpected Visit

It was still dark outside when Ainsley awoke the day after the concert. She made her way to the kitchen to enjoy a leisurely morning with a cup of hot tea. She put the kettle on to heat and contemplated having the weekend off. Rotating days off, though sometimes hard to keep track of, could be a blessing at times.

Click. Beep. The answering machine played back a recorded message when Ainsley pressed "play."

"Hello, Ainsley and Jesse. How was the girls' night out?"

Rose had been against Ainsley's original plan for Thursday evening—the date with her new friend Dale. The date got canceled and Ainsley let Rose know Jesse wouldn't be coming to spend the night. When Rose heard there were new plans, she accused Ainsley of keeping Jesse from her out of spite. There was no pleasing Rose.

Rose's attitude had toggled to glee when she found out they were going to the Sunset West concert. Ainsley suspected her mother changed her feelings about the plan because Ainsley may talk to

Tom. Rose wanted Ainsley to tell Tom the truth about Jesse. She wanted Ainsley to clear them both of the responsibility for the secret they kept.

The idea to keep a secret ten years ago was Rose's. Rose had given reasons when she presented the idea and Ainsley had been swayed. It was Rose's advice that got them into this mess. If Ainsley had learned anything, it was that her mother looked at things from one perspective only: hers.

Ainsley leaned against the counter and stared out the picture window, waiting for her kettle to heat. The morning twinge of light made Mrs. Dixon's backyard look magical, and Ainsley planned to enjoy this opportunity to experience the slow awakening of the world outside.

The rising sun touched treetops in front of the main house, and Ainsley's vision out the window became clear. She noticed a folded newspaper laying in the middle of her driveway, towards the street. It was Mrs. Dixon's. A locally produced weekly that contained all the news, happenings and community events of Sebastopol. In today's digital media world, Ainsley found it endearing that her landlady still read words printed on paper.

When the kettle began to boil, Ainsley extinguished the flame to quiet the whistle. She was focusing on keeping quiet so Jesse could sleep in a bit longer. Her desire to move about quietly made an unexpected knock at the door even more startling. The dog, who had been sleeping on the stairway landing, let forward a bark at the intrusive rapping.

"Brooke, quiet." Ainsley pushed out the words as she positioned herself between the canine and the door.

"Who's there?" Ainsley deepened her tone to sound bigger—more imposing—to the unexpected entity on the other side of the door. She peeked through the peephole to see Tom West's grinning face barely readable in the early morning light. "What on earth?" she muttered quietly, then flicked on the front porch light.

"What are you doing here?" Irritation replaced Ainsley's concern for her safety.

Tom stood there in her doorway in no hurry to explain anything. Ainsley's state of attire quite preoccupied him. Ainsley could feel Tom's probing stare.

Tom leaned forward to greet Brooke when he realized it might be inappropriate to keep staring. "Hello, girl," he said to the dog.

Tom straightened and looked at Ainsley, once again taking in the view. "Little Ainsley, you sure have grown up."

Ainsley adjusted her short satin robe to conceal the matching satin nighty she had on underneath. With nothing to shield her, this only brought more attention to the fact that she had on very little clothing.

Rude and creepy, Ainsley's brain told her regarding Tom's statement. *Flattering and arousing* were the words from her heart.

"What are you doing here?" Ainsley repeated the question, ignoring the emotional voices from her heart. The voice in her head that demanded logic clamored for an answer she deserved.

"I'm sorry to barge in so early and unannounced. May I come in?"

Ainsley held her ground, still in disbelief at who was standing at her front door. Tom stood looking at her and she side-stepped slightly, giving half of an invitation. Tom moved forward into the house. Ainsley shrugged her shoulders and shivered, perhaps from the cold or maybe it was Tom's sudden proximity.

"I just put water on. Would you like some tea?" The socially obligatory offer of a beverage to a guest seemed both appropriate and ridiculous, given the circumstances.

Ainsley cursed herself for good manners, hating that Rose's influence was keeping her from calling the police to report an intruder. "Please have a seat." Ainsley motioned towards the kitchen table.

Tom West was in her kitchen. Ainsley was in shock as the man walked away from her, grabbed a chair, and sat down, setting Mrs. Dixon's newspaper on the table. "I saw this in the driveway."

"Thank you, but that's my landlady's paper." Ainsley identified the item, then added, "I'll bring it back to her. She shouldn't be looking for it yet. Excuse me while I put on something more appropriate to wear."

Without waiting for any further conversation, Ainsley bolted up the stairs like a flushed game hen. She reappeared downstairs in jeans and a light sweatshirt. Tom was reading the paper.

"I made the tea. And, while it steeps, I figured I'd enjoy the paper. I miss this hometown rag." Tom's eyes paused on the pages of words with a nostalgic expression that was both satisfied and sorrowful. Then Tom lifted his head to look at Ainsley.

Ainsley smoothed her hands over her clothes, hoping Tom wouldn't stare again. "This is more comfortable."

"You looked fine dressed as you were," Tom grinned.

Ainsley turned her attention away, hoping to hide her crimson complexion and cursing her body's involuntary response. Was it to Tom she was responding? Ainsley decided he was acting creepy again and settled on putting her energy into behaving logically.

"What ever happened to quality journalism?"

"What do you mean? What are you reading?"

"A review of the concert. Did you see this?"

"I told you, it's not my newspaper. I didn't read it."

Tom handed Ainsley the paper and pointed to the headline.

Singer Wows and Woos. And the subtitle. *Local artist Tom West sings at LBC.*

Ainsley remembered the cheering crowds held captive by Tom's charms. And the talented musicians who brought depth and feeling to the emotionally charged lyrics.

Ainsley looked at the paper, then said, "Appears to be a favorable write-up based on the headline."

"You were there. Do you agree with their assessment?" Tom shook the paper at Ainsley. "The author makes it sound like I seduced the audience."

"I... uh," Ainsley felt unsure about how to proceed. She read, *A sold-out crowd welcomed singer-songwriter Tom West home to his roots last night in a one-of-one concert at Pearson Theater at the Luther Burbank Center in Santa Rosa. With mesmerizing charm and musicality, West and his bandmates covered all their favorite songs. West played the audience like the strings of his guitar with expert precision. The audience were dancing in the aisles and swooning in their seats.* Ainsley stopped reading and shrugged. "I always knew you'd make it big in the music business."

"What's going on?" Jesse rubbed her eyes with the back of her hands, then blinked two or three times. Then she smiled at Tom when recognition pushed through her sleepiness. "Why is Tom West here?"

"Hey, Lil' Beans." Tom greeted the child with the recently bestowed nickname.

"Jesse brings up a good point. If I may ask again, why did you come here?" Ainsley demanded. *And why have you given my daughter a nickname?* she added in her thoughts. This was all so confusing and highly irregular.

"I'm really sorry I barged in at this hour." Tom gave Ainsley the same answer as when she asked previously. She wondered if all celebrities were so tedious.

"That's okay. We always wake up early." Jesse was free with forgiveness. "Besides," she continued, becoming more awake, "I can't wait to tell my friends I met Tom West. Twice! They'll never believe me. And when I tell them you gave me a guitar lesson? Oh, man! They will be, like, 'No way!'"

With a smile, Tom interjected, "I came here this morning to see if you and your mother could help me out today." Tom found an opening when Jesse stopped talking to breathe. "We've added four concerts to our schedule and I am in town through the weekend. I am only free this morning and was hoping you could help me find the beach."

Ainsley couldn't believe her ears. Tom was asking them to go to the beach with him. Was he asking them to hang out? That Jesse skip school? What kind of irresponsible action is that to teach her?

Before Ainsley could speak, Jesse jumped in with a response. "Oh, we can help with that. We go to the beach all the time. Brooke loves to run along the shore. She would love to catch the seagulls, but when they fly over the water, she stops dead in her tracks. She hates to get wet."

Tom laughed, and Jesse continued.

"We can show Tom West where the beach is, can't we, Mama?"

"Mr. West knows how to get to the coast. It is easy to find the shore. Just head west 'til your feet get wet, then back up a step or two and you're at the shore."

Tom knew full well where the beach was. He grew up here. He was the one who showed Ainsley where to find the top-notch beaches.

"I can miss one day of school." Jesse began the campaign race. "I haven't missed a single day all year. Besides, today is Friday, and Friday is practically the weekend."

Jesse hadn't been absent from school since kindergarten. Like Tom West's band with their exemplary record of attendance, Jesse was a chip off the old block. Ainsley pondered the comparison, then regretted it. She didn't even want to think about how many ways they might be alike.

"Slow down, Jesse," Ainsley cautioned. "And since when is Friday part of the weekend?"

It was hard for Ainsley to believe she was having this conversation. She had gone to bed the night before thinking Tom West would head out of their lives, but instead, here he was in their kitchen.

"I only have a half day of freedom," Tom admitted.

"And then you leave town?" Ainsley asked with a glimmer of hope this nightmare would soon be ending.

"They added dates to our tour. Apparently, the demand for Sunset West concerts is huge. Got a show tonight, then two shows Saturday, matinee, and evening. We finish up with one show on Sunday."

"And we've all heard how you hold the record for consecutive concerts without a single cancellation." Ainsley flung out the words. "Give the people what they want, right?"

"Mom!" Even Jesse picked up on the sarcastic nature of Ainsley's statement.

"I thought it'd be nice to visit some of our old haunts and thought you and Jesse might come with me, that's all."

"Out of the question. Jesse will not be skipping class because it fits into some celebrity's busy schedule. That is non-negotiable."

Tom seemed stunned at how harsh Ainsley had become. Ainsley wished she hadn't spoken off the cuff. In her frustration at having her parental control undermined by a virtual stranger, Ainsley felt she may have gone too far.

Jesse's disappointment wasn't hard to see. To Jesse, there appeared to be no reason for her mother to treat Tom West in such a manner.

"That being said…" Finding an alternative that didn't look like she changed her mind, Ainsley made it known her word was still final. "Let's compromise. Mr. West shall pick you up at noon. You will attend school this morning and not receive an absence."

Jesse popped up like a rocket on the Fourth of July. "Yes!" she exclaimed and turned to exchange a high-five with Tom.

High-fives? Really? Ainsley was still furious with Tom for his antics, and the manner in which Jesse responded to him was maddening.

"This is so awesome! I'm gonna get ready. The sooner we start the day, the faster it'll be noon!" Jesse was already climbing the stairs.

"See you in a while, Lil' Beans."

Ainsley ignored Tom using the endearing nickname he created. She was trying to figure out how to orchestrate the day's plan. "So, you can get Jesse at her school. You remember how to get to Apple Blossom Elementary, right? And sometimes Jesse gets carsick on the twisty roads, so don't drive fast."

"I imagined both you and Jesse coming along, and thought I'd buy y'all breakfast on the way, but since it'll be noon, I'll grab us a lunch. I rather hoped you'd drive. All I have is my old pickup, and it's... well, old. It's on its last leg—or should I say, *wheel*? The other option is to take the limo, but Ed wouldn't appreciate us getting sand in it." Tom continued with the plan-making, unaware of the ire brewing under Ainsley's calm façade.

"Well, it looks as though you thought of it all. How clever. Does it ever occur to you that I may have plans? When you are plotting your next move, do you ever consider the consequences it may have on others?"

"I'm... sorry?" Tom tried to understand why he was apologizing. "I shouldn't have assumed you were free. Belle had mentioned you were off work, though, and I hoped we could do some catching up."

"Belle. Of course! My personal event planner. Now it all makes sense."

Ainsley paused to take back control of her emotions, then continued. "Belle is not wrong. I am off work, not that it's anyone's business. But I'm not going with you. It's not the greatest idea for Jesse either, but she really wants to. I don't want her to have a negative encounter with you."

"Fair enough." Tom couldn't make heads nor tails of Ainsley's moods. He showed genuine disappointment, but managed to muster a response. "I am honored you will allow Jesse to go with me."

"I will meet you at noon. We will be in the front parking area. There won't be many people out there at that time of day."

Tom said his goodbye and left the cottage with Ainsley spinning down the drain. She was tired of Belle's meddling, and tired of Rose's manipulations. Tom was inconsiderate, and she was tired of that, too.

Upstairs, Jesse was making plans. She was eager to explore with Tom the most excellent areas where the tide pools were.

"You know the beach I'm talking about, right, Mom? The one with all those rocks we climbed on."

"Yes, Jesse. It's Salmon Creek Beach," Ainsley answered. "Jesse, I see how much you enjoy Tom West's company and that's okay. He is a nice guy, a friend. Tom has a break and is spending it here where he grew up, but he is also very busy. He will leave in a few days because his singing takes up a lot of time."

"Of course I know he's busy! He's like the greatest country music singer ever!"

"Of course," Ainsley parroted. "I was being silly."

As Ainsley drove Jesse in, she explained she would not be going with them to the coast. Relief came to Ainsley when the child thought nothing of the plans and didn't ask why.

"I will have the office call for you from class right before lunchtime, okay?"

Jesse nodded as she climbed out of the Jeep.

"And remember, you are playing hooky, so don't be bragging to your friends about why you are leaving early."

Jesse nodded again. "I will try, but it'll be hard not to. I am, like, so excited!"

Ainsley waved as she pulled the Jeep away. She felt good about her decision to let Jesse spend time with Tom West. Someday, when she told Jesse the truth, they would both be better off for having had this time together.

After running a few errands and doing some housekeeping, Ainsley took Brooke to the park with her radio-controlled four-wheel-drive car. Border Collies were high-energy dogs with the need to herd livestock. Ainsley discovered they could exercise the dog using the RC toy. She sat on the table part of a picnic table with her feet on the seat and the panel that controls the car on her lap while the dog followed the toy in circles and back and forth until her energy waned. The dog sat near the table and watched the birds, squirrels, and people in the park while Ainsley dialed her phone.

"Hello? Dale?" she said, surprised when he answered. "I was ready to leave a message…"

Carrying on a casual conversation with Dale when compared to the events of the day had a comforting effect on Ainsley. Upon hearing his respectful voice and considerate manner, she was pleased when he asked her out.

"I *am* free Sunday and would love to get together." Her giddy smile showed through her voice.

After the plans were made, they talked a while longer, then Dale had to get back to work. Ainsley stepped down off the table and said, "Let's go," but the dog was already on her feet. Ainsley drove to Jesse's school from the park, as it was almost noon.

"Hello," Ainsley returned a greeting to the punctual Tom West, who rolled up in an unfamiliar vehicle as Ainsley and Jesse walked out of the office. "Nice truck," she added.

"Thanks, it's new." Tom turned to Jesse. "Hey Lil' Beans, are you ready for our adventure?"

"Are we going in this?" Jesse admired the shiny blue four-wheel-drive pickup with a decal with the word *Raptor* printed across the side of the bed.

"Yep, hop in."

"Not so fast." Ainsley's words stopped Jesse with one foot on the running board. "Someone let you borrow their new truck?"

"Well, I couldn't risk driving out to the coast in the old one. And I didn't borrow it."

"You stole it?" Jesse's eyes popped.

"No, hun." Tom laughed. "I bought it. Now, go on. Climb in."

Jesse waited for the nod from Ainsley before climbing up the side and into the cab of the rather large pickup. It was as if she were scaling a mountain.

"My goodness, Tom. Isn't this a little extravagant?"

"Are you impressed?"

"Pffffffffff." Ainsley was not.

"Not impressed that I bought a brand new vehicle, but maybe that I care enough to ensure a safe ride for your daughter?"

Tom's confession knocked across Ainsley's sensibilities like a wrecking ball. Why was she always misjudging Tom? He was a good guy when she knew him all those years ago, and he kept proving to her he still was.

"Are you certain you don't want to come with us, Ainsley?"

Ainsley was deep in thought—but not about Tom's question. She had to keep control regarding Tom. Yes, she had misjudged him about a few things, but Ainsley had to stay vigilant. *Was there a slight emphasis in Tom's voice when he said the words "your daughter"?*

"C'mon, Ainsley. What do you have to lose? Come with us." Tom mistook Ainsley's non-answer to the question as a sign she was thinking about it.

"C'mon, Mom. It'll be fun." Jesse leaned her arms on the sill of the cab window to join the campaign.

"Okay." Ainsley booped Jesse's nose. Even with her suspicions, she agreed to go. She sensed the potential for Tom and Jesse to do some talking and wanted to be there to steer the conversation away from certain areas.

"We'll follow you to the cottage and stash the Jeep." Tom jumped on the prospect, and Jesse cheered.

Ainsley parked the Jeep and ran into the house to grab her coat and some towels. Brooke was certain to pick up enough sand in her coat to fill a litter box, and Ainsley didn't want to mess up Tom's brand new truck.

"You should sit in front, Jesse. I'll take the back seat with Brooke." Ainsley directed her daughter, who scrambled up between the seats like a gymnast, then to Tom she said, "She gets carsick."

"Glad you are bringing a coat." Tom nodded his approval of the contents of Ainsley's arms as she opened the rear passenger door. "If memory serves me, and the wind picks up, it can be pretty chilly on the coast."

CHAPTER 9

Day at the Beach

"So, how does it feel to live on a bus?" Jesse wasted not a minute in silence as Tom navigated the roads west of Sebastopol.

"We don't live on the buses. Sometimes we have no choice but to sleep on the bus when the schedule is tight, but we try not to." Tom sounded eager to answer Jesse's questions as he cruised the highway towards the coastline.

Ainsley chuckled as she reclined on the roomy bench seat. Tom was unaware of how Jesse could talk, but he was about to find out. Jesse hadn't developed a sense of what a balanced conversation was and could talk anyone's ears off.

As the big, four-wheel drive continued west, the drone of the massive tires massaged Ainsley's mind. The tales of Tom's travels rolled along and Ainsley listened with only half an ear. For the first time in days, her thoughts were not racing.

When they arrived at Salmon Creek Beach, the shoreline was empty. After Jesse threw the Frisbee for Brooke a few times, the dog tired and became content to stay by Ainsley's side. The small group fell into stride and walked with bare feet the curved length of shore. Sometimes they left footprints on the firm sand, except when they walked in the surf through the arching path of a wave.

The ebb of the tide had created optimal conditions for exploring the pools of sea water teeming with sea life. Tom nabbed a hermit by the shell and Jesse squealed with excitement.

Ainsley was at ease in Tom's presence, even when he grabbed her and pretended to throw her into the breakers. Jesse came to her mother's rescue, jumping piggy-back onto Tom. Brooke sprang into action as Tom stumbled to avoid stepping on the dog, sending them all tumbling down in a heap, rolling and laughing on the sandy shore.

"Nothing looks more natural than a child and her dog," Tom said as he and Ainsley walked side-by-side, a short distance behind Jesse and Brooke.

"Jesse would be quite lonely without that dog," Ainsley murmured. "Me, too."

"That's quite a daughter you have there," Tom responded to Ainsley's statement, then said, "If I may ask, what happened to her dad?"

"Her..., he..., I mean...," Ainsley sucked wind, trying to replace the air in what felt like collapsed lungs.

Tom reached out to steady Ainsley, who looked pale and on the brink of fainting.

Ainsley stared at the ground as if transfixed, trying to get her mind right. She had let down her guard a little too far and needed a moment to plan a response that wouldn't involve more lies, nor reveal too many details, or raise more interest.

"Ainsley, are you breathing?"

"I, um..." Ainsley's heart beat heavy.

"Okay, you are breathing," Tom surmised. "I am so sorry. It is none of my business. The question just popped out of my mouth."

The grains of sand beneath Ainsley's toes crunched. It was difficult to balance while the ground seemed to move closer to her face, then far away again. She fought the urge to run away.

"You do not have to answer. Please forget I asked." It was undeniable Tom had hit a delicate subject but he didn't know the half of it.

As they continued to walk, Ainsley steadied her pace but didn't speak to or look at Tom. She found herself in an ethical conundrum. Tom deserved an answer. If Ainsley had been truthful in the beginning, Tom would already have known.

The ocean waves sounded in Ainsley's left ear but did nothing to drown out the pounding of her heart. For years, she had been able to bottle up the past. Now here it was, but she wasn't ready to face it.

As Ainsley gathered her scattered thoughts. She reasoned that though there was damage in hiding the truth, revealing the secret now would also cause pain.

"Can I sit in back with Brooke?" Jesse asked when they walked back to the truck.

"Yes, of course." Tom jumped to an answer, then added, "If it's alright with you, Ainsley."

"Of course, Jesse. You and the dog will both be sleeping before we make it to the highway, anyway."

Ainsley joked, though the thought of sitting with Tom in the front seat for the ride home made her uneasy. Tom might pose further questions Ainsley wasn't prepared to answer. What if he asked for more information about Jesse? If he was suspicious, he could ask Ainsley point blank.

As Tom drove away from the coast in a silent, contemplative mood, Ainsley grew nervous. The more opportunity Tom had to ruminate on the subject, the more likely he'd be to figure things out.

To Ainsley's relief, the expression on Tom's face seemed blank with relaxation. When they reached the highway she glanced back at Jesse. As predicted, the child's eyelids were already getting heavy. Jesse caught her mother eyeing her and smiled. Ainsley smiled back and her shoulders fell away from her ears a little. This trip was a good thing for her daughter.

"Thank you, Ainsley. I enjoyed getting to know Jesse." Tom broke the silence when he noticed Jesse had drifted off to sleep. "She is a wonderful girl, and it means so much to me you allowed me to meet her. I have little opportunity to be near children."

"It meant a lot to Jesse, too. She can be cautious and reserved before she warms up to new people, but with you, Jesse was all in from the start."

"Well, maybe she senses I am not 'new people.' I think I am not a stranger." Ainsley's classification hurt Tom. He and Ainsley had known each other for more than a decade, and though they hadn't kept in touch, they were not merely passersby.

Oh, if you only knew your actual status, Ainsley almost said out loud. The pressure to tell was threatening to blow through.

"I thought about you often over these past years, Ainsley."

"Tom..." Ainsley began, as she drew in a huge breath of the air that seemed short of oxygen.

"Wait. Stop, Ainsley. You don't have to say a thing."

"It's just..." Ainsley began. Maybe this was the opportunity to reveal the secret.

"Ainsley, please. Let's talk about something else. Tell me about the post office. How did you end up working there? I remember you talked about having a plan for after graduation. I had assumed your plan was to go to college."

Ainsley thought before speaking, then said, "That would have been my mother's wishes. My plan was whatever got me away. Rose had her plans. I had mine."

"So Belle mentioned you both went through training together. What was that like?"

Tom listened as Ainsley described how she and Belle met.

"They hired me and Belle in the same group, but we first met at the civil service test site in Santa Rosa."

Ainsley explained how different she and Belle were, but how quickly they had become friends and how they had been there for each other through a lot.

"What ever happened to Patti? You two were friends in school. I figured you'd still be close."

"I suppose I could ask you about Patti. Didn't she leave with you and the band when Paul was a crew member?" Ainsley was comfortable with this topic and wanted to continue on the safe subject. "What became of Paul?"

"Patti followed us for six or seven months, hoping to be Charlie's girlfriend, but when we got serious about the music, the work became more the focus. Somewhere between Tennessee and Alabama, Patti and Charlie had a falling out because she wished to party and we did not. Charlie couldn't pay enough attention to her, so she split. I had thought she returned home." Tom paused to study the screen on the console. "I'm not yet used to this truck. Where are the climate controls?" After fiddling with the touch screen, he located the appropriate window then continued his story. "And Paul wasn't as into the job when he realized there was no money in it, so he left."

"So how do you keep up your energy for touring from sea to shining sea across the country?"

"I have loved it. When the spotlight shines and the guys play, I'm transported to another world. The energy from the audience is tangible. The rush I experience from performing live is indescribable."

"That's the music, but what about the travel?"

"As much as I love to travel, it can be very lonely. I don't even have time to date, let alone have a serious relationship. The guys have all done okay. They have dated and had long-term relationships. Heck, Charlie is married now to a beautiful gal and they have kids. I guess I am not boyfriend material."

"That can't be true." Ainsley hated to see Tom down on himself but agreed that life on the road wasn't conducive to maintaining relationships.

"Enough about me. I will snap out of this pity party. The last thing I want is to depress you. Not today. Not on my watch." Tom winked and grinned.

The conversation stayed light as Tom talked about the off-the-beaten-path places they went. He told of the dive bars where the clientele were less than respectable and didn't let them play their own songs. "Eventually we played at better places and they wrote the rest of my story in the tabloids." Tom finished.

Ainsley remembered how Tom had been giddy with excitement about the band and their future. He had made it sound so romantic and thrilling. Tom's dreams had been Ainsley's dreams, too.

"It wasn't all fun and games, though." Tom continued. "After a while, seeing different places held less appeal. It was as if the newness got old. And the long, lonely miles in between are almost unbearable."

The emptiness in Tom's eyes revealed the sentiments to his words. Ainsley couldn't ignore his sadness and, not wanting to admit it, she could relate. Her life was bustling. Despite having a daughter, a job, and friends, she experienced a deep emptiness.

"I've made you sad with my stories of woe."

"It's not that," Ainsley tried to explain. "We've all got stories."

Tom pulled the pickup to a stop in Ainsley's driveway behind Mrs. Dixon's house. The conversation left Ainsley and Tom suspended in a moment between bygone days and the present. The years vanished, and they were the kids they used to be. Tom reached across the cabin of the Raptor and with his thumb caressed Ainsley's cheek in a tender, intimate gesture.

"Are we home?" Jesse said in a groggy voice as she and her furry companion sat up and looked around.

Tom and Ainsley turned away from each other to focus on the passengers in the back seat. Ainsley instructed Jesse to head up for a shower after she said goodbye.

"Thanks, Ainsley, for today. I'm at a loss how to express the great impact you have had on me."

"It was good to see you, Tom."

Tom leaned in and placed a kiss on her cheek.

Ainsley stayed in the driveway, watching Tom. He was returning to his life, his music career. They were two old friends catching up before returning to their separate ways.

"Good evening, Ainsley." Mrs. Dixon spoke through her screen door. The landlady may have been standing there for the entire scene. It's possible that she witnessed the interaction in its entirety, or even worse, only fragments. She might have questions, but to Ainsley's relief, Mrs. Dixon was too polite to ask.

"Good evening," was all Ainsley could manage before beating a hasty retreat into her cottage. Mrs. Dixon's questions were the smallest worry on Ainsley's mind. This afternoon's events were already more than she could contemplate.

"Let's not worry about it until tomorrow. On with our life." Ainsley said to herself, then to the dog she said, "It's dinnertime for us all."

Brooke's tail swayed and as if she agreed. Ainsley gathered ingredients and started assembling their meals. She noticed the open newspaper with the singer's photo. It felt surreal that she and Jesse had spent the afternoon with that guy. The man from Ainsley's past who had breezed into their lives, stirring up all kinds of inescapable trouble.

"Your turn for the shower, Mom." Jesse was pulling a towel off her wet hair as she descended into the kitchen. "Can we go to the barn tomorrow?"

"You must have read my mind." Ainsley smiled and hugged her recently washed child. "Nothing like a trip to the stables to bring some normality back into our routine."

Jesse tried to wriggle free from Ainsley's embrace.

"Not yet!" Ainsley held tight.

"Whatever," Jesse sighed, then broke free.

Ainsley heard her daughter mumble, "You're sooo weird," which only made Ainsley happier.

CHAPTER 10

Random West Sightings

"Good morning, Ainsley." Rose's terse delivery of the greeting did not match her words. "So glad you could join us."

Behind her customary church-mode façade, Rose's anger toward Ainsley bubbled. When Rose found out from Jesse that she and Ainsley were spending the afternoon with Tom West, she was hopeful the secret would be revealed. After the beach day, Ainsley admitted to Rose the subject hadn't come up.

"Morning, Mother." Ainsley returned a stiff acknowledgement with equal icy measure. Then she turned to her dad with open arms, speaking from the heart, "Hi Daddy."

Jesse also gave her grandpa a well-received hug, then linked arms with her grandmother. "C'mon. Let's take our seats."

St. Sebastian's was a small but active congregation with locals as well as newcomers attending. It filled Ainsley with joy, the spiritual fellowship in which she was about to partake. Ainsley also sensed a weight lift off her remembering Tom West would leave town today.

"You sure seem extra cheerful." Rose's left eyebrow pinched up at the corner. Rose's disdainful mood contrasted sharply with Ainsley's.

Father Lewellen kept the sermon short that morning, displaying foresight and evidence he knew his congregation well. He knew the difficulty he faced in trying to hold his audience's attention on a beautiful spring day.

"Let me leave you, my beloved people, with a thought about new beginnings. Observe the world around you and see it is in the full process of living. Think about the past only enough to use it as a tool to shape the future. Learn from it and take your cues from nature. Go for the gusto. Embrace the vitality of the season and grow with it."

Father Lewellen's words could have been created directly for Ainsley. Spring might be a good time to tell Jesse about her father. She thought about how it would play out. With the "Amens" still echoing from the pews, the guitar players broke out in song. The parishioners stood, knelt to the front, then turned and made their way out the double doors to exchange greetings and mingle. Everyone was squinting as their eyes were slow to adjust to the contrasting sunlight from the cooling shadows inside.

"Hi, Jesse." Emily wiggled out of the crowd.

"Good morning, Ainsley." Phillip emerged behind his daughter. Phillip exchanged greetings with Rose and William, then asked Ainsley about her and Jesse's trail ride.

"We had an amazing adventure. Thank you, Phillip, for letting us use Wally." Ainsley was grateful Phillip loaned her his late wife's horse. Ainsley's income could only support one horse, so she and Jesse would take turns riding Casey. It was nice they could ride together using Wally.

"Désirée would have wanted someone to enjoy riding her old horse."

"We caught the trail that goes behind the houses," Jesse chimed in, "and went all the way into the regional park. It was so much fun when the hikers saw horses." Jesse loved to be seen by the public on horseback.

"I know. The people at Taylor Mountain Park are not used to seeing horses either and they stare." Emily also enjoyed being seen by fellow park patrons.

"So, Ainsley," Rose pounced on a break in the kids' conversation. "Now that your plans for this afternoon have fallen through, you can join Jesse and participate in our weekly visit?"

Rose took the conversation in another direction as the children broke off and continued with theirs. Ainsley detected the edge when Rose emphasized the word "weekly." Though it was supposed to be the routine, Ainsley often successfully found reasons to avoid the standing invitation. Up until last night when Dale called to cancel their date, Ainsley had had the perfect excuse.

"I was hoping if you haven't any plans, Ainsley," Phillip interjected, "would you and Jesse join me and Em for Sunday brunch?"

"Two invitations at once. Jesse and I are so popular." Ainsley hid the awkwardness under her humor.

Rose expressed her displeasure at what she concluded was in poor taste. Phillip replaced her invitation to Ainsley with his own on the day preserved for loved ones.

"Actually, I wanted to stay close to home. I've got some things to do before I return to work tomorrow. We both need some downtime. Right, Jesse?"

"Well," Phillip snipped. "You and Jesse had ample time to have fun, beginning with the Thursday night concert and a whole day of horseback riding yesterday. But now you don't have any to spare for us?"

"You forgot to mention our visit at the beach with Tom West, Phillip." Hearing her name but missing the sarcasm, Jesse rejoined the adult conversation.

"What?" Phillip grunting at Ainsley surprised the rest of the group. "You and Jesse went out with Tom West?"

Agitated that Phillip was inserting himself into private matters, Rose preempted any further discussion. "Ainsley, you and Jesse will be there for dinner later today when you've finished your household responsibilities."

"Well, some other time then." Phillip regained composure. "C'mon, Em."

Phillip took his daughter's hand, and with a stiff smile, bid everyone adieu. "Rose, William, once again, a pleasure to see you. Good day, Ainsley."

Ainsley couldn't decide whether to be amused by Phillip's pithy dismissal or angry. She decided Phillip had only further embarrassed himself. As for Rose, her method for procuring their company that evening did not please Ainsley, but it put Phillip in his place.

"Bye, Em." Jesse said as Phillip led Emily away.

The smaller group stood in silence, trying to reformulate their thoughts. Ainsley hated how Phillip behaved towards her. Despite her honesty about her sentiments, Phillip continued to carry hope things between them would change. Him insisting her private affairs were his business bothered her.

"Well, Jess." William broke the silence as he took the child's hand and started towards the parking lot. "What do you bet Grandma makes biscuits tonight?"

"Oooo," Jesse played along, "I'll take that bet, but Grandpa, those are not the best odds. We almost always have biscuits on Sundays."

"Honestly, Ainsley. Must we air your personal matters in public?" Rose scolded her daughter as they fell in step behind William and Jesse.

"Which is it, Mother? Phillip? Or Tom West?" Ainsley listed two fires erupting in her life and wanted to be sure which of her situations had exasperated Rose the most before she defended herself.

Rose rolled her eyes and let out a huff.

"I value Phillip and don't want to lose him as a friend," Ainsley said. Though she didn't want to defend Phillip's behavior, she chose the lesser fire in order to avoid the second, much bigger problem. "I'm sorry he embarrassed you, Mother."

"It isn't your fault," Rose answered.

"See you later, alligator." William secured Jesse into the Jeep.

"We'll see you this evening, Ainsley," Rose said as Ainsley climbed into the vehicle. Rose's tone took Ainsley by surprise. There wasn't a thread of judgment in Rose's eyes, only understanding. It was foreign and threw Ainsley off.

"Look! There's Tom." Jesse pointed.

"Tom!" Jesse yelled and flapped her arms.

Tom acknowledged Jesse when he heard her shout and tried to move out of the throng, but the group of adoring fans was unrelenting. As she and Jesse drove away, Ainsley experienced a twinge of sorrow at what life was like for Tom.

It confused Ainsley that he was still in town, and at church. Had he not said Sunset West's last additional performance was a Sunday matinee? She thought he should be at the theater instead of here in Sebastopol.

"I'm going to do my homework first," Jesse announced when they got home.

"Good idea, sweetie. Tell me, Jesse. Given that you have this makeup work to do on a Sunday, was it worth missing class?"

"Mo-om. To even ask that question. Pfffff! Were you ever a kid? Of course it was worth it."

Of course it was worth it. The words echoed in Ainsley's mind. *To even ask that question.* Ainsley's thoughts drifted as she filled a basket with laundry to prepare for washing. She remembered her friend Patti having said something similar on the night they had snuck out to meet up with Patti's cousin Paul and the band.

"Of course we should go. To even ask that question. They invited us, didn't they?"

"They did, but they don't need us kids hanging around." Ainsley's decision was final. Ainsley had been feeling skeptical of Tom's feelings. He had become consumed with the band's planning for their first tour; a few dates at some local county fairs in the state.

"Suit yourself." Patti had disappeared into the foggy Sebastopol night, and Ainsley had started walking home alone down Main Street. She ducked into a storefront to avoid a set of upcoming headlights as her girl scout training instinct kicked in.

"Come on, Ains! Climb in!" The van stopped and the door opened. "Come to the beach with us! We're having a birthday bonfire," Patti implored.

"Tom won't come unless you do, and it won't be right for Tom to not be at his own party." Patti had drawn upon Ainsley's Catholic upbringing using guilt to change her friend's mind.

"Where is Tom?" Ainsley tried to look past Charlie and into the dark van. If he had wanted to see her, why hadn't he been there? Ainsley hadn't seen Tom for a couple of days. She had heard about the demo song the band was distributing in hopes of a potential record deal. Ainsley had considered it wise to spend less time with him, while the band was fulfilling legitimate performance dates at local fairs. This decision was music to Rose's ever-interfering agenda.

"If you wanna see him, come with!" Patti had jumped on the fissure in Ainsley's resolve. She had opened the slider door and taken Ainsley's arm, leaving little chance for protest. "Get in. We'll go back and pick up Tom."

"Mom, what is the capital of India?"

"What?" Ainsley pushed the memory away so she could focus on her immediate reality.

"Oh, never mind." Jesse yelled when she answered her own question. "The capital is both Delhi and New Delhi. It confused me."

"Do you need help, Jesse?"

"No thanks, Mom. I got it. It was a confusing question."

Jesse was a sharp and independent student. She needed very little guidance with homework. Ainsley never had to remind Jesse of due dates and assignments. Jesse turned in her work on time. A chip off the old block was Jesse.

"I always knew you got good grades," Tom had said on the night Ainsley joined the group at the bonfire. "Congratulations on the scholarship. In college, you will do well because that's where you belong. You have never seemed like a high school girl to me."

"Does it make you mad I am so much younger?"

"Where do you get that idea?"

Ainsley had shrugged her shoulders and had looked down into the yellow and blue flames. She had been insecure about her age around Tom.

"How else can I explain? I could never be mad at you over something you have no control of. It complicates things... but you'll be eighteen years old soon enough."

Ainsley had stared harder into the flames. She wished she could rise into the night air and disappear with the smoke. Their difference in age had come up regarding Ainsley's freedom to come and go under her mother's dictatorial rule. Yes, they had been over it many times. At this point, Ainsley had felt guilty for causing problems. She had hated that the only solution to the problem of her age was to wait.

"Ainsley," Tom had pulled her chin towards him so he could see her eyes. He took her hand in his and proclaimed, "I am falling in love with you. From the moment I met you, I have been so intrigued and have only become more interested in you. We are going to be together. I will do whatever it takes to make it happen."

"Ainsley Siobhan Tobin! What have you done?" Rose had towered over her broken-hearted daughter. "How could you be so gullible? How many times did I tell you? Guys are willing to say anything to get you into bed!"

"It wasn't like that," Ainsley had pleaded. "Tom didn't 'get me into bed.' He wasn't being manipulative."

"Well, he sure got you pregnant, so he must have gotten you in bed." Rose's fury towards her daughter had burned for hours after Ainsley had told her mother.

"I should tell your father. Send him over to the young man's house immediately. Make him face responsibility."

"Don't tell Daddy, yet. I can't handle him being disappointed in me. Let me explain it to him, Mom. Please."

The words had caught in Ainsley's throat. The thought of losing her father's love when she hadn't yet accepted losing Tom's was too much.

"Besides," Ainsley had sobbed, "Tom is gone. Traveling with his music. He doesn't know."

"He doesn't know?"

Rose had unleashed upon her daughter a life's worth of anger and resentment. After a little deliberation, Rose had approached Ainsley with their plan. She had decided not to take action against Tom West, nor his parents. She unilaterally decided they would not tell a soul and when it became necessary they would hide Ainsley's condition.

Throughout the few days following Ainsley's confession, Ainsley and Rose prayed—a lot. Ainsley prayed for wisdom and guidance. She was certain Rose prayed for a miscarriage.

To this day, Ainsley knew of no one else besides herself and her parents who knew the complete story. The Tobin family may have been disconnected from each other in some ways, but in matters regarding reputation, they had remained a united front.

From downstairs where she was ironing the shirts, shorts and culottes for the work week, Ainsley could hear music playing in Jesse's room. It was one of Tom West's hits.

> "I'll find a way to mend this broken heart
> Pick up the pieces and make a brand new start
> Though the nights may be long

and the pain is still strong
I know love will mend this broken heart."

"Come in, Mom." Jesse responded to her mother's soft knock. "I finished my homework." Jesse was lying on her back in the middle of her bed and appeared to be staring at the ceiling, listening with deep concentration.

"Love came in with the breeze on a summer day
Our nights spent 'neath a golden moon."
Ainsley lay on the bed beside Jesse and sighed.

"Do you think we will hear anything more from Tom? I mean, after he's done with the local concerts, what happens then?" Jesse whispered over the song.

"Sunset West has packed up and moved on to the next place," Ainsley whispered back, then added, "Why are we whispering?"

"That seems so sad." No longer whispering, Jesse continued in a somber voice. "How does he keep up with friends?"

"Maybe a little sad, maybe not. That's the path he chooses. It mustn't be all that bad."

Jesse's face stayed subdued, then the moment passed.

"I'd like to keep in touch with Tom." Jesse brightened. "In case he ever needs a friend to talk to. I'm wondering if he has an address where I could send letters. Maybe he'd give me his email or if I could text him."

"Jesse, I think those are some fantastic ideas." Ainsley was proud of her daughter for her thoughtfulness.

Jesse seemed satisfied with Ainsley's support and switched gears. "Can we go to Grandma's and Grandpa's now? Maybe we can all cook like the olden days."

"Olden days. You're not old enough to have olden days to look back on. Now, let's dress and tidy ourselves. I'll let your grandparents know we are on the way."

Dinner with Ainsley's parents had been an unusually positive experience. Rose had been generous with them all taking part in the meal preparations. She didn't complain once that they were doing things wrong. Ainsley cut up fresh veggies for a salad, William and Jesse were in charge of rolling out the biscuits. Ainsley noted Rose didn't get upset when they used a little too much flour on the counter. When they sat down to eat, the conversation flowed.

"Those buffalo could have gone through that fence." Ainsley recollected an incident during a family trip to Yellowstone. "Those thin strands of wire were barely a suggestion in stopping a charging herd."

"The look on those people's faces," William added. Then he and Jesse laughed.

"I wished we'd have filmed it." Rose joined in the laughter. "Watching those silly park visitors running away…" Rose caught her breath mid-chuckle.

"Even with all the warning signs…" Ainsley added. "Those folks thought they could get a photo with the buffalo."

The sharing continued as the little family enjoyed the meal and the merriment, then everyone helped with the kitchen cleanup.

"Work and school in the morning." Ainsley sighed as she dried the last cooking pot. "We have to leave early. Thanks for a lovely evening, Mother."

"It was nice to have you girls." Rose gave Ainsley a hug.

"Let's have lunch this week, Daddy." Ainsley wrapped her arms around her dad.

"I'll call you," William said to Ainsley as he hugged Jesse, then turned his back towards the child. Jesse followed by leaping onto William's back and riding piggyback as he carried her to the car.

"G'nite." Ainsley and Jesse waved their good wishes in unison as the Jeep began to crawl down the long, arching driveway.

"Hmmm," William said, hugging his wife from behind as they watched the vehicle disappear.

"She's driving slowly tonight," William observed.

Rose leaned into her husband and turned her head to glimpse his face. "What are you talking about?"

"Oh, just that this evening was pleasant and Ainsley didn't have to leave in a huff." William winked.

"William Tobin. Are you teasing me?"

"Yes, I believe I am."

With that, the older couple retreated into their home to enjoy a private evening.

"It's still early, Jess. Do you wanna…" Ainsley began.

"Go to Screamin' Mimi's for ice cream?" Jesse finished the thought. Screamin' Mimi's was the perfect way to end a memorable day.

"But don't tell Grandma." Ainsley knew Rose would have wanted her and Jesse to stay longer.

After choosing their favorite flavors, Ainsley was squaring up at the cash register when she heard Jesse squeal.

"Emily's here!"

Ainsley saw Phillip and his daughter coming into the shop.

"Hey, guys," Ainsley greeted them. "What a coincidence."

She wondered, half facetiously, if Phillip had put a tracking app on her phone.

"What a pleasant surprise," Phillip said. His goofy grin showed he was more than thrilled to have run into Ainsley and Jesse. "We couldn't have planned it better if we'd tried."

"Will you and Em join us? We'll save a table outside." Ainsley saw no other choice but to invite them.

Emily and Phillip got their scoops and joined Ainsley and Jesse in the little outdoor seating area on the sidewalk between the street and the front of the building.

"This is nice, isn't it?" Phillip was still giddy with his good fortune.

"Yes, it is. The ice cream is delicious here. I want to try the kind made using goat's milk. It's so rich. I'll have to be in the mood for that."

Phillip looked deep into the ice cream cone in his hand and laughed, at which point Ainsley realized he hadn't been talking about the dessert.

"Oh, you mean this..." Ainsley moved her cone in a circular motion to encompass them all sitting at the table.

"Yes, this..." Phillip mimicked Ainsley's gesture. "It's practically a date. Is there a chance we might do this more often?"

"Phillip. We've had this conversation. I don't know what else to say..."

"Wait, don't say a thing." Phillip put up his hand to imitate the halt command.

Ainsley tilted her head and spoke anyway. "It's just that Désirée and I were best friends. We all were friends. I never thought of you..."

"Stop. Don't say it. I was kidding." Phillip's short sentences copied his short temper. "You don't have to rub it in."

"Apparently I do."

"No, no. Ainsley. Please." Phillip backpedaled. "I'm sorry. All I meant is its nice when we spend time together, all of us. Doing this."

Phillip held eye contact, hoping Ainsley would accept his explanation. He cocked his head to the side and pushed through the self-inflicted discomfort with a goofy grin.

"Apology accepted, Phillip." Ainsley answered. His smile always made her want to smack him, even though—and maybe because—she also felt sorry for him.

"Look!" Jesse shouted and everyone looked in the direction she pointed.

"Dad, look!" Emily was pointing, too. "It's Tom West!"

From around the corner, Tom's old pickup came into view, heading down the street. Jesse and Emily's jumping and shouting caught Tom's attention—and everyone else's.

"Hey, Lil' Beans," Tom called out and waved and smiled as he came to a stop at the light. His smile dropped when he noticed the other man with Ainsley sitting at the table. When the light turned green, the smile reappeared and Tom waved as he rolled on by.

"Oh, my gosh." Emily squeezed Jesse's arm. "He called you Lil' Beans. Tom West has a nickname for you?"

"Yep," Jesse shrugged, as if it were nothing, and Emily stared down the road, watching the old truck disappear.

"He had one more show this afternoon. He should have already been done at the theater and left town," Ainsley thought out loud. "That's odd."

"What's odd?" Phillip asked.

"Oh, nothing." Ainsley realized she had been talking. Then she asked, "Why is he driving that old truck?"

"Why are you asking me? And why are you keeping track?"

"Jesse, come on. Let's finish up our ice creams. We should get going." Ainsley wished to escape before Phillip's attitude harshed the mellow she had come into at dinner. Seeing Tom again wasn't helping, either.

"You girls both have school and we have work." Phillip joined in the parental role.

CHAPTER 11

Withering Rose

"Ainsley. This is your mother. May I speak to my granddaughter?"

Ainsley recognized her mother's voice without question, but what confused her was the strained tone. Ainsley handed the receiver to Jesse in complete confusion. "It's… Grandma…?"

After leaving Rose and William, they went for ice cream. Was Rose upset they had left to go to Screamin' Mimi's without her and William?

"Hi, Gramma." Jesse spoke into the receiver, then paused.

"I'm watching TV." Then, another longer pause, followed by, "No." Pause. "No." Pause. "I don't think so."

Jesse finished her conversation and returned to the couch. "Aren't we gonna watch the rest?" she asked when she noticed her mother staring at the paused movie they had been watching.

"What was that all about? What did Grandma want?"

"She wondered if we had seen Tom. She said he was supposed to come over." Jesse wiggled deeper into the couch next to

Ainsley to finish watching the movie like there was nothing at all unusual happening.

"We were just with them a few hours ago. When would Tom have been here? For what reason? Why would Grandma believe Tom had been here?"

"Weird, right?" Jesse said, then shrugged, took the remote, and pushed play.

Ainsley pushed the pause button on the TV controls in Jesse's hand. "Did you tell Grandma we saw Tom West driving through town?"

"Oopsies. I forgot we saw him."

"No worries. It's okay, Jesse." Ainsley reassured her daughter, but her thoughts spun as she tried to add up the facts. All suspicions pointed to what Rose was capable of given the correct motivation. Rose was worse than a terrier on a rat when she set her mind to something.

"How could I have missed this?"

Jesse glanced over, then turned the movie back on.

Rose had been in such a cheerful mood at dinner. She was friendly, personable, polite, and almost comforting. Had she told Tom? That would explain her disposition. Rose had gotten what she wanted.

"I was enjoying the day and let down my guard. How could I have let Rose fool me?"

"What are you talking about?" Jesse couldn't ignore her mom and pushed pause.

"I have to talk to Rose. I must speak with her straightaway."

"Call her back." It seemed simple to Jesse. With a sigh, Jesse pressed play on the remote.

As resolute as Ainsley had always been to avoid speaking with her mother, she was now frantic, trying to get Rose on the phone.

"Mother," was all Ainsley said.

"Listen, Ainsley. I realize you must be confused. Obviously you have questions, but let me explain. Is Jesse still awake?"

"This is between us, Mom. Never mind Jesse. What is going on?"

"Ainsley, please be rational. I only called to check if Jesse was okay."

"Why wouldn't Jesse be okay? Mother, what have you done?"

"Let's not do this over the phone."

"This? What is this?"

"Okay, okay. Calm down, Ainsley," Rose patronized. "Call me after Jesse has gone to bed."

Ainsley's mind was reeling, but she concealed her angst. After the movie, she got Jesse tucked in for the night. She gathered the strength she needed in order to deal with Rose.

"I'm glad you're open to having a conversation, Ainsley, and I hope you have had a moment to calm down."

"I am further from calm than I have ever been. But I am focused on what is important." Ainsley's low tone should have sent warning shivers through Rose's veins if she had read her daughter at all. "I am scared to ask. Mother, what did you do?"

"Nothing that shouldn't be done." Rose used a double negative as a cover.

"Why would you have expected Tom to visit me and Jesse? Are you going behind my back?"

"Well, he is her father. He should be able to visit his daughter whenever he wants."

"You are not answering my questions. Do the Wests know?"

"Ainsley, let's face this situation. It has gone on long enough."

"Mother, so help me, if you have said anything to anyone..." Ainsley could not finish the sentence.

Rose knew she had better explain, so she began. "Your father and I ran into Tom and his folks at the market. It turned out Jim and Margaret were free this morning and accepted my invitation to have tea."

"Oh, no, no, no..." Ainsley groaned. "How can you be so casual regarding this?"

"It's okay. The Wests are agreeable people. Margaret is a gentle-woman and Jim is downright charming. We had a lovely visit."

"Really, Mother? You had a lovely experience? They are not the type you socialize with. In fact, I remember when you hadn't the slightest compliment or kind word to say about them."

"You're not letting me explain. They came over and Tom came, too. During the conversation, Tom asked about you and I mentioned you were staying close to home today. He mentioned he wanted to have a conversation with you and it surprised me he seemed comfortable enough to just drop by. His level of familiarity with you and Jesse made me suspect you were preparing to tell him and Jesse the truth."

"You expect me to believe all this happened earlier today? All this was bouncing around in your head, and you never said a thing to me at dinner? Why didn't you mention you had seen the Wests?"

"I couldn't risk talking about it in front of Jesse. You understand how important it is to tell them. You keep saying you'll handle it. I am patiently waiting. When will you be handling it?"

"This is about my daughter, and it is my decision. You don't get a say in this."

"Tom is leaving town soon and the opportunity will be lost. I hoped you and Tom planned to meet up to work it all out. I didn't want to interfere."

"Oh, my God, Mother. What the hell? You didn't want to interfere? That's all you ever do—thoughtlessly interfere."

"Don't swear, Ainsley. There is no need to use the Lord's name in vain."

"I am at a loss for words. I don't even understand what to do. This is… I mean…"

Ainsley couldn't think. It was all too much.

"Ainsley, I'm sorry if you are upset, but this needs to come out. The sooner the better. Just calm down. You are getting hysterical. We can better manage this once it's all in the open."

"Then what, Mother? What do you expect will happen? We have lied about this and there are going to be a lot of angry people when they find out. Do you understand the damage we have done? Can you imagine what others have lost because of our decision to keep a secret?"

When there was no response, Ainsley looked at the screen on her cell phone, checking to see if they were still connected. Rose was silent on the other end.

Seeing that Rose was still listening, Ainsley dropped her voice another octave lower and said, "I guess you hadn't thought of that, hmmm, Mom?"

"Of course I thought about the Wests." Rose rallied for a response.

"When, Mom? Did it cross your mind when you created this mess years ago? Maybe you didn't factor in the Wests before. Perhaps you weren't concerned about Jesse's extended family she knows nothing about, but it has tortured me for ten years."

Rose was silent once again. Then, she slowly said, "I tried to fix it. If you had followed the original plan…"

"And what if we had stuck to your strategy and—" Ainsley stopped mid-sentence and thought, *there would be no Jesse.* Rose originally planned to erase the past by giving Ainsley's baby up, thus removing the need to hide paternity.

The lines of communication dripped with silence.

"I was a child when we began this charade," Ainsley said, refocusing on the immediate subject. "I did not understand the depths of what we were doing. Now, after so much time, we can't just reveal the truth without any forethought."

Ainsley waited for Rose to speak. "Have you nothing to say, Mother?"

"You think I haven't thought of that?" Rose sounded far away. "I wish I could fix things. I have prayed for forgiveness." Her vocal timbre was almost like that of a child.

It was Ainsley's turn to be silent. That was the answer to all Rose's problems—praying. She never seemed to take responsibility for her actions, and when others were affected, Rose prayed for herself.

"The part I would change, Ainsley," Rose's voice crackled with emotion, "is what this situation means to Jesse. I regret how I felt about her before she was born. I can't make up for the resentfulness, the misplaced sentiments of blame. I didn't know her yet, and saw her as the thing that was hurting my child."

This was a new perspective. Ainsley hadn't considered that Rose's negative response to Jesse before the child was born might still be a burden.

"There were justifications for our actions in the past," Rose continued, "but now there are no reasons to keep the secret any longer and too many reasons to let the truth be known. Jesse needs to know her father, her grandparents. And they all should be acquainted with her."

"Your actions, Mother. Not mine." Ainsley held the phone in her trembling hand. "Maybe you can be forgiven by God and then go about your happy life, but that doesn't make things okay."

In the beginning, Rose's reasons to keep secrets were selfish. Now, in keeping with the narcissistic theme, revealing the truth would also benefit Rose. "And the reasons you list for telling them now existed the entire time."

Rose's manipulative narrative befuddled Ainsley. She dropped the phone away from her ear. Though she wanted to disentangle herself from Rose, there was no denying it. They were in this together.

"Then we agree." Rose confirmed. "They will be told."

Ainsley cut off the call to end the conversation. She wanted to say nothing more.

She needed fresh air, so she wrapped herself in a blanket and went out into the part of the garden where Mrs. Dixon had placed a bench in memory of her late husband.

"It's where I like to sit and pray." Mrs. Dixon had confessed. "I feel closer to God."

"Closer to God?" Ainsley thought God was everywhere and a specific geographic location shouldn't be necessary. Rose also bought into proximity of God physically. For Ainsley, the bench was a good place to gather her thoughts.

Ainsley often contemplated the concept of a deity who forgave so easily for the terrible actions people commit. The God Rose prayed to was not a God Ainsley trusted. This revelation made Ainsley sad as the tears flowed. Ainsley recalled the period during her pregnancy she had lived with Rose's sister, Ruth, in Arcata, California. It was her time with Ruthie that gave Ainsley a broader view of God.

As a child, Ainsley had always felt religion was imposed upon her. Rose enforced the rules as the law and used fear as a motivator. Ruthie, Rose's older sister, whom Rose described as hippy-dippy, led by example, but also gave Ainsley as much information as she requested for better understanding. Ainsley always remembered how her Aunt Ruthie's support helped her gain power, a voice and independence.

Ruthie, who was more like a grandmother to her, kept nothing from Ainsley but let her experience life in all God's glory—the good, the bad, the ugly. Her time with her aunt was a period of peace and joy despite her situation.

"They feel everything, hear everything. There is no filter," Ruthie had explained of the baby growing within during one of the many afternoons she and Ainsley spent together in the studio where she taught art.

"You're saying the baby from out here feels my grief inside?" Ainsley had hated what she might do to her unborn child, harboring these negative thoughts about her childhood, her mother, the baby's father.

"Let God be the filter, Ainsley. Give your grief, your worries, your fears to God. He wants to help."

Ainsley had wanted to be helped, but had lost touch with her faith. Ainsley had stopped believing in God as Rose presented Him. She believed in her aunt, though. Ainsley saw God better through Ruthie's eyes. Gaining her own perspective was beneficial. With Aunt Ruthie's spiritual support, Ainsley's time in isolation had become a period of inner growth.

The counseling service provided by the adoption agency, which to Rose was just a formality, had also become a regular thing for Ainsley. Through the service, Ainsley had found her voice. Ainsley had realized her true feelings. She had grown stronger in her own convictions and decided she was keeping the baby.

When Rose had discovered they had subverted her orders, she was furious. "Now, Ainsley," Rose had begun in her patronizing tone, "we've been over this before. The arrangements are all in place. You must accept this. It is in everyone's best interest."

"You mean what's best for you, Mother? All you think about is yourself."

Angry with how her daughter had spoken to her, Rose had lashed out at Ruth, accusing her sister of filling Ainsley's head with outrageous ideas. Rose decided Ainsley would come home to finish the pregnancy. Then, they would carry out the original plan.

The teenage mom, with her newly discovered power, dug in her heels about returning home with her domineering mother. "You will be fine," Ruthie assured her niece. "You are like the Casa Blanca Lily that blooms in the darkest of night. Even during the worst of times, Ainsley, you have grown and flourished. Your baby is destined to forever be the proof of the beauty that comes when you believe in yourself."

Ruthie had coached Ainsley on how to approach the situation rationally. "You are no longer obligated to take her seriously, Ainsley. Remember that. Your mother can have no power over you unless you give it to her. Don't give her the power."

Ainsley's return to the parental home hadn't been a peaceful transition because Ainsley had gone against Rose's wishes. When the going got tough, Rose refused to offer any support for the teenage mother-to-be. It was her way of saying, *I told you so.*

As the baby grew, Ainsley's physical discomfort was undeniable. "You know, this would have been so much easier if you had stuck to the plan." Rose had said when Ainsley was in her third trimester.

"You mean easier for you." Ainsley couldn't see how giving her baby up for adoption would have made this pregnancy any easier.

Remembering how Aunt Ruthie had helped her then, Ainsley realized how her auntie had always been there to support her for the hard times. It had been a while since they last spoke. Maybe it was time to bring Aunt Ruthie up-to-date and get her advice. Ainsley thought, *What would Ruthie do?*

Though it was late in the evening, she made the call.

CHAPTER 12

BFF Enlightened

"Well, well, well. If it isn't my long-lost friend," Belle teased Ainsley at work Monday morning.

"Was I lost? Well, now I'm found," Ainsley teased back.

"You seem in good spirits. I guess you needed that three-day weekend. You didn't miss a thing around here."

The two letter carriers began chatting through the space between their letter cases as they had done every morning since the USPS had hired them.

Ainsley had hoped for a normal day, and it was. Easy and uneventful. After work, Ainsley and Jesse came home and spent the afternoon together. They took Brooke to the park and grabbed takeout for dinner. They were about to sit down and watch TV when the phone rang.

"Hi, Aunt Ruthie."

"I was just calling to check in. That was some pretty heavy stuff we talked about yesterday. How are you feeling today?"

"I am okay, Auntie. Thank you for the late night counseling."

"Glad you reached out, hun. You and Jesse mean the world to me, and I want nothing more than the best. I know you are busy, but we should talk more often."

"Thank you, Auntie. We both care about you, too. And you are right, we should talk when things are good, too. You are the only person on this planet with whom I connect spiritually. Without you, I'd be blowing in the wind."

"Glad I could help. Are you still planning on coming clean about the past? It's a very complicated task. Are you sure you're prepared?"

"If not now, Auntie, when? It will not be easy, but it is long overdue. I will move forward with my plan with compassion and hope for understanding from those I have deceived. I will accept what happens. I will let the chips fall where they may."

"You sound as confident about this as you were yesterday. That is a good sign."

Ainsley chatted with Ruthie a while longer, then she joined her child in front of the TV.

"I already started the show. I'll catch you up." Jesse gave Ainsley a quick review of the comedy she was watching. With its simple plot, Ainsley needed only a brief explanation, and together they watched and laughed and snacked on popcorn.

At bedtime, Ainsley lingered beside Jesse, enjoying what had been a perfectly mundane day. She gave Jesse a hug, wished her sweet dreams, and turned out the light.

"It's been a while since we had a father-daughter lunch on a workday."

It had thrilled William when he got the call from Ainsley on Tuesday morning with an invitation to meet.

"I'm glad our schedules worked out." It made Ainsley happy she and William could occasionally make lunch plans.

"I am fortunate to have a decent supervisor who is happy to bend the policy on leaving the route as long as I finish my duties," Ainsley explained.

Ainsley and her father waited at the pick-up window of the local burger joint, Sequoia Burgers. Most folks agreed they were the best burgers in town.

"Did you catch the rerun of *Last Man Standing*?" William asked between mouthfuls. It wasn't surprising the network sitcom was among her father's favorites. The story of a hardworking, conservative, God-loving man dealing with his wife and daughters was something to which William could relate. He had his favorite episodes.

"I caught the last half. One of my favorite story lines. It was pretty funny. Jesse was watching it while I was finishing up on the phone. She likes that show, too."

"Your mother never let you watch TV when you were a kid." William took a bite of his burger.

"Dad, Mom never let you watch TV and you were an adult."

"She lets me watch now. She is loosening up."

"Phhhht." Ainsley hadn't been able to stop the derisive snort in response.

"I'm serious. Your mother is trying to change. She's seeing a therapist." William bit again into the overstuffed hamburger sandwich, like what he had said wasn't at all mind-blowing. Some tomato, onion and melted cheese escaped from between the buns when William squeezed his sandwich.

"Mom's getting therapy? You're kidding! Well, that explains some things." Ainsley remembered the phone conversation with her mother.

"No joke, Ains."

"Well, maybe I should go, too." Ainsley laughed. "Mother-daughter relationship counseling. Lord knows Mom and I fight no matter how hard I try not to. She is so difficult."

"I have gone to a few sessions with Rose. It is very helpful. She can be a challenge, but this therapist seems to dig to the root of what bothers her most."

"Rose makes things harder than they need to be." Ainsley wasn't ready to hang a medal of honor around Rose's stiff neck just because the woman had seen a therapist. "She is her own worst enemy."

"Well, she is learning about herself. I am seeing a change and I'm supportive."

"Daddy, I am going to tell Jesse," Ainsley blurted.

William stopped eating to give his daughter his full attention. After she reiterated the statement, William spoke.

"You and your mother are alike. She had to be strong and brave, too, when she tackled life given the cards it dealt her. You both had to cope with big life issues before you were ready."

Ainsley had expected nothing but a positive reaction from her dad upon hearing the news. She hadn't expected what he had to say next.

"Rose was quite young when she had to run a household, take care of a husband and baby all before she was twenty years old. Taking care of my father—she was the sole caregiver for his last days. She wasn't prepared, but handled it with grace."

Ainsley hoped her father had a point. She didn't want to talk about Rose, but out of respect, she listened.

"Before life happened, there were plans and she had dreams of her own. She was studying to be an anthropologist. She had earned several scholarships and a company in Reno hired her right out of high school with an offer to sponsor her further education. Your mother's achievements as a high school student left them very impressed. She was so fascinated with history and civilization, her passion was commendable."

Ainsley enjoyed the story her father was telling but wondered how it related to the big secret the three of them had kept. William picked up on Ainsley's need for clarity.

"Before your mother married me, she had done a great deal to prepare for university. One of her areas of research included the roles of females versus males in raising their young. She studied many species of organisms that had no parental contact with their offspring after birth. She compared them to others where both parents provided care. The final contrast was that for the more advanced creatures, females provided the most care. The most socially advanced among us earthly dwellers grow up in pods, packs, and herds but almost never are raised only by the male."

"Fascinating though that is, I can't see the connection."

"Among the many life forms on the planet, there are different versions of the ideal setting in which to raise young."

"Daddy, you're watching Animal Planet again!" Ainsley watched her father bite another chunk of his hamburger and waited for his conclusion. She hoped there was a point to his monologue.

William lifted his head as he chewed, savoring his sandwich down to the last morsel, before concluding his monologue with an accent on the purpose.

"I am relieved you and your mom are doing the right thing. The risks of telling the truth are no worse than what we have already lost in the keeping of secrets. Get started with your plan soon, but remember we make plans and God laughs. If you need more data, may I suggest Proverbs 3:5-6?"

William returned to his meal and began working on his basket of french fries, and it left Ainsley to ponder about what he had said. He had a point about the damage they had done in keeping such a monumental secret. It irritated her that it had been Rose's idea to lie, and it was Rose wanting to end the lying ten years later. No matter what Ainsley did, it would always be what her mother wanted.

Finishing her workday a half an hour later than most of her co-workers after her lengthy lunch break with William, Ainsley thought she was walking alone to the parking lot when, from behind, she heard Belle.

"Hey, wait up! Glad I caught you. Shall we meet up for some exercise?"

"Definitely. I had a huge lunch." Ainsley puffed out her cheeks, and both women laughed. "I'm taking Jesse riding. We can run through the orchards while she has her lesson."

"Sounds good. Five o'clock?"

"Yep. See ya."

When they got home, Jesse changed from school clothes to riding clothes, and Ainsley exchanged her uniform for the comfort of running shorts and shoes. She took extra time combing and clipping her hair into a ponytail.

"You look younger with your hair pulled back," Jesse commented.

"Maybe people will mistake us for sisters." Ainsley winked at Jesse's reflection in the mirror, then turned around.

"Not that much younger, mama."

Jesse laughed as they hurried out the door and into the car.

Jesse sat quietly as they drove to the ranch. Looking across at her, Ainsley couldn't deny Jesse was her father's child. The resemblance was undeniable. Fighting the desire to spill the truth right then and there, Ainsley bit her lip.

"There's Auntie Belle." Jesse waved and opened her door, letting the dog run across her lap and out of the vehicle. "Are you gonna watch me ride a little before you go running, Mom?" Jesse asked.

"We can do that. Of course."

"Hey, Jess." Belle hugged her goddaughter. "I haven't seen you since the Sunset West concert."

"Wasn't that the best night ever? I still can't believe I met Tom West and got a guitar lesson, too!" Jesse skipped past Belle, finishing her sentence and walking backwards. She then headed to the pipe pens where her riding instructor was preparing horses for riding.

"She has stars in her eyes." Ainsley excused her daughter's behavior. "And what about you, Belle? As I recall, you were pretty flirty with the bass player. Are you seeing stars?"

"Yes. Seeing stars. Brian and I have seen each other every day. I think I am in love for real this time."

"Seriously, you have said that so many times, it holds no truth. And besides, a musician is the last person you should get involved with. You'll end up with a broken heart. I'm surprised he's had time to see you every day." Ainsley held herself steady against the Jeep as she stretched her leg muscles in preparation to run.

"You are the biggest pessimist with romance and relationships. But I'm hoping you will give your heart to someone someday. Even a musician. If they are the right person, they won't break your heart." Belle started stretching, too.

Ainsley was certain Belle didn't understand that nothing could keep a musician from pursuing their dreams, not even love. "Trust me, Belle. It's not enough. Musicians are often on the road and love doesn't travel well when distance separates you."

"Like you would have any idea what you are talking about. I don't think you remember what it's like to be in love. That's assuming you ever were."

To end the conversation before she said too much, Ainsley whistled for the dog, who was enjoying the luxury of being off leash. Jesse and the other riders warmed up their horses while Belle and Ainsley watched. Afterwards, the two runners left the arena and took the dirt road that twisted through the apple trees.

"So, when are you planning to share with me the history between you and Tom West?" Belle asked when they had found their optimum running pace.

Ainsley knew Belle was dying for the chance to ask. "There isn't really much to tell."

"Then tell me what little there is, Ains." Belle was determined.

"You are correct. There is a story, but where to begin..."

They ran on in silence for a while.

"C'mon, Ains. You shouldn't have to think about it. Tell me the story. The truth."

"Belle?"

The thought of telling Belle about Jesse's father was forming on its own in Ainsley's mind. Her brain had momentarily relinquished control.

Belle must have felt her friend's anxiety. "Ainsley? What is it?"

"Jesse is Tom's daughter."

After the momentary shock, Belle listened without interrupting as Ainsley backfilled with a synopsis; she met and fell in love with—then got dumped by—Tom West in one short summer. When she could no longer contain her emotions, Belle began speaking Italian. "Non ci credo! Mamma mia! This is huge."

"It was a very hard time in my life." Ainsley confirmed.

After years of speculating, Belle now knew about the past, but the details were still missing. She wanted to know why the relationship ended. And why had Ainsley chosen not to tell Tom he had a daughter?

"It was obvious to me, when Tom sang that love song like there was no one else in the theater, that there was more. But not in a million years would I have suspected this," Belle said. "I did not see this one coming!"

With no energy to say more, Ainsley waited for questions, but Belle took her time digesting the information.

"Belle?" Ainsley couldn't discern her friend's thoughts.

They passed by the yard on the outskirts of the orchard where the barking dogs lived. The dogs lifted their heads but didn't move from their lookout on the deck upon which they lounged. The porch dogs ignored the pedestrians.

"Belle, say something." Ainsley grew impatient, waiting for Belle's response.

"I'm thinking." Belle paused. "I mean... give me a minute to process."

Belle breathed rhythmically with their footsteps, then let out an exasperated, "Unbelievable!"

"You don't believe me?"

"No?" Belle added an inflection, though it wasn't a question. "I believe you," Belle answered. "But I can't believe you lied. How could you keep this from me? And Tom. He doesn't know?"

"I can't explain in a few words, Belle." Ainsley gave her friend some more time to come to grips.

"I mean, it's not what I expected to hear. It's just... I thought I knew you, but this..."

"I know. It's a lot."

"I get that you value your privacy, but..." Belle left the thought unsaid, but she felt betrayed. "It hurts that you didn't trust me enough to confide in me."

The women had crossed the boundary of the apple orchard and began running through the Christmas tree farm on the adjacent ranch.

"I understand," Ainsley admitted. "I thought it would have been selfish to burden you with keeping a secret of this magnitude."

The questions flew from Belle. "You say you and Tom were in love? Were you engaged? How old were you? Had Tom left before you found out you were pregnant?" Answering one at a time, Ainsley discovered it an unfamiliar feeling to be this open on the subject, but it was good practice.

"There's one more thing, Belle. This is important. Neither Tom nor Jesse..." Ainsley's words were cut short when Jesse came riding around the bend at the corner of the property line.

"There you are." The horse was moving fast, and Jesse pulled hard on the reins as Casey's mouth opened and he braced his neck in protest.

"Don't pull so hard. You'll hurt his mouth," Ainsley scolded.

"Oh, sorry boy." Jesse gave the horse a pat, then leaped off. "He's here. Tom West is here. He said he wants to meet my horse and today he came."

"He's here now?" Belle said as she and Jesse walked with the horse following behind them.

"Wait, Belle!" Ainsley called to the retreating pair, trying to get their attention to no avail.

Ainsley caught up as Belle was asking Jesse, "Where is Tom?"

"He's with Pete. Pete is showing him a few horses. Tom says he's in the market for a couple of saddle horses."

"Belle!" Ainsley grabbed Belle's shoulder. "Stop."

"Ouch," Belle frowned, holding her shoulder.

"Jesse, you go put Casey up. Then come to the main barn."

Ainsley turned to Belle, who was rubbing the arm that Ainsley almost pulled out of its socket. "Jesse doesn't know."

"Well, I figured that out, Ainsley. I wasn't gonna say anything. Honestly, I'm not a dummy."

CHAPTER 13

The Telling Trail Ride

"If only it would rain," Ainsley said to herself as she stared out the picture window into Mrs. Dixon's backyard garden.

Sleepless and distraught following the events at the stables, Ainsley had kept her aunt Ruthie on the phone well into the night. Ainsley explained to Ruthie how her plan had derailed when she blurted out the truth to Belle.

Ainsley expressed how frightening it had been when, before she could give Belle all the information, Jesse had interrupted. "I barely got the chance to tell Belle she is the only other person who knows."

"It's obvious how horrified you are with this turn of events," Ruthie had said. "I can hear the angst in your voice and wish I was there to comfort you in person."

The phone conversation was helpful. Through their spiritual bond, Ruthie appealed to the Lord to guide them with His wisdom as she reminded Ainsley of the bigger picture.

"As uncomfortable as it seems, God has a plan. Hard to believe when you're in the thick of it, but everything is as it should be." Ruthie wouldn't let Ainsley off the phone until they had put it all into perspective.

Ainsley had expressed to Ruthie how she had been so surprised when Tom materialized at the ranch.

"I was certain he would have left town by now. Sunset West only had shows over the weekend. I assumed they had a running list of performances across the US."

"Regardless of how things unfolded, nothing has changed other than Belle knows." Ruthie had reiterated. "Have faith in her loyalty. She is a good friend and is smart enough to understand the gravity of the situation."

Ruthie was right. Ainsley hoped now that Belle knew the truth, she would have someone in which to confide. But things kept going from bad to worse. The horror had continued when Belle had inserted herself right into the mix. When Pete started negotiating a horse sale with Tom, Belle chimed in as if she were part of the deal.

"Pete," Belle had suggested. "Why don't you let Ainsley take Tom and the horses out for a test ride?"

Ainsley had resisted. "I can vouch for the quality of Pete's stock. Not a bad one on the ranch. You can't go wrong and don't need me to verify it."

"Nonsense," Belle had insisted. "A trail ride is just the place for horse trading."

Ainsley told Ruthie how hard she had tried to get out of the date. "It was beyond frustrating and Belle had to see I was uncomfortable."

Ruthie had listened without interrupting and then after hearing the story, she gave Ainsley assurance it wasn't bad at all. "The Lord is providing an opportunity for you and Tom to talk without interruption." Aunt Ruthie had explained. "Even though you intended for Jesse to be first, everything is on track, Ainsley. God is working His magic. Maybe telling Tom first so you and he can tell Jesse together is a better way of telling Jesse."

"If there is a God, and He wants to work His magic, He'll make it rain," said Ainsley. As she hung up the phone, she could hear her aunt chuckling.

The work day had sped by and when she got home, Ainsley put on her Wranglers and her old riding boots and gave herself a pep talk. "Calm down. This is what we want." She coached herself through the nerves that had continued from the night before. "Keep your senses and be prepared for what will be."

"I won't be long, Jess. Mrs. Dixon is home." Ainsley repeated the standard instructions she gave Jesse whenever she was leaving the child at home for a short time.

"Go, Mom. Say hi to Tom." Jesse sat at the table with her homework spread out before her and barely looked up from the book she was reading. "Be happy and have fun."

When Ainsley pulled into the parking lot at Green Gate Stables, she spotted a cowboy standing with Pete near his pickup truck and trailer. With his hat cocked slightly to the side, Tom West looked comfortable in this environment. Ainsley felt the opposite.

"Hey, Ainsley." Pete was the first to greet her. "Are you ready for a ride?"

"You don't need me, Pete. These horses will sell themselves." Ainsley joined the men, who were taking a quick look around the rig.

"Loaded and all set," Pete announced. "Now, remember, Tom. This is live cargo you're dealin' with here. You're not haulin' a buncha noise making music equipment. Don't be slammin' on the brakes or bendin' fast 'round corners."

"Got it, Pete." Tom remained respectful without mentioning he grew up on his parents' ranch as credentials.

"Ainsley will direct you to the park. You'll have a few hours of daylight."

"Are you sure you wouldn't rather go?" Ainsley asked Pete.

"I got plenty of work here. You two have fun. We'll talk business when y'all return. See ya in a while."

Ainsley dropped her head in defeat and hoped her nerves weren't showing through. Tom shrugged and said, "Let's go."

There was not much talking as Tom focused on his driving and Ainsley gazed out the window.

"I can't believe all the changes in such a short time." Tom commented when he began to relax behind the wheel.

"Hmmm," Ainsley responded. "Not so short, Tom."

"I haven't been gone that long."

Silence fell again as the occupants in the truck's cab became lost in their own thoughts.

"So, what do you know about these horses?" Tom asked.

"Dancer and Pepper are decent mounts with solid health records and good training. Dancer is a registered Quarter horse, about five years old, trained for cutting. Her owner was showing her when he hurt his back and couldn't ride. Probably why Dancer is for sale."

"Pepper is a grade horse of unknown origin, definite Appaloosa by his looks, but no registration papers. Pete got the gelding for his nephew, who decided a week later he'd rather ride motorcycles. I have ridden Pepper before when Pete let me and Jesse borrow him so we could ride together." Ainsley stopped talking when she noticed the traffic grew heavier as they approached the city.

Ainsley looked across the cab towards Tom. He was involved in handling the rig as traffic entered and exited the highway. "Do you know how to get to the equestrian parking lot?" she asked.

Tom shook his head as he glanced at the clearance on the right with his rear side mirror.

"When the freeway ends, continue straight at the intersection. That road continues and T's at Summerfield Road. Go left, then take the first right. That street will take us to the park entrance." Ainsley spouted off directions, then returned to her thoughts.

Ainsley glanced again at Tom. In contemplating his profile, she wondered what kind of person he had turned out to be.

"Here we are." Tom had followed the signs and was turning into the park.

"Hang right after the kiosk. The equestrian parking is up that hill."

Once safely parked, they exited the cab and set about unloading and tacking up. Within minutes, they had saddled the livestock. Ainsley had Pepper ready and was the first to mount up.

"Trailhead is this way." Ainsley moved towards the end of the parking area. When Tom mounted up, he followed.

The two rode in silent meditation, enjoying the surrounding scenery.

"Whoa." Ainsley noticed she was way ahead of Tom and pulled Pepper to a stop to let Dancer catch up.

"She seems lazy. Is there something wrong with her?" Tom wondered why Dancer was walking so slow.

Ainsley giggled and then explained, "Dancer is not lazy. If you saw her working cows, you would see a different horse."

"Well, then. What do I do out here to get her to move? How do I get her to keep up?"

"Dancer is relaxed because you are relaxed. It's a good sign. You are a quiet rider and Dancer is very comfortable with you."

Ainsley observed that Tom wasn't one of those types that assumed they knew it all. "Dancer gets bored when she's following another horse. Why don't you take the lead? The trail opens up to a fire road around the bend and we can continue side by side."

"Thanks for the advice." Tom said, and after Dancer took the lead, she perked right up. "You were right. And you are pitching a good sales line, too. I think I'm gonna have to buy them."

"If I may ask," Ainsley was at ease opening the dialogue up now that they were riding side by side, "why are you shopping for livestock, anyway?"

"Well, to be honest, I didn't come to the stable to buy. I wasn't at all in the market."

"Then why are you buying them?"

"When I came to the stable as promised to catch Jesse at a lesson, I met Pete, who told me Jesse was finishing up with her lesson and that you would be along shortly. He invited me to check out his place while I waited. Pete is very proud of his place, isn't he?"

"He works hard and takes pride in his ranch and his reputation."

"After he showed me the arenas, he gave a tour of the barns and announced which horses were for sale. I was admiring the stock and told Pete how much we miss having horses at the ranch since we sold the last ones. Pete suggested we should have a few horses and hire a part-time ranch hand to come for a few hours a day and tend to them. The idea of having a horse kinda took on a life of its own, and it's growing on me. These animals are nice, and riding with you is a special treat."

"I am not part of the deal, but thanks. It's nice riding with you, too."

"You can be. Do you like Pepper? If you do, he's yours. You and Jesse can ride him anytime you want."

"Thank you. That's a generous offer, but you haven't even bought him." Ainsley smiled with grace, but inside she felt uncomfortable.

Tom had spoken with such self-assurance. It reminded her of how sure he had been when he proclaimed his love for her that day on the beach all those years ago. He had a way of speaking off the cuff, but when it came down to actions, what Tom did wasn't always in line with what he said.

"I never meant to imply the deal included you. I apologize," Tom said. Then, he asked, "Is there a flat area we can trot or run a bit? I'd love to ride a little faster."

"Follow me." Ainsley changed the topic and the tempo. She squeezed Pepper with her legs and the sensitive gelding sped up to a gentle rocking-horse lope.

Tom followed suit, giving Dancer free rein to gallop alongside his herdmate. Ainsley could see Tom relax, and she felt his joy. It was nice to spend a moment enjoying herself, but there were reasons to return to reality: Jesse. It was time to have the talk with Tom.

From laughing with him and running free to averting her eyes, Tom couldn't have understood Ainsley's swings in temperament. Ainsley's forehead tightened as her eyebrows lowered. Tom rode beside her in silence, waiting.

When he could wait no longer, he asked, "It's Phillip, isn't it? You two are close. Are you dating?"

"What about Phillip?" Ainsley shook her head, struggling to make sense of the question. She found it odd for Tom to mention him. It was out of context, and she had to think. "Phillip and I are just friends. We've been friends since our girls were born."

"I see."

"What do you mean, 'I see'?" What could Tom West "see" about anything? It insulted her how Tom could assume to know anything about her life. She hadn't expected to touch on any other subject except the one she had come on this trail ride to discuss, but so far the conversation kept veering off course.

"Arrrrgh!" Tom let out a loud growl, causing Ainsley to twist her entire body and grip her legs tight around Pepper's barrel. Pepper took it as a cue and leapt forward. Ainsley, who didn't understand the reason for Tom's outburst, lost her balance.

"Sorry," Tom apologized as Ainsley regained her seat and Pepper regained composure.

Her reflexive response to the gelding's spook brought her adrenaline up. "What the hell, Tom? Why did you scream? Do you have Tourette's?"

"I'm sorry, Ainsley."

"Tell Pepper you're sorry. You spooked him good."

"Sorry, Pepper," Tom said. "I'm frustrated."

It was Ainsley's turn to ride in silence, watching Tom's forehead wrinkle while waiting for him to speak.

"We were having a moment," Tom spoke, "and then it was gone. I felt connected to you until, like a toggle, you switched off. Your mixed signals are confusing me."

"I am not sending mixed signals. There are no signals at all. Maybe it's mixed feelings you are picking up on because I am plagued by them. But I am not signaling you."

"That explains why I'm confused." Tom picked up on the mix of feelings with emotions of his own. "It feels good to spend time with you, Ainsley, as if we have never been apart. Then you say or do something so foreign and uncharacteristic, and it reminds me of the gravity of passing days."

"You have no idea how much has changed, Tom."

This was it. The opening she was looking for. The voice in her head screamed, *Tell him!*, but her words couldn't break through her fears.

Ainsley reached the summit of a hill and stopped to behold the vast expanse below. They could see the small community of Kenwood and to the west was the Santa Rosa Plain.

Ainsley urged Pepper to turn around. "Come look at this," she instructed Tom. She showed him the eastern side overlooking the Napa Valley. To the south, they could almost make out the San Francisco skyline with its distinct bridges and skyscrapers.

"What a fantastic view. I forgot how close Sonoma County is to the Bay Area." Tom studied the countryside below.

"Tom," Ainsley said. "There's something you need to know."

"Yes?"

Ainsley studied the mane on her mount's neck, unable to speak.

"Look at me, Ainsley. What's on your mind?" Tom said, unaware of the seriousness of her thoughts.

"I, um.. you should know that..." Ainsley looked into Tom's trusting eyes and couldn't seem to squeeze out the words. Aunt Ruthie warned her about getting caught in the emotions. In attempting to rectify the past, she wanted to avoid causing any pain. The idea of hurting Tom with all the baggage she had to unpack was overwhelming.

Ainsley panicked.

"We better head home. The park ranger closes the gates at sunset."

"Hmmm, okay." Tom turned Dancer to the trail they had taken to get up the hill.

'UGH!' Ainsley let out a growl of frustration while Tom's back was turned. He couldn't see her toss her head towards the sky, mimicking a coyote giving his high-pitched howls. Only hers were internal.

"Ainsley," Tom said, "thank you for riding with me today. It was supposed to be about testing these horses, but what I am getting out of this afternoon has more to do with my mind and well-being."

"No need for thanks. It is my pleasure."

"Those rocky crags over there—see them?" Tom pointed to the massive rock formations high above and on the other side of the canyon they were descending into. "Isn't it weird to think that the very grains of sand we walk on at the beaches along our coast could have come from those rocks?"

"Hmmm." Ainsley studied the jagged edges jutting out from the canyon wall.

"The caressing rains gently make even the most rugged cliffs smooth. The largest boulder becomes the tiniest particle of sand, yet remains unchanged at the core. Through the morphosis, only the outside appearance has changed."

Tom's poetic narration impressed Ainsley, though it didn't surprise her. "Maybe there is a song there. You should write that down."

Tom flashed his laid back grin that spread up to his eyes. Ainsley felt a tingle inside. She remembered why it had been so easy to have a crush on Tom West. As a young girl, she hadn't been able to appreciate the sexy man Tom was. Today was different.

By the time they had the horses loaded for the drive home, the sun had gone down.

"Hey, man." As they passed the park ranger at the gate, Tom slowed the rig, wanting to offer an apology for being there after sunset.

Before he could say another word, the young man exclaimed, "You're Tom West." His mouth stuck in an open circle.

The young ranger held the gate, too star-struck to say anything more. As Tom drove away, he waved his hat out the window like a rodeo cowboy.

"Doesn't that ever get old?" Ainsley blurted out.

"Sometimes the fans are overwhelming and then it is exhausting. Guys like the ranger are entertaining. It is flattering to be noticed and humbling to feel the love."

Love? Ainsley considered it an unusual word to describe the adoration of fans.

"They are just adoring fans. It is no replacement for real-life love," Tom answered, as if he heard her thoughts.

"Of course." Ainsley felt sorry again. "It might be an exciting and rewarding career, but there is a price to pay, isn't there?" She empathized, though she couldn't say she knew what it felt like to be a musician.

Tom appeared to think about it, then said, "You are lucky to have a place to call home. Someone for whom you return every night."

"Jesse is my world."

"You are an exceptional mother, if you don't mind the compliment. Jesse is getting everything she needs. You seem to manage quite a balance with her."

It was difficult to accept Tom's compliments. A good mother would not keep her child from her father. "It's difficult sometimes. Thank goodness we have family close by, and friends. Jesse has authentic examples of family dynamics and caring relationships."

The moment Ainsley spoke, she realized she'd created a segue— another chance to tell Tom he was Jesse's father. Before she could speak, Tom started talking.

"Remember my bass player and good buddy Brian? You met him on the bus the night of the concert."

"Yes, your bandmate Brian. I remember Belle mentioning she's been seeing him. Is that the same, Brian?"

"Yes, Belle and Brian are getting along very well." Tom said. "Brian and his ex-wife split up after several years into their marriage. Maryanne, Brian's ex, couldn't cope with the long periods of separation. She stayed home with the kids while he traveled with Sunset West, but she became resentful."

"It also frustrated Maryanne that Brian was not bringing her bundles of money. Her family was wealthy but disowned her when she took up chasing musicians around the country."

"Maryanne married Brian to irritate her parents, but he couldn't give her the luxurious life she was used to. Soon, the novelty of marrying a guy without her father's approval wore off and living without the perks of her wealthy family grew old. She left Brian and her family welcomed her back. With their support, Maryanne asked for a divorce. It hurt Brian and insulted him. It broke his heart when Maryanne asked for full custody of their sons."

"During their breakup, the popularity of the band had skyrocketed. We were putting in a lot of hours working and Brian had no way of caring for the children while we were gone all the time. We still weren't making much money, and Brian hadn't the means to pay child support to his estranged wife."

"When Maryanne presented a solution that would relieve him of all financial obligations, Brian agreed. He thought giving them up to be adopted by Maryanne's parents was a way of ensuring the kids were taken care of. He hadn't considered how Maryanne's parents felt about him, but he found out."

"Brian's ex father-in-law, who regarded Brian as a deadbeat before he gave up his kids, wanted his daughter to have less than nothing to do with him afterwards. Brian doesn't even have visitation rights!" Tom paused as if the indignation his friend and bandmate suffered was his to suffer, too.

"With every situation, there is more than meets the eye. Perhaps it was the best solution for them." Ainsley filled the silence.

"How could that be? Brian hasn't seen them in years. His children don't even know him."

Tom's words struck a nerve with such resonance, Ainsley's voice wavered, "Well, I don't know the situation, I only mean..."

She wasn't sure what she meant. She tried to explain. "It is better for kids to have stability, and a routine. Depending on the circumstances, when both parents can't give that to them, it's best for them to be with someone who can."

"I hadn't thought about it from that perspective. But shouldn't they at least have contact with Brian?" Tom didn't wait for an answer. "Brian probably thought it would be best, but I think he has regrets. He is making an effort to communicate with Maryanne. He would love nothing more than to reunite with his children."

Ainsley wished Tom would stop talking. *What does he know about this?* Ainsley fumed. *Tom, who is not aware of what it takes to be a parent, shouldn't have anything to say about Brian's situation.*

Tom assumed Brian was sad, but Ainsley considered that maybe he was relieved.

"Well, isn't Brian the perfect poster child for a situation that has played out a million times among you folks in the music industry?" Ainsley spoke without thinking.

"What are you talking about?"

Ainsley was certain Tom would have done what Brian did had he known he had a child. Would Tom have regretted it now, like Brian does?

Once she tells him, will Tom see Jesse as an unwanted burden?

"Musicians have so many opportunities when women are always throwing themselves at them." Ainsley further explained, "And when a child is the result, it's the woman who has to step up. The musician doesn't give up his dreams to take responsibility. It's the woman who pays the price of having a fling. The musician doesn't even care about it. Sometimes the public sees him as a victim, as if the woman is trying to trap him."

Tom stared at Ainsley, then returned his focus to the road ahead.

"What about you, Tom? Have you had your share of groupies? Have you sprinkled your seed across the country leaving behind kids as you passed through?"

Her ears felt numb from the words coming out of her mouth. The pounding in her head from her own blood pressure was no help as she attempted to figure out what she was saying.

It embarrassed her what she had said. Mortified, she tried to find words to free herself from her mess. "Not so quick to answer. Does that mean you are counting? Or that you can't remember."

Ainsley held her breath. She glanced at the side of Tom's face and saw a slight twitch on his left cheek. He turned to look her square in the eyes. Both Tom's cheeks lifted into a broad grin. "Ohhh, you... You're just yankin' my chain."

Ainsley laughed, and Tom concluded she was joking. Somehow, she had gotten out of that mess by faking it was a joke.

Pete was waiting when they returned. "So? What'ja think? Mighty fine horses, those two."

To Ainsley, Pete said, "We got this, hun," and took hold of the horses' lead ropes. "Thanks for helping. Tom and I will finish up any business." Pete gave her a wink, then turned back to Tom.

This was her chance for a clean getaway. Turning onto the familiar route home, Ainsley pushed down her emotions. Her only thought was to get to Jesse and the sanctuary of her home.

CHAPTER 14

Deeper

"When's your next day off, Ainsley? I'll take you out. You seem like you need a date." Even with headphones on, Ainsley could hear her co-worker's voice drifting over the cases that partitioned one route from the other. He was a self-proclaimed jerk, but that was no excuse for his saying and doing the wrong things.

"She can't hear you with her headphones on, Howard," Belle interjected from behind her case, "and even if she could, I guarantee she would not be interested."

"Relentless pursuit." A voice from over the top of the letter cases joined in. "Poor Howard. He'll never stop shooting the only arrow in his quiver."

"Some day Ainsley will say yes," Howard insisted. "And she'll be begging for more."

The other carriers in the vicinity offered a laugh or chuckle. Some let out disgusted groans.

"Speaking on her behalf, Howard. The answer will always be no."

"But she has been acting too serious. Ainsley needs to loosen up. What better approach to do that than to spend a night with me?"

Howard's level of inappropriateness rose to an unacceptable level. In defense of her best friend, Belle responded. "One night with you? Oh, cringe! I suspect you can make any woman switch sides. And weren't you aware? Ainsley and I are lovers. Your constant harassment has turned us gay. She will be with me this weekend."

"Ooooo," came a comment, followed by, "That is both offensive and a turn on!"

Ainsley cringed and kept working as the supervisor stepped in to end the rowdy interactions. She continued to process her row of letters, forgetting about the guys at work. She had other things to think about.

Days had passed since that terrible conversation while returning from the horseback ride. After telling Belle the secret, she had lost the courage to tell her daughter about Tom West. The inner conflict was gnawing at her, and it was showing.

"Ainsley, you can't keep everything bottled up inside." Belle had become concerned about the condition her friend was in. "Maybe you should seek the help of a professional. I am not being critical, but you look like hell."

"Thanks a lot. I agree to meet up for a run together, and this is how you treat me?"

Belle and Ainsley finished stretching and started their run towards Ragle Ranch Regional Park, a path they had taken many times. Before they entered the park, they zigzagged through the surrounding neighborhoods. "You'll feel better if you talk it out and I'm here to listen," Belle offered.

Ainsley remained quiet. After having kept a secret for so long, she felt unable to casually converse casually with anyone.

"It's fine, Ainsley. You can do what you want for yourself. That's your choice. But Jesse is seeing a change. She is attuned to you. And you are sending her off to your folks to avoid her. Jesse knows something is up."

"Jesse is fine. She suspects nothing at all. It is normal for Jesse to stay with her grandparents. I'm doing it for her good."

"And what is good for you, Ains?"

The question evoked self-pity. Ainsley projected her feelings onto Jesse and conflated the issue. "Based on Tom West's disappearance, it seems for the better that Jesse doesn't know who he is. It would upset her to find out he's a parent who is always gone. The last thing I aim to do is bring grief into her life."

"I am not telling you what to do. You wouldn't listen, anyway. I recommend you talk to Tom. Give him a chance to be there for his daughter. How could you assume he wouldn't care?"

"It's complicated."

"Then please explain. Help me understand."

Ainsley ran on past the tract homes built in the seventies. With their weedy yards and outdated windows, one could deduce, based on the lack of demonstrated pride, the homes were rentals, or on their third owners. Time had done those houses no favors.

"Nothing ever gets better with time."

"Which is why you should not waste another minute on this secret. What about your Aunt Ruthie? Have you talked to her?" Belle understood the close bond Ainsley had with Rose's older sister.

A stingy head shake was all Belle got in response.

"Look at me, Ainsley," Belle said. "For too long, you've cut yourself off from others."

Ainsley stopped when Belle took hold of her arm, then freed herself and started running.

"You've been pushing away anyone who cares." Belle stopped Ainsley again. "Nobody can reach you and soon we'll stop trying. But we won't stop caring."

Belle spoke the truth, but Ainsley was too deep in denial. It locked her in a prison of loneliness. She couldn't believe anyone would understand.

The days following the horseback excursion were darker than when Tom went away for the first time. When Tom left Ainsley, pregnant and alone, she had the moral high ground. Now, Ainsley had no ground at all. Once the truth was out, Ainsley's actions could be viewed as criminal. Would it be worth the risk? What if Tom is so mad at Ainsley for hiding the truth that he files for full custody?

"Damn...!" Ainsley stopped running and bent to hold herself up, hands on knees.

"What? Do you got a leg cramp?" Belle stopped running, too.

"I can't keep going."

"You brought this on, Ainsley. In avoiding me, you've also missed out on exercising and your body is rebelling. We should have stretched more before starting."

"No, no, no…" Ainsley stood up, moved her hands to her hips and started walking, shaking her head to the rhythm of her words.

"Here, let's stretch it out." Belle motioned towards a picket fence they could hold on to for balance.

"No, dammit. It's not a stupid muscle." Ainsley huffed. She wished it was only a cramp.

"It's Rose's fault." Ainsley made fists. "I messed everything up and I can't regain control."

Slamming her heels into the concrete with each foot fall, Ainsley walked forward without direction. Belle followed.

"I've got to…" Ainsley paced. "There must be…" She shook her arms to loosen the involuntary clench. "I… need a better plan."

"You need to quit obsessing." Belle stopped Ainsley's cyclic pacing. "Come here and sit."

Ainsley was on the verge of a breakdown.

"Breathe from the bottom of your lungs." Belle led Ainsley to a short brick wall between the sidewalk and a raised lawn bed in a front yard along the lane. "Not another word. Just breathe."

Belle waited for Ainsley's breathing to return to normal.

"You are in love with Jesse's father."

Hearing the words gave Ainsley's emotions an outlet. It was a relief that Belle had figured it out. Ainsley couldn't admit it out loud, and Belle had spared her the pain of having to utter the words herself. Shaking and sobbing incoherently, Ainsley nodded.

The next morning, the ringing of the telephone woke Ainsley, but before she could reach for the receiver by her bed, someone picked it up.

Ainsley sat on her bedside, gathering her wits. She looked down at her running shorts and realized she had slept without putting on jammies. *Why?* she wondered, but couldn't remember.

The implication was she had also not showered the night before. Though still foggy around the edges, Ainsley remembered the anxiety attack, and getting home thanks to Belle. Ainsley stood up and her head spun. On unsteady legs, she followed her nose down the stairs to the source of the smell of coffee.

"Your mom asked if you are coming for Jesse today," Belle stated when Ainsley descended.

"Thanks for making coffee." Ainsley went to the cupboard. "You spoke to Rose?"

"She said it's fine if Jesse stays longer. They don't have any plans."

"Thanks, I'll call her." The cup of coffee was ready to be consumed, and Ainsley hoped the brew would ease her headache. "Who knew you could have a hangover from an anxiety attack?"

"Drink this first." Belle handed Ainsley a glass of cucumber water. "You're dehydrated."

Ainsley drained the liquid from the glass, then choked. "Wait, what time is it?... What day is it?... Am I late for work?"

"Hold on there, sister." Belle put her hand in front of Ainsley's face and tilted it back and forth like a windshield wiper. Erasing Ainsley's questions as the blade wipes clean the raindrops, Belle said, "You are gonna get yourself agitated again. Take a few deep breaths."

Ainsley did as she was told while Belle supplied some contextual facts.

"Today is Friday, your long weekend off. You are not late for work, but I am. I called in sick."

"No. You shouldn't have done that." Ainsley hadn't meant to have caused Belle to miss work.

"Hey, I was up all night with you. There is no chance I was going to work today. I have lots of leave stored up. Only bummer is I broke my record of most consecutive days without calling in."

"Belle, I'm sorry."

"It is not that big a deal anymore, and here's the bonus. With us both absent from work today, the guys are gonna believe we are lovers."

It took Ainsley a moment to comprehend Belle's odd statement. Then she remembered their peers were teasing them the day before. "Ohhh!" Ainsley's laugh came from deep in her abdomen.

"We should totally put them on. Play up the ruse. Then at least Howard might leave us alone."

"That'll encourage the guys to bug us more," said Ainsley. "It's how guys react to girl-on-girl love. For them, it's the best kind of porn."

Ainsley laughed more than the subject warranted, but it felt good to release some more toxic energy in a healthy manner. "What'll people think?" Ainsley made an exaggerated shocked expression. She was committed to furthering the game.

"I hope the news doesn't travel to Brian!" Belle imitated Ainsley's face.

Belle's last contribution to the frivolity took the fun out of the game, and she regretted it. Mentioning Tom's bandmate snapped Ainsley out of the frivolity. "I'm sorry, Ains. It just slipped out."

"No worries." Ainsley looked up. "I had the anxiety attack yesterday, and it's out of my system. I'm fine now. You needn't tiptoe around. I realize you're seeing Tom's bandmate, but I'll get past the association and be happy for you. I promise."

Belle studied Ainsley, looking for signs of the tension that poured out of her the night before but saw none. Maybe Ainsley was indeed fine.

"I heard you last night, Belle. What you said makes sense. This should have never gone on for so long. Putting it off only makes it worse. I won't be afraid... I will be fearless."

"Fearless is a misnomer. It implies there is no fear. What you need is to be brave. Brave means sometimes you have to do things despite your fears."

"There you go again, being serious and all logical and philosophical."

"Well, don't expect it to last too long. I am not the sensible one. I have a reputation to maintain."

The girls lingered for a while, enjoying each other's energy.

"Well, this slumber party was a blast, but I must get home. It is possible for me to make use of this unplanned day off by doing something constructive. Will you be okay now?"

Belle stood, and Ainsley lifted herself off the chair to give her best friend a heartfelt hug. "Thank you so much for everything. And I promise, I will follow through. I am starting off first with Jesse. I want to help her digest the information before I bring in Tom. Then, what comes next will depend on her. I am going to follow Jesse's lead."

"Have you thought about telling them together?"

Ainsley could feel the twinges of fear spiking through her heart when pondering Belle's question. Thinking only about telling Jesse was scary. Facing them both at the same time? That was unimaginable.

"Either way," Belle offered assurance, "I support you. It's time for action. Jesse is the most important thing. And I am just moments away if you or Jesse need me." Belle hugged Ainsley. "Take care of my goddaughter and yourself. Siamo una famiglia. We are family."

Belle went home, leaving Ainsley to plan.

The sooner the better, Ainsley had heard more than once, and she intended to take that advice. If holding onto the lie made her look and feel this way, then telling the truth couldn't be any worse. She had descended to the bottom and was tired of the view. There was no place else to go but up. With her mind set, she got ready to collect Jesse from Rose and William.

Ainsley had done what she could with makeup to improve her appearance, but the shocked look on Rose's face showed she had failed to conceal her suffering.

"You look so thin," Rose announced.

"Thanks, Mom."

"I didn't mean it as a compliment."

"I know. I'm not doing so well, so I guess it makes sense."

"Come. Sit. Jesse is with William. There are some things we need to discuss now that you're here."

"I'm not interested in talking at the moment, Mother." Chatting with Rose was exhausting under normal conditions. "I am ready to tell Jesse. I thought we'd head to the coast where I can think clearly."

"You want to go to the beach? The beach. That's your solution to everything. Running away."

"When have I ever ran? From what have I run?" Ainsley and Rose were falling into their old pattern. Ainsley clawed her way out. "No, Mom. Let's not do this today." Ainsley pushed past Rose. The last thing she had energy for was sparring with her mother.

"Ainsley, wait—" Rose called out as Ainsley had reached for the sliding door in the family room that led to the backyard.

When she reached for the handle, what she saw made her freeze in place. She must have been dreaming. Never in her wildest imaginings had she expected to see Tom West sitting by the fish pond. Worse was the moment she realized Jesse was out there with him.

"I tried to warn you." Rose came to the slider and took Ainsley by the elbow. "Please come into the kitchen before you do something rash."

"You said Jesse was with Dad. Why did you lie?" Ainsley's shock turned into anger.

"Ainsley, please. I hoped to spare you the alarm." Rose's hand on her elbow carried an energy that made Ainsley oblige. "Sit down in here."

Rose led Ainsley from the kitchen to the family room, but Ainsley resisted before they reached the chairs.

"You told them?" Ainsley jerked her arm free. "You did, didn't you! How could you?"

"Stop being so dramatic. I wished I had told them. Then we could all move on and heal. If you'd quit behaving like a toddler and let me explain."

Ainsley started counting backwards in her head, a trick Aunt Ruthie suggested. *Three, two, one.* Ainsley breathed in, then out. "Go ahead. I'm listening."

Ainsley applied the technique believed to have a calming effect on people, but she lacked faith in its application.

"First, I have said nothing to anyone. I wasn't aware that Tom was coming—he unexpectedly showed up. Jesse acknowledged she received a few texts from him over the last few days. Maybe they made plans?"

"Tom has been communicating with Jesse without my knowledge?" *Three, two, one.* Ainsley inhaled and exhaled. Aunt Ruthie's antidote to control emotion wasn't working.

"Not the immediate concern, Ainsley. If you overreact, you will confuse Jesse. From my perspective, they are not talking about anything serious. Only things a ten-year-old kid would talk about."

"Well, then we won't be interrupting anything. I am going to retrieve Jesse's things. Please have her meet me in the car."

"What do I tell Tom?" Rose was at a loss.

Ainsley let the backdoor close on Rose's question. Jesse was the most vulnerable. She was Ainsley's sole concern.

"What's taking so long?" Ainsley whispered as she waited in the Jeep, expecting at any minute Tom would come strutting out. If Rose had said anything, he would want to speak to Ainsley. Was he going to announce he wanted custody and was taking Jesse? Over her dead body.

"Hi, Mama." Jesse greeted her mother and struggled to get in with her belongings. The excited dog gave Jesse a slobbery welcome. Jesse snapped the seat belt buckle and leaned over to give Ainsley a half hug. "Are you okay?"

"I'm fine. And how are you?" Ainsley pretended Jesse's inquiry was merely a standard greeting.

Maybe Jesse knew. Maybe Tom found out and had told Jesse. Tom likely instructed Jesse not to say anything. *Three, two, one.* Ainsley tried to stop the creeping paranoia. She was losing the battle.

"Are we going to the stable?"

"We can. I called Pete this morning thinking we wouldn't be coming today, so he turned Casey out in the pasture, but let's fetch him."

"We don't have to ride or anything, I just want to see Casey." Jesse continued. "I hope you aren't mad, but Grandma couldn't take me out yesterday."

"Why would I be angry? We shall go to the stable, if that's what you want, Jess."

"Yes, please. I miss Casey when I cannot see him every day."

Jesse was such a sweet child. She was a good kid, the best a mother could ask for. She had more grace than some adults and lived a grateful and appreciative life. It seemed as if she was born having mastered the secrets to happiness.

Rip off the bandaid. Ainsley heard the words of advice. *Get it over with fast.*

"Jesse, there is something I've been meaning to share with you." Ainsley paused. "I've been waiting for the right time. I am uncertain if there is a right time."

The breeze from the open-air vehicle blew Jesse's hair around her face. Looking at Ainsley, Jesse pulled gently on Brooke's ear as the dog watched the scenery go by.

"I need to share more regarding your father." Ainsley paused, but Jesse's expression remained unchanged. "You are familiar with the basics—he was my boyfriend, and we loved each other, but we went our separate ways before you were born."

Jesse nodded.

"I have been waiting to find out if you wanted to hear more. You haven't asked, but now that you are ten years old, I think you should have this information."

"I have been curious," Jesse confessed. "My friend Beth, on her fifth birthday, her parents explained she was adopted. And they waited 'til her tenth birthday to tell her about her birth mother. Beth told me she doesn't know much about her birth father. She said parents can sense when to do these things and she is waiting for them to discuss her dad with her. I was expecting you to talk to me like Beth's parents did when you were ready, so I never asked."

Jesse was so matter-of-fact. It made Ainsley smile. It also left her a bit more ashamed about the secret she had kept. It amazed her how much faith children put in adults. They had no choice. Ainsley couldn't help feeling she had betrayed that trust.

"Parents are not always aware of when it is time, Jesse. Most of us struggle. Don't tell anyone, but parents are clueless about raising their children. We are lucky when our kids turn out okay."

Ainsley stopped in the parking area at the ranch among the staged horse trailers, a tractor, and a ride-along lawn mower. Ainsley turned in the seat to face her child. "Jesse, let me ask you. Do you want to know about your dad?"

Jesse turned with a serious face to her mom and nodded. Even the dog, who usually jumped around with excitement as soon as they entered the ranch property, sat quietly.

After a deep breath, Ainsley began, "When I was young, I fell in love with a musician and you are the gift given because of that love. We had planned to be together, but your dad wanted very much to play his music, so I decided he would go and I would stay with you."

"He was a musician? Like Tom? Cool."

"Yes, Jesse."

"Is my father still a musician? Is that how you know Tom West? Was my dad in his band?"

Ainsley saw no other option but to put it straight up. She studied her daughter's face.

"Jesse, Tom West is your father."

"My father IS Tom West?"

"Yes."

"Tom West is my dad?"

Ainsley nodded. "Tom West is your dad."

"He's my dad."

Ainsley sat still, holding her breath as the youngster processed the information.

"Tom is my father... and you loved him." Jesse repeated to the tempered glass of the car window, then turned to her mother. "Do you and Tom still love each other?"

"We were kids then, but now we are adults. Everything about our lives has changed."

"You loved him back then. What's changed?"

Ainsley wanted to have an answer to satisfy Jesse's question. "Tom and I have grown into two different people than who we were when we were in love."

"You stopped loving each other? Did Tom not love me?"

"Nobody has stopped loving you." Ainsley hadn't expected the question. "Parents never quit loving their kids." Ainsley paused to quiet the pain of Jesse's question. "Sweety, Tom doesn't know about you. I never told him."

"What?" Jesse exclaimed, then asked, "Why?"

Jesse's question was legitimate, and she deserved an answer. Ainsley found it hard to look into Jesse's eyes when all she saw was innocence.

"It was a decision I made based on what was happening. I believed it was the right choice. Like I said, parents don't know what we are doing." Even as Ainsley said it, she hated her own words.

Jesse turned away and stared through the window again.

"That's really lame." Jesse opened her door. "Okay, Brooke." Jesse released the dog without another word to Ainsley. Jesse started across the gravel yard towards the barns without a backward glance and headed towards Pete when he beckoned her to come.

PART TWO
Freedom from Fear

CHAPTER 15

Circle of Disclosure

The following day, Saturday, at three o'clock, Ainsley heard the knock.

"Come in. The door's not locked." The door was already opening.

"Hello, Ainsley." Tom stepped in.

"Have a seat," Ainsley said, trying to quiet the fluttering butterflies inside. Tom's irresistible smile was always enough to throw Ainsley's thoughts into disarray. "Can I offer you a drink? Soda?"

"A soda would be nice, thanks."

"So, I hear you bought the horses?"

"Yes, I brought them home and Mom and Pops are spoiling them rotten. The apples we sell to the processing facility are disappearing from the trees. The horses are loving the arrangement and my folks are happy to have all the fun, none of the work."

"That's nice for them," Ainsley said. "Most folks leave their horses on the ranch for Pete to manage."

"I plan to manage the horses myself. As promised, Pete arranged for one of his hands to swing by every other day. The horses will be more than well taken care of."

"I wasn't implying you would put the horses' well-being at risk by keeping them at your folks' ranch." Ainsley sought to avoid starting on a point of contention so early in the conversation.

Tom focused on the soda can Ainsley had set on the table in front of him. Popping the top and pouring the contents into the glass, Tom enjoyed a satisfying swig, then said, "I was glad Belle and Brian reached out to let me know you were asking to meet up. I was hoping we could get together."

"It surprised me to see you at Rose's the other day. I thought you had left town."

"We should be in Nashville, but there was a change of plans." Tom seemed slightly vexed. "I was at your mother's place when you came to get Jesse."

Why were you there? She wanted to ask. Remembering her annoyance with Tom for approaching Jesse uninvited, she hesitated, then said, "I had no idea you were so friendly with Rose and William."

"Our folks have been friends a long time."

Ainsley hadn't ever considered the Tobins and the Wests to be very close at all. "Our parents?"

"It's a small town, Ainsley. Your father and mine are both in the building industry. Our mothers volunteer at the same church."

Ainsley detected more irritation. "I know that. I meant friends in the social context."

Sounding like a snob, Ainsley had irritated herself. *Three, two, one.* This was not the topic she aimed to discuss.

"What I mean is," Ainsley tried once more, "I wasn't thinking you'd be returning home so soon. What about your tour dates?"

"Ainsley, I'm certain you have no interest in discussing my schedule or my equine acquisitions. Nor do you wish to converse about family. Why am I here?"

"You're a busy guy, so I'll skip the small talk if you wish." She turned to face him again. The gnawing feeling in her stomach replaced the fluttering she had felt before. "There is a very important reason I asked you here."

"I'm all ears." Tom waited.

"That is such a funny expression. 'All ears,'" Ainsley said. Her nerves were getting the best of her. She started laughing as she pictured Tom with huge ears all over his head.

Tom looked at her and breathed through his nose, trying not to join in the mirth. He kept composure, while waiting for the laughing to subside.

"'All ears.'" She repeated. With her hands on either side of her head, Ainsley motioned in an arch from her hair to her neck, showing the size the ears would be if a person was 'all ears.' "Get it?"

"Mm-hmmm." Tom tilted his head. "So, you were saying?"

Ainsley's laughing faded and her smile disappeared as she studied the kitchen floor. Then she blurted it out. "Jesse is your daughter."

When Ainsley mustered the courage to lift up, Tom was looking at her with sparkles in his eyes.

"I knew it. When I first saw her that night at the concert, I felt a magnetic pull. And the day at the beach? It's as though Jesse brought out something deep inside my heart. We were suspicious, but it is so good to hear you confirm it."

"We?" Ainsley asked, "Who's 'we'? How long have you been suspicious?"

Tom ignored her question. Still with enchantment but touched with sorrow, Tom asked, "Why, Ainsley? Why did you keep this secret? All the time I have lost. All the things I wasn't a part of." Tom wasn't angry, only sorry, it seemed, for the lost time.

Ainsley was stuck on Tom's use of the word 'we'. "What do you mean, 'we were suspicious'? Who else knew?" Ainsley wanted to know.

"My parents suspected your baby was mine. When they found out you were pregnant, they kept asking me if I heard from you, but they never informed me of your condition. I never knew you had a baby. Why didn't you tell me?" Tom implored. "My parents knew where I was. You could have asked them."

"I was always afraid you might not have a place in your life for a child."

"My mother wanted me to contact you. She admits she had a feeling about Jesse, but she never said it to me. She felt it wasn't her place to interfere. How could I have understood I should reach out to you?"

"I was busy having a baby and raising a baby and working to make a life for the two of us. I didn't have the energy to hunt for you as you went traipsing around the world."

"It was painful for me to be on the road. Thinking of you and longing for you was the hardest part." Tom twirled the empty soda can and relived the sadness as he spoke.

"There were times I almost quit the band. The guys were sick of my moodiness and lost patience with me. I realized I had to keep my feelings inside, so that is what I did. Staying away was easier than facing the pain of rejection."

Ainsley saw a slight lift in his expression when Tom paused, remembering. She waited.

"I know we lost touch, Ainsley, but I never stopped loving you. And now we have a child together. We have a lot of catching up to do." Tom stood and stepped towards Ainsley, who had never sat down. He caught her in a full embrace. "You don't know how happy you've made me."

With his arms still around her, Tom leaned forward to kiss Ainsley. He put his hands on her back and pressed her into his chest. She surrendered to his cues. All she was aware of was his nearness, and the warmth it fueled inside. With no room for logic, reasoning stepped aside and instinct took its place. Her lips kissed him back with equal passion.

"Oh, Ainsley. How I missed you…"

Tom's words broke the spell as he had to stop kissing her to speak.

"Oh… no." Ainsley's arms fell to her sides and Tom's grip eased. It only took a moment for her to remember who she was, who she was kissing, and the conversation they had just had.

Tom pulled away from the embrace, trying to read Ainsley's face. He remained confused.

"This is not right. We mustn't do this. I can't bear to be hurt." Ainsley spread her hands over her face.

"I don't understand."

Afraid to speak in fear of saying the wrong thing, she hesitated. Nothing had changed except him knowing. He was still a musician and the pain of his departure remained. She couldn't help but feel it was presumptuous of him to think he could just have her now after everything.

"This is not about us, Tom. This has got to be about you and Jesse. You and Jesse need time to focus on your relationship."

"What are you trying to say?" Tom asked.

"You and I are the past. Jesse is the future."

Ainsley's heart ached at the disappointment and confused look on Tom's face, but loving him now would only complicate an already out-of-control situation. There was no going back, and for Jesse's sake, she and Tom had to create clear boundaries. "Maybe you should go." Ainsley heard herself say.

"You want me to leave? Why did you bring me here if only to tell me something this big, then kick me to the curb?"

Ainsley chose not to take into account Tom's feelings. "I brought you here to confirm you have a child. Apparently, you already knew."

"So, what you're saying is you have a daughter, and I have a daughter, but we are not a parental unit? You are a parent. I am a parent. Separate." Tom almost fell backwards as he backed away. "I don't... I can't even..."

Tom's look of disbelief hit Ainsley hard. He wasn't mad at all. Hurt.

Ainsley found it necessary to look away. Upon hearing the click of the doorknob, Ainsley knew the worst had happened. Her worst-case scenario hadn't even been this bad. Tom had left, and she had been the one to send him away.

Ainsley was alone in the little cottage behind Mrs. Dixon's house and couldn't even cry. She hadn't the right to.

CHAPTER 16

Ainsley in the Dark

"Are you coming to church, Mom?" Jesse's voice drifted up to Ainsley's sleeping ears. "If you don't get up now, we will be late."

Ainsley growled, then rolled up to sitting.

"I'm up," she lied as she sank back down. Lately, Ainsley, who was always quick to rise, found it difficult getting out of bed. Revealing the long-kept secret to both Jesse and Tom was supposed to be a relief for her, yet nothing had gotten better. The truth did not set her free, as promised in the Gospel.

"Phillip and Emily are coming by to pick us up," said Jesse as she climbed the stairs to check on the wake-up progress. "Mo-om!"

"Okay, okay." Ainsley dragged herself out of bed. Hearing that Phillip was giving them a ride did not improve her outlook. "I'm up."

"That's what you said, and then you went back to bed." Jesse kept watch, making sure her mother went into the shower.

Wanting the running water to wake her up, Ainsley realized there was little hope of it. She was weary when she went to bed the night before, and the hours of restless sleep had done nothing to restore her energy.

Ainsley hadn't spoken to Tom since she sent him packing, and Jesse had acted as though nothing had changed for her.

Ainsley wished to converse more with him, his parents, and hers. She reached out to Belle who seemed to have gone radio silent and Aunt Ruthie hadn't returned her call either. Without input from her confidants, Ainsley remained aimless.

As promised, Phillip and Emily showed up at the cottage to drive them all to church. Ainsley spotted Rose and William sitting near the front and started towards them when Phillip stopped her with a hand placed on the shoulder.

"We can all four fit here. Let's sit together." Phillip's hand guided Ainsley, who showed little resistance.

Rose noticed them, but Ainsley questioned whether Rose was showing approval or condemnation.

Oh, who cares anymore? She thought.

Ainsley remembered nothing about the sermon. She was present in body, but not in spirit. As the congregation collected out front afterwards, Ainsley scanned the parked cars, wondering if she could find one with the keys in it. How she longed to drive off and get lost. Then she heard Phillip and Rose talking and tried to focus on that.

"Thank you, Mrs Tobin, for the invitation. We'd love to come for brunch." Phillip accepted Rose's offer, lifting his arm over Ainsley's shoulder in an inclusive gesture.

Ainsley wished she had been paying attention. Getting together with Phillip for family meals was the last thing she wanted, but it was too late. Phillip had already accepted.

"Yay!" Ainsley jumped when Emily and Jesse squealed in stereo. It thrilled the girls to spend their Sunday at the Tobins. Smiling from ear to ear, Phillip acted like the girls, except he stifled the squeal.

A bald-headed man Ainsley recognized came up behind William while they were standing at the church front. "Great work on the repairs at the Nagler's, Will." Dan Taylor patted William on the back. "Nagler was ecstatic that you could bring that old house up to regulation, and in time for the inspection."

"Of course." William was proud to take credit on behalf of his employees. "Glad to do it. We aim to please."

"We can always count on you," Dan Taylor said. "I am putting in a bid for a renovation at Orchard Hill Middle School. Their bathrooms need updating to comply with the water conservation regulations. Government contract, man. You interested in the job?"

"Dan," Rose interrupted before William could answer. "I'd like you to meet Ainsley's friend Phillip Martin and his daughter Emily."

"Phillip, this is Mr. Dan Taylor from Taylor's Top-Hat Contracting."

"Nice to meet you, Mr. Taylor." Phillip held out his hand and the two men shook.

When Rose suggested they all should prepare to leave, Ainsley had the urge to bolt, but Phillip was still holding onto her shoulder.

At the Tobins' farmhouse, Rose served her guests lunch in the garden, and everyone agreed it was the perfect setting for a beautiful spring day. Ainsley sat in a lounge chair and let the warm sunshine soothe her frayed edges. The girls frolicked on the lawn and climbed the ladder to the tree house. She could hear their childish chatter.

"Let's play house." Emily suggested.

"Okay. Pretend we're horse trainers and the tree is our ranch. The trunk is the barn, and the tree house is the part we live in," Jesse added.

Ainsley could also hear Phillip and William engaged in a conversation she didn't care to follow but couldn't shut out.

"I usually golf on Saturdays. Should you be interested in going, I have a standing tee time," Phillip offered. "It would be a great way to network for plumbing jobs."

Phillip's cringeworthy offer to take William on the golf course to schmooze was insulting. William's company did not need to go through any efforts to secure business. His reputation stood for itself and was the best form of advertising.

"Thanks, but you don't have to waste a standing reservation on me. Not much of a golfer."

Ainsley closed her eyes, and the garden grew alive with sound. She heard the birds twittering and the pond's waterfall bubbling. As she relaxed, she thought she could even hear the butterflies dancing in the breeze.

"Ice tea?" Phillip broke through and set a tray on the table by Ainsley's chair.

"Oh, thank you."

"My pleasure." The perpetual grin on Phillip's face remained.

Ainsley still ignored it. *Let him wait on me*, she thought. *I don't have the energy to stop him.* In her state of resignation, the afternoon slid by without further incident. Jesse and Emily's game of make-believe continued as they migrated from the tree house to the pond, where they became anglers in a fishing contest.

The next day Ainsley went to work still exhausted but made it through her route on autopilot. Her three-day weekend had been everything but restful. She was facing her six-day workweek already on empty.

On Tuesday evening, Ainsley met with Dale for dinner and a movie. It was nice to put all the drama aside and breathe a little of the simple pleasures.

Dale was attentive without demand. She felt comfortable around him and didn't pull her hand away when Dale set his hand over hers on the armrest between them. There was another goodnight kiss at the door and loose plans were made for the next date.

Upon returning home, Ainsley got the questions she was expecting from Jesse regarding her date. She smiled as she explained she had had a nice time. The joy she had felt was wiped out when Jesse asked, "Have you heard anything from Tom West? I texted yesterday, but he hasn't responded."

"Maybe he'll call soon and give you some better contact information. Remember, he is a busy guy." Ainsley presumed this would be a regular question to be dealt with. She had expected Jesse would have to adjust to Tom's ability to drop out as quickly as he had dropped into their lives. She remembered her father implementing damage control with her life when Tom had left her when she was pregnant with Jesse.

"Ainsley, you have got to stop tormenting yourself." William had said to his expecting daughter when he had observed her jumping from a knock on the door or the ringing of a phone. "If you want to talk to Tom, you should."

"No, Daddy. Tom knows where to find me. He must not have any reason."

"You could give him a reason," William suggested.

A reticent pregnant teenager proved impossible to reason with. William let it go, but Rose was determined to snap her daughter out of a funk. Using her unique brand of critique and blame, she said,

"Stop acting like a child, Ainsley. Tom West left you. He ruined your life and then disappeared. Why do you want him back?"

"He said he would call. He wanted me to go with him, Mother." Ainsley debated.

"And then what? You are having a baby, remember? The best place for you is right here at home."

Rose had been thorough in manipulating her vulnerable daughter by digging down to the emotions. It had overwhelmed Ainsley with the situation, and she believed her mother's opinion. Her own beliefs regarding her relationship weakened with each day until there wasn't even a glimmer of hope Tom would call. The rejection still stung deep in her heart.

Ainsley didn't have to worry for long that Jesse would suffer the same hurt. Tom, who asked to speak to his daughter directly, called the house the next day.

"He's flying in from Texas." Jesse had called Emily to tell her the news. "Just for me. And I'm going to meet my other grandparents."

Ainsley didn't like listening to the details of the plan from outside Jesse's bedroom door, but Jesse was excluding her and as a parent, Ainsley had an obligation to know what was happening. It is what a responsible parent should do. How else was she to keep track of Jesse?

"Can you believe it?" Jesse exclaimed into the receiver. "Miss Meg is my grandmother."

Margaret West, or Miss Meg as the children called her, had been the teacher's aide in all Jesse's classes. Miss Meg had moved up the grades with Jesse. Had that been a random coincidence? Ainsley stopped herself from being suspicious. Even if Margaret West had intentionally followed Jesse from grade to grade, there could be many legitimate reasons that it had nothing to do with anything. Ainsley continued to listen in on her daughter as she peered through the almost closed door.

"He has to fly back tomorrow night, but he promised to be back real soon." Jesse was lying back and staring at the ceiling with a dreamy look on her face. Ainsley hoped Tom would follow through.

Tom came for Jesse at six a.m. on Saturday as planned. Jesse hugged her mother and then ran up the gravel drive where Tom was waiting. Tom gave a weak wave. "I'll bring Jesse home at six tonight," he said, and they were gone.

At work, Ainsley inserted the earbuds from her iPod to listen to music, hoping her co-workers wouldn't bother her.

"Hey, look at this." Through her headphones, Ainsley could hear John talking from over the top of the letter cases. "They addressed this envelope to a Mr. Thomas West." John stepped out from behind his case, holding a legal-sized mailer for all to see.

A few guys stopped working to get a closer look.

"Do you think it's the same Tom West as in the famous singer?" Ainsley heard another voice asking.

"Isn't that address up in the hills above town?" A third carrier inspected the address.

"It's a new name at this address," John informed the group. "The house was vacant and on the market."

"You've got Tom West on your route. And look. The return address is for the American Title company. These are title papers." The group buzzed.

"Tom West must have invested in real estate."

"Tom West lives on John's route." Other carriers joined in with their comments.

Ainsley sorted through her parcel tub, then dropped a package with a loud crash. The carriers all turned to her, but she kept working. At least she had gotten them to stop saying "Tom West." Hearing the carriers repeating the name bothered her. It was as if her every nerve were being twisted into knots with each mention of the country music singer. She finished the mail prep and hit the street only to realize her thoughts were still revolving around Tom West. Was the envelope from the title company addressed to Thomas West really for Tom? She wondered if Tom had indeed bought a house.

She spent the rest of the day trying to stop the dialogue in her head. When she got home, she wanted to go for a run but hadn't the motivation. She played in the yard with Brooke, then busied herself studying Jesse's school year-end celebration packet. Ainsley left her world behind for a spell while she read about what was to be in Jesse's academic future for the next year.

It startled Ainsley when her cell phone chirped.

"Hello?"

"Ainsley? This is Dale."

"Hey, Dale. How's it going?" She left Jesse's school information on the dining table and retreated to the living room. Talking with Dale was a comfort and a boost to Ainsley's low mood. She sat and relaxed on the couch with her feet up on the ottoman, once again taking a break from her strife. They chatted for a while then Dale promised to phone back and arrange a get-together, to which Ainsley agreed. She liked having something to look forward to.

"Mom, I'm home." Jesse's voice carried into the cottage from the front door.

"Sounds like your daughter is home, so I'll let you go. I hope I can meet Jesse next time we get together."

"We'll see. Thanks for calling, Dale." While Ainsley appreciated talking to Dale, she was eager to switch gears and focus on Jesse.

Jumping up from the living room chair, Ainsley stumbled over the footstool. She was relieved at the sight of her daughter crouched in the doorway, scratching Brooke on the scruff of her neck. The dog stretched her head forward in sheer pleasure.

"Hi, baby." Ainsley stooped down, lifted Jesse to upright and squeezed her tight, looking over her shoulder through the open door.

Reading her mother's body language with accuracy, Jesse announced, "The limo dropped me off. It's taking Dad to the airport. Doesn't that sound weird? I love saying the word 'Dad.'"

Ainsley closed the front door, and Jesse entered the kitchen in full chattering mode.

"My new grandparents are so nice. Isn't it funny, Mom? I have known Miss Meg from school all along. She has been in my classrooms, and I didn't even know she was my grandmother. They said I could call them Gramma and Pop-pop if I felt comfortable with that. Isn't that cool? I told them I'd think about it. And Tom... uh, I mean, *Dad* bought a house at the top of Bloomfield Road. You can see Pete's stables from his yard."

Gramma and Pop-pop? Tom had bought a house? The letter in the mail to the house on her co-worker's route wasn't a coincidence. Wait... Jesse had been to the new house?

"The house is ginormous, Mom, and we have a pool. Tom said we can go swimming soon. He said there wasn't enough time today."

"Oh, Jess. I'm so glad you're home now." Ainsley hovered like a drone.

"You're acting weird, Mom," Jesse proclaimed.

"Sorry. I'm just glad you had a good day and I'm happy you are home." Nothing was more important than seeing Jesse happy. They were going to be okay, she and Jesse. They had come through the day's stormy events with no apparent collateral damage. Now their lives could go back to normal.

Ainsley left Jesse alone to unwind and decided she needed to call Belle.

"Hi Belle. It's me again. Where are you?" Ainsley left another message on her friend's phone.

"She went to Texas with Brian and... my dad." Jesse heard her mother making the call.

"Oh, yeah." Ainsley made it appear she knew and had forgotten. "But she could still return my calls. There are cell phone towers in Texas, too."

It hurt to think Belle hadn't told her of her travel plans. Ricochetting from the sting of exclusion from parts of Jesse's life, Ainsley was facing being cut out of the loop with Belle, too. Acting upon impulse, with the receiver still in her hand, she dialed.

"Hi, Mom. How are you?" Ainsley called Rose.

"Hello, dear," Rose answered. "I'm fine."

Ainsley waited for Rose to say more.

"Was there anything you wanted?" Rose asked.

"Nothing in particular. I just called to chat." Ainsley had hoped to discuss Jesse's busy day with her mother, but chatting with Rose wasn't something they did. When Rose did not inquire, it threw Ainsley off track.

"Can we talk some other time? Maybe tomorrow after church?" Rose said.

"Sure, Mother. Sorry if I caught you when you're busy."

"Not at all, Ainsley. We'll see you tomorrow." Rose hung up.

Just as Ainsley was setting the telephone down, it began ringing.

"Hello?"

"Hi, Ainsley. It's me, Phillip."

"Phillip. What's up?" She cringed at how chipper she sounded. After all, she rarely wanted to chat with Phillip either, but at the moment, he was available. Not wanting to encourage him further, she reigned in her enthusiasm.

"The reason I'm calling is I'd like to take you and Jesse to church tomorrow."

Phillip phrased his request as a statement, showing he thought it was unnecessary to ask. Ainsley didn't want to encourage this Sunday go-to-church-like-a-family routine. If she agreed to go, Phillip would start assuming there was more going on.

"We have plans in the morning. But we will see you at church, Phillip."

It wasn't a total lie. She and Jesse were planning on getting ready for church. She imagined Phillip's smile turned into a sad expression during their call.

"That's fine." Phillip made it clear that it irritated him at being turned down. "Can Jesse come to the phone? Emily wants to talk to her."

"Jesse," Ainsley hollered, "it's for you."

CHAPTER 17

Conversations and Choices

"Mom, hurry." Jesse called for Ainsley to get out of the Jeep parked in the nearly full church parking lot.

Ainsley obeyed, but it irked her. Not because she was being ordered around by her ten-year-old child, but because she was once again rushing on her day off.

Her intentions were to be punctual, yet here she was, the last to arrive. The grand exterior leading into the edifice was empty except for Phillip, who stood waiting, grinning like the Cheshire cat in Alice in Wonderland. "Good morning," he whispered.

"You needn't have waited." She spoke in a low voice. She was Alice teetering on the precipice of the rabbit hole as Phillip held open the massive door into the vestibule.

"No problem. I wanted us to go in together," Phillip whispered as he reached to open the smaller door that led to the interior. His manipulating the situation to suit his agenda added to her ire. Ainsley wished to slip in undetected, but Phillip wanted the opposite. In a grand demonstration, he flung open the door with force. The whoosh of the displaced air was enough to disturb the liturgy.

With so many eyes now peeled on them, Ainsley reckoned the congregation of worshipers were wondering about the rumors that she was somehow connected to the famous country music star but also seemed to have an attachment to Phillip Martin. The priest nodded to the latecomers, and the sermon resumed.

Father Lewellen had more thoughts to express on this Sunday, but nobody appeared to mind. It was going to be hot, the predicted high in the 80s outside. The collection of listeners were enjoying the cool, soothing atmosphere in the church.

As soon as the mass ended, Ainsley rose to leave. Phillip stepped behind, placing his hand on her waist to steer her to the exit. Once outside, Ainsley walked towards the stairs, but Phillip stopped her.

"Shouldn't we wait for your parents?"

Ainsley hadn't intended to—avoidance was her go-to response to matters regarding Rose—but couldn't formulate a reason for avoiding her.

"Mr. Tobin. Miss Rose." Phillip waved when he spotted Rose and William stepping out.

"Good morning, Phillip," Rose greeted as the older couple navigated across the exterior space that was becoming crowded with folks wanting to extend the fellowship experience.

"Good morning, everyone," William addressed the group. "You arrived a bit tardy."

"Traffic." Phillip took possession of the infraction with an exaggerated chuckle. Ainsley wondered if he smiled in his sleep. And why was he making an excuse when he and Emily had been there on time?

"Ainsley." Rose made a request. "Will you be joining us for our Fourth of July celebration?"

"Of course. We'd love to." Phillip accepted without even knowing the parameters of the lunch gathering.

Ainsley felt her face flushing at Phillip's presumption that the invitation included him. If given the chance, she'd have declined Rose's offer herself. Now an afternoon of social obligations seemed unavoidable.

"Jesse," Ainsley called, as she motioned with her arm. "Time to go."

"We'll see you in a while," Phillip addressed the group courteously then took hold of Ainsley's arm.

"I want to stop at home and change clothes," Ainsley heard herself say, almost as if she were asking permission. What she pictured herself doing was shaking free from his grip, saying, "Take your hands off me." *Why*, she wondered, *am I acting like I'm brainwashed?*

"Emily and I will head home and change, too. We'll meet you at your place and all ride to your parents' house together." Phillip held her car door open. Ainsley climbed into the Jeep, thinking how chivalry, while it seemed to be a basket of charming formalities, could be a caldron of oppressive gestures men used to impart control.

"No, we'll meet you there. I have errands to run." Ainsley said, hoping Phillip would pick up the clue.

"Nonsense. It's Sunday. Nobody has errands on a Sunday. We'll pick you up in ten minutes." Phillip didn't buy the excuse. He refused to acknowledge the hint.

Noting that Jesse was belting up, Ainsley pushed in the clutch and started the engine while closing the car door, almost hitting Phillip with it. She had nothing else to say.

The answering machine was flashing on the home phone line when Ainsley and Jesse slipped into the cottage for the quick wardrobe change. She pressed play and Tom's voice filled the kitchen.

"Hiya, Lil' Beans! We arrived in Texas. The flight was pleasant. Oh, and the flight attendant's name was Brooke. Isn't that a coincidence? I told her my daughter's dog's name is Brooke. I'm not sure if she was flattered or offended. It's difficult sometimes to read people. Anyway, I'll get in touch with you if we finish up here sooner. Otherwise, I'll meet you in two weeks as planned. Call the cell number you have if you need anything. I miss you and I'll be home soon. Bye, luv."

Ainsley watched Jesse's expression as they both listened to the sincere message. She could tell Jesse already had a deep bond with her father, and she meant the world to him as well.

But wait—what was that? They had plans in two weeks? Why didn't they include her in the making of plans?

"Two weeks!" Jesse's squeal startled Ainsley. "I can hardly wait!" Jesse spun around in the kitchen, then danced upstairs to change out of her Sunday dress.

Ainsley stayed put and imagined the sense of security Jesse felt knowing Tom would "be home soon."

"C'mon, get different clothes," prodded Jesse to her absent-minded mother. She had come down in shorts and a T-shirt.

"Whose shirt is that?" Ainsley asked as she sidled past Jesse on the stairway.

"This is a Tom West shirt, see?" Jesse hunched her shoulders to show the other side of the shirt had a list of cities on the band's tour.

"Oh, yes..." Ainsley's words trailed behind as she proceeded to her room.

New plans, new clothes, Tom coming home to Jesse. Ainsley was battered by the rapid-fire changes.

When she heard Phillip and Emily arrive, she resented that they were all going to her mother's garden party. Out of frustration, she tied the sash around the waist on the sundress she had changed into in an ugly bow. With great effort to be less aggressive, she retied it.

"Stay." She shifted her attention to the dog and patted her head.

"Bring the dog," Phillip ordered.

"You don't mean that. In your nice, fancy car?" She questioned his decision to allow Brooke into his vintage 1968 Mopar muscle machine.

"Yes, I mean it. I'm trying to be more flexible." His statement didn't match his expression.

Ainsley knew the vehicle was his pride and joy. She remembered Désirée had complained about how much time and money her husband spent with his precious automobile. Désirée had told Ainsley to appreciate being a single mom. "Phil is so disengaged sometimes, I feel alone," Désirée had said. "At least if I were a single parent, it'd only be me spending all the money."

Phillip grimaced as the border collie jumped onto the rear seat. Ainsley winced at the image of her dog's claws on the flawlessly renovated vinyl surface.

"I hoped the dog would ride on the floor at your feet," he muttered when they were underway. Ainsley ignored his utterances. It had been his own idea that Brooke join them. With her dog sitting on the seat between Jesse and Emily, Ainsley allowed herself a half smile of schadenfreude.

When they arrived at the family farmhouse, they observed a luncheon event in full swing. The driveway was lined with little flags and

William had strung a huge red, white, and blue banner at the end between the house and the trees. The banner read, 'Welcome to the Tobin Family Fourth of July Celebration.'

Ainsley scanned the backyard full of guests. Near the tractor barn, William had captured the attention of a few guys who were intrigued by his latest addition to the farm—a compact version of the most popular tractor used in their orchards. "This unit has more power, uses less fuel and skirts an apple tree with nary a scratch on the trunk or branches."

When they saw other kids gathered around the pond, Emily and Jesse ran to fetch the fish food being distributed by one of the moms. After the pellets were divided amongst the outreached hands, the children flung the meal into the water for the swarming koi and goldfish.

Ainsley hesitated at the entry to the garden, then shrugged her shoulders and headed to the shade of an enormous umbrella. With the dog at her heels, she took a seat in a chair near a couple of ladies who appeared to discuss something on which they had differing opinions. The debaters stopped and looked at her.

"It's gonna be a hot one." Ainsley succumbed to the protocol that dictates she says something to appear to be social. The weather was an appropriate subject.

Acknowledging her polite comment, the women dipped their heads in unison as their floppy-brimmed hats wobbled. Neither woman replied. Before another awkward moment could pass, Ainsley got up. "Can I freshen your drinks while I'm up?" Both women graciously declined. Ainsley excused herself and as she turned, she could sense the exhale of relief from the guests.

Once inside, Ainsley went to the refrigerator, found a bottle of Fresca, her dad's favorite, and got a glass. She grabbed some ice from the freezer and poured the soda over it. Holding the frosty glass to her forehead, though she wasn't warm, she moseyed into the living room. From her comfortable position in her father's recliner, she found solitude inside the home, but it proved to be short-lived.

"Hello, Ainsley. I'm not sure if you remember us..." Tom's father, Jim West, entered the family room. "May we come in?"

"Hi, Mr. and Mrs. West." Ainsley clanked the recliner to the upright position, startling Brooke, who was laying at her feet. "Of course I remember you. Nice to meet you again." Could this be the most awkward thing Ainsley had ever been through? "Please sit." Ainsley motioned towards the sofa.

The tension was off the charts. If there was a God, Ainsley needed a miracle right about now.

"It's been a long time." Margaret West stated the obvious.

Ainsley nodded. She braced herself for the likely scenarios she had imagined could happen if she ever had to face the family she had hurt by keeping the secret. Intending to control the dialogue, she pulled up her courage by the bootstraps and dove in.

"I am so sorry for what I have done. It was selfish and I hurt many people. I hope you will accept my apology."

Even as she spoke, she realized it sounded pretty lame. She waited but the Wests said nothing.

"I am grateful that you have welcomed my daughter into your lives. She is blessed to have such a loving family."

"Your daughter? She is our son's daughter, too." Margaret's icy façade crackled under the pressure.

"We know this is not a very comfortable situation, and we want you to know we only want what is best for our son and, of course, Jesse." Jim forced a deep breath. "Out of respect, and to show we hold nothing against you, we were interested in having a conversation. We want to assure you, we love Jesse already, as though she's been a part of our lives all along."

"Of course." Ainsley hoped for a good relationship with Jesse's grandparents. She would give the Wests as much access to their granddaughter as they requested. "Anything you want."

"Thank you for hearing us out."

"Of course," she repeated, lacking something better to say.

The senior Wests rejoined the festivities, but Ainsley stayed behind. This was usually the time she would run away. Without a car of her own in which to speed off, she thought she might climb on William's old Farmall tractor and ride it home.

She could relate to the tractor's obsolescence and decided both she and the farm machine could disappear with no one taking notice. She took another swig from her glass of Fresca, wishing she had mixed in a shot of Seagram's.

Ainsley forced herself to stand and walk outside. Phillip noticed her and led her to a loveseat in the shade. With Phillip sitting much too close, Ainsley bristled and wished he could read her mood. Across the yard, William was now giving Rose a lesson in swinging a golf club.

Rose stood on the lawn which had been drafted for duty as a putting green. With her feet apart, hands holding the club, she stood while William mirrored her position from behind. There was no air between them and William's hands covered over Rose's on the handle.

Rose turned her head towards her husband as he explained something, and William traced a finger along her arm. Then the two figures moved in unison as William slowly guided his wife in slow motion through her first attempt at a golf swing. There was something sensual about the display, like it should have happened in private.

"See, nothing to it." William complimented his wife's effort.

Ainsley could hear their voices as the couple laughed in celebration, and the surrounding group smiled and clapped. Rose then giggled like a schoolgirl and beamed. Not sure how to feel about it, Ainsley acknowledged she had never seen her parents act this way. The older couple had never so much as hugged each other in public. Once she overcame the unsettling sensation children feel when observing their parents' intimacy, she had to admit it was pleasant to witness. She presumed the couple's therapy must be going well.

"Can Jesse stay the night?" Emily came up to her father after they had tagged her "out" during a tag-you're-it game the kids were playing.

"Sure she can." Phillip volunteered.

"You should stay home for a change, Jess." Ainsley spoke when her daughter joined in the conversation. "And besides, you both have summer school in the morning. You know the rules about school nights."

"Rules are made to be broken. Jesse may sleepover. You two go play." Phillip dismissed the children, much to Ainsley's dismay.

She couldn't wrap her head around the circumstances. Were there no limits to the number of ways he could annoy her?

"That's okay, right?" Phillip asked after the fact. "It is your Monday off, and I have a free day, too. In fact, we should do something special."

It was her day off from work, but she had made plans with Dale. And since when did Phillip keep accurate track of her days off?

Taking advantage of her silence, Phillip said, "We are settled, then."

"NO, we did not settle it." With emotion threatening to push her over the edge, Ainsley fought to squelch her anger.

"It's okay, though."

"No, it's not okay," she burst forth. *Three, two, one*, she remembered. "But it's too late to confirm with me now."

Ainsley surveyed the small assembly of guests and made the choice not to air their personal lives in public any further. What she needed to say, but couldn't, would have to wait. "You gave them the green light."

She stood up and Phillip also came to his feet, unsteady from the amount of alcohol he had consumed. Wanting to escape from him, she declared, "You stay here. I'm getting another Fresca, and maybe I'll add a shot of liquor to help me deal with you."

"I'll get it for you, honey." Phillip seemed oblivious to her sarcasm.

"No." Her abrupt retort was louder than she expected. Then through tight teeth she added, "Thank you. And don't call me honey."

As she walked away, she noticed the outburst had attracted some attention. She heard a hiss from the people who didn't even attempt to hide their whispers. Ainsley heard, "Rose told me she has been under stress," and "She looks thin and pale," before reaching the sliding door to the sanctity inside.

Let the ol' biddies gossip. They haven't any lives of their own, Ainsley thought to herself.

Ainsley was no stranger to the scratch of the barbs thrown by gossiping words.

After refreshing her glass with Fresca, she added the shot she wished she'd had in the first drink, then started moving about the kitchen, finishing lunch preparations. Looking over the prep-work Rose had done the previous day, she recognized each dish.

There were pin-wheel sandwiches, mini carbonara quiche tarts and little red peppers stuffed with a cream cheese spread. All the goodies she knew and loved. Stumbling upon a tray of little rolls sprinkled with toasted sesame seeds and stuffed with something that looked yummy, she picked one up, examined it visually and with her nose then said to the tiny morsel, "And what are you?"

"Those are mini-masala sausage rolls. They are delightful." Rose hustled in and joined Ainsley. "Try one, dear."

Ainsley did as instructed, then continued to transfer the circular sandwiches onto a platter for serving. "Yummy."

It elated Rose to have Ainsley helping with the lunch. "It's like old times, us working together."

"Just how you raised me, Mom."

Rose stopped working to squeeze her daughter's hand. "I am proud of how I raised you."

"Thanks, Mom."

Then Rose asked, "So, tell me. What is going on between you and Phillip?"

"We are friends, for now, but that is in jeopardy if Phillip continues to pursue more than that."

"So, there are no romantic feelings? You had better tell him that. Appears to me he has other intentions."

Ewww, Ainsley thought, but said, "I keep hoping he gets the idea with each rejection, but he is relentless."

"You need to clear things up. You have enough to worry about sorting out your life issues."

Ainsley slumped forward over the counter she had been leaning on and waited for the lecture, but Rose said nothing else. When she straightened up, to her surprise, there was genuine sympathy in Rose's eyes. "It sure is a mess." She pitched a general statement of agreement.

"I regret my contributions to one predicament you are in. I am aware of how all this is taking its toll."

There was nothing Ainsley could add to her mother's confession.

"You should rest awhile, Ains. I can do this luncheon in my sleep. Why not enjoy the warm air and sunshine? Maybe mingle a little."

Ignoring her mother's suggestion, Ainsley creeped up the stairs to her childhood bedroom, where nothing but the sheets on the bed had been changed since she and Jesse lived there. Ainsley sat on the twin bed Jesse now used when she stayed with her grandparents.

From the open window came the breeze that lifted cool air through the magnolia tree beneath the window. The fragrance from the blooming flowers was intoxicating. It brought her back in time to a day late in summer ten years ago. The day Tom left. On a late summer afternoon, Ainsley had decided to share with Tom some big news.

"Hey, if it isn't Tom's little honey. How are you, little lady?" A musician coming from the house had been bringing snacks to the garage where Tom's band was practicing when Ainsley arrived.

She had smelled the liquor on his breath when he got close. Were they having a party?

"Come on in. Tom's in the back."

She had followed the intoxicated man into the garage and headed for the area behind a curtain where they stored their equipment. There had sat Tom, strumming his guitar and singing:

> "I don't take for granted this life I live
> With open arms, I'll embrace what it has to give
> And I'll spread some kindness, love, and hope
> And take this gratitude with me down this
> country road."

"Hey, com'on in. Aren't you a sight for sore eyes?" Tom had spotted her in the shadows. His welcoming look said it had not disappointed him to see her.

"I have some great news," Tom had said before she could speak. "Our single is climbing up the billboard charts. I have booked us to play some gigs in Nashville."

"That is great news." Her voice had sounded stupid in her own head. It had not been great news at all.

"Your mouth says 'great' but your face says otherwise." Tom had beckoned her to move closer. "Why are you so sad? Is it because I'll be leaving?"

"I am not sad." Not a lie. The sadness was a minor part of the larger problem. "I am happy for you."

"Good, because I want you to come with us."

"I can't," Ainsley had trembled in Tom's arms.

"Yes, you can. This is your chance to escape. Show Rose that you can make your own choices. We'll be back by summer's end. You'll be back for college, but it'll be your choice and your mom will realize that."

"It wouldn't be right." Ainsley had felt more shaky and Tom had increased his hold around her.

"We'll make it right. I want you in my life."

"You are heading towards a new life." She had wished to tell Tom his life had changes other than his music career.

"I can't understand. Are you saying you don't love me?"

"It's not that simple." Ainsley hadn't been prepared to talk about this. She knew she was in love, but was unsure how to express it without sounding like a silly teenager. If Tom had said, "Would you marry me?" rather than that he wanted her in his life, his intentions would have been clearer. She needed that clarity.

"Ainsley, it isn't so difficult. Either you love me or you do not."

"It's complicated." She had wished to explain, but instead she had stared at him, afraid to speak. If she had told him at that moment, he might have scrapped the tour and stayed. He may have married her out of a sense of obligation. Ainsley hadn't told him then she was carrying his baby because it would have trapped him. The last thing she wanted to be was another person's regret. She had had enough of that with Rose.

"What's complicated about it?" Tom repeated himself.

Ainsley was confused and had to look away to avoid seeing the hurt in his eyes when she didn't answer.

"Ainsley?" Tom had begged for an answer. She hadn't been able to give him one.

"There you are, Ains. We've been looking for you." William stood in the bedroom doorway looking at his daughter sitting on her bed.

"Oh, hey, Daddy." Ainsley hid her face and swiped her hand across the cheek with a tear trickling down. "I was enjoying the breeze." Ainsley deflected to the weather hoping her dad wouldn't notice she was crying.

"Fog is on the way," William responded without missing a beat, then sat down by her side. "Why are you crying?" he asked. "Ainsley, what is it?"

"I was walking down memory lane," she uttered when she could speak. She brushed her wet cheeks and forced a smile. "I've been doing a lot of that lately."

"Too bad we can't only remember the good times."

"Do you remember only the good times, Daddy?" Her dad's face appeared blurry through her wet eyelashes.

"I'd be fibbing if I said yes." William moved his arm into a side hug. "That's just not how our brains work. You will get through this. Better memories will smooth over the painful edges of this diffi-cult situation."

"You sound so sure of it. Wish I had the same level of confidence."

"You are struggling with a lot of changes, Ains. But remember, life gives us more than we can handle to remind us of our need for God."

In his special, fatherly way, William paraphrased the Bible. The way he did it never seemed contrived or preachy, as when Rose quoted the Bible.

"Thank you, Daddy."

The comforting sentiment behind William's biblical language was helpful.

"Stop your crying, sweetheart. Don't dwell on it. What's passed is gone. Can't change a thing. All we got is the future."

"Do you have any regrets?"

"Hmmm... that is a tough question."

"I mean, is there anything you did that you now wish you could do differently?"

"I've been around a long time, Ains. With lots of chances to mess up. If I grieved for every mistake I've made, I would be the world's most depressed man. The trick is to reconcile with yourself first. Then try to make things better."

Ainsley leaned in and repeated, "Thanks, Daddy."

Her father's words did little to help, but the fact that he cared enough to try was a tremendous lift for her grieving heart.

"Let's mosey down and see if the party is over so we can watch TV."

The shiny leaves on the old magnolia seemed to peek through the open window as if to emphasize William's words. How many father-daughter conversations had that tree witnessed through the years? Only God and the tree knew.

CHAPTER 18

Resisting the Change

"Dad called," Jesse said as Ainsley lumbered through the door wheeling her bicycle beside her.

"Oh?" Ainsley attempted to sound indifferent as she leaned the bike against the wall and proceeded across the kitchen to the cupboard for a glass. It was still warm outside after highs in the 90s and she was parched.

She still hadn't gotten used to the frequent phone calls Jesse got from her father. She understood it had been a process of change for Jesse, too. At first, the child had vacillated between calling him "Tom" and "Dad." Regardless of how Jesse referred to him, Ainsley grimaced at the mere mention of him.

Jesse watched her mother down a glass of water, noticing the pained look, then said, "Why do you torture yourself, Mom?"

"What do you mean?" Ainsley had been attempting to hide her discomfort whenever Tom West was the topic. She had hoped Jesse wasn't noticing, but maybe, despite her efforts, Jesse was reading the truth.

"The exercise. If you ask me, you are too thin," Jesse continued. "As Grandma Rose says, you exercise too much."

Ainsley released her held breath. "Well, thank you for your concern. They say, 'No pain, no gain.'"

"I almost forgot. Phillip called, too." Jesse opened the freezer for a fruit-juice popsicle.

Ainsley did not hide her pickled face upon hearing Phillip's name. "Grab me a popsicle, please." She removed her helmet and wiped her sweaty forehead with a cloth. This had turned out to be an unseasonably warm August. So far, they had had days of ninety-degree heat and no fog to relieve it.

"He wants you to call him," Jesse said.

"Tom?" Ainsley exclaimed. "Me?"

"No, silly. Phillip." Jesse handed her mother the frozen treat. "I think all the exercise is keeping oxygen from your brain."

"So now you're a scientist?" Ainsley joked. "For your information, exercise increases the circulation all over the body."

Ainsley went outside to sit in the waning sun, and Jesse followed. They sat together on the bench just to the left of the front door. Ainsley removed her clunky biking shoes with the pedal attachments on the soles and wiggled her toes in the cool grass. Jesse launched into a lecture about circulation, explaining what she had learned in science class.

It had been two and a half weeks since the luncheon at Rose and William's and Ainsley hadn't spoken to Phillip, but not for his lack of trying. Not wanting to deal with his annoying behavior, she knew she couldn't cut ties with him altogether. She and Phillip had depended on each other's support regarding Jesse and Emily.

"... blood brings the good stuff to the brain," Jesse was in the middle of explaining, "and carries the bad stuff on its way out."

Ainsley caught the send of Jesse's lecture on the cardiovascular system and noted that the child needed to recall what the "stuff" was.

"So, we know the blood carries oxygen. Have you learned what else it delivers to the various organs and tissues of the body?"

"Oh, yes." Jesse rattled on as she sucked on her fruit pop. "There are nutrients... and glucose..."

Ainsley sat back and listened, enjoying her daughter's enthusiasm as the endorphins ran through her veins from the recent exertion.

Work and exercise were the main activities in Ainsley's life. As Jesse forged ahead with her relationship with her father and Belle extended her vacation to be with her new love, Brian, Ainsley felt lonely and somewhat depressed.

Ainsley was relieved when Belle returned, but after a small blow-up between them at work, Belle had been keeping her distance. Ainsley recalled the fight.

"Talented, good-looking and sweet as anyone could be," Belle had gushed when describing Brian to Ainsley, "And he adores me."

"Phffffff," Ainsley had snorted with derision. "May we change the subject?"

"I finally find Mr. Right and I can't share it with my best friend?" Belle had expressed her disappointment. "Fine, I won't mention Brian."

Neither woman had any suggestions for an alternative subject to discuss, so they worked their mail in silence.

On their walk to the parking lot after work, Belle recounted a memory of sitting in on a recording session at Tom's studio in Nashville with a new song.

"Ugh! Enough about the band. Can't you think of anything else?"

"This is exciting for me." Belle beseeched, "I want to share it with you. Please don't take away from my happiness."

"It's not my intention to drop negativity on your joy," she started explaining. "I just want to talk about something else."

"It's always about you, Ainsley. I'm sorry, but you are not the only one with a personal life. I have heavy stuff, too, and I'd love to have a friend I could confide in. You are always so hung up on your own drama..."

Ainsley understood Belle's complaint. She had apologized and listened to Belle talk about her adventures with Brian and the band, but getting no feedback, Belle soon stopped talking.

"The chrysalis is the caterpillar's skin, which becomes hard and protective." Ainsley realized that while she was thinking about Belle, Jesse had switched gears and was talking about butterflies. "The chrysalis mustn't taste good to birds. If it was tasty, there'd be no butterflies. All chrysalises would get eaten before the butterfly could emerge."

Ainsley finished the last bite of her melting treat and reflected on how Jesse was like a caterpillar. As if right before her eyes, Jesse was transforming. Intellectually, physically, and emotionally. Jesse would all too soon be the butterfly emerging from the chrysalis of youth.

"He will be in town for the weekend." Jesse had once again switched the subject. "He said it took him a little longer, but the arrangements are all made."

Ainsley got up and held out her hand for Jesse to deposit the remnant stick upon which had been her just-eaten popsicle.

Arrangements? The word stuck in Ainsley's head, refusing to be ignored.

Jesse followed her mother into the house and continued, "He's throwing a party in my honor. He said he wants everybody to meet me." With a childish giggle, Jesse held open the cupboard door under the sink for Ainsley to discard the popsicle wrappings.

"That sounds nice, Jesse. Where will this celebration take place?" she asked.

"At his new place. This Sunday. He's taking me shopping on Saturday for a birthday gift, even though it's not my birthday. He says he wants to catch up on the ten birthday presents he missed."

Yes, we all know how much Tom has missed, said the voice in Ainsley's head.

She was sick of the topic and worn out by the guilt it induced. "He better catch up on Christmas gifts," she said. "He's behind on those, too."

"So I can go?" Jesse seemed confident she knew the answer.

"Of course. You must go. The party is for you."

Ainsley found it irritating that Tom didn't inform her of the plans. It was as if Jesse was at his disposal, available for his every whim. Tom should have been courteous enough to at least let her in on the bare minimum of his plans for their daughter.

Later that evening, Jesse came down from her room with heavy footfalls. "Emily isn't answering the phone."

Jesse had dialed Emily several times to invite her best friend to the party. It hurt to see Jesse's disappointment. "Why don't you see if Auntie Belle is available to chat? Have you invited her to come?"

"We invited Auntie Belle. She is coming. Everybody is."

Everybody? Ainsley realized that was a sizable group of which she herself was not a part.

"No wonder she wasn't at home. Emily's here!" Jesse exclaimed, and from the corner of her eye, Ainsley detected movement out the picture window looking up their driveway. It was Emily and Phillip.

Jesse sprang forward and pounced. "Emily, guess what? We're having a party and you're invited!" The two girls sprinted up the stairs, twittering like parakeets.

"Good evening." Ainsley could hear the grin in Phillip's voice, though the dim dusk light spared her the sight of the smile.

"C'min." She motioned with her arm. She wanted to keep the door closed to minimize the loss of cool air the A/C unit was struggling to supply.

"It's a warm one for sure." Phillip noted her urgency.

"May I give you a cold drink?" Ainsley offered.

"No, thank you. I came prepared." In one hand, Phillip held up an insulated sleeve with a beer inserted and in the other, a cool box. "I brought my own."

"Sorry to barge in," Phillip continued, setting the mini-cooler he had brought on the floor before taking a seat. "We were stuck in the house hiding from the heat and had to escape. We took a shot, assuming you and Jesse would be home."

"No worries. Jesse and I have been hanging out today, too." Ainsley pulled out a chair from under the table. It was obvious Phillip had turned the unexpected arrival into a social visit.

"So what's this about a party for Jesse?" Phillip asked, pulling the empty bottle from the foam sleeve to be replaced by another bottle from the cooler.

"I'd rather talk about something else."

"We can talk about anything you want. We have plenty of time, Ains. Let's start with Tom West."

Phillip ignored Ainsley's request to talk about something else. "So, he's Jesse's dad?"

"Yes he is." She decided Phillip might as well hear it from her. Leaving out most of the details, she explained a bit about Jesse's father, skipping the part where, for the last ten years, she failed to tell either of them about each other. She mentioned Tom had been busy with his career, but at present wants to be a bigger part of Jesse's life.

"Wow, Ainsley. That's a lot to unpack." Phillip said. "I assume this is a good thing, no?"

Ainsley admitted it was a great deal, and having Tom West in the picture would entail some adjustments, but that she was okay.

"I've often wondered about Jesse's father. Who'd have thought he would turn out to be a famous country music star? That only happens in the movies." Phillip seemed entertained.

Ainsley relayed the information she had gotten from Jesse regarding the celebration and that Jesse had been dying to invite Emily.

Phillip became contemplative. "I am glad Jesse had some exciting news to share with Emily. She could use the distraction."

Taking up the prompt, Ainsley asked, "Is Emily okay? Why does she need a distraction? Distraction from what?"

"Emily is fine, now." Phillip paused, and Ainsley grew concerned.

"What has happened? Please tell me?"

"It may embarrass Emily but, I'm going to tell you." Another pause as Phillip took a long swig from the brew in his hand. "I need to vent. Today my little girl grew up. She's not even eleven years old. I looked it up online. It is quite normal."

"What is normal?"

Phillip didn't answer. Ainsley wondered what could be so traumatic as to keep Phillip from talking about it. She knew Emily was okay. She was at this moment upstairs with Jesse. Then Ainsley understood.

Her mouth went round. "Oh, Phillip, that is huge. And you had to research online?"

Ainsley found it amusing. She tried to hide it and remain sensitive. "I'm so sorry. It must have been very awkward. Is Emily alright?"

"From what I could gather, she's fine. She said she had everything she needed." Phillip ran his fingers across the top of his head and down the back side.

She waited for him to gather his composure.

"I felt so bad, Ainsley." Phillip was no more enlightened than most men. A woman's menstrual cycle was still somewhat of a mystery to him. "Emily was comforting me. Poor kid. She told me the teachers taught them all about it in science."

Phillip emptied the last drop of the comforting elixir, then continued, "They are just children, Ainsley. How is this possible? And all she needed from me was a ride to the drugstore. She didn't want me to come in!"

Ainsley once more suppressed her amusement. Poor Phillip. She could only imagine the picture of distress. The idea of Phillip standing outside the store or sitting in the parked car, overwhelmed by a feeling of uselessness, was entertaining.

"I am sorry I wasn't there for Emily. I could have minimized the drama for you both."

Phillip popped the top on a third bottle and sucked hard on his beer, waiting for the effects of the alcohol to ease his nerves.

Ainsley understood the six-pack of Coors Light in the mini ice chest; she gave Phillip a pass for being crass with it.

"With your permission, I can join them for some girl talk. I'll get an idea of how Emily is feeling."

Phillip let out the longest sigh of relief and a soft "Thank you," which she interpreted as permission.

"We'll let them alone for a while longer, then I'll see if they want to talk."

"So, Tom West." Phillip shook his head as if he had difficulty comprehending. "It sounds like the superstar is going to be around. That's likely to be challenging."

Ainsley sighed. Tom West was a force to be reckoned with at every turn.

"I detect a sense of wistfulness. You're not still in love with the guy, are you?" Phillip teased, unaware he may have hit the nail on the head.

Ainsley laughed a little too nervously, but Phillip continued, "Should I be worried? Are we going to compete with Mr. Music Man for your time and attention?"

"Compete?" Ainsley winced at Phillip's attempt to be coy. His snide nickname for Tom caused her to cringe. "I have always been here for you and Emily. Our friendship will not change." With emphasis on the word friendship, she hoped Phillip picked up on the prompt.

"Emily and I have grown very attached to you," Phillip winked.

Feeling creeped out again by Phillip, Ainsley declared, "I'll go up now and look in on the kids."

"I hear we have reason to celebrate Emily's major life event," Ainsley announced when given consent to enter after her soft knock.

"He told you?" Emily rolled her eyes. Jesse giggled.

"Yeah, he told me." Ainsley imitated the eye-roll. "And boy, did he overreact!" When she saw the girls relax, she continued, "Jesse's grandmother did the same thing to me. Parents can be such a pain."

"No kidding," Emily agreed.

"Grandma Rose freaked out on you?" Jesse said. Ainsley and the girls talked for a while, then made their way downstairs. Phillip had set himself up in front of the TV.

"Si'down, girls, and I'll find something we'll all enjoy watching," Phillip slurred.

The girls sat on the floor, and Ainsley took a spot on the couch. Soon they were all laughing at *America's Funniest Videos*.

"Is it okay for Emily to have some ice cream?" Ainsley asked, and Phillip nodded.

"Who wants ice cream?" Ainsley threw it out as a question, knowing there was only one answer. She then stood up and headed to the kitchen. Moments later, she came out with three bowls and handed them out before returning to the kitchen to clean up.

"You are incredible." Phillip had followed her and was standing too close behind as she wiped the surface of the counter. The beers he had consumed fueled Philip's courage to make a move.

Attempting to slide away, Ainsley turned but found her space further invaded by Phillip and they were now facing each other.

With bedroom eyes, he reached out like he was going to cradle her face and kiss her. When Phillip looked into her eyes, he stopped and made no further movement. Without offering an apology, Phillip declared himself drunk and returned to the couch.

"ERRRR!" Ainsley growled and shook her head, trying to forget seeing Phillip that way.

"Damn," she cursed under her breath. This went beyond ruining a friendship. Phillip was jeopardizing more than his relationship with Ainsley. She had to find a way to change the direction before Phillip's behavior affected the girls.

CHAPTER 19

The Wrecking Ball

"Ainsley?" Belle peeked around the corner of her letter case Friday to say good morning. The two had kept their distance, drifting farther apart because of their divergences. Ainsley was too moody and melancholy, Belle was too bright and enthusiastic.

Ainsley removed her ear buds. "What's up?" She tried not to sound suspicious.

"I think I owe you an apology. I was being insensitive."

"Oh, Belle." Ainsley whispered, trying not to invite the entire office into the conversation. "I'm the one who should be apologizing. I have been very self-involved."

"I have missed you." Belle slid from around her case to give Ainsley a hug.

"I have been missing you, too."

"Why don't you two girls get a room?" A carrier noticed the embrace and alerted the others.

"Hey, guys. Look," said a co-worker casing his mail across the room. "We got us some girl-on-girl action. Where's my camera?"

"Ignore them." Belle eased her hold, and the women stood apart a little, still holding each other's hands. "Do you want to meet up for a run after work?"

"Do I ever! I hate working out without you." Ainsley swung Belle's arms fondly and gave the guys something to stare at.

"Sounds great."

"I haven't been exercising at all and I'm so out of shape," Belle confessed when she and Ainsley met up later that day. "It will not be easy keeping up with you." Belle assessed her friend's physique. "I have gained weight, and it looks like you have lost. You are absolutely skinny."

"Well, I think you look great. If you have gained any weight, it doesn't show. They say that's a sign of fulfillment."

The two athletes began a slow run through the neighborhood. Ainsley sensed Belle's scrutinizing glance. She could tell Belle was hesitant to speak.

"You can talk about Brian. I am fine with it."

"Are you sure? Because I need to talk to you about something, but I won't if..." Belle paused, wanting to give her friend a chance to change her mind.

"Yes, Belle. Go ahead." Ainsley went into consolation mode. She thought maybe Belle needed a shoulder to cry on. In the past, Belle's relationships had always come with an expiration date. Her budding romance with Brian must have reached that point.

"I want to ask you for something."

"Ask me anything."

"I want you to be my maid of honor, Ainsley. Brian and I are getting married!" Belle burst out.

"Married?!"

Belle was so excited to share the news, she failed to see how completely shocking it had been for Ainsley to hear. Luckily, Belle continued talking, sparing her the need to respond.

"We haven't made an official announcement. I wanted you to know first," Belle gushed.

Ainsley remained speechless. They had gone from the streets into the park where the multi-use trail would take them for a loop.

"So, what do you say? Will you do me the honor?" As she asked, Belle finally noted Ainsley's condition. "I knew it," Belle gasped. "I shouldn't have led with that. Please don't freak out. You said you were fine."

Ainsley tried to speak but, without words, her mouth opened and closed as if she were mimicking a fish. She kept running instead. She was unsure of her emotions.

"You don't have to decide immediately."

"It's not that." Ainsley found some words. There was no question she would be a part of Belle's wedding.

"I know, you're shocked. It is a shock to me, too. But I guess because I have dated so many duds, it wasn't long before I realized Brian was Mr. Right."

"Brian is Mr. Right?"

The shock was waning as Ainsley acknowledged the reality. Belle had no need for someone to console her through the burn of a fresh affair that had run its course. She needed someone with whom to celebrate. Ainsley wanted to give her that.

"Oh, Belle. You are getting married!" Ainsley exclaimed. "I am so happy for you."

Ainsley held it together as the women finished the loop through the park and ran up the streets of the subdivision. When they got to the turnoff for Belle to return to her house, Ainsley congratulated the bride. "I wish nothing but the best for you and Brian." It sounded like a phrase taken off a Hallmark greeting card.

"Thank you, Ains." Belle gave her friend an honest hug. "I'll see you tomorrow."

It was a relief to separate from Belle and all her cheerful updates. Ainsley put down the act and allowed herself to experience what she felt inside. She couldn't accept that her best friend was engaged. Marrying a guy with whom she was barely acquainted was the definition of imprudence. A whirlwind romance destined to fail.

After dinner that evening, she sat outside in the peaceful garden between her cottage and the main house. To escape from her own thoughts about life and all its complications, she enjoyed the gentle breezes and listened to the evening crickets' serenade. From the distance, she could hear the voices of kids playing in the waning light..

As it was a sound faint enough to be coming from a neighbor's house—and even if it wasn't, she didn't want to pick up—Ainsley ignored the summons of her ringing phone. When the ringing stopped, she closed her eyes and braced for impact.

"Hi, Dad." Ainsley heard Jesse's voice, which grew more muffled as the child moved farther into the interior of the house.

Ainsley rocked herself from side to side on the stone bench. Her eyes were still closed as if choosing not to see the presence of Tom West in her and Jesse's lives. Ainsley snapped to attention when she heard Jesse's voice sounding louder.

"... I think so. Let me ask her..." Jesse's little face appeared from inside. "There you are. When can I go with Tom shopping?"

"Oh, that's tomorrow?" Ainsley aimed to sound as if she hadn't been giving it any thought.

"I told you he was taking me shopping Saturday."

"Shopping. Right." Ainsley stalled. "Tomorrow is Saturday." Ainsley dragged out her response. Why did they bother her now with details? They had left her out of the plan-making up to this point. Why include her now?

"I'll be at work. You'll be at Grandma's." Ainsley deferred parental authority.

"I'll be at my grandma's." Jesse's voice faded again as she moved out of the doorway.

Ainsley sought to regain the peace she had felt briefly when she first sat in the garden. Using a mindful technique she learned to clear her worries, she imagined each thought as a chain of words attached to a balloon that floated from the top of her head into the atmosphere. Through determination, she reached a state of blankness.

When she gave Jesse what she thought was enough time to finish her conversation, Ainsley called Rose.

"Hi, Mom."

"Hi, dear. Are you okay?"

"Why wouldn't I be?"

"I wasn't criticizing." Rose paused, as if stopping herself from speaking, then continued, "What can I do for you, dear?"

"Ummm..." Ainsley's thoughts had jumped their track.

Capitalizing on the pause, Rose blurted, "I was about to call you."

"Oh...?" Ainsley said, as if her vocabulary contained only the one-syllable interjections.

"Instead of spending the day with William and me while you're working tomorrow, is it possible for Jesse to stay with Phillip and Emily?"

"Wait, what? Why?" Ainsley's glossary was expanding.

"Your father did some work for a client who has a place in the Sierras. The customer offered us to use his condominium this weekend. We took him up on the offer and were planning on taking off after we drop Jesse home tomorrow afternoon. But we could leave early if Jesse..."

"Don't worry, Mom. You and Daddy go have a great weekend. Jesse has other options. She'll be on a spending spree sponsored by Tom West."

"Why, that is wonderful for Jesse. Tom is sure diving into this parenting role head first. Well, that's perfect. It all works out for everyone."

"A cozy hideaway in the mountains?" Ainsley changed the subject.

"Yes, it's north of South Lake Tahoe up Highway 50 towards Kingsbury, eight miles from Stateline. A little golf course on the Nevada side called Glenn Brook." Rose seemed to brim with excitement.

"They offered us a tee time, and it's membership and guests only. The course isn't open to the public. William has only started playing since Phillip introduced him to the sport. He is a little intimidated by his lack of experience, but his client assured us nobody on the course will even notice."

"Sounds like a wonderful opportunity for some rest and relaxation." Ainsley pictured her parents on an immaculate expanse of turquoise green grass lined by stands of pine trees. She could even imagine the gentle scent of vanilla emitting from the crevasses of the bark of the conifers. "You guys have a good weekend. Don't worry at all about Jesse."

Ainsley returned the phone to its charging dock, then turned her blank eyes to the window. The air outside had taken on a marine quality as the ocean influence eroded the dominant high pressure, and it begged her to come back out. Ainsley was certain there would be fog by morning. Ainsley headed upstairs to talk to Jesse about the change in plans.

"Jess?" Ainsley knocked on her daughter's bedroom door. "Grandma and Grandpa are going away for the weekend, so you will stay home tomorrow."

"You mean while you're at work? But Tom was gonna get me from grandma's house." Jesse had gone from sleepily watching a DVD on her mini TV to being alert and almost panicked.

"I gotta call Dad and tell him to come here to get me."

She watched Jesse pick up the phone on the charger by her bed. "Are you calling Tom? You can't call now. It's two hours later in Texas."

Jesse ignored her mother.

Ainsley didn't blame her. Even she couldn't understand her own logic. It made no difference what time it was in Texas. Jesse's father would either take her call or call back.

"My dad is not in Texas, Mom. He's in Sebastopol, remember?"

The spicy edge in Jesse's response revealed the child was becoming annoyed at her mother's lack of focus.

"Oh... right." Ainsley backed out of the room, leaving Jesse alone to make her plans, all the while thinking, *This is out of control.*

CHAPTER 20

Family Dynamics

Just as Ainsley had foreseen the evening before, the fog descended with resolute commitment overnight, blanketing everything in its path. The thick mist emitted a dampness that caused the gutters to drip. On the towering trees surrounding the cottage, the dew collected, forming large droplets that created a soothing pitter-patter as they landed on the roof.

"Come in… please," Ainsley said, thinking it might be rude to force Tom to stand outside under the dripping trees. "Jesse will be right down. Please excuse me, I'm preparing for my workday."

With a yielding glance, she noted Tom's appearance as he bent forward to greet the dog. Subdued, he seemed. Uncharacteristically unsure. She wondered if he felt as uncomfortable in her presence as she did in his.

"Good morning, Dad." Jesse came bounding down the stairs and leapt into Tom's open arms.

Tom lit up at Jesse's entrance, his energy transformed. He held his daughter tight, then thanked Ainsley for letting him come so early. Jesse released her father to cross the kitchen. "Bye, Mom. I love you." The father and daughter joined again and walked together out the door without a backwards glance.

The workday, governed by its redundancy, sped by and to Ainsley's relief was ending on a good note as she made her way to the parking lot.

"You know anything about a grand shindig happening at Tom West's mansion?" John caught up to her and asked. Her coworkers knew about Ainsley's daughter's father. The whole town did.

"Maybe." She wondered what it would require to end John's inquiry.

"'Cuz there were moving trucks and delivery trucks and catering vans everywhere. Must be some big party."

"You take it upon yourself to be way too familiar with the people on your route, John."

"Is it a public event or private?" John bulldozed forward with questions. "Do you believe it's a music event? Are you and Jesse invited?" He was a worse gossip than the coffee group that met at the community center. Ainsley continued walking to her car, leaving John's questions unanswered.

After work, Ainsley went to do laps during the open swim session at the public pool at Yves Park. As she swam the length of the pool, she let the water ease the tension in her neck and back. Carrying the mail bag every day took a toll on a carrier's body, and it was important to relieve the pressure that built up in the muscles. Jesse's swimming instructor, Brandon, approached Ainsley as she was drying off after her swim.

"Hi, Ms. Tobin. Where's Jesse? I wanna say hi." The seventeen-year-old had been teaching Jesse's swimming class for the past three summers.

"Jesse is not with me today. She is with her father."

"Jesse has a father?" Brandon asked. "She never talked about her dad."

Ainsley chuckled at the absurdity of Brandon's question while wrapping the towel she used to dry off around her waist.

"He has only recently had a bigger role in Jesse's life."

"I didn't know. Are you and he divorced?" Brandon was still too young to recognize the improper questions.

"We were never married."

"Oh," Brandon's complexion developed the faintest touch of red. "No wonder Jesse hadn't talked about him."

Ainsley then explained to Brandon the changes in Jesse's life, giving the facts—and nothing more. Then she changed the topic. "I heard you are going to West Colorado State University this fall. Congratulations."

"Thanks, yes. I'm so ready to leave this town." Brandon's teenage need to flee the nest was clear.

"I'll bring Jesse around before summer's end. She'll want to wish you luck and say goodbye."

Swimming had improved her spirits, and knowing Jesse would be home soon gave Ainsley an additional boost. When she rounded the corner a block from her house, there was Tom's truck parked in front. She turned into her driveway, pushed in the clutch, turned off the ignition, and coasted to a stop. Before she could exit the vehicle, Jesse sprang from the front door of the cottage.

"Hi, Mom. Where were you?" Jesse's arms encircled her mother's neck. "Oh, you were swimming," Jesse answered her own question as she tugged at a ringlet hanging low on Ainsley's forehead. "Your hair is wet." Jesse hugged her mother tighter. "I missed you."

"I missed you, too." Ainsley gripped Jesse, and the pre-teen did not protest. It was their way of apologizing for their differences the day before.

"I have so much to tell you. We had gobs of fun. Wait till you see the stuff we got today. I got to help pick out furniture for the new house, and guess what?" Jesse remembered to breathe. "There's a pool right in the yard! Well, it's not really a yard. Not like our yard, or Brooke's yard. More like the park. And Dad says Brooke can swim in the pool. Won't that be fun? She's gonna love it. Com'on, mom. Come with me. I wanna show you the outfit Dad bought me."

"Slow down, Jess. Your tongue is gonna get whiplash. And Brooke doesn't swim. Remember?" Ainsley noticed Tom leaning against the picket fence when she reached into her Jeep for her beach bag.

Tom acknowledged her with a nod. "You shouldn't freewheel your clutch when you drive in. It's detrimental to long-term performance," Tom advised.

Tom was giving her driving advice? It seemed so out of context. Ainsley hesitated before responding.

"It doesn't hurt a thing. And once the ignition is off, the only concern is the compromise in steering and brakes without the electrically driven components."

"Bye, Dad. And thanks for everything." Jesse broke away to give Tom a quick hug, threw a "See you tomorrow," over her shoulder, and followed her mother inside. "I'm gonna call Emily."

Jesse was still on the phone with Emily when Ainsley finished her post-swim shower. After thinking about what to make for dinner, she decided something warm and comforting—a bubbly casserole of some sort would be nice. With the return of the ocean mist each evening that developed into a full cast of fog by morning, there also came a dampness that lingered even after the morning burn-off allowed for temperatures to warm. Running the oven would take off the chill from the air inside.

As she sliced zucchini for a pasta-free lasagna, she reflected. She loved seeing her daughter with such energy and enthusiasm. Aunt Ruthie had been coaching Ainsley on letting go so Jesse could be free to experience life. It wasn't easy but Ainsley resolved herself. Thanks to Aunt Ruthie's words of wisdom, she was learning to ease up the control on every aspect of her daughter's life.

As Ainsley was sliding the casserole dish she had been preparing into the toasty preheated oven, Jesse appeared. "Yay. Zucchini casserole. My fave."

"Your 'fave'?" Ainsley teased. "Are we too busy to even finish our words?"

"My fav-or-ite!" Jesse emphasized the word, then added, "Emily said her dad wants to talk to you when you get a chance."

Ugh, Phillip. Ainsley's reaction was becoming a reflex akin to gagging. "Okay, thanks for the message. I'll call him." But she didn't. Instead she retreated to the garden bench.

She hadn't spoken with Phillip since the night he had tried, in a drunken stupor, to make a move. Perhaps embarrassment kept him from apologizing. It was possible he hadn't remembered what he did at all.

"The timer says 22 minutes. I'm starved. Can't we speed up the cooking process?" Jesse ventured out and joined Ainsley in the garden.

"Good things come to those who wait." Ainsley lifted the blanket she had brought outside and opened up her arms for Jesse, who willingly sat in her lap. Reclining against Ainsley's chest, the child was a bit too big for this custom, but neither mother nor daughter minded.

"Emily and Phillip are coming to the party. I told Dad I wanted to invite Emily, but I didn't want Phillip." Jesse tucked deeper into her mother's arms.

"You'd rather Phillip not come?" Ainsley asked.

"I'm worried, is all."

"Worried? About what?"

"Well," Jesse began, "I saw him and you in the kitchen. He made you uncomfortable."

"Oh, Jesse. You saw that?" Ainsley was dismayed. "I am sorry for that, but you don't have to be worried. He had a few beers and wasn't behaving as his usual self."

"The beer doesn't make it okay. It isn't right. What if he drinks beer tomorrow? I would be so embarrassed if he acted that way in front of other people too." Jesse's little face fit in the crook of her mother's neck as she expressed her fears.

"Oh, sweetie." Ainsley felt terrible for her daughter.

"I'm glad you will be there. Maybe there's a way to keep him from getting drunk?"

Jesse's expecting me to go? Ainsley had thought she wasn't invited. Her own self-doubt surprised her. She had been acting a fool. Of course she should be there. She and Jesse were a tight unit. Not even Tom West could break them apart.

"I shall monitor his every move. I promise. Not to worry." Ainsley rocked Jesse the way she did when Jesse was a wee infant.

"I feel sorry for Philip. He is lonely and unhappy."

"How do you know he is unhappy, Jess?"

"Emily tells me he is sad her mom is gone. It's hard for Emily because she lost her mom and feels as if she's losing her dad."

"What do you mean?"

"Emily says sometimes he sits alone, in the dark, in his bedroom or sometimes in the garage."

Ainsley listened as Jesse shared her concerns. When she paused, Ainsley asked, "Does he get that way a lot?" Ainsley wondered how often Phillip was isolating himself. "Does he do that when you are over?"

"Sometimes," Jesse nodded, and the soft, lacy hairs on her head tickled Ainsley's cheek. "That's why I stay over. If I am there, Emily says he is more happy."

"Thank you for telling me. I am so proud of you for how you are taking care of your friend. Losing her mother has been hard for Emily and her dad is struggling to mend their lives. You are a loyal friend to Emily and I will help them too. I will offer support to Phillip."

"How can you help him? You can't bring back Emily's mom. How can anyone help them?" Jesse's upset went deeper than the surface.

Ainsley knew Jesse was a sensitive child and an old soul. She considered how much Jesse should know about such adult issues, then began to speak. "I can encourage him to talk to someone. He continues to miss Aunt Desi. There are people, psychologists, who help us when we need it. They are called therapists. Phillip can talk to a therapist who will help him and teach him how to be happy again."

Ainsley evaluated Jesse's response to check if she was understanding. "Do you get what I'm saying?"

"I think so... No offense, Mom, but kids are better at being happy. Adults suck at it."

"You are not wrong, my child. Adults could learn a thing or two from you kids." Ainsley was glad Jesse had lightened up. "I am going to be more like you."

Jesse stood straight up. "Was that the timer? Dinner is ready."

After dinner, Jesse went into the living room to watch TV and have a little couch-cuddle time with the dog. With the phone in hand, Ainsley went to her room, dialing as she climbed. She would not let another minute pass without talking to Phillip. Unfortunately, Phillip didn't answer his phone. Ainsley left a message, then stood with her hands on her hips, staring into her closet. She had a party to attend and needed to put together a nice outfit.

After finishing the wardrobe portion of the preparations, she moved on to cosmetic fixes that included a facial mask and eyebrow tweezing. Immediately after applying the mask, she heard the phone ring. *Dang*, she thought, *it must be Phillip calling*.

"Jesse, will you please answer the phone?" Trying not to interrupt the hardening of the damp concoction on her face, she shouted without moving her lips. She figured Jesse must have understood her cryptic request when the ringing stopped.

Jesse ascended to the upstairs.

"Was it Phillip?" Ainsley tried not to crack the now dry, caked-on mud.

"It was Belle," Jesse answered. "She had some news. She and Brian are getting married and they want to announce it to everyone tomorrow at the party."

Even through the therapeutic mud covering Ainsley's face, she couldn't hide a wince as Jesse announced the news. When Ainsley's face was clear of the mask and she had applied a clarifying cream to nourish the fresh layer of skin cells brought forth by the mud mixture, she noticed Jesse hadn't gone downstairs to watch TV. She knocked on Jesse's bedroom door and it opened. "Are you in bed already?"

"I'm in bed. G'nite."

Through the darkness, Ainsley detected in Jesse's voice something was wrong. Was she still concerned about Phillip?

"Can I come in?"

"I'm going to sleep. I am tired."

"Jesse, I can tell you're upset. Please tell me why?"

Maybe the girl was simply worn out. She had had a busy day. She had been fine at dinner, but since then, her mood had changed. Jesse had spoken to Belle. Had Belle said something to upset her?

"Was it something Belle said?" Ainsley's pupils were adjusting to the low light in the room and she saw Jesse bury her face in her pillow. From Jesse's reaction, she gleaned it must have been Belle.

"Is it Belle and Brian's announcement?" Ainsley sat bedside and put her hand on Jesse's shoulder. "Belle will understand if you don't want her to announce it tomorrow. After all, it is your party and nothing should be there to divert the attention you deserve."

"Errrr!" Jesse growled into her pillow.

"What is it, Jess?"

"It's not Auntie Belle, Mom. It's you. You are against weddings."

"I never said that," Ainsley defended.

"When Grandma talks about marriage you always tell her people should never get married. Why are you so against it?"

"Oh, honey, no. I'm not against marriage. I think sometimes people get married too fast. Belle and Brian hardly know each other."

"But they should get married right away. Waiting means they won't get married at all." Jesse sat up and pushed away the covers.

"If they truly love each other, waiting won't change that. Sometimes waiting means they become well acquainted before they marry. They might find that even though they love each other, it doesn't mean they should be married to each other." Ainsley was walking a fine line between being honest and brutally so.

"You're talking about what happened to you and Dad." Jesse drew the parallel.

In the night-light lit bedroom of a child, the subject seemed out of place. Jesse was far more perceptive than her young age would suggest. Here, in front of an audience of assorted stuffed, plush toy animals, and a shelf full of model horses, Ainsley wanted to fix this. Looking for inspiration, she searched around the room at the picture of a cartoon unicorn dancing on a rainbow with the words "Dreams Can Come True."

Taking a deep breath, Ainsley explained. "Your father and I loved each other very much, but we were too young for marriage. In our hearts, we were as close as two people can be, but we weren't meant to be married."

The sorrow in Jesse's expression was that of acceptance and an acknowledgment. "That is just so sad, Mommy."

Jesse's words tied Ainsley's heart into knots. There wasn't any way she could explain to Jesse why she and Tom weren't together. She couldn't even explain it to herself.

CHAPTER 21

Jesse's Celebration

Ainsley's eyes fluttered open to the melodic strains of music drifting up from the radio down below.

The familiar tune, a Tom West hit, filled the air, accompanied by the sound of Jesse's voice intertwining with the melody. Not only singing along but also harmonizing. Jesse was a natural.

"Reelin', Smilin', hours on the pier. Castin' lines and tall tales, sippin' ice-cold beer.

Through the laughter and the tears, we stick by each other's side. Good friends and good fishin'. That is life's joyride."

"Good morning, sunshine," Ainsley said when she reached the little kitchen filled with music.

"Morning, Mom." Jesse turned the volume down and handed Ainsley a glass of orange juice.

"I was thinking of making a quick trip into town," Ainsley announced.

"What about church?"

"The Lord will forgive us for missing one day."

More often, they were obligated to go to church, but since Rose and William were on a weekend getaway, they could play hooky.

Rose encouraged Ainsley to keep religion in Jesse's life, even though she knew it wasn't as important to Ainsley. Unlike Rose, she was more of a spiritual person than she was religious.

"Why are you going into town?"

"I thought I'd shop for something nice to wear to your party."

"There isn't enough time. How long will that take?"

"Not long. If I find nothing right away, I'll wear what I have."

Though Ainsley had chosen an outfit from her closet, she rather wanted something new to wear to the celebration. She was less confident this morning about attending Jesse's event than she had been the day before and hoped to find something to wear that brought her courage.

"I'll stay home," Jesse declared as she sat down at the table with her plate of toaster waffles swimming in a pool of syrup. She dipped her finger into the puddle of sugary sap and stuck it in her mouth with emphasis. "Yummmm." She teased when she saw the look of disgust on her mother's face.

"All that sugar," Ainsley said. "Don't come crying to me..."

"... when my teeth rot right outta my head." Jesse finished the sentence and gave her mother a toothy grin with her mouth full of perfect teeth.

"Okay, okay." Ainsley winked and finished her glass of OJ. "I'm going to the Santa Rosa Mall. My phone is with me and charged. Call if you need to."

It was comforting to see Jesse's playful nature had superseded her somberness the night before. Seeing her eating breakfast with a hungry dog watching was a tonic for the heart.

Arriving early at the shopping mall meant there was ample parking, so Ainsley got a spot near the entrance. She would start at the department store—and hope she needn't go further into the labyrinths of the interior. The high ceilings, escalators and vast openness of the edifice often put her on edge.

Keeping a close watch on the clock, it didn't take Ainsley long to find what she was looking for—a cool and flowy, light-colored floral print dress drawn in at the waist with bell sleeves. She found a wide-brimmed sun hat that suited the style to finish an outdoor event look that would meet Rose's approval. Struggling with the multiple bags, she wrestled them into the Jeep's back seat and headed west.

"I'm home!" Ainsley called as she grappled with the bags and, once in the house, let them fall to the floor. The silence that followed told her she was alone.

"Jesse?" she called. She thought maybe the child had taken Brooke for a walk, although she was not in the habit of leaving when Ainsley wasn't home.

Ainsley felt her blood coursing. *Maybe she is with Ms. Dixon.* Then she noticed a note sitting on top of the kitchen table.

Ainsley began her counting exercise to calm herself. It was very unlike Jesse to do anything without at least a call to the cell phone. Not even a text was showing on her screen. The note explained that Jesse and the dog had gone to the party early with Tom.

Ainsley carried her packages upstairs and got dressed. As she was descending, the home phone rang and she stepped across the empty kitchen to answer it.

"Hi, Ainsley. I'm glad I caught you before you left."

"Hey, Phillip. What's up?"

"Earlier today, Tom West and Jesse dropped by to take Emily with them for some pre-party festivities. That leaves you free to ride to the party with me."

Ainsley felt her skin begin to itch. First Tom had come for Jesse without Ainsley's knowledge, and now Phillip was arranging for her transportation. When did she give up her autonomy to everyone else? Ainsley had fought hard and won her independence from Rose. She wasn't about to give it up for a couple of men. "I think it's best if I take my car, Phillip."

"If we go together, maybe we can chat. I wish I'd have spoken to you sooner, and I know this is not the best timing. There are some things I have been working through, and I may have come across as avoiding you."

Ainsley listened. She didn't want to admit to Phillip she was avoiding him, too.

"The other night I may have messed up, and I owe you an apology. I just don't know how big of an apology it should be. I blank out after I've had a few beers." He seemed apologetic, but avoided taking responsibility for anything.

Poor Phillip. She wondered how to handle this. If his recollections were sketchy, she could downplay it all. "Boy, you really can't hold your liquor, my friend."

"No, I cannot." Phillip chuckled.

The expulsion of air behind the nervous laugh showed Phillip's relief and told Ainsley he had been as unsure of how to proceed as she was.

"So, shall I swing by and pick you up?"

"No, Phillip." Ainsley wasn't eager to let bygones be bygones. She had an excuse, not that she needed one. "My parents are out of town this weekend and I have to stop in and check on the old barn cat. I'll see you at the party. Bye."

Ainsley hung up the phone, giving Phillip no chance to negotiate further.

When she arrived at her mother's house, it did not surprise her that Spencer, the cat, was nowhere to be found. After waiting and calling out his name, knowing the feline wouldn't come running, she gave up. Placing the food in a bowl inside, she reasoned Spencer could use the kitty door when he was hungry enough. She would check up on him later. With envy, she contemplated Spencer's straightforward existence. His was a life of few changes and surprises.

With part of her sensing urgency, and the other part wanting to procrastinate, Ainsley made the trip to the address Tom had left on Jesse's note. She entered the driveway leading to the house.

No, not a house—Tom's estate.

"Man, oh man." Ainsley exhaled the words as she steered through the ornate designer wrought-iron gates.

A breathy "Wow," came out when she saw the mansion, complete with a covered drive-through entry and a valet motioning for her to come through. She rolled past a ten-foot tall goldfish spouting water into a Brobdingnagian pool at its base.

On her right was a mowed expanse of field where she saw rows of parked cars, exotic sports types, fancy black SUVs with multiple antennae, and private limousines. Beyond the empty field were crops; mounds of rounded, dark green foliage from which shot forth spears of fragrant lavender blossoms.

"Who are these folks if this is what they drive?" Ainsley hissed, evaluating the cars as she drove past the parking area towards the valet parking sign, as instructed. She was doing all kinds of judging. It was her defense against feeling intimidated.

Ainsley drove towards two young men standing beside a podium in the covered area at the entrance. *They must be the parking service.* she thought. Then, handing over her keys, Ainsley said, "The best spot in the shade will get you a better tip. Mind you, don't scratch it."

"Yes, m'am. I mean, no m'am." The flustered kid took Ainsley's keys, and she was sorry her nervous attempt at humor made him uncomfortable. *Wait until he tries to drive the manual transmission,* she thought.

As the young kid drove her Jeep away, only killing the engine once before jerking forward, Ainsley stood in the vast open space that served as the porte cochère of Tom's new domicile. "Wow," she repeated.

The roofed passageway was bigger than her entire cottage. The ceiling was over two stories high and in the middle hung a chandelier as big as a truck.

"Who has an exterior chandelier?" Ainsley continued talking to herself to expel some more nerves as she stepped through the massive double doors that stood propped open. Inside was the formal entry hall.

Upon entering, she noticed the stunning starburst pattern on the parquet floor. It looked too beautiful to walk on. Through double doors on the left of the entry was a room furnished with a large, artisan-carved desk and leather chairs—a den or office. To the right was a formal living room whose furnishings looked to be straight out of an old Victorian inn.

Straight ahead of Ainsley was a massive stairway that split at a wall of glass and continued up both sides. Overlooking the valley, the landing was like an observation platform that made her kitchen picture window seem like a portal on a ship. Craning her neck, she looked up at the ceiling and hanging there was another chandelier. It was a carbon copy in design, though bigger than the one hanging over the exterior entry.

"Ms. Tobin?" A well-dressed man appeared before her.

"Yes. And you are?" Ainsley had never met this man who gave the impression he was familiar with her.

"Name is Adams."

"Adam what?"

"Just Adams, Miss Ainsley." Adams spoke with a comfortable accent. "The Boss asked me to be on the lookout for y'all."

"The Boss?" Ainsley questioned.

"I reckon Tom was concerned you'd get lost in this cavernous place he wants to call home." Adams held out his arm. "Please accomp'ny me to the garden," he said with a wink.

Ainsley linked arms, questioning why she had such a strong sense of trust towards this man with a discernible southern drawl. Adams led Ainsley around the other side of the immense staircase and out to a covered veranda that ran the entire length of the main house.

There were several tables around which sat a multitude of guests drinking and engaging in conversation. Not wanting to stare, Ainsley looked away but thought she recognized Tom's folks, Jim and Margaret, Jesse's new grandparents.

The terrace transitioned into an open patio that was filled with more tables and chairs for guests who had yet to arrive. Beyond that was more lawn, manicured to perfection. There was a large tent under which was set a disk jockey and her equipment.

It was all so over the top. To Ainsley, it seemed ridiculous.

Ainsley heard splashing and found the source. She had caught sight of Jesse among a group of kids swimming in the Olympic-sized pool. From the far side, Brooke bounded towards her for a joyful reunion.

"Thank you, Adams. I'll go say hello to my daughter."

"Of course. Tom is over yonder." Adams pointed, then went in that direction.

"Hi, Mom!" Jesse shouted from across the pool when she spotted her mother, and Brooke appeared at Ainsley's side. "Isn't this pool crazy big?" Jesse said as she stepped out.

Ainsley grabbed a towel and squeezed her soggy daughter. "I was thinking the same thing."

"Wait till you see my room. I picked out the furniture myself."

Jesse led the way into the main house and turned right, walking down a corridor with closed doors on either side.

"This is the actual part where we live," Jesse explained. "These rooms are called 'sweets,' like candy, I guess." Jesse giggled. "Isn't that a funny word for rooms?"

Ainsley smiled, but didn't explain the difference between "suites" and "sweets." She would remember to do so at a later date.

"This one is where Brian and Belle stay," Jesse walked past a door, "and Charlie and his family stay here." She pointed to another closed door farther down the hall.

Ainsley followed Jesse past the other doors, trying to keep up. It surprised her how familiar Jesse was with the names of the bandmates.

"And this is where we live." Jesse held the doorknob, and Ainsley held her breath.

She was having trouble wrapping her mind around what Jesse was saying. She mentioned "we" when referring to the area they occupied. It was weird that Jesse said she "lived" here and was a part of someone else's life. From her perspective, it was as though she and Jesse were wandering through someone else's house. "Shouldn't we be knocking?"

"No, silly. My room is in here." Jesse pushed the door open and stood aside for her mother to pass.

With trepidation, Ainsley stepped in, but it wasn't a bedroom. Rather, it was a living area, a comfy one at that. In the middle was a soft-looking sofa that squared up to a fireplace, and above that hung a large, flat-screen TV. On the right side of the fireplace were several guitars on stands, and to the left, between the fireplace and a big sliding doorway, was a baby grand piano. The far wall had two doors and in between them was a glass case packed with awards and plaques representing Tom's illustrious career in music.

"This is Dad's room," Jesse pointed, "And this is mine."

Into the room they went, and Ainsley couldn't believe how well furnished and decorated it was. Everything in there had Jesse written all over it, from the shelf with a few model horses to the posters of Taylor Swift and Carrie Underwood.

The room was large enough to accommodate a queen size sleigh bed, set up high, with a two-rung step ladder at the foot. On the bed was a pink and purple print bedspread with a matching dust ruffle. Brooke brushed past Ainsley and leaped onto the bed from the floor with ease, turned in a circle three times, then lay down in the middle of the pillows.

"She always wants to lie down right where I put my head," Jesse commented.

Jesse moved to the mahogany dresser and pulled out a crochet swimsuit coverup. After slipping it over her head, she walked past the bed and disappeared. Ainsley glanced in and saw Jesse standing at the mirror in her own bathroom, brushing her wet hair.

"You have got to be kidding me," Ainsley whispered as she took in the entire scene. Though not as large as their own bathroom, this bathroom was more than big enough for a ten-year-old. "You have your own bathroom?"

Through the suite door left open, Ainsley heard Adams calling. "Miss Jesse? Your public awaits."

"What did he say? Oh, no. Not a chance." Ainsley flew out of Jesse's room to confront Adams. There was no way she would let them showcase Jesse to the paparazzi like a prop.

CHAPTER 22

Garden Gossip

"Miss Ainsley?" Adams seemed confused by her reproach.

"Please excuse my frankness, but I will not let this happen." Ainsley remembered her manners and her calming breathing technique. This wasn't Adams's fault. He was merely following orders.

"It's not what you're thinking. I was only teasing Miss Jesse. Believe you me, Tom West never seeks attention of any kind. Never has, never will." Adams spoke highly of his "Boss" and Ainsley admired Tom for having the unconditional support of a guy like that.

"Forgive me for jumping to conclusions, Adams. I may have overreacted."

"No sweat, Miss Ainsley. Tom warned me you can be quite the 'Mama Bear.' I admire that quality." Adams was nothing but helpful. "This is all so new to Jesse, and Tom worries about overwhelming her. That is why I am here, to protect y'all. I can answer your questions and shield you from any discomfort, too."

"That sounds very noble."

The breathing method had once again calmed her nerves. Ainsley had made a deal with herself to stay unemotional and she intended to honor it if it was the last thing she did.

Jesse went outside to reunite with her friends, and Adams stayed in the suite with Ainsley.

Ainsley asked Adams where he was from, how long he had worked with Tom, and whether Adams was his first or last name. Adams, whose last name was Pinchard, said he was from Louisiana and had worked with Tom for eight years. Before that, he served as a Green Beret in the military, participating in counterterrorism missions. After over a decade of service, he moved to the private security industry.

Ainsley found Adams impressive and intimidating due to his background and was reminded that, as a superstar, Tom needed such security. After reassuring her, Adams led Ainsley through a secluded brick patio and a Japanese garden to the mansion's family wing.

"There you are."

Ainsley turned and observed Tom coming up behind them. Tom was a welcome sight. Finally, a familiar face. "Hello, Ainsley. I noticed you met Adams. Don't believe a word he says. This guy has been trying to stab me in the back since he met me."

Tom turned to his bodyguard, and they exchanged the synchronized moves of a short, private handshake. A communication method Ainsley could not interpret. This liaison intrigued her; the men must have had more than just a business relationship.

Adams excused himself to tend to business, leaving Tom and Ainsley alone in the Japanese garden.

"Hi Tom." It felt strange to address him so casually when they had hardly spoken to each other recently. When he came to her home to pick up or deliver Jesse, it felt like such an intrusion. Here, his appearance inspired in her the desire to grab his arm and run away to the past, or anywhere things made sense. She stifled the desire to flee by reciting numbers backwards in her head.

"I trust Adams has been treating you with kindness. Has anyone given you a tour of the place?"

"Jesse has shown me some of the important parts. It's all so ostentatious. This mansion must surely have quite the story behind it. You can show me the place some other time." Ainsley found it to be tedious, this unnatural environment, and would rather not see the entire complex.

"Not much of a story," Tom confessed, ignoring her dismissive energy. He explained as they strolled through the garden, getting farther away from the hoopla of the celebration gatherers. "The previous owners built the house and the surrounding grounds to run a lavender farm. They planted English lavender on the acreage below. It was a dependable crop for farming, because it was easy to grow and useful."

"I noticed most of the land is without crops of any kind. Have you some other plans? Some other crops in mind?" Ainsley scanned the expanse below when they reached the hedge that defined the lawn and ran the perimeter of the area. Beyond the short boundary of vegetation was a drop-off. A retaining wall had been built there to shore up the hillside.

"Initially, we chose this estate for the multipurpose usefulness as a studio. It was to be a satellite location where we could come to write, collaborate with other musicians, and take a break."

Standing there in the garden overlooking the lavender fields, Tom became contemplative. "I had no interest in the farming aspect. I come from a long line of ranchers. Not a single sodbuster among us. But Charlie pointed out that the lavender could become a great side-hustle business for his wife, Claire."

"Side hustle?" Ainsley could figure out what the term implied, but thought it to be a poor choice of vocabulary for the business world. An unprofessional slang word.

"Claire has an entrepreneurial knack." Tom was quick to defend when he picked up on Ainsley's judgment. "Based on her marketing savvy, Claire did some research. She'll plant a few other varieties of lavender—French, and a hybrid known as Blue Cushion, which is used in culinary applications."

"Hmm." Ainsley considered how romantic it would be to be a farmer growing lavender. Working on the farm, wearing a wide-brimmed straw hat and coveralls with a sprig of lavender in her pocket. She imagined riding through the fields with Jesse on horseback, inspecting the crops.

"...it made sense for us that with the farm for fun, spending time here for retreats might not be enough. With a little planning and rearranging, we can run our entire music operation from here."

Ainsley nodded, but hadn't been paying close attention to what her host was saying. She regretted her previous attitude.

"I want to put your mind at ease knowing where Jesse is when she is with me. I intend to provide nothing but the best for her."

"Please don't think you have anything to prove. I have no doubt you will do anything for Jesse." Ainsley stared up at Tom.

Tom looked down at her as if he was on the verge of speaking. Just then Phillip walked up with Adams. Tom and Adams exchanged glances as Phillip stared at Tom. Ainsley sensed the intensity of the non-verbal conversation taking place.

To diffuse the energy, Ainsley spoke up. "Hi Phillip. I see you found the place."

"Yes, Miss Ainsley." Adams remained on edge. "This gentleman insisted he be brought directly to you."

"Thank you, Adams, for bringing Phillip over," Tom said, never losing eye contact with Phillip. The two men shook hands. Tom stared at Phillip's arm, which had come to rest possessively around Ainsley after they shook hands. Ainsley repositioned herself, shifting her weight away, but Phillip didn't ease his hold.

"Dad!" Emily, who had been with Jesse since the morning, came running up from behind and broke the tension.

Phillip released his hold on Ainsley to hug his daughter and handed her a tote bag. "I packed you a few more clothes in case the fog rolls in."

"Thanks, daddy." Emily took the canvas sack and trotted back to Jesse and the other children, who were now enjoying a game of croquet on the lawn.

"They'll play in the sun until they are all wrinkled up raisins." Phillip remarked. With awkwardness anew, Phillip returned his arm to Ainsley's shoulder, but the posturing game was over.

"If you all will excuse me, I have responsibilities to tend to. Phillip," Tom spoke, "welcome. Please, make yourself comfortable."

Phillip nodded. "Thanks, man."

"Ainsley?" Tom dipped his chin. "I'll catch up with you later." The brief but powerful communicative exchange with Adams before Tom stepped away wasn't to be ignored. Then Tom was gone.

"Shall we join the celebration?" Adams said, giving Phillip an icy glance.

Ainsley took hold of the arm Adams offered and walked with him. Phillip clung to her other arm and followed. Sandwiched between the men, Ainsley felt like an Oreo cookie. To Ainsley's relief, Belle and Brian were the first people she saw.

"I've been looking for you." Belle turned her shoulder to invite Brian, who had stood behind her, into the conversation. "Ainsley, this is my fiancé, Brian Carter. Brian, this is my best friend and my maid of honor, Ainsley."

"It is a pleasure to see you again." Brian and Ainsley exchanged pleasantries. "This is my friend, Phillip."

Then Belle interrupted.

"Look," she squealed and held up her left hand, "we picked it up from the jeweler. And booked the church for next month. Labor Day weekend."

"Congratulations." Phillip shook Brian's hand while Adams looked on with scrutiny, the natural position of body guards.

"Come with me," Ainsley moved away from the book-end men. It was time to free the creamy filling from the hard cookie constraints. "Let's sit. We have a lot to talk about."

"Good idea. We have a wedding to plan, and there's no time to waste."

When Phillip tried to follow, Adams intervened, "So, Phillip. I hear you're in the import business. What exactly does that entail?"

"It means I bring in products from overseas." Phillip answered with a condescending edge as he watched Belle and Ainsley walk away. He seemed irritated by Adams's intervention. His irritation subsided, and he changed his tone. Phillip puffed up with self-importance.

"I am an interim CO for an international company based in San Francisco. We work with many countries bringing all varieties of handmade products to clients that run online shops. As interim CO, I am on the short list for getting the position…"

"Can you believe it, Ainsley? I'm engaged." Belle was bursting.

"Yes, Belle. I'm excited, too."

They found a gazebo on the far edge of the lawn, a perfect shady spot for a comfortable private conversation.

"So?" Belle questioned. "I know you have so much more to say. Get it off your chest."

"Do you think you and Brian are moving a little too fast?"

"I have never felt this way about anyone I've dated. Brian makes me feel like I am the most important person in the world. He is so considerate, and he makes me think of someone other than myself. He inspires me to want to make him happy. Does that make sense?"

Ainsley understood, and her eyes softened with approval.

"I am not getting any younger. Brian has two children from a previous marriage, and I want a family. I'll be a mom and won't have to compromise my body."

There it was, the old, self-centered Belle that Ainsley knew and loved. "You have considered everything," she smiled. "I wouldn't try to change your mind, but let the record show. I was in favor of slowing things down."

"Okay, okay. The record shall reflect." Belle mollified her friend. Coming from cynical Ainsley, this was the closest to a blessing she and Brian could expect. Belle was on the verge of suggesting they move to the veranda to socialize when the DJ, who had been spinning a variety of music, cut short the current song playing.

"G'day, mates and welcome to this first annual celebration that will o'ways and fo'evah from he'yah on out be known as Jusse's Day." The DJ had a strong accent. Ainsley speculated she was from either New Zealand or Australia. The way she pronounced Jesse was endearing.

Ainsley searched for Jesse, wanting to be sure her daughter wasn't uncomfortable with the attention. She scanned the area and spotted Jesse and Tom. Jesse was looking up with admiration at Tom, and he was staring back at her. The DJ handed the mic to Tom for his announcement. "It is with pleasure and an immense amount of pride, I introduce you all to my daughter, Jesse, the latest addition to our ever-expanding family. Jesse, welcome home."

"Ay-oh," the DJ took back the microphone, "one big happy family right he'yah. And the cater'ahs are announcing the victuals ah ready. Let the nosh begin."

A palpable hum of excitement surrounded Jesse as guests clustered to greet her while others gravitated to the tables laden with a diverse multiplicity of cuisines. They were serving crispy fried chicken, coleslaw, pasta dishes, green salads, and casseroles such as black-eyed peas and cornbread.

"Shall we get some of those vittles?" Belle asked. "I am going to find Brian and we'll meet you over there in a few minutes."

Belle excused herself, leaving Ainsley alone and self-conscious. From the gazebo, she surveyed the gatherers. She stood up for a better look and Brooke, who had been laying beside her, bounced to her feet. Along the outskirts, Ainsley walked, and as she approached the privacy screens in the Japanese garden area, she heard voices filtering through the shrubs.

"I wonder which woman is her?" One voice said.

"She's the one with the black and white dog who follows her everywhere," said the other gossiper.

"I haven't seen her yet, but I'll look for the dog. I heard she has some guy with her and she's showing him off to poor Tom," was the response.

"You know he has been pining for her for years? All for nothing. She broke his heart. Again."

"At least he found his daughter. She's a cutie. And now, with that woman out of the picture, Tom is available. He's up for grabs." The reply came as two women emerged up the path from the Japanese Garden.

Ainsley couldn't be certain she was the subject of their conversation, but who else could they have been talking about if not her? Mortified that they should see her, Ainsley hung back as the gossipers passed. She heard one of them say. "Now's your chance, Diane. You should go for it. You have been waiting long enough. Let Tom know how you feel."

Ainsley remained undetected by the two women, who continued chatting as they walked out of sight.

CHAPTER 23

Lost in the Dance

"There you are, honey. Join me." Phillip caught sight of Ainsley and, shouting from his place in line for dinner, beckoned her to stand with him.

Phillip put his arm around her and proclaimed to the couple behind them, "She's with me." Ainsley smelled alcohol on his breath.

"Loosen up, honey." Phillip did not let go. "We can tell people we are dating. I've been in mourning long enough."

"Phillip, have you been drinking?" Not looking for an answer, she wanted Phillip to understand she knew he had been.

It was the right moment to assume control.

Taking hold of Phillip by the wrist, she removed herself from his clutches. "I am very sorry," Phillip confessed with drawn out spaces between words and syllables. "I've upset you. Please forgive me, Des. Don't be mad at me." He had moved from a spiky drunk to an emotional sap. He had called her Des, his nickname for his late wife, confirming he was conflating the two of them.

"I'm not mad. I am concerned. And I am Ainsley."

Phillip stared as if to refocus his mind, then began quietly sobbing. In his intoxicated state, Ainsley's response had sobered him enough to know what was happening.

"I'm sorry, Ainsley." Phillip rested his forehead in his palm.

As the food line moved forward, Ainsley built Phillip a small sandwich with the bread and cold cuts and he accepted the sustenance.

"What a mess I've made. This is so embarrassing."

"Yes, you have, and yes it is. And now, you will do better."

"It scares me. Being alone. I am trying to keep her memory alive but, with each passing day, I lose Désirée, bit by bit. We are replacing the memories with her with more recent memories without her."

"You will never forget Désirée. Her spirit lives on all around us. Let her rest in peace. Honor her by being happy and taking care of her most precious gift: Emily."

Nodding in agreement, Phillip ate his sandwich and Ainsley summoned a server for a cup of coffee.

With Phillip sobering up and settling down, Ainsley headed off to get him a piece of birthday cake to go with his second cup of coffee. On the way to the cake table, she remembered she needed to use the facility. She was reluctant to leave Phillip alone, but she really had to go. She took a detour to the bank of portable toilets the service crew had delivered for the occasion.

"Excuse me, are you waiting in line for the bathroom?" Ainsley asked the woman she then recognized as the gossiper talking behind the screen in the garden.

"Yeh," the woman responded. "Why is there always a line?"

"Most people drink too much, and need to evacuate more often. Then when they have to urinate excessively, they refrain from consuming water, become dehydrated, and the alcohol has an even stronger impact."

"Hi," the woman held out her hand. "My name is Wil." The pinched expression on her face indicated Ainsley's scientific answer to her rhetorical question might have caused her head to ache. "It's short for Wilhelmina."

"Nice to meet you." Ainsley replied. "It'd be faster to go inside and use the facility there."

"No guests are allowed in the living area of the house. Tommy made it clear we are forbidden." Wil waggled her pointer finger in "no-no" fashion before Ainsley's face. "I'm family, and they won't even allow me to access the living quarters."

"My daughter lives in there, so I think it's okay."

"Oh, who is your daughter?" Wil asked. Then her mouth opened round as she sucked in the air. "Oh, wait. You're Jesse mom? That means you're Ainsley. I was told you'd have a black and white dog with you."

Ainsley stepped to the side so Wilhelmina could see Brooke. A few others waiting in line noticed the conversation and then Tom rushed in.

"Come with me. You can use the bathroom inside." Tom led Ainsley away towards the entry to the family wing. "Of all the people with whom to strike up a conversation, you choose Wilhelmina?"

"She called you Tommy. Do you prefer the name Tommy now?" Ainsley teased when she noticed Tom's discomfort.

"That's Wilhelmina. She is a groupie and also Charlie's sister."

"She seems nice." Ainsley hid her true feelings towards the woman she had previously characterized as a gossip. "Why isn't she allowed to access the family wing? She seems harmless… Tommy."

"Hardly." Tom said through stiff lips. "She is always hanging about stirring up drama and sometimes seems lost and out of sorts. For Charlie's sake, we permit her to take part in stage design. She is talented but inconsistent."

"And she calls you Tommy?" Ainsley couldn't resist.

Tom lifted his chin to the ceiling, suppressing the desire to react to the undesirable nickname. Then he looked down. "I have been hoping to catch you without Phillip. Can we talk?"

"Talk and walk, please. I have urgent business with a man about a horse." Ainsley's bladder was not to be ignored any longer.

After she had taken care of business, Tom, who had waited for her to come out of Jesse's room, asked her to sit for a minute.

"You want me to stay alone in the family quarters with you? According to Wilhelmina, guests are not allowed." Giving Tom a hard time proved to be entertaining.

"Wil said that? How long did you two talk? What other nonsense did she tell you?" Tom was showing signs of frustration.

"Okay, okay. I'll stop." Ainsley turned serious. "She said nothing incriminating. I was just bustin' your chops. Forget about Wil. What is it you have to talk to me about?"

"I have been thinking, and I don't intend to take any action before first talking to you."

Tom had her full attention when he used the words "take any action."

"I'm listening," she responded with trepidation.

"Do you think there's a chance Jesse would want to—and only if it's okay with you—that Jesse could come to the studio in Nashville? We have a few matters to tend to and she'd be back before school starts."

"Wow, that got real serious, real fast." Ainsley could tell Tom was choosing a gentle way to present his case.

"I'm sorry to be abrupt. I had doubts about when we'd get the chance to talk about it." Tom continued. "They need me at the studio. We are making changes and I have a lot of arrangements to make. We bought this place so I would have room here to bring our setup from Tennessee. There is enough space to build a couple of recording studios if we want with the highest-quality equipment. There is room for everybody to stay when we are working. I am making it permanent, Ainsley. I don't wish to be away any longer from my parents or Jesse."

"Wow, I mean..." she took a breath. "Wow, that's a lot to process all at once."

"You don't have to decide right away. I have not mentioned this trip to Jesse. I haven't asked her about coming to Nashville yet."

Ainsley did not oppose the idea of Jesse taking the trip, and she didn't mind that Tom was moving his entire operations from Tennessee. Before she could say, "I'll think about it," she remembered she had left Phillip alone. Hopefully, he had stayed out of trouble and was waiting for her to bring him some cake. "I gotta get back."

"Don't overreact." Tom followed her into the corridor, mistakenly interpreting her haste.

Ainsley kept walking towards the exterior. She had to find Phillip. "I'm not overreacting."

"Then why are you running away?"

"I'm not." She crossed the parquet floor and headed out the door.

"So you will think about it?"

Adams appeared next to Tom as they looked at Ainsley retreating. "She didn't take it well?" Adams asked.

"I thought it was fine. We were talking. No flares, no gunfire. Then, poof—she was gone."

"You should have prepared her better, softened the news. Maybe give it to her in small doses," Adams advised.

"There's never enough opportunity for small steps with Ainsley."

Ainsley found Phillip chatting with a group at the cake table. To her relief, Phillip had stayed away from the bar.

Tom approached the DJ, who gave him the microphone. Facing the crowd, he called for their attention.

"Family, friends, and colleagues. I have a few announcements."

After waiting for the bustling group to settle, he revealed the joyous news that Brian and Belle were engaged to be married. Next, he presented the plans to set up shop in Sebastopol.

"Along with these geographic changes will be an expansion of our endeavors. Securing new talent, our team of new agents will handle young artists who emulate the freshest sounds in country music. So, let's have a toast."

They passed out champagne with sparkling cider for the kids, and everyone raised their glass to toast Tom's new enterprise. Shortly after the toast, Phillip gathered Emily and her belongings and bid them all adieu.

Phillip and Emily were not the only ones leaving. The parking area became a flurry of activity in the fading light of the late summer sunset.

The DJ invited the remaining guests out to dance, and Ainsley watched her daughter join in. Jesse was nothing like Ainsley regarding social interactions. She was outgoing and gregarious, with no effort. When the group of kids that had grown smaller took to the floor to dance, Ainsley was proud that Jesse was dancing without embarrassment.

"May I have this dance?" Tom snuck up behind her as she sat watching the dancers.

Ainsley looked up as Tom circled around to face her. She grasped his outstretched hand, and for a moment they stared at each other.

"Please, just dance with me?"

Ainsley couldn't refuse. The DJ switched to a slow song, and Ainsley released her death grip on inhibitions.

In each other's arms, as if it was the most natural thing to do, they rocked and swayed to the mellow beat of Keith Urban's song "Blue Ain't Your Color."

Tom eased Ainsley only far enough away so that he could see her face. It seemed as though Tom intended to speak, and she waited. The moment passed, and he pulled her close again. With his chin dropped low and close to her ear, Tom repeated, "Let's just keep dancing."

Ainsley sighed in response and danced as if the music would never stop. But like all the greatest moments in life, the music eventually ends.

PART THREE
Letting Go

CHAPTER 24

Oceans of Emotions

After tucking Jesse in at Tom's after her party, Ainsley arrived home that night to an empty cottage and realized this new reality would not be easy. Jesse was staying with Tom, taking advantage of her summer vacation. Tom would soon be a permanent resident and a big part of Jesse's day-to-day life. Sharing Jesse meant she would spend frequent periods alone.

Waking up after a short but restful sleep, Ainsley had Monday off this week and decided a pleasant walk at the ocean would do both her and Brooke some good. The beauty of having rotating days off meant she could make the most of an almost deserted beach. She permitted Brooke to run loose, and after chasing a flock of sandpipers just to the surf, the dog walked by Ainsley's side.

As she swished barefoot through the waves, Ainsley contemplated the events of the previous day. Tom had been there for some of the best parts. With each step through the sand, she sensed again the warmth of Tom's nearness, and it reminded her of how intimately they were connected once upon a time.

The waves rushing to the shore rolled past her as she drifted from the present into the past. The memory of her loneliness and her healing stay with Aunt Ruthie stood as a powerful reminder of how much Ainsley had had to overcome.

The waves of time had been pounding away but had had little effect on her feelings. In her head, she had reconciled with the past and no matter how much her heart wanted to be acknowledged, her head had the final say. From her head to her heart, the distance was greater than the expansive ocean that lay before her.

"C'mon, Brooke." Wanting to escape the relentless torment of thoughts, she called to her faithful furry companion. "Let's run."

On the homeward drive, still carrying the energy she absorbed from the pounding waves and the exhilaration from her run, Ainsley turned on the radio.

In between songs, the radio host teased about an upcoming announcement that the entire country music industry was waiting to hear, followed by a Tom West tune. Ainsley let the radio play.

"I'll be singing my songs from the front porch swing,

With a guitar in my hands and the love that it brings,

Back to my roots, where I truly belong.

In the arms of the ones who've loved me all along."

Ainsley listened to the old hit she had heard before, but the words seemed to hold more meaning now. When the song ended, the announcer delivered the promised revelation.

"That's right, all you single ladies. There are big changes in the life of country music's most eligible bachelor. He has a steady girl. Singer/songwriter and music producer, Tom West announced he has a daughter and rumor has it they might sing a duet. Yes, folks. Ten-year-old Jesse can sing, too. She's a chip off the old block." The host proceeded, saying there were no further details but encouraged listeners to stay tuned.

A duet? Ainsley wondered when they had formulated that idea. Her maternal instincts were triggered by what she thought sounded exploitative. She hoped Tom had Jesse's welfare in mind when making such plans.

As she slowed the Jeep to cruise past the half dozen buildings that lined the main street of the town of Bodega, Ainsley's thoughts collected in a more logical manner. Nothing about the way Tom carried himself, be it business or personal, showed he was anything but responsible.

She used the rest of the drive to secure feelings of ease and contentment. She had to accept things as they were. Turning into her driveway, Ainsley eased in the clutch and shut off the engine at the right moment, allowing the vehicle to coast to a stop in the exact spot she always parked. She smiled when she recalled Tom admonishing her for this method of driving.

Feeling sleepy when she got home, Ainsley decided to lie down. She grabbed the afghan from the foot of the bed and slithered under it. The rays of light that radiated through her bedroom window fell on the bed where she lay, coercing her into slumber. She slept for what could have been moments or hours until the ringing of the landline roused her.

She fumbled for the unit on her nightstand. "Hullo?"

"It's me. What's a matter with your voice?" It was Belle.

"What time is it?" Ainsley focused on the digital numbers of the clock by the bed and identified the numbers five, two, and five. She glanced out the window but couldn't tell if it was dusk or dawn. At this time of year, the light in the sky before sunrise and after sunset looked the same.

"It's five twenty-five." Belle's response did nothing to clear Ainsley's confusion.

Ainsley rubbed her eyes as if better focus would help. She strained her brain and concluded it was her Monday off, and she and the dog had gone to the beach. It had to be evening.

"Hey, Belle."

"Pretty exciting stuff yesterday, huh?"

"Yeah, a lot of stuff."

"Jesse had a blast, and you did okay, too."

"Yes, Jesse did."

"You don't seem to be in a talkative mood," Belle noticed.

"Sorry, Belle. I was taking a nap. I am in recovery mode."

"No matter, I'll do the talking. There will be no surprises because I wanted you to be the first to know. I'm putting in for early retirement.

I did the paperwork today and I'll be there tomorrow morning to say goodbye to everybody."

"So you are gonna go through with this?" Ainsley had listened yesterday as Belle mused about being a full-time mom to Brian's two kids.

"Brian and I talked about it a lot. And Ainsley?" Belle paused in typical dramatic fashion. "Brian and I are thinking of having a baby."

"You're planning on having a baby?" Ainsley made it seem as if the decision to reproduce was the most alien concept for a human. It wasn't so much the reproductive aspect, but the deciding.

She had had a baby with no cognitive process. She had never considered that it could be a choice. Not that she regretted it, but for her, it hadn't been optional.

"Yes, Ainsley. A baby. Me." Belle laughed as if she thought it was a foreign concept, too, but for different reasons. "Did you ever think you'd hear those words out of my mouth?"

"To be honest, I imagined no one deciding on such things." Ainsley laughed along. "And you? Of all people," she teased, "You have never even had a dog or a houseplant to care for."

"I know, right? I guess I needed the right person to bring out the maternal instinct."

"You will make a fantastic mom. Look at how much Jesse loves you. And I will be there with you every step of the way, as you've been there for me."

"I was hoping you'd feel that way. I can't do this without my best friend by my side."

Ainsley and Belle talked a while longer, and she got the feeling Belle was more nervous about the idea than she revealed. It was a rewarding feeling to be giving Belle reassurance.

When they'd finished talking, Ainsley got up from her nap and went down to make some dinner before she would start getting ready for her work week.

At quarter to eight, the phone rang.

"Hi, honey. We're back." It was William.

"Hi, Dad. How was your trip?"

"We had a wonderful stay. Amazing weather, plenty of relaxation. Your mother and I even did some fishing."

"My mother?"

"Well, Rose didn't exactly do any fishing, but she helped." William chuckled.

Ainsley chuckled, too, wondering how one person helps another fish. "That's great, Dad. I am thrilled you had an enjoyable weekend." Then she inquired about the cat. She confessed she hadn't seen Spencer all weekend. William assured her the cat was fine. The food bowl was empty, so he had eaten.

"Well, I better hang up, Ains."

"Okay, Dad. Thanks for calling."

"We want to hear all about Jesse's weekend celebrations. Maybe tomorrow after work?" William invited.

"That sounds good, Dad. See you tomorrow."

At work the next day, Belle showed up out of uniform to say goodbye to her work family. Belle's coworkers congratulated her and offered their best wishes.

"We are going to miss you, Belle." John hugged his retiring coworker, and then, as if planned, each carrier took their turn wishing her well. Some teased that she had found herself a rich man. Others said the guy must be a saint to handle her. Darryl jokingly asked if Belle's fiancé was okay with her and Ainsley's lesbian relationship. A comment for which he literally got the boot when Ainsley tipped her toe to his backside.

Then Belle came to Ainsley and though it wasn't goodbye, it was the end of their professional partnership. The tears flowed.

"C'mon, you two. It's not like you'll never see each other again." John showed his sensitive side.

"Yeah," Darryl chimed in, "you'll be seeing each other for a three-some. Brian is one lucky dude."

"Shut up, Darryl." A half-dozen voices in unison flew from the group. Then they all laughed.

"This," Belle looked around. "This is what I will miss the most."

"Creepy guys making inappropriate comments?" Ainsley smiled.

In an instant, Ainsley's work world became a lonely place. Yet another aspect of her life that had changed. She did her job that day mechanically, keeping the raw edges of her emotions at bay. She didn't allow herself to contemplate anything—not a single thought could she entertain. Thanks to Aunt Ruthie, Ainsley had made tremendous improvements in her coping skills. But the task was draining.

"I miss her already, Mom." Ainsley lowered her defenses when she stopped by her folks' house after work.

"You'll always be friends. You might have to be more deliberate and plan to stay connected. It won't be so easy. You can't peek through your desk areas to chat."

"They're called cases, Mom." Ainsley corrected Rose and started tearing up. "And it won't ever be the same. Everything is changing. Everyone is leaving me."

"Yes, there are changes, but no one is leaving. They are growing. Without growth, things become stagnant." Rose hadn't become annoyed by Ainsley's emotional outburst and was being comforting. If this was because of her therapy, it was not only benefiting Rose.

"I am happy for Belle, but it is going to take some getting used to." Ainsley couldn't even think of bringing Jesse's changes into the conversation.

"I understand, dear." Rose offered genuine sympathy and Ainsley believed her. They chatted for a while longer, then Ainsley went home. Alone again in her empty cottage, it suddenly became imperative that Ainsley speak to her kid.

"Hello?"

"This is Ainsley." Feeling self-conscious, she wished she had mulled it over before dialing. "May I speak to Jesse?"

"Hi, Ainsley honey. What's up?"

Ainsley recognized Adams' distinct accent. "Hi, is this Adams?"

"Yes, dear. What can I do for you?"

"I was hoping I could speak to Jesse, if that's okay."

"Nonsense. You have permission to call anytime, hun. Just a minute, I'll get her."

The silence that followed on the line revealed he had put her on hold. *A home where a caller gets put on hold?*

"Hi, Mom."

"Hi, Jess." Ainsley's voice caught in her throat when she heard her daughter's voice. "How are you doing?"

"I'm doing great. We were hanging out and playing music and I can play on the piano. We went to the stable today and Pete gave me a lesson. Casey was a super good boy. We got to do some jumps and Dad was worried they were too high. You know, Dad has never jumped, like a real jump. He mentioned he has been on trails where there were little logs to step over and sometimes the horse had to hop a little." Jesse snickered.

Ainsley could hear Tom in the background with a comeback of some sort and Jesse laughed. He must have picked up on the ribbing he was getting. Then Jesse said, "We are teasing, Dad."

Ainsley could tell Jesse and Tom had great chemistry. "I'm glad you got to have a riding lesson and I'm sure your dad will get used to you jumping. Pete would never ask you to do anything unsafe."

"I know. Pete said to be patient with Tom. He's still new at being a dad." Jesse giggled again.

Jesse told her what they had for lunch and dinner and described the enormous kitchen facility right there in the mansion. "It's too big, and clean. I'm afraid to dirty it up, but Dad said never mind. He said the staff can handle it."

"Oh, my goodness." Ainsley tried to hide her alarm.

"Don't worry." Jesse read into her mother's shock. "I tried my hardest to be neat about cooking. I didn't want someone else to clean up after me."

"That makes me very proud, sweety."

It was humbling to realize what a good kid her daughter was. What had shocked her sensibilities was that Jesse had a "staff member" to rely on.

"Well, let's say good night, then. I'll see you tomorrow. Sweet dreams."

"Nite, mom." Jesse left the conversation, but Ainsley hung on to the phone a few seconds longer. A goodnight wish spoken over the phone was nowhere near satisfying.

CHAPTER 25

Co-Parenting Trap

Wednesday began, wet and drippy, but Ainsley's spirits remained undampened. It had filled her with joy as the day progressed to know Jesse would be there that night. Tom was dropping her off before he left for the airport. They were due to arrive by six. After work, Ainsley went straight home, managed some wedding duties, fit in a workout, and started the preparations for dinner.

It was six-fifteen, and she was about to send forth the National Guard when her landline rang.

"Jesse?" There was only a slight crackling on the edges of her voice.

"No, m'am. This is Ed. Mr. West's driver?"

Tom's limo driver? She needed more info.

"We dropped Mr. West off at the Sonoma Jet Center. They called him in to Nashville a little sooner. Jesse is with me and I am bringing her to you."

Ainsley breathed. Jesse was fine. She was coming home. "Thank you, Ed."

"Traffic was heavier than expected. We'll be there shortly."

"Take your time. Thanks for calling."

Ainsley had to sit down. What a relief, and thank goodness she hadn't shown she was freaking out. Letting go of control of her daughter's every waking moment was difficult. Ainsley had to believe Jesse was as well protected in Tom's care as she was with her.

It irked her, though. Why hadn't Tom informed her of the change in schedule?

As promised, Ed came with his precious cargo. Jesse ran into her mother's open arms. The dog jumped and spun around them, demanding to be included. They thanked Ed when he bid them fare-well. Arm in arm, they retreated into the cottage for some serious reacquainting. One would have thought by the looks of it they had been apart for years.

"I missed you so much, Jess."

"I know, Mom."

"You are impatient with me," Ainsley felt the need to explain, "but please understand. This is a lot to get used to."

Jesse gave her mother a big hug. "Okay, I missed you, too. Now, shall we move on?"

"Excuse you?" Ainsley said using a motherly tone.

"Sorry, Mom." Jesse understood.

"Traveling back and forth between houses is tiring. Still, that is no excuse to get snippy," Ainsley explained. "We will all adjust to the new routines."

Along with their home life, Ainsley was also adjusting to working without Belle at the office. They saw each other every day anyway, meeting up for lunch or exercise. Belle kept Ainsley busy by helping plan her small, intimate wedding.

One afternoon, Jesse joined them with bridal preparation duties.

"I want flowers everywhere, a mixture of all shapes and colors. Is that too much to ask?" Belle was losing her patience with the florist.

"When are we going to the mall?" Jesse interrupted, showing signs of agitation. It was unusual for her to be so demanding. Belle had been quite the difficult bride-to-be, but was her attitude rubbing off on Jesse? Or was Jesse being a typical preteen? Had the time with her dad spoiled her?

"We're done here." Belle proclaimed. "Jesse, let's go. *Abbiamo finito qui.*"

Ainsley cringed when Belle began speaking Italian.

"We only have two weeks," Ainsley protested, reaching out for her friend's hand to stop her exit. "If you walk out, we won't have any flowers at all. This is the only florist willing to fill our order on such short notice."

"Then you talk to her." The bride fumed. "You know what I want. See if you can explain it."

"C'mon, Jess." Belle motioned for Jesse to follow her.

Ainsley waved them off with a good riddance. She would deal with Belle after she had calmed down. And Jesse? She would catch a few breaths first. The importance of handling Jesse when she was certain she could react calmly to her daughter's behavior was paramount. Dealing with Belle would come first.

The florist stood behind the counter waiting for further instructions. Ainsley explained the bride was a little stressed and was micromanaging.

"I understand. If I had a nickel for every bride that wasn't a stressed-out mess, I'd be broke." The florist was nothing but professional, and explained to Ainsley that filling their order would actually be easy since Belle wasn't specifying a certain blossom or color. Leaving the shop, knowing Belle would be delighted with the flower order, Ainsley was on to the next items.

Ainsley found a bakery to accept the cake order on short notice, as the baker was the brother of her co-worker, John. They had secured a tasting appointment.

"This shouldn't be so difficult," Belle lamented, putting down her fork beside the plate without taking a bite. "Why are there only two samples? Chocolate and white. Can't they give us a few more examples of what they offer?"

Brian, who had joined them for the tasting, was experiencing what Ainsley had endured in dealing with his bride.

"Let's at least try what they have." Brian tried to console his fiancée.

"This bakery has the best reputation," Ainsley added. "There is no need to try each kind."

"I can't decide without knowing how their cakes taste. And the two of you plotting against me won't accomplish anything, either.

"Belle, honey, don't leave." Brian begged when the bride stood up.

"I'm going to the bathroom. Maybe when I return, the baker might figure out how to run a tasting appointment. *Questo è ingiusto.* An outrage."

While Belle was in the bathroom, Brian bought several other cakes for Belle to sample. Belle tried the Champagne cake, a fruit basket, a white cake and a chocolate; one with raspberry filling and buttercream icing.

"The cakes are all so delicious. But I think the simpler, the better. I choose the white chiffon with buttercream." Belle was proud of her decision. Ainsley and Brian looked at each other with tight-lipped smiles.

Being the maid of honor overwhelmed Ainsley. With all the duties that came with the title, she had no time for anything else.

"I'm sorry, Dale. I really would like to see you. I am just so busy." It wasn't like Ainsley to make plans and not follow through, but there she was canceling on Dale for the third time.

"I can meet you for lunch." Dale was patient. "Maybe tomorrow?"

Ainsley knew her lunchtime would be spent making phone calls on behalf of Belle. It made little sense at all. Since her retirement, Belle has had all the freedom in the world. Why wasn't she doing some of the work herself?

Meanwhile, Tom had returned to the West Coast, and Jesse was spending most days and some nights with him while she was still on summer vacation. Ainsley noticed some more attitude transgressions.

"It is natural for kids to push boundaries." Ainsley spoke to Tom, and he promised to be mindful of Jesse's attitude and agreed to be more strict with her.

The mother and daughter talked by phone. "Can I trust you to be courteous and well-behaved when you are at your father's house?"

"Yes," Jesse quipped.

"You are still under the same rules as you are at school or Emily's or anywhere else."

"I know how to behave in public, Mom."

"See, Jesse?" Ainsley remarked. "Right there. The sarcasm. Are you responding with respect?"

Jesse's frustration was evident, and Ainsley sensed they were about to identify the problem.

"Are you upset because your trip to Nashville never happened? You have reason to be disappointed."

"Sometimes," Jesse paused, then explained, "when I'm in the kitchen, a stranger walks in and that makes me uncomfortable."

"I understand. That would make me feel uncomfortable, too. When you meet someone new, just be polite, but you have the right to set boundaries. You do not have to be friends with everyone."

Afterwards, she took up her concerns with Tom, who assured her he would make changes.

"Please tell me what you think we should do." Tom admitted he wasn't sure how to handle it. "How do I make sure Jesse is one hundred percent comfortable?"

They talked until they resolved the issues. They established safe zones to give Jesse her space. When Jesse saw someone with whom she was unfamiliar, she could ask who they were. Everyone at the mansion was briefed on this delicate issue.

And so went the days of summer, Jesse dividing her time between her parents, Tom and Ainsley working through co-parenting issues, and everyone making adjustments. Ainsley became better at being alone as the weeks went by. The school year began and the transition was smooth.

When the Friday before Belle's big day dawned, Ainsley was relieved. Juggling work and wedding duties had been a challenge, but this was her three-day weekend. Plus, with Labor Day Monday off, she had a built-in recovery time. The next two days were to be all about Belle, and after that, she could focus on managing her own affairs.

Upon returning from taking Jesse to school, it caught her off guard to notice Tom waiting in the driveway. Leaning up against his new Raptor truck, Tom was wearing his scruffy cowboy hat and worn-out boots. He resembled the cowboy in an advertisement for Ford pickups. The thought made her chuckle.

Standing there in her driveway looking casual and comfortable, Tom West had the charms to sell ice cubes to a snowman. It was difficult to stay logical regarding the father of her child. No matter what her head had been saying about Tom West, her heart had dibs regarding the chemistry she felt seeing Tom there.

He stayed in place as Ainsley climbed out of her car, then straightened up and removed his hat to say good morning. His ability to be both polite and imposing, and confident with no hint of arrogance, was disarming. "Apologies for my unannounced visit. Do you have a moment to talk?"

Their conversations had been over the phone until now.

"I am always available to chat." Ainsley was agreeable. There were a few phone calls she needed to make regarding the wedding, but she could do that later on. "I am free this morning. Let me get Brooke. I have an idea. Get in the truck."

Ainsley went inside and grabbed a ball cap, pulling her ponytail through the hole. She took Brooke's leash off the hook, and she and the border collie leapt into the tall truck where Tom was staging.

"Where to?" Tom waited for directions at the top of the driveway.

"Turn right on Bodega."

Tom did as he was told.

"And a left here."

"Here?" Tom questioned as he turned into a turnout for a bus stop next to a complex of townhomes.

Ainsley nodded. Tom maneuvered the truck through the cut-out. The pavement curved left at the end of the bus stop and ran along past the condos. To the right was the cemetery, and in between was where she directed him to drive.

"Here." She pointed. "We can catch the trail here."

"Trail? I'm wearing cowboy boots." Tom pointed out his attire was not fit for a hike.

"It's a short walk. You'll be fine." She chuckled.

Tom followed Ainsley past a wooden gate, mumbling about breaking an ankle. "You take a great deal of pleasure in my pain."

"Stop being dramatic. If you weren't always expected to look sexy, you could wear tennis shoes once in a while." She enjoyed teasing him.

"You think I'm sexy?"

"That's not what I said."

"You think I'm not sexy?" Tom struck a manly pose, sticking out his chin and adopting a furrowed brow.

"I never said that either." As Ainsley's complexion grew tinted with a slight blush, she continued talking, ignoring her own response to the inviting twinkle in his eyes. "This is a historic site called Goldridge Farm. A satellite location. Famous botanist Luther Burbank built the cottage and experimental farm."

Tom was listening with interest. "I never knew this was even here."

"Luther Burbank is most popularly known as a historic figure from Santa Rosa. Though his gardens and primary residence were in Santa Rosa, he stayed out here where he did most of the work inventing plants. His old residence on Santa Rosa Avenue in the downtown area is a museum and has been a favorite tourist stop for many years. Tourists come to walk in the original gardens planted with the many hybrid fruit trees, shrubs and flowers he grew. Hybridizing plants to create new varieties was his specialty."

They continued walking up the path that meandered across the three acres that remained of the original ten-acre farm Burbank owned.

Tom admired a tiered garden brimming with color and variety. He literally stopped to smell the roses, then said, "I grew up here and never saw his house or his farm."

Ainsley filled Tom in on some facts she could remember and repeated herself distractedly. Just standing there in the garden with Tom was a pleasure. She was close to making stuff up to prolong being near him.

"Very interesting." Tom watched Ainsley as she spoke about Burbank and the history, but he seemed to be thinking of something else.

Ainsley remembered how Tom could bring out her emotions with his disarming charm. He had been back then, and was still both exhilarating and calming.

On a bench in the shade, Ainsley sat down. "This is a good meditative spot." Tired from having romped around, Brooke laid down beside the bench as if this was part of their routine. "So, shall we talk?"

Tom glanced behind them almost suspiciously, then sat beside Ainsley.

"Are you looking for the paparazzi?"

"It's not that I expect them to be here. It's become second nature." Tom's statement made her feel bad for celebrities.

"No wonder you have Adams."

"It's not only Adams. There is a team of professionals that all answer to Adams. That way, I don't have to think about it."

"And yet you do." She stated the fact, then paused.

"You didn't come over to talk about your security department. What's on your mind?"

Tom sighed. "I am over the moon having Jesse in my life. She is a remarkable young lady, and it has been a privilege to connect with her."

Tom looked down at his boots as if they would tell him what to say. Ainsley waited for him to continue.

"I'm finding it difficult to be your friend." The words flew off Tom's tongue as if he had no control of his mouth.

Ainsley stared at Tom's boots, too, puzzled and unsure if she heard right. "I thought things had been going well," she replied.

"Ainsley, you still affect me. You always have. The years, the miles of separation—nothing has allowed me to forget about you."

Ainsley stood up, and Brooke, who had been lying at her feet, rose to standing. "I'm not sure how to respond."

"You don't have to say a thing. I felt it necessary for you to be aware of how I feel."

She took a step, and Tom stood up, too.

"I still love you, Ainsley. If you can believe it, I love you more. I am eager to ask you to marry me. I want the three of us to be a family."

The dog followed as Ainsley moved aside, shaking her arms like she was warming up for a run. "Us being together for Jesse is no more right today than it was ten years ago."

"That's what you got outta what I just said? Ainsley, I wanted to marry you then. I know the reason you chose not to go with me to Nashville, and I understand. But it was a mistake to push me away. It was wrong to leave me out of Jesse's life."

"You never asked me to marry you." She remembered how she longed for Tom to propose.

"You never gave me the chance. Give me a chance, now."

"It's not that easy."

"Ainsley, it doesn't have to be difficult."

It troubled her to witness his vulnerable condition. "I'm not the same naive girl, Tom, and you are not the aspiring singer on your journey to the top of the charts. A lot has changed."

"All I want is a chance to show you that even though we have changed, our love remains the same. I am more confident about how I feel today. You didn't give us a chance ten years ago. We have a second chance. Don't take it away again."

He had laid it all out there. A man whose heart was ripping into pieces by her soul-crushing obstinacy. She hated it was her fault.

"Tom, please. Stop torturing yourself."

Tom dropped his head with his chin on his chest. "Well, alright, then." Tom spoke, but there was no energy behind his words. "Let's go. I'll take you home."

"I would have given anything to change the way things went, Tom."

Her words fell as if unheard between them. Tom had only recently become an important part of Jesse's life, and Ainsley wanted that. She also knew that his lifestyle could be very disruptive and not conducive to the healthy development of their daughter. By removing herself from the situation, she could be the sanctuary of normalcy for the kid living in the shadows of her famous parent.

"I think I will walk," she said in a low voice.

Before he drove off, Tom leaned out the window. "You know, Ainsley, I was older than you, but I was just a kid, too."

Ainsley returned home to a plethora of tasks yet to be done for Belle, and hadn't time to think about Tom. At one point, she was on her cell phone with Belle and talking to the caterers on the landline for a last-minute detail check.

The afternoon flew by, and she was about to load the dog and collect Jesse from school. Afterwards, she would pick up the bouquets, corsages, and boutonnieres from the florist. Ainsley was working her tail off, planning a ceremony and reception for her best friend, whose fiancé could afford to hire a dozen planners.

"I thought I'd bring Jesse from school," Tom said when Ainsley answered her cell phone.

"Thank you, but no. I am already on the way."

"I am here at the school. Why not get your errands done? I'll hang out with Jesse at your place and help if she has homework."

Tom seemed to be a different person than the one she had walked away from only hours ago. His businesslike tone made her wonder how he could turn off the emotions that had poured out of him earlier. *I guess he's good at compartmentalizing, too*, she reasoned.

Jesse was doing her homework when Ainsley returned with the flowers, and Tom leaped up to help with the heavy box. "Why are you picking them up? Can't they deliver?"

"Why, you ask? Because 'brides be crazy,' that's why." Ainsley began making room in the refrigerator.

When the posies were safely stowed, and she had caught her breath, Tom reached towards her. In his hand, he held what looked like a personal check. "I want to give you something."

"What's this?" She realized she was staring at her name on a check with a lot of zeros in the number.

"Consider this the first installment. I want to reimburse you for raising our daughter."

"You've got to be kidding." She could tell this was no joke and couldn't understand what Tom was thinking. How could he not realize how denigrating this was?

"I will send money to your account once a month from here on out. Half for the past, and half for current expenses."

He was serious. She didn't have the chance to calm her rage with a counting exercise. Her breathing techniques were not enough.

Her eyes narrowed. "You... you are so..." *Arrogant. Insolent.* She couldn't find a derogatory term to describe him in front of Jesse. "Keep your money. You can't pay me back for something unquantifiable. What we needed from you can't be compensated."

"Now, hold on." Tom did not shy away from the wrath that had quickly descended.

"I told you she wouldn't accept it," Jesse chimed in.

Ainsley glanced at her daughter, then redirected her attention to Tom. "You talked to Jesse about this?"

Tom's mouth opened, then closed when he realized it had been a bad idea to include their daughter in the matter.

"Jesse," Ainsley spoke to her daughter and never took her eyes off Tom. "If you could please..." She searched for words. "Brooke could use a walk."

Jesse took her time leashing the dog as the adults silently stewed. As soon as the duo had cleared the front door, Tom jumped in. "You can't blame me for not being there for Jesse. You didn't even tell me I had a daughter until a few months ago. That's on you."

Tom's words cut deep. She knew what had been her deception and needed no reminder of the damage. No matter what, it seemed Tom had the power, and it was Ainsley being hurt. She felt certain this dynamic would never change.

Fighting against the emotions, she spoke through gritted teeth, "I had my reasons. I stand by my decision. It was based on logic. It was what was best. I will make no apologies anymore. Jesse and I have been fine for ten years, and you owe me nothing."

Silence fell between them as they both retreated.

"Please tell Jesse I'll see her tonight." Tom reached for his hat that had sat on the table, pushed it low on his head, and stepped out the door.

Ainsley stood in the vacuum of his departure.

CHAPTER 26

Rings of Promise

"The flowers are not here yet? You should have gotten all the arrangements yesterday." Belle was in the church courtyard scolding her maid of honor. She was in a state of panic since daybreak. The florist was one item on the list of things which Belle decided to obsess over. She had been searching for the florist and the decorations for twenty minutes.

"I picked up the bouquets and boutonnieres," Ainsley explained. "I didn't have the space to store any more than that. We needed the florist anyway to set them up."

"This should already be done. I shouldn't have to worry."

"Then why are you worrying?"

It was more of a statement than a question. Ainsley had run out of patience trying to calm Belle's nerves. She had tried to keep away the pressures, to no avail. *To heck with the bride*, she thought with resentment. She had her own stress to manage.

After the drama of the day before, Ainsley got through the rehearsal ceremony and dinner without incident. Ainsley tried to

243

avoid Tom, but as they were the maid of honor and the best man, their duties required some interaction. When rehearsing the walk down the aisle, Tom had the demeanor of someone going off to war. Ainsley had sensed her feet itching to run. It had been a taxing effort to get through the evening.

Ainsley squared up with Belle and looked her in the eye. "Please lighten up or you won't be able to enjoy your special day. You are getting all my organizational skills for the bargain price of, let's see... free, but remember, I am only working up to my paygrade."

"Don't joke around, Ainsley. You know how important this is to me."

"Seriously, Belle. I'm not joking. This is the happiest day of your life. It will be perfect. I've got this." Ainsley led Belle to the sanctuary to show her where the florist had placed the arrangements.

"When did the flowers arrive?" Belle's relief was momentary. "You mean I've been worrying for nothing?" She turned to storm off and almost ran over Jesse.

"How do I look?" Jesse had come out from a side door in a lacey, lemon yellow dress. Pinned below her chin and to the left was a corsage made of a single lily.

"She has a corsage. Where did you get that?" Belle descended upon the child like a hawk on a mouse.

"The box we brought from home. It was in your dressing room." Jesse leaned away from the assaulting vibes.

"Stay calm, Belle. Jesse has distributed all the corsages and boutonnieres to their rightful recipients." Ainsley ran interference. "You would have known that if you weren't out here micromanaging. I told you I got this."

Ainsley seized Belle by the shoulders and drove her through the door Jesse had come out of and into the women's lounge. "Do we know if the florist brought the fresh flowers to decorate the cake?" Belle asked, returning to her flower obsession.

"Brian!" Belle broke free from Ainsley's grasp when she caught sight of her betrothed and ran into his open arms.

The couple remained locked in an embrace while Tom, who had come over with Brian, stood to the side.

"Hey, hey. Take it easy," Brian whispered to Belle. "You are so wound up and tense."

"The florist was absent and there are no flowers for the baker to decorate the cake," Belle wailed.

Brian tried to mollify his bewildered bride while looking to Ainsley for answers.

"Everything is fine, Brian. She is overstimulated." Ainsley resented Belle was the one being consoled when it had been she who carried the strain.

Brian turned to Belle. "We should have eloped. I told you all this silly stuff wasn't necessary."

Ainsley's eyes opened wide, and she shook her head, hoping Brian would stop talking. Did he refer to the wedding as "silly stuff"?

He didn't catch the hint and continued, "If it was so important, we could have taken more time to plan. If we'd have hired a planner, we could have carried out this event without us having to lift a finger."

"What do you mean 'silly stuff'? This is very important," Belle replied. "I have been dreaming of my wedding since I was a little girl. I couldn't simply turn it over to a planner." Belle was on the verge of tears.

"Without us lifting a finger?" Ainsley glowered, as it was she, alone, doing all the lifting. Nobody caught the irony.

When he saw the faces of the women, Brian recoiled. "Did I say 'silly'? I meant 'sensational.'" With the bride and maid of honor scowling at him, Brian started digging himself out. "Everything is going to be sensational. You look amazing. Ainsley has done a remarkable job of getting everything you wanted. This wedding will be unique and all your own and perfect."

Belle turned to her maid of honor with a questioning expression.

"Yes, Belle." Ainsley nodded. "What Brian said. It will all be okay."

"Wow, Brian." Ainsley heard Tom saying, "You were about to make things worse."

Brian shrugged his shoulders, then winked at his departing bride. "Yeah, but I didn't."

"You're not supposed to see me before the ceremony. Stop looking." Belle flirted with Brian and blew her beloved a kiss.

"I never understood that superstition..." Brian was saying as he and Tom headed for the priest's chambers to wait for the nuptials to begin.

Ainsley left Belle with her mother and sister and headed out to the garden area. Belle insisted she check if the baker had decorated the iced layers of cake as directed.

The reception was to be held in the large grassy area outside the main wing of the church complex. Each of the tables set out under the circus-sized tent had a floral centerpiece of different colors and types of flowers. There was an arch of mixed blossoms under which to take photographs and a dance floor towards the far end of the canopy. Gossamer curtains hung from the sides of the canopy, and in each corner there was a three-foot tall vase with assorted arrangements of—you guessed it—flowers.

Ainsley saw the cake, and to her relief, it was perfectly decorated with fresh flowers as ordered. Ainsley stepped away to capture a picture. She was texting the picture to Belle as proof when she saw Rose coming up.

"The cake looks lovely. Everything looks so good, Ainsley. You did a wonderful job."

"Thanks, Mom, but these are all Belle's ideas. I merely executed her dreams."

"Well, it's very impressive. It's easy to have ideas. But you adopted her ideas and transformed them into reality. That's the talent. Your ability to listen and execute a plan is remarkable."

Ainsley never expected compliments from Rose.

"Hey, Ains. How are you holding up?" William joined the two women and put his arm around his daughter.

"Hi, Dad." Ainsley leaned in. Having her folks there was a comfort. Pushing into William's arms, she wished he and Rose could dash her away. Maybe if she closed her eyes for a few minutes, all her troubles would evaporate and she'd be a child once more. In her father's arms, it wasn't hard to believe she was safe.

"I better return to help Belle. She has been driving everyone nuts with her panicking." Ainsley forced herself away from the hug.

"You are taking care of yourself, aren't you?" Rose was mindful of her daughter's stress level.

Ainsley detected the genuine concern behind her mother's question and nodded. "Thanks, Mom. I know you and Dad are always here for me. It feels good to have unconditional support."

When the pianist started playing and more guests had arrived for the ceremony, William, Rose and Ainsley made their way into the church. Once inside, Ainsley heard the vocalist sing.

"She sounds okay today," Ainsley noted. A last-minute decision by Belle, the pianist asked for his sister to be included in the ceremony.

After hearing the girl sing the song during the rehearsal, Belle freaked out. The poor girl did not sound good at all. Belle had ordered Ainsley to fix it, but Ainsley had refused. "You said yes to the girl."

"It will be embarrassing to have a soloist performing poorly at a wedding attended by professionals in the music industry," Belle had said.

"I guess the pianist thought this was his sister's shot at being discovered." Ainsley made light of the dilemma, and Belle conceded.

As the church pews filled, Ainsley waited for the song they chose as a cue to bring out the bride. She hurried her charge from the bridal lounge into the reading room off the left side of the vestibule. "That's your song."

Belle seemed as if she couldn't move.

"Belle, it's time."

"Jesse, you're first. Wait by the door. We'll be right behind," Ainsley instructed. Jesse obeyed and moved through the doorway. She looked back and gave a thumbs up.

"The guests are all standing for you," Ainsley said. Belle didn't budge.

"I can't do it. I can't follow through with this."

"Of course you can. And you will." Ainsley saw Belle's father standing at the open door with a questioning expression on his face.

"No. It'll never work. We are much too different. His music is bound to pull us apart."

"What are you talking about?" Ainsley was ready to push Belle if need be. She glanced across the antechamber to see Tom striding towards them.

Belle spun around, sat down on a bench, and buried her face in her hands.

"Don't cry, Belle. You'll ruin your makeup."

"I'm just not sure. We come from different worlds, Brian and I. How will we adjust?"

"Don't be ridiculous, Belle. You and Brian love each other. See how he looks at you? Brian would let nothing, including his music, come between you."

Taking a deep breath, Ainsley formulated her thoughts. Belle was acting out of character. Where was her self-assuredness? What happened to her confidence? "You listen to me. There is a guy who is standing at that altar and he will commit to you today and for the rest of his life. There are no guarantees. Life happens, but what better way to experience it than with Brian by your side?" Ainsley gently pulled Belle's hands away from her face. "Take it from someone who's done it all by myself. It isn't as glamorous as it seems."

Ainsley hoped a joke would bring Belle around. She couldn't believe her own ears. Her words seemed hypocritical, but she hoped Belle would do as she said.

"So what I'm hearing is where there is love and commitment, there is happiness? Love conquers all? And two people can overcome any obstacles if they have each other to help them through?" Belle raised her face with bright eyes, appearing to have done a complete one-eighty.

Ainsley was confused. "Well, not in so many words, but yes. If it'll get you to the altar, that's what I'm saying." Ainsley was trying to understand Belle's weird behavior.

"Great!" Belle jumped up like a cattle prod had zapped her. "Did you hear that?" Belle glanced at Tom, who was standing behind Ainsley, and gave him a wink. "Let's go. What are we waiting for?"

Belle's display bewildered Ainsley. The pianist had started the song for their procession.

"You are nuts, Belle." Ainsley muttered.

Belle gave her maid of honor a shove towards Tom before linking arms with her dad. Tom caught Ainsley's arm to keep her from stumbling. Momentum landed her a little closer to him than she expected. Her forward motion stopped when she fell square against his chest. Tom reached out and caught Ainsley in his arms to steady her.

"Hello," said Tom with a smile as he peered down into Ainsley's surprised face.

Ainsley held onto Tom longer than she needed to steady her balance. "Thanks," was all she could think of to say.

As the bridesmaid, Jesse was the first to be escorted to the altar by Brian's oldest son. So stoked to play an important part in this momentous occasion, they were a vision of sweet innocence.

Although Tom had steadied her balance, Ainsley still felt knocked off her feet. His smile drew her attention.

Was that a twinkle in his eye? Has everyone gone mad?

"Go, you guys," Belle demanded. "You're messing up the timing." Belle sounded angry, but she had the same peculiar smile Tom had. It was like they were up to something.

Ainsley's feet moved forward, and with everyone watching, she felt self-conscious and her grip tightened on Tom's arm. Tom reached across with his free hand and placed it over hers.

At the altar, Father Lewellen was smiling, and Jesse was motioning with her hand for Ainsley to walk towards her. Ainsley thought she heard some whispers from the congregation and a chuckle or two. Were they laughing? Had the audience noticed her unsteady gait and Pitbull-style squeeze on Tom? She was feeling embarrassed in front of the crowd. *Get it together,* she said to herself as the pianist played the Bridal Chorus.

Everyone stood up and turned as Belle began her walk, slowly and elegantly. Escorted by her proud father, Belle made her way towards them, towards Brian. There was no fear, no trace of doubt. It struck Ainsley, a wave of emotion, as she felt the love.

"Who supports this woman in her marriage to this man?" The priest asked when the bride reached the front.

"Her mother and I do, as well as everyone here today, to witness." Belle's father gave her a kiss on the cheek. Belle held onto her dad and whispered, "Nailed it, Dad."

Once again, Ainsley found herself overcome with emotion. Then Ainsley noticed Jesse's elbow bumping her hip.

"Mom, the bouquet." Jesse reached for the posies from Belle and handed them to Ainsley. Ainsley was certain she heard whispers and giggling among the pews.

Wishing she could disappear, she focused on Belle and Brian, but her attention didn't stay on the bride and groom. Instead, all she saw beyond them was Tom. She wanted to walk across the aisle and stand next to him. She wanted to feel again the security and comfort he had provided.

Belle recited her vows, and Brian then recited his. Other than having put some thought into it beforehand, the couple spoke from the heart. Ainsley listened as they each described what it was about the other they loved. Then they expressed their future dreams. During the vows, Ainsley put herself back together emotionally, but it didn't last. She looked beyond the couple about to tie the knot, and Tom was looking at her with such intensity she could not look away.

"By the power of your love and commitment, the authority vested in me, and the love of all the individuals gathered here today, I now pronounce you husband and wife. And now with a kiss, you seal your union in holiness under God."

Brian and Belle faced their family and friends, and the congregation cheered. The priest introduced them as a new couple, and again, the crowd hollered.

As the newly wedded couple started up the aisle, Ainsley and Tom reunited for their turn to follow behind. Gone was the dreadful demeanor Tom had exhibited when escorting her at rehearsal. In him she saw love. With all these emotions in the air, Ainsley realized how deep her own love was for this man walking beside her.

CHAPTER 27

Bells for Belle

It was a quiet Saturday, late in the summer, on an afternoon in the middle of the Labor Day weekend. The residents of Sebastopol went about their business, but for some, it was not just another day. Through the streets and over the housetops, the bells of St. Sebastian tolled. Such a joyful sound enhanced the small-town charm of the little city.

The sound of joy echoed over the heads of the people gathered at the church for their loved ones' wedding. An intimate gathering of folks made it the perfect wedding for Belle and Brian.

After the ceremony finished, the newly married couple walked up the aisle inside the chapel, shaking outreached hands and accepting brief hugs from those seated in the middle, and Father Lewellen invited the gatherers to continue the celebrating outside. While the attendees began filing out, the bridal party stayed inside for a photo shoot.

The photographer wanted pictures with everyone; the wedding party with family, one with the bride's family only, followed by the family of the groom. Ainsley and Jesse were both released from photo duties after the first few shots and headed out to the reception area.

Outside, the merriment had begun. To Ainsley's relief, everything seemed on track. Rose and William had found their name tags on a table near the bridal party's table and spread the word among guests to find theirs. The ritual repeated until most everyone had their name displayed for all to see.

In the beginning, Ainsley had questioned Belle's idea of name tags, thinking it was tacky and might make some folks uncomfortable. In counterpoint, Belle explained how awkward it was when she forgot people's names.

Ainsley compromised by agreeing to include the name tags, and as an added incentive for initializing conversation, the tags were color coded to make it more interesting. Yellow for those on the bride's side, blue for those connected to the groom. Green was for those few that were musically associated, having a business connection. There weren't many with green, as Belle had requested Brian separate business from their important celebration. Rose and William wore yellow.

"Ainsley, you have done an amazing job."

"You already said that, Mom, but I don't mind hearing it again."

"I had no idea you knew so much about weddings. You showed no interest. Unlike other girls who dreamed about their future, your dreams were not to be found on the pages of bridal magazines. You've shown there is a more romantic side to you." Rose had noticed the details for which Ainsley was responsible. Small touches that further enhanced everyone's enjoyment of the celebration.

"It's all the Hallmark movies we watch—me and Jesse."

Ainsley had invented a fun game. On a table were a few pens, a blank notepad, and a chalkboard with instructions. Players were to contribute on a piece of notepaper, a fact or favorite memory of either the bride or the groom without mentioning names. Later, they would read the notes and the participants had to guess to whom the message on the note was related. A small crowd gathered at the table to play the game.

From family and friends, Ainsley had requested old childhood photos of Belle and Brian to create a digital slideshow that ran on a continuous loop projected on the white linen hanging behind the center table where the wedding party would sit. The ooo's and ahhh's uttered by the gallery of viewers as each picture came into view were proof enough the display was being enjoyed.

"It was a lot of work, but worth it." Though there was some resentment for having most of the duties fall into her lap, she was also happy to do it for her best friend. The hard part was done. The party was going off with nary a hitch.

"Well, you accomplished it and you earned the right to relax and enjoy it."

Rose was right. Ainsley deserved to revel in the accomplishment. She was proud of her efforts and as surprised as her mom to discover, hidden under her layers and layers of pragmatism, there was within her a trace of idealistic romance. There was nothing saying she couldn't be carefree for a change.

As soon as Ainsley let down her guard, what immediately popped into her mind was Tom.

She recalled the feelings she had experienced during the ceremony. Though more subtle than before, she encountered more ripples of emotion. These feelings were uncomfortable, but she was trying to roll with them. Ainsley figured that because it was such a joyous occasion celebrated by a small, intimate group of people, she would tolerate the surplus of heartfelt emotions.

Incongruous was the memory of her and Tom's interaction in the afternoon before the rehearsal dinner, but she pushed that memory aside. At present, she dismissed it as an anomaly and felt the good vibes she most recently experienced.

When the photographer finished with the photo shoot, everyone joined the reception. The DJ announced that the luncheon was ready and invited guests to enjoy the buffet. Belle and Brian took their seats at the front and center table with the still shots slideshow running above them.

Ainsley and Jesse sat together on Belle's right; Tom and Brian's son were seated to the left. While they waited for the others to serve themselves, Tom visited Ainsley and Jesse at their side of the table. Squatting down between them, he placed his hands on the backs of each of their chairs.

"Jesse, you did an excellent job leading the party. You are the go-to girl under pressure. Nice save on the *almost* bouquet disaster." Tom gave Jesse a high-five, then turned to Ainsley with a wink and an understanding smile.

There it was again—that wave of emotion. When Ainsley looked into Tom's eyes, she saw nothing there but caring and compassion. Tom seemed to have forgotten how intense and destructive their last conversation had been.

His behavior was as perplexing as Belle's meltdown prior to the ceremony. More inexplicable was her abrupt recovery. Belle went from a cold-feet breakdown to almost sprinting to the altar in the flip of a switch based on Ainsley's words of wisdom. She couldn't remember the verbiage she used to defuse the bride's panic, but was happy it worked.

The food was a simple display—cold cuts and cheese, rolls and condiments. There were plates of fruits and vegetables, bowls of melon slices, and a variety of salads. Belle's parents were underwhelmed by the spread. It was too American for their wishes, but Belle believed the food at her wedding shouldn't be the focus. The caterers embraced the simplicity with grace—especially since it was such short notice.

The people present enjoyed the offerings but were more engaged in interacting than with satiating their appetites. Belle's plan worked. When everyone had finished eating and the staff had cleared the plates, the moment had arrived to pour the champagne and give the toasts.

Belle had insisted her wedding include a baldachin, a ceremonial canopy usually present at the church altar. St. Sebastian's had one inside, but Belle decided she wanted a mini baldachin over the table with the wedding cake and she wanted the maid of honor and best man to give their speeches from it.

Though she thought it was a silly request, Ainsley had dutifully pleased her best friend. From the rafters of the canopy under which the reception was being held, she hung a mosquito net. She decorated the frame ring with silk flowers and suspended the fabric on each side to form an opening.

The party supply company that brought the tables and chairs had a palette upon which they laid a piece of plywood for the floor of the baldachin. To cover the floor, Ainsley spread more fabric. When it was finished, she was pleased with the result and had to admit the cake sat beautifully on its table, up high for all to admire.

Ainsley was already a hulk of self-consciousness at the prospect of standing to speak. The baldachin, a tastefully done replica of simplicity, only magnified her nerves when she stepped up on the raised portion. Why did she have to go first?

Starting her speech with a self-introduction, her nerves were threatening to expose her fear of giving public orations. "What insights about Belle and Brian haven't we shared here already? We all know them well enough to believe theirs will be a fairy-tale story..."

As she spoke, a wave of emotion smoothed over and she couldn't remember what she had wanted to say. Her words seemed stupid. What had been her point? Everyone waited; some were looking on with sympathy.

"So," she concluded, pulling a joke out of thin air to ease her embarrassment, "before the bubbles disappear from all our glasses, raise them high. Cheers to Mr. and Mrs. Brian Carter."

She held up her champagne, and the revelers, probably relieved her speech was over, called out almost in unison a hearty, "Cheers!"

Next, it was Tom's turn to give his version. Holding up his hands, his fingers in air-quotes, he began, "I was going to say, 'what she said,' but that would be cheating." Tom paused for laughs.

Tom shared a story about his and Brian's friendship. He spoke fondly of how their musical collaborations were made better because of their slightly competitive personalities. Then he joked, "So, I guess it's true, after all this time we've been friends, partners, and each other's best critics, with witnesses to prove it, Brian admits I am, in fact, the best man."

Tom, with all his charisma and natural showmanship, was shining. It figured he'd have the crowd eating out of his hand.

"All kidding aside, I admit how lucky I am to have Brian on my team and even more fortunate that Belle is a part of our family now. And if I may quote something our maid of honor shared with the bride before she made that leap of faith and walked down the aisle."

Tom paused for dramatic effect, and Ainsley grew uncomfortable. Why was he putting the spotlight on her?

"The lovely Ainsley expressed, and I quote, 'There is a guy who is standing at that altar ready to commit to you for the rest of his life.'"

Tom looked right at her, and his eyes did that thing that stirred her emotions.

"Then Ainsley said," he continued. "'Life happens, but what better way than to make the journey with someone by your side?'"

"Brian, Belle, we are gathered here to celebrate with you this joyous event. Love is most powerful when shared. Cherish each other, and it will keep you two together. Cheers and congratulations." Tom raised his glass to the couple, and the crowd expressed their delight with whoops and hollers.

After they had enjoyed the champagne and cut the cake, there was a mixture of guests dancing and others sitting and visiting. Amongst the hustle and bustle of bridal duties, Belle caught a moment with Ainsley and seemed delighted.

"Look!" Belle exclaimed. "Everyone is eating the cake, all the cake. There isn't an excessive amount of icing to be cast aside and left on the plate. Nor are there any dry pieces of cake in the trash."

Ainsley couldn't help feeling pleased that her bride was happy. "We did it, Belle. Your wedding was the most beautiful I've ever been to, and I am only bragging a little."

"You deserve all the credit, Ains. You brought my vision from page to fruition. Thank you for putting up with me. There'll be no complaints from me when you are the out-of-control bride and, as your maid of honor, I am the one following orders."

"We make a good team, and you needn't worry. There's no marriage in my future."

"Oh, you poor, oblivious girl. You can't see it."

"See what?" Ainsley asked.

"Remember what you told me? In your own words, you prophesied your future. We heard it and can't unhear it."

"What did I say?"

Both Tom and Belle had alluded to something she said. Tom even quoted her in his speech. Ainsley's suspicions were right. Tom and Belle were up to something. "I verbalized whatever I could think of to get you down that aisle."

"The truth comes out when you can't think of anything to say."

It was time for Belle to throw the bouquet, so she and Ainsley put a pin in their conversation, but Ainsley intended to set things straight somehow. Whatever the shenanigans Belle and Tom had conjured up, she was certain they had drawn some inaccurate conclusions.

Ainsley didn't take part in the bouquet tossing ritual, but she stood by with Jesse, who insisted. The embarrassing pile of young women and girls scrambling for the aromatic bunch of flowers was a frivolous custom and not for dignified women.

Afterwards, Ainsley followed Belle into the dressing room, where Belle changed out of her gown. She had chosen a stylish blouse and a comfortable skirt for her departure. She also loosened her hair from the updo, and as Ainsley brushed it out for her, Belle brought up the subject of their earlier conversation.

"You need to practice what you preach."

"What do you mean?"

"You said there are no guarantees, and that I had a guy waiting for me at the altar. You have a guy waiting for you, too. He is ready to commit and be a family. Why do you resist?" Belle was serious, more serious than Ainsley had ever known her to be.

She was talking about Tom. She had tricked Ainsley with a fake cold-feet pre-ceremony breakdown. And since Tom heard Ainsley, Belle must think it was logical that they profess their love and it would solve all their problems.

"You were playing a trick? I suspected your emotional display was not sincere."

Belle ignored the insinuation. "No, Ainsley, I was doing you a favor. I know you have a heart in that chest of yours. It beats, and it loves and it wants you to listen to it, but your head keeps getting in the way. Tom and I didn't conspire. It was a fortunate coincidence he was there to hear you speaking from the heart. It seems to have given him renewed faith. He is certain you still love him. You're the only one in the world who is oblivious. You are resistant, but give yourself a break. I can only hope that when your head figures out what is in your heart, it won't be too late."

Ainsley considered herself schooled by her best friend in the most uncharacteristic way. "Wow," was the best word to illustrate her reaction.

"I don't know how to interpret your response." Belle took the brush from Ainsley's motionless hand and added a few strokes to her hair, then pushed up on her waves to give them some bounce. "Hug me—now. I have to go."

Ainsley did what she was told. Then Brian appeared in the doorway to escort his bride to the limo. They had a plane to catch. Brian leaned in and gave Ainsley a hug, too. "Thank you for everything," then as he and Belle walked through the front entrance of the church, he added. "And think about giving Tom a second chance."

"Brian!" Ainsley gasped, following the newly weds outside. *What did he know about it?*

"You should listen to them."

"Daddy!" Ainsley exclaimed when William and Rose joined the group to see the bride and groom off. "You are in on it, too?"

"In on what? I'm not in on anything. All I heard is Brian saying something about second chances. It sounds like solid advice to me," William conceded.

"Makes sense to me, too," Rose agreed with her husband.

Out in front of the church, the guests were gathering. Everyone stood together, waiting to throw seeds at the bride and groom as they departed. Another wedding practice in which Ainsley had no intention of taking part.

The new couple reached the limo and, with a wave, they were gone, a string of cans chasing behind them. The crowd dispersed, some heading out to the parking lot, others who weren't ready for the party to end stayed.

As the designated planner, there were closing duties to be done, but there was no hurry. In a meditative state of limbo, Ainsley sat down to catch her breath. The warmth of the late afternoon sun on her shoulders eased the tension.

Belle had been her focus for the past few weeks, but that duty had ended. She could give her attention to other matters. Leading up to today, she had to divide her energy, giving Jesse the short end of the stick. Plans were made for Jesse to accompany Tom to Nashville following the reception. She finally had time for her daughter, and Jesse was about to leave. The decision to allow Jesse to fly to Tennessee left her with regret.

She surveyed the dispersing group until she saw Jesse. Beside Jesse, chatting with two white-haired gentlemen in western suits and fancy boots, was Tom. Watching him conversing with great composure and presence of mind, she understood why those in the industry admired him. He had a knack for handling business seamlessly, both musical and personal. The feelings she had experienced during the ceremony and once more at the reception resurfaced.

She could explain the emotions from before as stress-related. It had overwhelmed her with the planning and responsibility. She had been nervous about making the speech and toasting the couple. All good excuses for her to have been sensitive. But what was it this time? What logical reason was there at present for the waves of feelings washing through her?

Lost in her own thoughts, Ainsley was caught staring at Tom as he and Jesse approached her directly.

"Well, I guess we're off, too." Tom's resolute stare was unnerving.

Ainsley experienced a reaction to his coming closer and almost uttered a soft hoot-owl "whoo!".

This novel sensation she experienced in response to Tom, which originated from memories of the past, was pushing through the years and into the present. She could recall the effect he had had on her emotions when they used to be together.

His unwavering confidence and self-assuredness with which he carried himself were things about him that attracted her back then. She could not deny it attracted her to him still. But with an abundant supply of water under the bridge, all she was experiencing was pressure.

"Won't you please come to the airport with us?" Jesse broke the energetic exchange between her parents.

Ainsley turned to Jesse, and the emotions found an outlet. "Oh, baby. I miss you already."

With things wrapping up in Nashville, Tom had to ensure he tied all the strings of responsibilities. He was taking Jesse with him. Inside, Ainsley was not in favor of it, but she kept that to herself. It was a significant amount of travel for a brief stay, but Jesse had presented a logical case in support and she could only agree.

Tom had stayed out of the debate as they worked out the pros and cons. He had stood back in a neutral position, but his very presence had been an influence. His confidence had won over her hesitancy. His certainty that Jesse was coming with him had given Ainsley no option but to let her go.

"I want to say goodbye from right here." Ainsley poured herself over her child. "It is a way better place for getting all gushy than in a crowded airport, don't you agree?"

"I guess'so. But I'm a kid and I don't care about other people like y'all do." Jesse spoke the truth from her ten-year-old perspective. Her vernacular surprised Ainsley. It didn't seem like she could have adopted a southern drawl so quickly. Adams obviously spent a good deal of time with them.

Rose and then William joined in on the goodbyes, each taking their turn hugging their grandchild.

Then Ainsley moved in for one more hug. "You have a good time and be a good girl."

Tom stepped forward, taking Jesse's hand in his. "Just two days and she'll be home."

Tom didn't say goodbye. There was sadness when he met her gaze, and Ainsley experienced the emotions, but it was more of a sense of loss. She couldn't ignore the urge within her to, for once, be included among those leaving.

Ainsley stood hand in hand beside her father, who gave her a couple squeezes as if to convey support. William had experience with the punch in the gut watching his child leave. Rose stood on the other side with her arm around Ainsley, and the three people watched their most important person in the world climb into the waiting limo.

CHAPTER 28

Replenishing the Hollowness

"Now what?" William asked after the black sedan disappeared from view.

Good question, Ainsley thought. Then, out loud she said, "I must close things up here. Make sure the professionals leave the place the way we found it. I have to move the flower arrangements into the church, and that's about it."

"We can help," William offered, and Rose nodded.

"Let's get started."

The three of them got busy, and it was gratifying to have the support. When the rental place and the caterers had gathered their contributions, and the DJ had packed up the sound system, a church staff member inspected the facility and signed off the OK. In a short time, the only evidence there had been an event was the canopy under which it took place. The crew that assembled it would arrive soon.

Ainsley sensed her father was about to speak. "Don't say it again, Dad."

William protested in fun. "Now what?" he repeated, despite his daughter's warning.

"It's only four-thirty. Would you like to come over?" Rose invited.

"No, thanks, Mom." It was Ainsley's go-to response.

"Then will we see you tomorrow for Sunday service?"

"Yes..." Ainsley answered affirmatively.

Rose had skipped a step in their exchange. She left out the part where she would urge Ainsley to accept her invitation by extending a second offer to join them that evening. When asked again, Ainsley would have answered yes.

On the drive home, she reflected on how differently her mother had behaved. Rose hadn't criticized her once. She had been above complimentary when acknowledging what she had done with Belle's wedding. Then she agreed to stay and help when William suggested it? Rose usually snubbed her nose at doing what she considered work the staff should be doing.

Finally, there was the single invitation to come over for the evening and no protest when Ainsley declined. All these new behaviors resulted in her ending up alone in her own abode when she could have been spending the evening with her folks.

Once inside, she received a greeting from a dancing dog, who celebrated her person's homecoming. First thing was to walk Brooke, so Ainsley went upstairs to change clothes. Moving past Jesse's bedroom, she glanced at the door that sat slightly ajar against the frame.

Feeling compelled to reach for the door, Ainsley wanted to sweep it aside to see if Jesse was there lounging on her bed, maybe listening to her iPod. Knowing Jesse would not be there, Ainsley was afraid the emptiness in the room would overwhelm her. The conflicting imaginings rendered her immobile.

Jesse had been gone on previous occasions. She had gone on vacations with Rose and William. She had sleepovers with Emily. Jesse had been staying with Tom, and Ainsley hadn't felt so disturbed by her absence as she did at this moment. Though she had made some headway in adjusting to life in Jesse's absence, her resolve was being tested. Why was this hitting her so hard?

Ainsley let her arm drop, then turned to see Brooke staring at her with a curious expression.

"None of this makes sense to you, either, does it?" The border collie cocked her head to the side and perked up her ears. Ainsley changed her clothes. There was ample time to take the dog for a romp in the park.

Brooke had a copious amount of energy to burn after having slept while waiting for her people to return, so Ainsley grabbed the ball and Chuckit! stick. Brooke loved to run across the park's massive lawn for a game of fetch. As they ambled to the park, Brooke took care of business, and after Ainsley threw the ball for her at least a dozen times, the dog seemed satisfied.

"It's easy for you to be happy, isn't it, girl?"

She reflected on a recent conversation with Jesse, in which they compared the happiness of dogs and children. Jesse had been upset with adults for having a hard time being happy. Dogs and children were also alike in other matters. They loved without considering the consequences. If only it were that simple.

She then remembered Belle's parting comments. Belle had suggested she was thinking too much. Even Brian had asked her to listen to her heart. Ainsley had gotten by for a long time being rational and ignoring what was in her heart. Now that everyone was with someone, and she was still alone, maybe she should consider their advice.

"Ahoy, Ainsley," came a voice from afar.

"Dale?" she greeted the aerospace engineer warmly as he approached. It was comforting to see the smile of a familiar face.

"I was just taking one last walk through this lovely park before I return to the base in Arizona. I am going to miss this town."

"It's nice to see you." She held out her hand for a shake and he reached in for a half hug. "You're heading back already?"

"I've finished the upgrades at the Air Base and trained the personnel on the new protocols we implemented."

Embarrassed she hadn't returned his calls, it seemed wrong to make excuses. Within her silence, Ainsley was aware of the awkwardness.

"I'm sure I'll be visiting Scott while he is stationed here."

Ainsley understood what Dale was hinting at. She wanted to feel hopeful about him. She wanted to say, "Maybe we should get together," but that wasn't the truth. Her silence must have conveyed enough.

"Well, Miss Ainsley Tobin. It was a pleasure to meet you. In the brief period I knew you, I could tell you are a very special woman."

"You take care, Dale." She offered him a hug, which he gallantly accepted.

"If you're ever in Tucson, look me up."

Dale turned to go, gave a look back and a wave, then strolled out of the park.

After Ainsley called for the dog who had wandered off about twenty yards looking for marks that the other dogs had left on one of the giant redwood trees, she filled her lungs deep and let out a soulful breath.

During the return walk, she considered her feelings towards Dale. When they first met, she could admit to feeling excited. He was attractive, and they had chemistry. In comparison, their accidental meeting today exposed a clear lack of connection.

She realized there was no reason to pursue a relationship with Dale. She had been so busy and had forgotten about him over the past few weeks. It hurt to think she may have missed an opportunity, and it added to her emptiness.

Spurred on by the farewell meetup with Dale, she longed to fill the hollowness within. She needed to be with people. She called Rose. "Does the offer still stand? Can I come over?"

Ainsley knew the answer and was grateful for the opportunity to spend time with her parents. A few months ago, this would have been the last thing she would feel. Leading with her heart, she headed out in the darkening dusk towards comfort.

Leaving the pavement, the tires squealed under the Jeep as Ainsley rounded the corner and headed up the driveway to the old familiar farmhouse. The light coming through the windows invited her, and she realized how long it had been since she was traveling in a hurry towards the house instead of away.

As she approached her parents' farm, she was fighting waves of emotion. Why did these waves keep coming?

She tapped on the familiar front porch screen. When no one came out, she tried to go in, but the door was locked. Around the corner, she went to the side door, knowing it was always open.

Through the shadows of the dark kitchen, she caught the blue of the television glowing under the swinging family room door. She could hardly believe her eyes when she swung through the door and saw her folks cuddling on the sofa, both pairs of eyes glued to the screen. Rose motioned for her to come in, so she sat down quietly in her father's recliner.

The news story her folks were concentrating on was about a rescued hiker that became stranded on the cliffs above the sea near Salmon Creek Beach. She waited for the segment to end and for Rose to turn off the volume. Instead, Rose stood up and offered to make some tea. Rose didn't even demand Ainsley join her in the kitchen when she left the room.

"Lots of changes, Ains. Look." William proudly held the television remote. "She even leaves me the controls."

Ainsley wore her reaction to her parents' transformations on the outside but remained speechless.

"In the beginning, it was unsettling, but there are benefits. Your mom is becoming a new person. You'll adjust to it, too." William soothed.

"I'm going to help her with the refreshments." Ainsley nodded and stood up, still uncertain she wasn't in the wrong house. In the other room, Rose was busy preparing hot beverages.

"Have you had dinner? Your father and I ate leftovers. Truthfully, we were not that hungry after the late lunch at the reception." Rose was chatting as soon as Ainsley stepped through the threshold.

"Thank you, but I'm not hungry for dinner, either. But are there any cookies to eat with the tea?"

"You have always had a taste for the sweets. We have the lemon ones you like." Rose reached into the pantry.

Ainsley remained silent. Why wasn't Rose giving a speech about the importance of a balanced meal? Cookies for dinner?

"Mom?" Ainsley expected to discover an imposter had invaded her mother's body.

"What is it, Ains?" Rose hadn't called her by her nickname since, well... she couldn't remember when her mother stopped calling her Ains. Hearing the nickname brought a sentimental wave, not unlike the ones she had been experiencing repeatedly. Rose waited for her to speak.

"I just thought we could talk."

Rose waited again, then began, "I remember the day you and Jesse moved out on your own. It was mid-winter and Jesse was so tiny. It was freezing cold, and I was so worried." Rose paused and her eyes drifted as she recounted the memory.

"How I yearned to follow you. I questioned, who will protect you? How could you manage without me to predict the future and steer you away from harm? Keeping you safe had been my only thought. All my interfering prevented you from experiencing life."

"I know how you feel. It's taking all my energy to stop myself from jumping on a plane to Tennessee."

"Jesse is experiencing life, and I admire you for allowing it."

"It is the hardest thing I have ever done." Ainsley continued to share her fears. "I acknowledge it is irrational. Tom will do everything and more to protect Jesse."

"Yes, Tom is an attentive father. He slid into the role with no experience. He loves Jesse, and she loves him. It seems to come naturally to them."

"For both of them."

The conversation faded when Rose became focused on the tea. Ainsley's mind wandered as she reflected on how easy it had been for Jesse to love Tom. She was happy for them but sad for her own self. She heard again her best friend's advice to listen to her heart. And Brian and William both told her something about following her heart. She understood the concept, but the need to protect herself was paramount.

When Ainsley was talking to Belle, she had been speaking from the heart. Tom had heard her speaking to Belle, and it encouraged him. Maybe that was why every time they locked eyes, she noticed the wave of emotion. The feelings were normal for most humans, but for her, they were foreign. It had been a while since she had allowed herself to feel.

"Are you okay, Ainsley?"

Ainsley looked up from the surface of the kitchen table on which she'd been concentrating. She became startled by Rose standing before her, holding a tray with a kettle of tea, cups, and cookies.

"Of course. I'm fine…"

"Then follow me. Let us all have tea and cookies and watch TV."

Ainsley wasn't tripping any more over her mother's softer, more easy-going side. Snacking in front of the TV with guests? The old

Rose wouldn't have allowed it. As her father predicted, she was liking the new Rose.

They sat as a family would, the three of them all sipping tea and crunching shortbread while watching TV. After watching a movie, William was the first to call it a night.

"Good night, sweetie." William addressed his daughter.

The dog who had been dozing by her feet lifted her gaze when she stood up and put her arms around William's neck. "G'nite, Daddy."

"It's bedtime for me, too." Ainsley remained on her feet. "I should head home."

Brooke understood and jumped to standing, followed by a brief stretch and a yawn.

"You're welcome to stay here tonight. No sense in being lonely while Jesse is gone."

"That is a wonderful offer, but I am feeling so much better. Thank you, Mom. For everything." In that blanket thank you, Ainsley felt thankful for all the caring and concern Rose had provided over the years, and apologetic for being difficult when what Rose did was only try to help. In hindsight, it was tragic to have wasted so many precious moments being resentful.

Mother and daughter hugged, and the healing energy that moved between them was undeniable. They each knew without speaking that the past was mending, and they could move forward.

Ainsley drove home feeling very different. All the positive changes Rose had been implementing since seeking the advice of a therapist were spreading. William was happier than ever, and Ainsley was benefiting, too.

She and Rose were dancing with different choreography, and she felt the safety and security a daughter should expect. The cottage didn't seem empty at all that night when Ainsley returned, and when she turned out the light for bed, she slept in peace.

CHAPTER 29

Releasing the Toxins

Waking up without Jesse in the house, though not ideal, had its perks. Ainsley had the bathroom to herself. Taking time for self-care in the shower, Ainsley wasn't worried about using all the hot water. She luxuriated in the soothing steam, felt relaxed by the comforting aromas of her various hair and skin products, and allowed herself an extended post-shower routine of pampering.

Once finished in the bathroom, Ainsley collected the ingredients for a detox smoothie. Watermelons, cucumbers, lemon juice, apple cider vinegar, and cranberry juice—everything she needed. With the concoction delivering the expected healing effects—rehydrating and replenishing—Ainsley slipped a Mindful Yoga disk into the player and followed along. There was just enough time for stretching and meditating before church.

After church, Ainsley went to see the horse. With all the preparation for Belle's wedding, Casey hadn't been ridden for days. He was feeling a little frisky, so Ainsley turned him loose in the arena to let off some steam. As soon as she unsnapped the lead, the horse took off bucking and kicking up his heels.

First, he ran in one direction, then the other just for the fun of it. He stopped to sniff the arena flooring, which was a mixture of sand and dirt, and blew up a cloud of dust when he snorted. The dust must have been too good to leave alone because Casey pawed up an even bigger cloud before lowering himself down to roll. When coated with a thick layer of dirt, he jumped up, ran, bucked, and kicked out.

When Casey had had enough of a romp, he came over to the side and Ainsley retrieved him. It was time to meet up with Phillip and Emily for a trail ride through the orchards.

It was a pleasant afternoon with plenty of California sunshine. The coastal influence of fog that was normal for summer was absent in the fall and, on this September afternoon, things were warming up.

"So, Em," Ainsley engaged with the youngster she had come to love as her own, "how is it to be back in school?"

Emily, who wasn't near as talkative as Jesse, seemed to open up without Jesse there to monopolize the conversation. She told Ainsley she was happy with the sixth grade teacher and glad she and Jesse were in the same class.

"How does it feel to be the big kid on campus?" As sixth graders, this was Emily and Jesse's final year at the elementary school.

"The teachers told us, as the oldest students, we had the responsibility to set good examples for all the little kids," Emily explained. "But I like that we can boss the younger ones around and not worry about getting beat up."

The adults laughed, and Emily seemed pleased to have told a joke. The trio of riders rode on and talked, sticking to general topics until Emily galloped ahead.

"This being friends," Phillip said as he had found an opportunity to talk to Ainsley, "It might take time to adjust."

"We have always been friends. Nothing has changed." Ainsley was hoping Phillip hadn't regressed back to obsessiveness.

She thought it ironic that both Tom and Phillip mentioned it would be difficult being just friends. An interesting coincidence, in her opinion, as the two relationships were completely different.

"No, I know we are only friends. I am so grateful my foolishness didn't ruin that. But I also am afraid of how things are still going to change."

"Everything changes, Phil."

"I'm talking about you, Ainsley." Phillip was straining to say what was on his mind.

"Me?"

"I can see great things for Jesse now that you and Tom will be co-parenting. It seems to make Jesse happy. Maybe it makes you happy, too…"

"What do you mean?" Ainsley asked, thinking. *Here we go again.* Another person acting like they knew something Ainsley didn't know.

"I'm just saying you and Tom have a connection. At one time, there must have been something there. That kind of chemistry only comes once in a lifetime." Phillip looked straight ahead, focusing on his horse's ears.

Ainsley felt Phillip's emotions and suspected he was thinking of his late wife. "Oh, Phil. Désirée was your 'once in a lifetime,' but don't seal yourself off from having that again. With an open heart, you will find someone again." Though Ainsley said it, she wasn't sure of it herself.

"Remember what you just said, Ainsley. Think about that with Tom West."

"Me and Tom?"

"I'm just saying." Phillip paused, then continued, "He isn't the only fish in the sea."

Phillip then squeezed his horse's sides with his legs and galloped away to catch up with his daughter, leaving Ainsley to ponder.

"Oh, fiddle-faddle!" Ainsley exclaimed in frustration and urged Casey to quicken the pace. She would contemplate Phillip's comment later. Right now, she wanted to enjoy the rest of the ride. When she caught up with the other two riders, they all rode on together, talking and joking and laughing.

"That was fun. Thanks for inviting me," Ainsley said as she pulled the saddle off Casey's back.

Standing next to his horse, Phillip said, "I'm glad you had fun. I love seeing you happy. Don't forget how much fun you can have with me and Emily."

"What are you trying to say?"

"As your friend, I feel compelled to wish you a happy future with Tom West, if that's what you want. You and he will make a solid team as parents, or whatever else. I just don't want you to forget about us," Phillip answered.

She could see he was struggling to wrap his mind around her connection with Tom. Phillip knew a small amount about the history between Tom and her; that their relationship had ended in hurt. Was Phillip feeling protective?

"You and Emily are an important part of my life, Phillip. I will never forget about you. And I assure you, I am happy, and I'm not planning a future with anyone."

"I know. You say you're fine by yourself." Phillip had heard the speech before over the course of their friendship. "But you deserve to share your happiness with someone. If that someone is Tom West, then so be it. Just be careful."

The slight sneer in his voice when Phillip said Tom's name brought out defensiveness in Ainsley. "Tom is not a bad guy, and I have a good reason to get along with him. He is Jesse's father and as long as he is good for her, there is no problem."

"Okay," Phillip retreated. "Message received."

Columbus Day was a freebie, not part of the weekend, nor a regular day off, and Ainsley woke up wishing she had the same restful sleep as she had had the night before. The only thing that shone a light on the day was that Jesse was coming home. Jesse and Tom would fly from Nashville and touch down in the late afternoon.

With nothing to do while waiting, Ainsley needed a distraction. Something that required focus—exploring new recipes. First, she spent a good chunk of time deliberating over what to make and creating a plan. She was going to use the stove and the oven, making several recipes at one time because she liked the challenge.

She chose a pop music playlist on her cell phone, connected her phone to Jesse's little bluetooth speaker and began to sing. While her creative juices were flowing, time slipped by. When she realized, according to the itinerary, that Jesse and Tom were in the air, her breath got caught mid-exhale.

Jesse had asked Ainsley if she would be there to greet them when they landed, but Ainsley explained to Jesse that as long as Tom had made the arrangements for a limo, Ainsley decided it would be fine to let the professionals do the driving. Well, now she had changed her mind. She wanted to see Jesse as soon as possible. She would go to the airport and surprise her daughter.

She arrived an hour before the flight was due. Upon checking in at the front desk of the private airport, they gave her directions to the lounge, where she could wait. Instead of waiting in the private airport, she made the short walk to the main entrance of the Charles M. Schulz-Sonoma County airport.

Inside, the airport was teeming with activity. Ainsley found a comfy chair in a spot she could do some people watching. When it was time, she moseyed back to the separate part of the airport where private charter jets departed and arrived and stood looking out the window of the lounge. She knew Jesse's plane tail number by heart, but couldn't read the tails of the planes as they landed and departed. She was gazing out the gigantic wall of windows when from behind her she heard, "Surprise!" Jesse came running to her mother.

"I was going to surprise *you*." Ainsley had planned on greeting her daughter with calmness, maybe a hug and a kiss. When Jesse lunged through the open door of the lounge and Ainsley saw her child's face, it was as if the girl had been born all over again.

"Hello, Ainsley." The words broke into her reverie.

"Tom?" The moment their eyes connected, Ainsley realized a strong desire to be in Tom's arms, too. Defusing the intense feelings and redirecting the awkwardness she felt, she asked, "Do you have baggage?"

"Doesn't everybody?" Tom answered with a grin.

"You know what I mean." Her discomfort amplified the perplexing situation.

"Yes." His brief answer to her absurd question did nothing to assuage the interaction, and his grin widened as he sensed her embarrassment.

"Yes, you have baggage?" She asked in a deflective move. "Or, yes, you know what I mean?"

Amusement danced in Tom's eyes as he enjoyed this bantering game.

"You two are acting like you've never seen each other before." Jesse was getting impatient. "How long are you going to stare at each other?"

Ainsley and Tom turned back to their daughter and laughed. Tom started looking around. "Where is Ed? I thought I ordered a limousine for Jesse."

"I canceled Ed and drove myself."

"Well, ain't that a hoot? Now, I have no ride."

Ainsley hadn't considered Tom. She felt bad for an instant, then Tom and Jesse laughed.

She hadn't a clue what was funny until Jesse explained, "The car service called Dad as soon as you called. We knew you were coming to the airport."

Tom and Jesse exchanged an inside glance. Tom winked. Jesse giggled.

"What is going on?" Ainsley asked.

"Nothing." Jesse shrugged.

"Nothing at all," Tom agreed, "but, since you canceled my ride, I'll need a lift home. If it's not too much trouble?"

"Didn't you say the driver came anyway for the others? Why didn't you ride with them?"

Ainsley winked at Jesse, who knew her mother wouldn't just leave Tom stranded at the airport. The three of them walked out together.

"It's a good thing we don't have many suitcases, Dad." Jesse said when they got to the Jeep. "We don't even have a trunk to store stuff."

"When are you going to get a proper car?" Tom teased as he folded his long legs into the front seat area.

Ainsley and Tom laughed with too much exuberance at his comment.

"Not that funny, Mom." Jesse seemed well aware her parents were acting peculiar.

Ainsley took the highway instead of going over the back roads that cut across the county, even though it was a longer drive. Jesse recited stories of their adventures in Nashville and Ainsley listened with interest. The pauses between Jesse's stories grew longer and soon the stories stopped. Glancing back, she and Tom looked over their shoulders at their child, whose head had fallen to rest on the roll bar. Her eyes were closed and so was her mouth.

"Finally, she sleeps," Ainsley said.

"I noticed it's the only time she's not talking." Tom sighed.

"She is a talker. If it's quiet, it means Jesse is sleeping."

"Jesse is so lively and full of energy. She seems to know a lot about so many things for such a youngster." Tom continued to look straight ahead as he spoke.

"Well, when she's not talking or sleeping, she has her head in a book." Ainsley continued on the subject, keeping her eyes on the road.

"In some ways, she is like an old soul."

"It is a tricky balance because, in most ways, she is still just a little girl. She has had a lot of adult situations thrown at her. Made her grow up fast."

"Growing up fast seems to run in your family," Tom observed.

"An accurate statement."

"That's another reason I didn't stay in Nashville," Tom confessed.

"Another reason?" Ainsley invited Tom to elaborate.

"I am worried about Jesse. I want her to have a normal childhood."

Ainsley knew without a doubt Tom was head over heels in love with their child. He had fallen hook, line and sinker. Something told her he was operating entirely out of concern for her.

"We were on the go a lot this weekend," Tom said. "I wore her out. I won't ever plan such a busy schedule again."

"Kids live their lives on too much planning these days. I know some parents who button down on a calendar every waking moment of their children's days. There's nothing wrong with having a schedule, but at this age, there needs to be a lot more downtime."

"I thought this was going to be a simple transition for me." Tom leaned on the headrest. "I have been around kids, and we get along great, but being a dad is a novel experience. It seemed easy at first. Make a few adjustments in my routine, delegate more responsibilities to the band, and outsource more of the business duties to my manager. I want to have all the time with Jesse I can get."

"The responsibility of having a child is a sacrifice from day one. That's why I never told you about Jesse. I gave you the option."

"The option? Telling me would have given me an option. Keeping Jesse a secret? That was criminal." Tom's frustration turned to animosity and resentment and he was letting it out on Ainsley.

"That seems harsh." Ainsley had enough guilt without having Tom to remind her. "A criminal? You left me, not the other way around. Child abandonment. Also, a crime."

"I didn't know I was leaving you with my baby. I can't be guilty of abandoning a child I didn't know existed."

"We made love. What do you think happens when you have sex?" Ainsley attempted to keep her volume down, though her need to defend herself made her want to shout.

"You had heard of birth control, hadn't you?" Tom asked.

"Had you?" Ainsley shot back. "I wasn't even eighteen years old. You were an adult. I don't recall you taking care of the issue. I don't remember you putting on a condom that first time."

Tom backed down as his voice trailed off. "You seemed so mature, so much older... I just thought..." Tom looked out the side of the car, "Weren't you taking the pill?"

Fighting the urge to be angry, Ainsley let the subject drop. The absurdity of his confession. He thought she was on birth control. Shaking her head, she realized it was all water under the bridge. They rode the remainder of the trip in silence, with both Ainsley and Tom having retreated to neutral corners to nurse their wounds.

Tom used his cell phone to open the gate at the end of his driveway, and Ainsley drove through. The formal turnaround looked cold and unfamiliar in the fading twilight.

"What? No valet service today?" Ainsley brought the Jeep to a halt and waited for Tom to exit.

"Can I say 'good night' to Jesse?" Tom asked.

"She's asleep."

The exhausted child was out like a light in the back seat. Ainsley refused to look at Tom. She felt bad but couldn't stop herself from being mean.

"She can sleep here tonight. We can put her right to bed. I hoped you might come in so we can talk some more." Tom stepped out of the Jeep.

"Your weekend with Jesse is over." Ainsley showed no mercy.

CHAPTER 30

The Pool Date

It was a short drive home from Tom's mansion. Ainsley cut off the engine and let the vehicle free-wheel to a rest in the desired spot in the driveway. With the motor now silent, and the tires stationary, Jesse's eyes fluttered, then opened. Disoriented, she asked for her dad, then showed her disappointment when she discovered he wasn't there.

"Your father promised he will see you tomorrow." Ainsley soothed. She didn't know that for certain.

"Will he pick me up from school?" Jesse asked.

"He didn't say."

The fury that controlled her at the mansion had since dissipated to be replaced by remorse. She had struck out with a broad swing to punish Tom, and her hurtful blow had hit Jesse, too.

"It's late, Jess, and we have to get up early. Run up and take a shower."

Jesse did as she was told, but seemed to be in a daze.

In denying her daughter the chance to say goodbye to her dad, Ainsley had blindsided her. She realized the mistake of taking such actions and hoped to be in better control of her emotions regarding her daughter's relationship with Tom.

Ainsley tucked her freshly showered daughter into bed. Jesse had never fully awakened from her roadway slumber, but she did not fall to sleep right away when she hit the sheets. As soon as Ainsley left the room, she heard Jesse's soft voice and knew her daughter was talking to Tom.

With no right to hear the conversation, Ainsley went to bed wondering how many times Jesse would forgive her for being a jerk. She rolled over and flipped her pillow to the cool side. Eventually her train of thoughts switched off and she fell into a fitful slumber.

Dropping Jesse at school the next day, Ainsley was relieved to begin the week with their normal routine. Her relief disintegrated when she arrived at work to face mountains of mail, backed up from the non-delivery holiday. By nine-thirty, Ainsley realized she would not get the job done in eight hours. She asked the supervisor for help.

"We are short-staffed. There will be no route assistance," said her supervisor.

"I can't work overtime. You know I have to pick up my daughter."

"Of course, and you know I always do my best to accommodate carriers with family obligations. We are down seven carriers, and three routes are not covered. It's always this way after a holiday," the supervisor explained.

"So what you're saying is *mandatory* overtime." Ainsley knew the policy. An employee's family was a personal issue and not the responsibility of the post office. Her supervisor routinely went above the policy and tried to be as sensitive to his carriers as he could. She knew her manager was in a bind.

Managing the extra volume as best she could, Ainsley clocked off only twenty-five minutes later than her actual quitting time. She had texted Jesse she was going to be late, and got a text back saying that Tom had met her at school, where they were both waiting.

When picking up Jesse at the normal time, there was a line of cars waiting to pick up students. Since she was late, Ainsley drove right in and circled the area. She searched through the few remaining people still gathered in front of the school and her eyes caught the tallest figure in the crowd. As she drew closer, she noticed a crew of Tom West admirers clustered around him.

Jesse pulled Tom away with her and climbed into the car. Tom asked, "Can I hitch a ride?"

"Hop in." Ainsley took no time to respond. If she hung out any longer, the assistant principal who oversaw the student pickup process would be on her case.

Ainsley tried to, but could not decipher how Tom was feeling today. Was he angry? Would he be cold and distant? She wasn't sure what the next steps would be.

"Where's your truck?" Ainsley asked after they had left the pickup loop.

"At home." Tom's answer didn't help Ainsley decide on what direction to drive.

"You want me to deliver you to your house?" she asked.

"How are we going to do this?" Tom answered Ainsley's question with a question.

"Do what? What way do you need me to drive?" Ainsley was no stranger to "the question game." She glanced at Jesse in the rear-view mirror. At the moment, the child was unaware of the adults' unusual conversation.

"You are something else, Ainsley," Tom said, still not giving her driving directions. His behavior was unsettling.

"I'm assuming you need to go home," Ainsley announced. Tom's behavior caught her off guard. He wasn't angry or aloof, nor was he warm and friendly. He was on the border of creepy and psychotic.

Tom looked away, Ainsley presumed, to take a moment to think of where he needed to go, a question that should have been easy to answer. He twisted his neck to look at Jesse, then he asked, "How would you like to come over and go swimming?"

"Goodie!" Jesse exclaimed without hesitation. "Can we, Momma?"

Going from uncomfortable to bizarre, the situation took a turn she could never have predicted. With Jesse waiting for an answer, Tom had put Ainsley on the spot.

"Homework comes first." Ainsley avoided being the bad guy.

"You are welcome to come, too," Tom offered.

Except for her eyes, which narrowed in response, Ainsley stayed neutral regarding the invitation.

"Are you gonna come swimming?" Tom pushed for a commitment. "You look like you could use some leisure time."

"What's the matter with the way I look?" Ainsley was not interested in how she looked, but wanted to answer with a question.

"Not a darn thing." Tom held his eyes on Ainsley as she drove.

When Ainsley dared to glance at him, Tom's expression remained unchanged.

Upon arriving at the huge entry to Tom's place, Ainsley left the engine idling in neutral, waiting for Tom and Jesse to disembark.

"You are staying, right, Mom?" Jesse asked.

Ainsley had no intention of doing so and didn't want to give the two other people an opportunity to change her mind.

"Please, Mom?" Jesse asked again as she and Tom looked at Ainsley. His way of using her daughter against her was disgraceful, but he seemed unashamed.

"It won't be much fun if you don't come swim with us. Pleeeeze," Jesse beseeched.

"We'll see," Ainsley said as she drove away.

Brooke was jumping and falling over herself when Ainsley arrived at the cottage. Ainsley packed her canvas bag with her suit, a towel, and sunblock.

"Let's go swimming!" she called to the dog, who was ready on the spot.

"I knew you would come," Jesse said when she and Adams met Ainsley in the driveway. "Adams and I made a bet. I won."

Adams winked at Jesse, then said to Ainsley, "Good to see you again, Miss Ainsley." Together they walked to the main house.

"Tom has some matters he's tending to but will finish shortly. Meanwhile, he would like you to make yourself at home."

"C'mon, Mom!" Jesse's excitement wasn't just because she won a bet. "I'll show you to the room I picked out for you."

Ainsley followed Jesse through a side door behind where Tom parked his truck, along with several other cars. Once inside, they walked past what looked like offices where Ainsley observed a number of people hustling and moving about. Continuing on, she and Jesse skirted the perimeter of the formal entry hall and arrived at the double doors she recognized as the family wing. She decided Tom's house seemed more like a corporate headquarters than a home.

Jesse led them down the hall of the family wing to a room just to the other side of the doors she recognized as Jesse's and Tom's quarters. Jesse opened and quickly closed the door. "Oopsies. Wrong room."

"Who's in there?"

"Nobody, at the moment. I think it's Adams's room. I always get lost in this place." Jesse was still adjusting.

Jesse moved down the hall to another door and peeked in. "This is the one."

Ainsley glanced around the room and felt like a hotel guest, as the house that had seemed like a building full of executive offices morphed into a luxury resort.

"We didn't pick the furniture for these rooms. Someone on the staff did," Jesse commented. "I'll be right back."

Looking at Jesse as if she didn't recognize her, Ainsley asked her retreating daughter, "Someone on the staff?"

Jesse lived in a household with a staff. Ainsley stepped into the room Jesse offered and set her bag on the four-post pine frame bed. Brooke then leapt onto it.

The room was decorated in a southwestern style with a pine dresser and nightstands to match. Hanging on the wall at the front of the bed was a giant woven dreamcatcher. On the other walls hung a sand painting and an oil painting depicting a rodeo action scene with cowboys riding horses and roping and handling cattle. Making the luxury spa resort feeling of the room complete, Ainsley saw, through an open door, a private bathroom. "I bet there's a walk-in shower," she said to herself. Upon further investigation, she was right.

Jesse came back to the room and together, the two made their way out onto the veranda and onward to the pool. The late afternoon sun beat down, and the water was inviting. Ainsley did some laps while Jesse practiced diving. Starting at the bottom rung and working her way up, Jesse was soon diving from the top rung. "Just like how Brandon taught me." Jesse said proudly. Next, she graduated to the pool's edge.

"Watch. I'm gonna do a dive off the board!" Jesse called, and Ainsley stopped to tread water and offer advice. Jesse had dove into the water from the concrete rim of the pool at Yve's Park, but this was her first time from a diving board. With her arms over her head and pressed against her ears, she stood with her little toes on the edge, but she seemed frozen in place.

"Bend your knees." Tom's voice from behind them was low and calming. "When you lean forward, point your hands towards the water, then just lean forward and straighten your knees."

As if in slow motion, Jesse followed her father's advice, and *swoosh*—she made a beautiful dive.

"Good job, Jess. You look like a pro." Tom was clapping when Jesse came to the surface.

"Way to go, Jesse! Your first dive from a diving board!" Ainsley was proud of her daughter, and complimentary about her efforts. Most first dives end in some aborted abomination that comes nowhere near an actual dive. "It will surprise Brandon when he sees how you can dive."

"Who's Brandon?" Tom stopped clapping and adopted a strict expression.

"My swim coach," Jesse answered, climbing out to do another dive. "Remember? You met him at Yve's Pool."

"Oh, yes." Tom recalled he had taken Jesse to the public pool so she could say goodbye to her teenage swim coach, who was off at college now.

Ainsley had to laugh when Tom's stern manner softened. Had Tom's reaction been that of a protective father? Or was it jealousy? Maybe both, she theorized.

"Stand down," Ainsley teased. "Jesse doesn't have a boyfriend." The very thought of Tom thinking he would already have to scare off the boys was amusing.

"I wasn't thinking about Jesse having a boyfriend." On the defensive, Tom chose a seat under the pool-side umbrella and set down his cell phone on the table.

From the chair, Tom sat and surveyed Ainsley as she climbed out of the water. "I thought there might be yet another man in your life, Ainsley. You could have many boyfriends for all I know." Tom's smile showed he was teasing.

"Yes, I suppose I could." She laughed and snorted at the same time. "There is Brandon, whom I've known since he was a sweet child. He is grown up now. But I am no Mrs. Robinson."

"So, you're not a cougar. Do you still prefer older men?" Tom seemed pleased to continue the game.

"I don't have a type and I have no spare time to develop one."

"Oh, no, Dad." Jesse was making her way up the ladder after another dive. "Here comes Mom's 'I don't have time to date, I'm happy the way things are' speech."

"Jesse." Ainsley shook her head at Jesse for mocking her. It surprised her how much Jesse was paying attention.

"What about you, Tom? Are you a happy single guy? Do you date? What is your type?" Ainsley wanted to shift the focus off herself.

"I've dated a few women here and there. Been on some blind dates. Don't have a type either. Just never clicked with anyone else." Tom took his eyes off the view of the valley and rested them on Ainsley. "Does that satisfy your curiosity?"

Satisfy her curiosity? Ainsley stared back at Tom trying to think of an answer. As they focused on each other, neither Tom nor Ainsley saw Jesse sneaking up from behind until she unloaded a bucket of water over the top of Tom's head.

"I'll get you!" Tom lunged for Jesse and got her by the arm.

Jesse squealed in fake distress as Tom scooped her up into his arms and tossed her into the water. The commotion had startled the dog, who ran around the pool barking in frustration. The mock fight seemed serious to the dog.

Jesse came to the side. "It's okay, girl. We were just playing." Brooke licked the water from Jesse's face to make sure. Jesse climbed up the steps and collapsed on a chair, out of breath but still laughing.

Tom was out of breath, too, as he lifted himself out of the deep end and turned to sit on the edge. The muscles in his toned arms flexed and the T-shirt he had been wearing when the assault began clung to his torso. Tom peeled the soaked garment over his head, then shook the water off his hair. With a final flick, he cleared it from his face.

Ainsley couldn't take her eyes off Tom and noticed his chest and stomach flexing as he caught his breath. This was not the body of the younger version of him she had known. This was the physique of a man that brought pleasure by just looking at him.

As soon as Tom and Jesse caught their breath, they went back in for a playful game of Marco Polo. When Jesse had run out of energy,

Ainsley wrapped her in a towel and sat her on her lap. "All this activity must have given you quite an appetite. We best be getting home so I can start dinner."

"I was just about to invite you two to stay. Adams is making lasagna." Tom took a towel from his chair.

"Adams is your cook?" The minute details of Tom's life intrigued Ainsley.

"Not officially. We all just cook when the mood strikes and then we share meals with each of our own contributions. It's potluck night every night, and we invite everyone."

"Please, Mom, can we stay?" Jesse asked.

Ainsley wanted to present a reason she and Jesse should go back to their own home but lost focus as Tom was drying off his arms and legs.

"Can we stay?" Jesse prompted for an answer.

Tom stopped rubbing with the towel and returned Ainsley's stare. "She's caving, Jesse. Tilt your head sideways and say 'Pleeeeze.'"

Jesse did as she was told and joined in. They both smiled at her with their ridiculous smiles. Ainsley gave in. "I can't win against the two of you." Ainsley rested her face in her hands.

"Was that a 'yes'?" Tom asked, feeling almost sorry for the vanquished.

"Probably as close to a 'yes' as we're gonna get." Jesse could have inherited her sense of humor from either of her parents as she joined in the banter.

It seemed so beyond normal to be sitting by a pool wasting away the day. Ainsley had to admit she couldn't remember the last time she and Jesse had had a vacation. Pretending she and Jesse didn't have to get up early for work and school the next day, Ainsley decided to enjoy the afternoon for a little while.

The late September angle of the sun lit the area with a warm glow. Jesse was reading a book at the table, resting her feet on the silky, furry dog stretched out beneath her chair. Tom had reposed, still shirtless, on a lounge chair with a paperback book over his face. His rhythmic breathing suggested he was napping.

Even in a relaxed state of slumber, Tom's physical fitness was clear. The muscular legs were the perfect amount of toned and his tanned skin said he spent enough time in the sun to stay healthy. Did celebrities hire out their fitness regimen to be done by staff members? She chuckled at her own joking thoughts. The soft laughter awakened Tom.

"What are you reading?" Ainsley asked, to change the focus before Tom could realize she had been staring.

Startled, Tom sat up and the book tumbled forward. "This is Louis L'Amour," he said when he had recovered his surprise.

"You were deep in sleep. Sorry I woke you," Ainsley said.

"I was dreaming." Tom ran his fingers through his rumpled hair. "I imagined what it would be like to have you and Jesse here with me. Then I woke up to a dream come true." Tom was conscious again and back to his teasing ways.

Ainsley didn't mind being referred to as his dream come true. It was all in fun. "So, Louis L'Amour?" she questioned.

"My dad reads these Western themed novels, then gives them to me. It's not timeless literature, but it's something to share with my father. It makes me feel closer to home when I am so far away."

Tom's candor touched Ainsley. She never thought about Tom's strong family ties. She assumed he swept aside all that when he took up his musical career.

Tom retrieved the bookmark that had fallen to the concrete when he bolted upright. With the placeholder in the book, Tom swung his legs to the side of the chair to face Ainsley.

"It's a shame you chose not to come with us that morning." Tom's face turned a little away, and the dreamy expression disappeared. "How different things would have been, Ainsley."

Ainsley allowed herself to imagine what could have been had she and Tom stayed together and traveled the world and raised their kids and lived happily ever after.

"We have wasted so much time," Tom continued, "but I feel like I no longer have to race to catch up. You and Jesse coming into my life has made me so happy."

"Glad I could help." Ainsley left the fantasy of her dreams and stepped back into reality.

"I am sharing my thoughts and feelings and you act like you are sharing a seat with a stranger on a public transit bus."

"Your dream world is a great place to visit, but the fact is we went our separate ways and there is no going back. You look at me and see the same person, but I have changed. I grew up." Ainsley had retreated, snuffing out the fire Tom had ignited.

"I know how much I hurt you, Ainsley. It's devastating for me to witness such pain, and I've only begun to understand it. On the day we parted, I left without my heart. Despite time passing, I still feel connected to you and seeing you again confirms that nothing has changed for me. I will not stop trying to repair the damage I have done, no matter how long it takes." Tom stood up as he continued to speak. "I will keep showing you how committed I am to you. I will keep trying for me, for Jesse, and for you."

After having spoken his mind, Ainsley watched Tom stride across the veranda, into the kitchen and out of sight. She then noticed Jesse with her head buried in her book. She decided Jesse may or may not have heard Tom's declaration, but she had received the message loud and clear.

Just because Tom was handling his feelings for her with the same fearless conviction as before didn't mean she should abandon her protective ways. His strong confidence hadn't been enough to keep them together once upon a time. She did not expect things to be any different now.

Lying back in the lounge chair, she closed her eyes and let her thoughts rest. The late afternoon breeze feathered across her bare-skinned legs and arms. She took in a deep breath and floated off to gentle slumber.

It was dark when Ainsley awoke. The veranda was bathed in lights and the pool glowed a blueish-green. She wasn't at first sure she wasn't dreaming. Clarity was slow to set in as she looked for Jesse and felt her chin touch upon a Navajo blanket that covered her body.

"It was getting chilly, but I didn't want to wake you. You were resting." Tom's voice wove itself into Ainsley's awareness.

"Where's Jesse?" Ainsley also wanted to know why Tom was there beside her on a lounge chair.

"After dinner she wanted to watch TV, and if your next question is 'Did she finish her homework?', the answer is yes." Tom was catching on to her way of thinking.

"What time is it?" Ainsley glanced at her wrist, then remembered she had taken off her watch before her swim and hadn't buckled it back on.

"It's around eight-thirty." Tom glanced at the digits on his cell phone screen.

"In the evening?" Ainsley always woke from a nap a little grumpy. She realized she was in this picture-perfect scenario of the happy family on a typical evening at home. But this wasn't reality. Reality was her job to go to, and bills to pay. There were babysitters to be arranged and homework assignments due. Ainsley pushed the Navajo down and set her feet to the ground next to Brooke. The dog sat up.

"You must be hungry. Can I heat a plate of lasagna?" Tom asked.

"No, thanks. I have to go home."

Brooke, who had been lying just to the right of her chair, jumped to her feet when she recognized the words 'go home.' Ainsley stood up. "Thank you for your hospitality."

"Why don't you and Jesse stay the night?"

Ainsley knew this was coming. He was becoming predictable.

"I have to go to work in the morning. Jesse's got school," Ainsley stated the facts.

"Jesse is already in bed. And the guest room is ready for you."

"My uniform is at home," Ainsley responded on her way into the house. Tom followed behind.

"I can take Jesse to school and you'll have plenty of time to stop off for your clothes in the morning." Tom was pushing his case hard.

Ainsley continued walking with the dog and Tom followed. She gathered her things from the guest room and found Jesse's bedroom door was ajar. Inside, Jesse's TV was on, but the screen was watching her. Jesse had fallen asleep and was nothing more than a motionless lump, safe and cozy in her bed.

"Now will you stay?"

"This changes nothing. *I* still need to go home."

"I don't want you to go. You're tired, and it's late. I'm not asking you to marry me tonight, Ainsley. I just want to keep you safe."

The quiver in Tom's voice almost made Ainsley agree. This wasn't just about getting his way. His concern was genuine, and it scared her. She crossed the massive entry room to the front doors, where Brooke stood waiting. Her fluffy tail swayed and her dancing eyes said, "Let's go for a ride!"

It wasn't until Ainsley belted herself in the vehicle and the engine rumbled that she dared look into Tom's face. "I'll talk to you tomorrow," she said.

"Can you please let me know when you get to the cottage?"

Tom stood by the fountain as he had done the night before and watched the Jeep circle around before heading to the gate. Ainsley arrived home in under ten minutes and sent Tom a text.

CHAPTER 31

A Message from the Universe

The alarm on the nightstand buzzed, and Ainsley struggled to make it stop. Her hand fumbled around the top of the appliance until she located the little knob. With much more effort than should have been necessary, her fingers located the little mechanism and slid it into the off position.

"Stupid alarm!" She sank into the pillow, hoping to slide back under the covers and return to dreaming, but the magic was gone. She heaved her disappointed self up and into the bathroom.

Splashing water on her face, she evaluated her image and put on a smile to build up her attitude. The positive outward expression began to work on the inside and followed her to her workplace, giving a reason for some teasing from her fellow carriers.

"Look who woke up on the sunny side of the bed." Darrel was the first to notice Ainsley's light spirit and commented.

"Maybe she didn't wake up on either side," Howard chimed in. "Maybe Ainsley woke up in the middle."

"You guys are bad." John tried to come to the rescue, but the heckling continued.

"Maybe she slept in someone else's bed altogether." A voice Ainsley didn't recognize came from Belle's route.

"Was it not your Jeep I saw in West's driveway yesterday afternoon?" John kept the thread alive, much to Ainsley's dismay.

Despite initially deflecting the heckling comments, John switched sides and joined in.

"What, are you spying on me? I expected better from you, John."

"I saw your car, didn't I?"

Ignoring the question, she checked out of the conversation, and the other carriers lost interest. John, however, did not let it die.

"Well? Are the two of you an item?"

"Tom West is my child's father." She was certain John knew this already. Nothing beyond that was anyone's business.

"So, are you two dating or not?" John continued to fish for information.

"We are co-parents. Nothing more. I guarantee you'll see my vehicle at his house and his car at mine. There is nothing more to it than that." Ainsley paused. "And you people need to get a life."

Walking towards the supervisor's desk, Ainsley ended the conversation with John. Still drowning in piles of backed-up mail following the Columbus Day holiday, Ainsley asked for route assistance. Again, she was turned down.

"Sorry. There is nothing I can do. You will have to do your own overtime."

His response did not surprise her. Her supervisor was leveraging against her integrity, and Ainsley knew it was her own fault. When she had more mail than she could deliver in her regular shift, she often absorbed the extra mail and ran her route without proper breaks.

Before leaving the office to begin the street portion of her duties, she texted Tom, asking if he could collect Jesse from school. When Ainsley finished that afternoon, she had put in over an hour of overtime.

On the drive home, Ainsley received a text, and when she pulled into her driveway, Tom's truck was there. The text from Jesse said, "Pete called. He wants me to practice. Dad's taking me to ride."

Jesse met Ainsley as she was getting out of her car. "Pete entered a bunch of us in a playday show at Fieldstone, and I have to practice if I want to be ready."

"Give me a second. I'll drive you to your riding lesson." Ainsley rushed towards the front door. Feeling the urgency, she remembered Jesse had missed a few lessons, and Pete liked his students to look good at horse shows.

"I can run Jesse over right now," Tom offered.

"No, you've already helped so much. I've got it from here." Ainsley was certain Tom had much to do and many other people depending on him. She ran up the stairs, two at a time, tore off her uniform and grabbed her jeans. In less than two minutes, Ainsley was racing down the stairs.

When she tried making the turn at the bottom landing, her leg buckled and her ankle twisted. She experienced an intense pain that ran up her leg as the joint strained. Landing on her backside facing the direction she had come, her momentum continued backwards and her head hit the tile floor.

"MOM!" Jesse got to Ainsley first. "Are you alright?"

"What happened?" Tom asked, not needing an explanation.

"I fell. I think I twisted my ankle." Ainsley still hoped she would be on her feet in a second, but when she tried to sit up, a dizziness overcame her.

"Don't get up just yet. You may have hurt your spine." In an instant, Tom was on his knees beside Ainsley and cradled her head. He could feel a bump already pushing out. "We should get you to the hospital. You could have a concussion."

Spurred by the threat of a hospital visit, Ainsley ignored the spinning walls and sat up. She experienced a darkening from the inside of her eyes.

"Her face is white!" Jesse noticed the change in her mother's complexion. "Is she gonna faint? I've seen people faint on TV but never in real life."

"I'm not gonna faint." Ainsley fought against the urge to lie down. "Let me get up. If you are gonna ride today, we better be going."

"Forget about the riding lesson, Ainsley. We should go to the Emergency."

"Absolutely not. I hate hospitals."

Ainsley's refusal was to be expected, but Tom was taking charge. "No one likes the hospital. Jesse, call 9-1-1."

"No, Jesse." Ainsley ordered.

Jesse froze in place. The dueling orders bewildered her, and she was uncertain which parent to obey.

"It's okay, Jess." Tom saw his daughter's confusion. "You don't have to call. I'll drive your mother myself."

"No, take me to Urgent Care." Ainsley also noticed Jesse's frightened expression.

"Good. We are all being rational." Tom lifted Ainsley up now that he had permission.

"What are you doing?" she protested.

"Taking you to the doctor."

The 20-minute trip to the nearest facility was painful. The ride made Ainsley carsick. Still unable to put weight on her foot, Tom carried her into the waiting room.

"Do I recognize you?" the receptionist asked. "Wait… You're Tom West. We went to school together. I'm Mary."

"Mary Belmont, right?" Tom smiled upon recognizing his classmate from grade school.

"It's Peterson now." Mary held up her left hand, wiggling her fingers, wanting everyone to notice the one with the big rock on it. "I can't believe it's you. You are back in town? Wait 'til I tell Jamie and Christine that Tom West is in my clinic. Do you remember them from school? They are also big fans and we all follow you on social media."

"Well, thank you, Mary. I appreciate that."

"Uh-hum," Ainsley interjected.

"Oh, sorry." Mary returned her attention to the patient and finished with the intake information. "Please wait out here and we'll bring you in shortly."

"You have a social media presence?" Ainsley found the idea amusing, but giggling rattled her brain.

"I have people who handle my accounts. I think there's Twitter and some other ones." Tom lifted Ainsley and carried her from the front desk to a chair in the nearly empty waiting area. There was an older gentleman who seemed unimpressed that there was a celebrity among them. He was more interested in watching a young woman being hoisted around like an invalid to notice who was doing the lifting.

"I could've hobbled, you know."

"Yes, but this is so much more fun." Tom seemed to enjoy holding her in his arms. He paused for effect. "We might as well give my fans a show."

Even in her injured state, she saw the humor, and she leaned forward to place a kiss on Tom's cheek. "How's that for showmanship? Now, will you put me down?"

They called Ainsley for an examination within minutes, and once again, Tom lifted her up, and cradled her into the room.

"They have a wheelchair." Ainsley was so close to Tom's face she could see his five o'clock shadow.

"I enjoy doing it this way better."

"I'm Dr. Davis." The doctor introduced himself as he walked into the exam room.

After a quick look, they ordered an X-ray, which ruled out any broken bones. The doctor's diagnosis was, as Ainsley expected, a moderate sprain on the joint and a major strain on the ligaments and tendons. He also diagnosed her with a hematoma on her head, but no concussion.

"Well, at least they won't have to examine your brain," Tom teased and placed a quick kiss on the crown of her head. "That's a place nobody should look inside of."

"Hey," Ainsley protested, though she knew Tom was teasing. "You are not wrong, though," she admitted in earnest.

Dr. Davis paused and smiled as he witnessed the interaction, then went on with instructions for Ainsley's recovery. "Stay off your feet for at least five days. You may use an over-the-counter anti-inflammatory. Here's a prescription for pain. Depending on your level of discomfort, I recommend filling the order right away."

"Stay off my feet for five days?" Ainsley had heard nothing else that he said. "I have work."

"You shouldn't walk on that leg. Keep that ankle elevated and on ice for the next three to five days, minimum. There will be significant swelling regardless, but if you don't follow instructions, you'll have more pain and less healing."

Three to five days? her thoughts ran around. *I have used all my vacation for the year and have only two days of sick leave accrued.*

"There is no way I can miss any work," Ainsley said, after she tuned out of her mental narrative.

"Don't worry about money. I'll cover you for lost wages," Tom whispered as he lifted her once again into what was more like a protective embrace than a means of transport. "Let me take you home."

Tom fixed up the couch in the cottage for Ainsley when they got there. He retrieved pillows for her leg, then stepped outside to make some calls. She suspected it was about business.

"Hey, Mom," Jesse said upon coming home. Before Tom took Ainsley to the doctor, they had made sure Jesse could stay with Mrs. Dixon while they were gone.

"Hey, baby." Ainsley opened her arms and Jesse snuggled in. She felt the tension in her daughter's little body ease. "I'm fine, Jess."

"And no concussion?" Jesse asked.

"No concussion, but I have a gnarly bump." Ainsley took Jesse's hand. "Here, feel."

Jesse wrinkled her nose when her fingers encountered a lump. "Does it hurt, Mommy?"

"Not really." Ainsley lied.

Tom came in from the front yard and slipped his cell phone into his jeans pocket. He had a concerned expression. It must have been hard for him to witness Jesse so worried. "I am going to pick up your prescription."

"Don't get the drugs. I won't take them." Ainsley kept her arms around Jesse and spoke in a deep, low voice. "I won't do drugs."

"These are not drugs, it's a prescription," Tom clarified.

"What's the difference?"

When Ainsley stayed with her Aunt Ruthie, she learned about all the homeopathic remedies for anything that ails you. "I plan to take something, but it won't be a narcotic. There are some arnica tablets in the cupboard."

"Maybe you do need your head examined," Tom said.

She had her own approach to things and wasn't sure if Tom admired her for it or it annoyed him. Responding to Tom's snarky remark with a pinched face, she moved on to other business. Returning to maternal matters, she turned to Jesse. "I'd better call your grandmother. It looks like we're going to need her help."

Tom went to retrieve the home phone, but when he came back, he chose not to hand the device to Ainsley. "I will take care of you. Both of you. We don't have to bother Rose."

"That's very generous, but you can't run your music business from here." It seemed to Ainsley she and Tom were always at odds.

"It's only for a few days. I insist. This is an opportunity for my staff to demonstrate their ability to handle things."

"It's out of the question. End of story. You should be where you can conduct business. Retreating to my front yard to make deals and arrangements is not how to handle your affairs." Ainsley held out one hand and rested her forehead on the other.

Tom gave in and handed Ainsley the phone. "C'mon, Jess. Let's see what we can rustle up for dinner."

Jesse reluctantly left her mother's arms, and Ainsley dialed, preparing to talk to her mother.

Rose handled the news well. There was no criticism about how reckless Ainsley's actions had been.

"Your father and I were leaving tonight. Ken is managing the shop, so we are able to spend the rest of the week in Mendocino."

"Another couple's retreat?" Ainsley said. "Mom, that is wonderful."

"We can stay home, if you really need me." Rose emphasized the word "need" in such a noticeable manner. She understood her mother was being polite and, for once, she didn't perceive it as patronizing.

"We'll be fine." She knew her parents were working on their relationship, and she admired her mother for it. "You and Dad go. Have fun. Jesse and I will manage. Who's looking after Spencer?"

"We have taken care of the cat. Our neighbors volunteered to replenish his cat food and water bowls.

The decision to excuse Rose from babysitting them was the right one. Rose sounded relieved. But that meant Ainsley was still in a bind. She allowed herself to feel temporarily defeated and lay herself back to rest. She didn't open her eyes when she heard a knock at the door, some conversation she chose not to hear, and a rustling of bags changing hands.

Tom had called the pharmacy for Ainsley's prescription and ordered takeout for dinner. When the commotion at the front door died down, she looked at Tom coming towards her with a fresh ice pack. The ankle was painful, and she couldn't control a wince when Tom lifted the limb to position the ice on the pillow.

"Hurt?" Tom caught Ainsley's cringe and handed her a glass of water.

"A little." Ainsley lied again. It hurt a lot, yet she declined the capsule of pain medication he offered in his open palm. It was irresponsible for her to use even a mild, mind-altering drug when she had Jesse's safety to consider. She took the homeopathic arnica tablet, placing it under her tongue to be absorbed sublingually.

"So?" Tom questioned. "Is Rose coming over?"

"Not exactly." She hedged around the truth.

"There is no room for gray here. Rose is coming, or she isn't. Which is it?"

"She isn't."

"That settles it. Adams shall cancel my flight to Nashville. The responsibilities I can manage over the phone. I'll send someone else for the hands-on part." Tom left the house to make more phone calls, thus ending the debate before it could begin.

She was in no condition to perpetuate a fight. Reaching for the glass and the opioid pill Tom had left sitting in a dish on the lamp table, Ainsley resigned to her fate. "If he insists on staying, I might as well use the drugs."

Within a short time, the effects of the prescription took hold, and she drifted off to the edge of consciousness. She could hear Jesse and Tom talking, but made no sense of their words. At some point she dozed off.

"No, Dad." Jesse's voice coming from the kitchen woke Ainsley. "We don't put on the dressing straight. We wet the leaves or else the dressing tastes too rich."

"Oh, okay." Tom listened as if he had never made a salad before.

Ainsley's nose told her there was food being handled. "What are you guys doing in my kitchen?" Her voice was soft, but audible.

"Oh, you woke up." Jesse came to the couch. "Grandma called my cell number and told me to tell you as soon as you woke up. She wanted to talk to Tom."

It irked her that Tom involved himself, but she couldn't think of a technique to express it that didn't come across as ungrateful.

"Everything is all squared away, Ainsley." Tom brought in a replacement ice pack. "You may not want to admit it, but you could use a hand. You are wasting energy fighting with me, and you should reserve your strength for healing."

"Hmmm." She let out a weak sigh and let go of the last bit of resistance. "Whatever," she whispered.

"I hate feeling like I am forcing you to accept help. I wish you would give in this once. You push yourself too hard and this accident is nature's way of saying, 'Slow down.' Allow yourself to rely on someone, Ainsley. I promise the sky won't fall and no giant fissures shall open on the earth's surface and swallow you up."

The imagery of Tom's words evoked in Ainsley's mind a surreal scene in which she was falling through the earth and floating in the clouds at the same time. She welcomed the vision and drifted away.

CHAPTER 32

Jesse with an "E"

The pain and swelling in Ainsley's ankle persisted for days and did not subside as quickly as the doctor's best-case scenario. She refrained from thinking about what her absence was doing to her status at work.

Tom went back and forth between his house and Ainsley's, taking care of them while keeping the operations running at the studio. At the end of each day, he would head home for the night after making sure he'd met their needs. He would be at the cottage before anyone else was awake.

After dinner Thursday evening, Tom lingered at the cottage with them.

"So, what can you tell me about our little Jesse when she was a baby?" Tom asked.

Ainsley was aware there were many details about Jesse that Tom didn't know, and she wanted to share. "Ask me anything."

"Ugh." Jesse squirmed. "I'm going upstairs."

"Why?" Tom protested in mock astonishment.

"Because this will be embarrassing." Jesse stood up to leave, but the smile on her face said she wasn't against it.

"Tom is your father. I want him to understand what makes you the most special kid in the world," Ainsley said, joining in to tease.

"I'll be in my room." Jesse headed upstairs. "Please come up and say good night before you leave, Dad."

"Of course," Tom answered. Then he turned his full attention to Ainsley. "So?" he asked.

"Where to start..." She paused.

"How did it feel being pregnant? Did Jesse sleep, or was she a crier? How did Jesse get her name?"

"Oh, Jesse's name, that's a fun one."

Ainsley told Tom how William wanted a boy and even took to calling her belly Jesse, the name Ainsley chose if she was having a boy.

"The gender neutral name stuck and when Jesse was born, the hospital asked for birth certificate information and I told them her name is Jesse with an 'e.'" Ainsley finished the story.

"I remember those exact words at the meet and greet," Tom said. "Belle said 'Jesse with an *e*' when I signed the CD case. So it's not a nickname for Jessica, nor is it spelled with the traditional 'ie.'"

"Nope. It's just Jesse. It is Hebrew and means 'the Lord exists' and 'gift.' It describes Jesse as a gift that renewed my faith in God."

Emotion drifted across Tom's face as he listened. Then he spoke. "I wish I had been there when Jesse, with an 'e', was born."

"For a while," she continued with the tale, "William struggled to remember his grandchild was not a boy. He had been so certain she would be a he. We often teased him and referred to her as 'Jess-she' to remind him."

Tom reached out and gently took her hand. "Thank you for sharing." He moved his thumb in comfort.

Her hand in Tom's felt nice but she pulled away. She didn't deserve his loving touch after having taken away from him so much. No more baby stories or memories today. It was too painful for them both.

"Well, I best be going. Promised Jesse a good-night kiss." Up the stairs, he flew as if he could run back in time and be with his daughter in the past.

Within a few minutes, he came back down and asked if Ainsley was ready for a lift up to bed. Not wanting to keep him there any longer, she took him up on the offer, even though she wasn't ready to go to sleep.

"There is a busy schedule at the studio," Tom announced when he came into Ainsley's bedroom the next morning carrying her breakfast on a tray. "After I drop Jesse at school, I am going straight over to the complex. I'll bring you downstairs before we leave."

Every morning, Tom had brought her breakfast in bed, then carried her to the couch for the day. She was certain she could climb the stairs by herself, though she was beginning to enjoy the closeness of the lifts.

"Let me stay up here this morning." She had gotten a whiff of herself, and to say she was smelling funky was an understatement. Until she could spend some more time on hygiene, she would forgo enjoying his proximity.

"Okay, I'll come around before lunch and bring you down."

"You needn't do that. I'll be fine. I have everything I need."

"Nonetheless…" he went downstairs without finishing the sentence.

Ainsley eyed the tray of breakfast food. She smelled the scrambled eggs and acknowledged the effort taken to prepare the meal, but wasn't hungry. Though she had no appetite, she was certain Tom would notice if she only ate a few bites. He would try harder to create a more appetizing dish, which she didn't want him to do.

For two days, Tom was the epitome of professionalism in caring for them. She wished she could relax and enjoy it, but she was worried. In spending time with them, had he disregarded his own responsibilities?

The moment she heard the front door close, she knew Tom took Jesse to school. When she was certain they were gone, she whistled, hoping Jesse hadn't let Brooke outside in the yard.

"Brooke," she called, and the canine bounded into her room. "Would you care to share my breakfast?"

She took a forkful of the eggs and had to admit; it was pretty tasty. Fluffy and perfectly cooked so as not to be runny nor scorched. She detected cheese and maybe parsley flakes. After she took another bite, she set the plate on the floor. Brooke licked the platter clean.

"Okay, Brooke," she slumped down against the pillows Tom had fluffed with expertise, "in a minute I'll have a shower." The border collie curled up beside her and she patted her head. "You are a faithful nursemaid."

She realized taking a shower by herself was a risky idea. Common sense roared to wait until someone else was home, but she hadn't bathed in two days and it was embarrassing. Opting for crawling instead of hopping, she would avoid the risk of losing her balance. Swinging her injured limb and her healthy leg together over the side of the bed, she sat up. The discomfort in the joint was intolerable as the fluids pulled by gravity rushed down the leg.

"I need my body to adjust to being upright." Talking it out with the dog was helpful. She believed the dog looked at her with reassurance.

Raising herself off the bed, she put all her weight on the intact limb as she achieved equilibrium and confidence, then dropped to the floor. Crawling over to the dresser, she raised herself to her knees and grabbed some yoga pants and a sports shirt. Ironically, she was dressing for an activity she had no intention of doing. Dropping to all fours, she crawled the remainder of the journey to the bathroom.

"Write this down," she instructed the dog, "*Ask Dad to deliver those crutches.*"

After her shower, she smiled triumphantly. She had executed the task without incident, and feeling refreshed had bolstered her spirit. To be clean and to have gained a little independence was encouraging progress. She was about to roll her discolored joint with a fresh stretchy wrap when she heard the front door crackle.

"Tom?" She glanced at the clock with surprise. Less than an hour went by since he and Jesse left.

"Ainsley?" the feminine voice belonging to Belle drifted up.

"Up here!" Ainsley called to Belle as if she were lost and about to be rescued.

"Oh, my dear," Belle went to her knees in front of Ainsley, sitting on the edge of the tub, and gave her a full hug. "What have you done to yourself?" Belle stared at her friend with consternation.

"I'm so glad to see you. How is the honeymoon?"

"It's been a fantasy come true." Belle gazed up in a dreamy stare. "But never mind that for now. How is your ankle and what are you doing out of bed?"

"I was stinking up the place. I had to drag my rotten carcass to the bathtub."

"So, Tom's been helping, but not with shower duty. It surprises me you are allowing him to help at all. It's so unlike you to be pampered."

"I'm not allowing anything. He is insisting. Are you here just to bust my chops?"

"Of course." Belle softened. "We give each other a hard time. Or at least we used to."

Ainsley understood. They had been spending less time together since Belle left the post office, and she may have missed their workplace camaraderie. "Everyone at work misses you, Belle."

"Of course they do." Belle smiled, then helped Ainsley finish wrapping the limb before they hobbled to the bed. Curled up with her, Belle told Ainsley all the details of her honeymoon in a Hawaiian paradise. It pleased Ainsley, knowing Belle was happy.

"What does Jesse think about having Tom around?" Belle changed the subject.

"It has been love at first sight for Jesse and Tom. She loves her dad and has been in heaven these past days."

"That is great. Tom seems to be a natural at this parenting stuff."

"I am concerned about it, though."

Belle encouraged Ainsley to elaborate. Ainsley explained, "I'm worried she thinks of it as her mother and father being together. Whenever Tom and I are interacting, she gets this twinkle, and she smiles."

"Oh, let the child be happy. It's beneficial for her to see you two getting along."

"I wish it were that simple. She shouldn't have a false sense of reality. I don't want her to build up hopes. What happens when Tom goes to Nashville?"

"Are you talking about Jesse's hopes or your own?" Belle asked.

Ainsley flinched when Belle smacked the nail with a direct hit from the hammer. "I'm talking about protecting my daughter from harm when I see it coming."

"Just as Rose protected you?"

Belle hit another nail, and Ainsley reacted with indignation. "Rose? Protecting? She made my life a living hell."

"I don't know if you will ever have a different outlook," Belle began in a calm voice, "but I hope someday you open your eyes."

"Oh, boy. Here it comes." Ainsley stared at the ceiling. "You go right ahead with the lecture. Please tell me all about my relationship with Rose. Because you are married, you think you are the expert on relationships? Okay, Miss Expert, fix me."

"Errr! You can be so infuriating." Belle lifted her chest, drawing in a larger amount of air, then exhaled. "I intend to capitalize on this opportunity when you're unable to run. Please hear me out."

Ainsley lay back and glazed over in defiance.

"Where to begin." Belle gathered her thoughts. "Let's not talk about your relationship with your mother. That's reserved for another day."

Ainsley smirked. "Good, because what you don't know is Rose and I have been working out a lot of things already."

"I will ignore your snarky attitude for the sake of progress. Now, sit here and listen."

"Like I have a choice." Ainsley wondered how her best friend could seem so mean as to take advantage of an invalid.

"Tom hurt you when he left, that is true, but you hurt him when you declined to go with him. He wanted you to go, but you were too scared or stubborn or whatever cockamamie reason you use."

"I was pregnant with his baby." Ainsley lifted, then pushed down hard on the pillow behind her.

"All the more reason you should have gone with him. You didn't tell him he had a baby. You gave him no choice. He would have stepped up. He might have looked after you both. You deprived him of the chance to try."

"And he also might have resented me for it. Have you ever thought of that?" Ainsley remembered how her mother lived with her own mistake and punished her with resentment. She vowed not to repeat that history. Rose and William had to get married because of her. Her parents' marriage had been the example Ainsley used as what to avoid.

"You want to talk about resentment?" Belle asked. "You are so lucky Tom forgives you for deceiving him and keeping Jesse from him. Tom has a reason to be resentful, but he's not."

"Tom was following his path and finding his dream. The last thing he needed was to be chained down." Ainsley still believed in her reasons.

"Given Tom's plans to include you, how can you character-ize him as having abandoned you? I understand how you felt. But what about Jesse? Tom couldn't have deserted her. He wasn't aware of her existence."

Ainsley opened her mouth to speak, but Belle placed her finger on Ainsley's lips. "Still my turn to talk, and you are the listener."

Turning her head away, it frustrated Ainsley that she was a captive audience.

Belle continued, "You feel forsaken, but Jesse does not. Don't punish her for what you experienced."

Belle paused, giving Ainsley a chance to gather a lungful of air. Belle had spoken her mind. Now it was her turn to share what was on hers. "I have told the truth. I am making amends. If I could change the past, I would."

"You are missing the point," Belle interrupted. "Can't you see how, even though you say you won't repeat the past, your resentfulness is harming your daughter?"

"I am letting her go. She traveled without me halfway across the country. During this visit, they introduced her to people I've never met. I can't vet these people. Not knowing if Tom is off doing busi-ness while Jesse is hanging out somewhere else, I have to trust that my daughter is being looked after. You think I am causing harm? Do you have any idea...?" Ainsley paused when her voice wavered. "I think I am being very understanding and accommodating."

"Accommodating? It's only fair to provide a man with the oppor-tunity to spend quality time with his daughter. You are lucky he doesn't ask for full custody."

"You think I haven't thought of that? It crosses my mind every day." The air left Ainsley's lungs and she gasped for breath. The pros-pect was paralyzing.

"Oh, sweetie." Belle turned comforting, "I am sorry I said that. I didn't mean to scare you. Tom will not take Jesse from you." Belle pulled her frightened friend into a hug. "But one day, Jesse will be old enough to make her own decisions. Don't alienate her, or you will have lost her long before she's even gone."

"Alienate her? Jesse and I have a great relationship."

"You do now, not unlike you and your mother. But you and Rose drifted apart."

"We didn't drift. She drove me off. Our relationship is completely different." Ainsley shook her head, refusing to entertain Belle's analogy. Belle only saw the situation from her own perspective.

"I have known you for almost eleven years, Ains, and I have watched you and Rose dance around each other, pushing buttons, causing pain. If you fight to control Jesse's life the way Rose fought to control yours, you'll end up repeating history."

"I am nothing like Rose." Belle had put Ainsley's deepest fear into words. "Nothing at all like her. I won't let that happen to me and Jesse."

"How do you know you haven't already started it?" Belle must have sensed the effect her declaration was having.

Unswayed by the tears forming in her best friend's eyes, Belle went for the target. "It appears to me that you are trying, but be truthful. Remember to check yourself. Are you doing the right thing?"

"The right thing," Ainsley whispered.

How many times had she heard that phrase? How often had she struggled with knowing what that was? The fresh moisture in her eyes was spilling over, refusing to be held back. "What does anybody know about the right thing? Was it wrong for me to keep Jesse's existence from Tom? Should he have stayed for Jesse even though he left me despite our love?"

"He hurt you so badly. But he was hurting, too. Have you two talked about this?" Belle switched from antagonistic to understanding.

"I had gone to see Tom with every intention of telling him about the situation. It was the day before he departed for the band's first tour." Ainsley was sharing things she told no one. "Confident in his love for me, I hoped he would be okay with it. Then when he announced his upcoming trip, I questioned whether our love was enough. When he left, I realized it wasn't. He didn't love me enough to marry me for love. To have him stay because we were pregnant was not how I wanted it. I didn't tell him that day."

"What stopped you?"

"I was scared and confused. Chickened out, I guess." Ainsley had never spoken about that day with anyone. "Maybe I wanted the fairytale, and in what Disney version, does the princess get knocked up? The prince always wants to marry Cinderella because he loves her, not because he feels some sense of moral obligation."

"I am not telling you what to do, Ainsley, but I suggest you and Tom should talk. You are not kids anymore. It's time to address all of this."

Before Belle could continue, the phone rang. Belle's quick reflexes got her to the landline before Ainsley could reach it.

"Tobin residence." As a gag, Belle used a phony professional voice for entertainment. "Yes, she is here, but she's not available. May I give her a message?" Belle winked.

Ainsley waved her hand, indicating Belle should give her the receiver.

"Oh, hey, Bob, the supervisor from the USPS. This is Belle, the ex-carrier. How are you? How is my old route?"

Ainsley couldn't believe Belle's casual tone. Management hadn't called to socialize. The post office was calling for information from Ainsley about her leave from duty.

Belle continued conversing, "I can vouch for Ainsley. She definitely has an ankle injury. It's positively black and blue."

Belle poked at the bear even further. "No, I am not a doctor, but I don't need a medical degree to say that Ainsley is in all kinds of pain here."

"Belle, stop," Ainsley whispered. "You are making things worse."

"Yes, I am aware of the company policy. As is Ainsley. You'll get your documentation."

Belle paused and listened to the supervisor, then responded, "This is turning into harassment."

Ainsley hated to guess what was being said on the other side of the conversation. "Belle, please." This was a bad idea. This was about her livelihood, her ability to support her family. Belle was messing with her job.

Belle ignored the plea. "I'll give her the message."

Ainsley scolded her friend. "I guess that was fun for you. You may have nothing to lose talking to a supervisor in that manner, but I still work there. I am in enough trouble as it is."

"You need to stand up for yourself. Don't let them push you around." The chat with management had gotten Belle riled up. "You are an exemplary employee, better than ninety percent of the carriers. They have no reason to treat you this way."

"They are only enforcing the policy according to the contract, not pushing me around. It's easier to follow the rules and avoid being punished. The policies and protocols are here to protect both me and the company. Call me straight-laced, call me uptight. I refuse to compromise my ethics."

"You crack me up." Belle's words did not match her expression. "You are the only person I know who thinks being a goody-two-shoes is a compliment. Being well-behaved got no one anything except stepped on." Belle flung her hands and face skyward.

Before Belle glanced down again, Ainsley broadsided her with a pillow. "Who needs to lighten up now?" She grinned.

Looking towards Ainsley with shock, Belle fake-threw the pillow back.

"Who did you say is the goody-goody? You won't even throw a pillow at me." Ainsley further inspired Belle's ire.

With that, Belle let loose and the flying projectile missed Ainsley and sailed across the room to the open door. The girls had been talking so intently they hadn't heard Tom come in. He picked up the weaponized bag of feathers.

"Did somebody lose this?" Tom heaved the pillow toward the women. "It seems the patient is in a better mood."

"Hey, Tom." Belle retrieved the wayward pillow and pushed Ainsley forward. "I was about to leave. I have suffered enough abuse from this one for the time being." Belle shoved the cushion behind Ainsley. "She's all yours." Then to Ainsley, Belle said, "I will see you soon. If you need anything…" she mouthed the words "call me" as she stepped out of the room backwards.

"Thanks, Belle. I appreciate you."

Tom walked Belle out and the two of them spoke, but Ainsley could not catch the words. After a few minutes, they said goodbye, but Tom did not come upstairs.

Ainsley stared out the half-opened window noting the season she loved the most, autumn was upon them and she was stuck inside. The breeze floating in through the slightly opened window had a tweak to it that said cooler weather was in store. Thinking she was missing out on all the things she depended upon to keep her biological rhythms balanced was depressing.

When she heard Tom climbing the stairs, her spirit brightened.

"Your hair is damp," he said. "Did Belle help with your shower?"

"Yeah," she said with a grunt. "Belle is always a big help."

Tom came all the way into the room and sat down. Ignoring the sarcasm, he looked at her as though she were a fresh snack. "You smell nice. I hope you feel as healthy as you look."

"I am much better," she assumed he had been noticing she was looking pretty shabby before. "Now, if I could get up on my feet and out of this house." Ainsley hoped Tom would offer to drive her around town. It wouldn't be as rewarding as a hike or bike ride, but through the windows of the truck, the air of the changing season would pass over, giving her a tangible experience.

"Belle updated me about the work situation. I spoke with Dr. Davis and he agreed to complete the required documents for your employer."

"It's standard procedure," she said, wishing he hadn't gotten involved.

"Well, then they shall have their paperwork. This afternoon I plan to stop by your work office and secure their forms on my way to pick up Jesse from school. I can swing by the Urgent Care and leave the papers for Dr. Davis. I'll take the finished documents to your office as soon as they fill them out."

Tom was leaving the room as he spoke. It frustrated her that by exiting, he had cleverly ensured she couldn't argue. She heard him in the kitchen and figured he was probably making her next meal. If she could have followed him down, she would have prepared a sandwich on her own.

After having skipped most of her breakfast meal, she bit into the sandwich with a ravenous appetite. She consumed the sandwich and graciously finished the rest of the lunch, then realized she needed to go potty. She crawled to the bathroom to take care of business, then got brave and scooted down the stairs on her backside.

"What are you doing?" Tom exclaimed when he saw Ainsley.

"I'm fine, look." Ainsley looked up in victory at the second floor, whence she came. "I reached my goal."

"Yes, you did. But it was risky." Tom picked Ainsley up without asking, and she didn't mind. "It's encouraging to witness your progress."

As Tom carried Ainsley the remaining distance to the living room, she felt an irresistible urge to give him a kiss. Would that have been weird? It would have been a sign of gratitude. She appreciated his efforts. He was so kind and attentive.

Tom lowered his chin and stole a lungful of the fresh smell of her clean scalp. It reminded her of how she did the same thing to Jesse's head when the child was close enough. This tender behavior was endearing. The closeness of his lips when he set her down became her focus. He hesitated, as if her lips were the only thing on his mind, too.

"I'm gonna run these errands before I pick Jesse up from school." His voice was unsteady when he spoke. "See you in a bit."

He placed a kiss on her cheek and if she had turned her head, they could have been lip to lip. Tom appeared to be unaffected by the current that passed between them. He took his hat from the rack, tipped it, then disappeared.

Ainsley sat quietly and allowed the effect of the kiss on her cheek to linger. She imagined the possibilities of another such close encounter with Tom and wondered where it would lead, given the right circumstances.

CHAPTER 33

Going Postal

"Where are they?" Ainsley asked the dog, who started looking around as if she was supposed to find somebody. Ainsley expelled a relief laugh at Brooke's silly antics, then went back to worrying.

"Hi Momma." Jesse came in first and sprinted past Ainsley and up the stairs as if pursued by wolves.

"What's the rush?" Ainsley called after her retreating daughter.

"She gets that behavior from you." Tom evaluated Jesse's method of levitating to the second floor. Coming straight towards Ainsley, he had an unusual expression on his face. She decided he looked frazzled.

"I don't see how anything gets done at your workplace. That the mail gets delivered correctly is a tribute to the carriers because nothing else about that place runs smoothly, does it?"

She couldn't help but laugh at his reaction to the chaos he must have experienced.

"Tell me, what happened?" She chuckled, knowing this promised to be entertaining.

"At first, nobody came to the dock despite me ringing the service bell. The sign on the door says, *Not an Entrance. Postal Employees Only*, so I waited. Finally, a short man wearing gloves came out, informed me the loading dock was for businesses dropping off bulk mail or employees only. He seemed annoyed and disappeared before I could ask if I could speak to your supervisor."

Tom continued. "I pressed the doorbell, and a different employee responded, but not right away. I asked if there was anyone else who could give me the papers you needed and the employee informed me he was on break." Tom threw up his arms like a goose trying to fly.

She laughed at the picture Tom presented in his flustered state.

He ignored her and continued, "A carrier who was returning from the street said his name was Dave? He told me he used to be in management and he knew where they keep the forms. Dave was back in minutes with the packet for Dr. Davis. He wished you a speedy recovery, then disappeared through the great swinging doors." Tom's eyes were cartoonishly wide. He bent his still extended arms and smacked his hands on top of his head. "How can they run a business when the right hand doesn't know, or care, what the left is doing?"

It was a rhetorical question, and there was no satisfactory answer. "It is the government." Ainsley smiled. "Welcome to my world."

She scooted over and patted the cushion. "Sit down. You're getting all worked up."

Tom took no offense to her patronizing tone and sat down as directed.

"Most of the people do their job," she explained. "When everyone handles their responsibilities, it's amazing how much mail we process. It makes me proud to be a part of it."

"No wonder employees go postal." Tom held onto his belief that the public service designed to receive, transport, and deliver letters, documents, and parcels could not remain fruitful based on how they ran their business. "I am surprised you don't hear more often about crazed postal workers running amok. If I managed my affairs thusly, I'd never succeed. I admire you for being as stable as you are under those conditions. You'd have to haul me off in a straitjacket if I had to deal with that kind of dysfunction."

"Your affairs thusly?" Ainsley teased, repeating Tom's vernacular. "C'mere." She pulled Tom towards her to give him a shoulder-to-shoulder side hug. "The postal service does not differ from any government institution. You should only approach it in small doses. It takes some getting used to."

Tom leaned in and dropped his shoulders. "I am not accustomed to incompetence. At least with my business, I can make changes. If we are not happy with something, we find better ways. If someone isn't doing their job, we move them on."

"Don't worry, I won't let you go to that awful place ever again."

"You're patronizing me," Tom said in a moment of introspection. "I suppose I am acting childish."

"That's the spirit." She reached across with her other hand and started massaging his tense shoulders. "Now you relax and I'll make it better."

Tom shook himself like a dog shaking water off its coat, then shifted so Ainsley had easy access to both sides. "I will take this treatment." He closed his eyes. "Mmmm, that feels nice." He focused on the tension-mitigating action of her hands kneading his tight trapezius muscles.

"You're not ticklish, are you?" Ainsley dropped her hands to his sides. She couldn't hide her delight when he squealed in surprise.

Tom predicted what she was about to do next. He was very ticklish but also smart. Before she could tickle his sensitive sides some more, he turned and caught *her* off guard. Holding her hands to stop her, he said, "There is no way to answer that question that won't end in a... tickle fight!"

He moved so quickly, she took a defensive position with her arms wrapped around her middle. "Oh, oh, no." She squirmed and twisted but was outmatched. He tickled her before she could get to him and seemed to revel in her predicament.

"Oh, ouch," she exclaimed, and he stopped tickling.

"Sorry, sorry. Did I hurt you?"

"Psyche!" Ainsley capitalized and pounced.

Her attack rendered Tom helpless and gasping for breath. "I surrender."

Ainsley stopped tickling, but left her hands at Tom's sides.

"You play dirty. I will have to remember that."

The wrestling had ended with him lying back. She was almost resting on his chest. The closeness of their bodies, the proximity alone, created an electric heat between them. Motionless, they remained.

"I wonder if…" His voice was low, his words spoken slowly.

"If…?" Ainsley asked.

His breath touched her face as her gaze went from his eyes to his lips, then back.

Then he finished the sentence, "if Jesse is ready to go for her riding lesson."

Tom opted not to move or take his hands from Ainsley's sides.

"Hey, you two," Jesse announced herself from the hallway.

"Hey, Jess." Ainsley recovered from the ethereal experience but remained near Tom on the couch.

"I'm ready to go riding."

"Did you finish your homework?" Tom returned to parental mode.

"Da-ad." Jesse elongated the word. "You sound just like Mom. It's Friday. I have all weekend for homework."

"Okay, then." Tom sat up straight, lifting Ainsley to upright at the same time. "Guess we better get going."

Jesse moved towards them. "Bye, Mom," she said with a hug.

"Bye, guys." Ainsley answered with little expression.

She sat for a while after they left, contemplating. There was no doubt in her mind she and Tom still had chemistry. History shows that in their youth, they were weak regarding their passion. Were they still slave to their carnal desires? To spare herself the risk of disappointment, she wouldn't read anything more into it. "Just let it go," she advised herself. They were adults now, and she decided they would handle their actions with much more control.

Tom stayed with Jesse for the riding lesson and brought her home afterwards. Since Jesse began spending her time between households, the carpooling to and from the stable with Phillip and Emily fell out of the routine. It was a sad, but normal progression in their lives. She knew Phillip was not happy with the changes.

When Tom and Jesse returned, Tom made dinner while Jesse shared the details of her riding lesson. They ate together, then Ainsley and Jesse cuddled while Tom cleaned up the kitchen. After Jesse turned in for the night, Tom asked if Ainsley was ready for bed. "I'll take you up before I go," he offered flatly.

Even as he held her in his arms to carry her upstairs, she couldn't read his body. Gone was the heat she was certain she felt earlier.

She went to bed wondering how he could turn off so easily. Had she been feeling something that hadn't been there in the first place?

"What are you doing?" Tom rushed in on Saturday morning without even bothering to shut the door behind him.

"I am making breakfast." Ainsley stood at the refrigerator on her good leg with the bum leg propped at a bent-knee, resting on the mobility knee scooter he had bought for her the day before.

"You shouldn't be in here. You came down the stairs alone *again*?" His panic was coming at her from all directions. "You are supposed to keep that ankle elevated."

"Relax. I'm not alone. Jesse's here." She closed the icebox door and lost her grip on the container of eggs.

Tom lunged forward and caught the carton before it hit the ground. One wayward egg escaped the secure confines and fell to the floor.

"Ooopsies."

Placing the remaining eggs still intact onto the counter, Tom grabbed some paper towels. "I'll get that." But before he could clean it up, Brooke had availed herself.

"Sorry about that. Thanks." Ainsley continued preparing the meal. "Brooke does a pretty good job of keeping the floors clean."

"Let me do the cooking." He took her by the elbow to lead her out. "It is important that you elevate that leg."

Ainsley flopped on the couch with a thud. It frustrated her to admit she had made more work for Tom. She had picked up on his annoyance at her, though he tried to mask it.

Their voices awoke Jesse and, still half asleep, she came waddling in for a snuggle against her mother. Tom busied himself with the meal preparations.

"Hey, Lil' Beans," he called, "why not play the tune I taught you on the guitar?"

Jesse retrieved Tom's six-string from where it rested on its stand by the TV. Tom brought it over the first day so he could take advantage of even the shortest downtime and continue to write. Tom had also played for comic relief and had written a short song about Ainsley's accident.

"In a hurry, there she lays with twisted ankle, on the stairs
Saving time it didn't pay, gravity got its way, so laid-up she must stay"
Ainsley had laughed out loud when he played her song. "That sums it up."

Jesse plucked the strings and strummed. "I am warming up my fingers." She mirrored what her father did on stage and copied what he said to the audience. Ainsley was reminded of the quote by Oscar Wilde, "Imitation is the greatest form of flattery…." Glancing up at the object of Jesse's mimicry, she was proud of them both.

When Jesse played, Ainsley recognized the song. It was "Achy Breaky Heart." Jesse started with confidence in the first verse.

From the kitchen, Tom caught up and sang. It thrilled Jesse when her father joined in, but it made her lose focus.

"Take it from the top. Two, three, four…" Tom encouraged her.

"You can tell the world you never were my girl
You can burn my clothes up when I'm gone
Or you can tell your friends just what a fool I've been
And laugh and joke about me on the phone."

The father-daughter duo did two verses and the chorus. When breakfast was cooked, Tom took the meals out to the folding table he had set up in the garden, and the three of them sat together family style.

"Well, isn't this the perfect picture?" From the driveway, Phillip and Emily came walking up.

"Oh, they are here already." Jesse grabbed her empty plate and went inside. The girls were chattering with excitement about going to the barn together like old times.

"She'll be ready in a minute, Phillip." Ainsley assured him.

"Sorry to ruin your little morning gathering." Phillip's words were not in sync with his attitude as he took a seat uninvited in the chair Jesse had vacated.

Phillip was staring at Tom with disdain. Tom gathered his and Ainsley's empty plates to take them inside. "May I offer you a cup of coffee, Phillip?" Tom was aware of but chose to ignore the other man's attitude.

"No thanks, man." Phillip declined the offer, and as Tom walked away, he turned to Ainsley. "So? What, does he live here now?" Phillip asked, not caring whether Tom had heard.

"Not that it's any of your business, but no. And what's up with your attitude?"

"I warned you to be careful. Remember, he hurt you once. It could happen again." Phillip's words seemed to show concern, but they were laced with anger.

Ainsley remembered their last conversation the day they took a trail ride. "I am grateful for your concern. If this is about anything more than that, I'm warning you, you'll be crossing a boundary."

She was growing weary of the same issue with Phillip, and she had no intention of discussing her personal life with him, so she stopped the conversation. They waited in silence for Jesse and Emily to come back out.

Phillip stood up when the girls emerged.

"Bye, Mom and Dad," Jesse said, and the girls climbed into Phillip's Prius.

"Bye, guys," Ainsley responded to the group.

Phillip grunted, then turned to leave.

"That is an uptight and conflicted guy. I feel bad for him," Tom said after they left.

"You heard us talking?"

"I couldn't hear a word you were saying. His body language says it all. It's obvious how he feels about me. So, I guess I am right about him?"

Ainsley told him a brief history of her and Phillip's friendship. She needed a sounding board. Tom listened with unbiased interest.

"Your relationship is experiencing some changes."

"Everything in my life is changing." Ainsley sighed. It felt good to talk about it. It had been a tumultuous summer with many unforeseen twists.

"It's like weeding a garden. Friendships, like gardens, need constant tending. You have to make changes, rip out the old growth when it has died, and make way for new crops. Phillip is afraid of being thrown out of your garden like a weed."

"You should write a song about that." Ainsley teased. "And if he acts like a weed, he will be ripped out."

"You are ruthless."

After breakfast, Ainsley wheeled herself into the house on her scooter while Tom finished cleaning up. She unwrapped her wounded limb and studied the tissue as she elevated and iced her healing ankle. Tom picked up his guitar and started plinking strings and doodling with the lyrics to a song. It thrilled her to imagine him writing a hit song from her own little cottage. As he wrote and played, she flipped open the Louis L'Amour novel he had left on the back of the couch against the wall.

It was a Western novel about an enigmatic character who interrupted the travel plans of a family from the East who were embarking on a trip across the West. So engrossed in reading about the mysterious traveling cowboy was she that she failed to notice Tom had stopped plucking the strings on his guitar. He was staring at her, and she wondered for how long he had been watching. Tom grinned mischievously when Ainsley looked at him. It was funny how she felt embarrassed that Tom was watching her read.

"Do you like the book?" Tom asked.

Ainsley raised her arms overhead and stretched, thinking about a response. "So far, yes."

"When my dad first gave me a Louis L'Amour, I read it because he wanted me to. It turned out I liked the story. After the next book my father sent, I looked forward to reading them. Now, I am a fan."

Ainsley lifted her elevated leg off its support platform of pillows preparing to stand up, and in one motion, Tom set his guitar on its stand and was at her side. "Where are you going? What do you need?"

"I need a snack." She breathed deeply to expel her annoyance, then stood up. She wanted Tom to stop hovering.

Tom stood by while Ainsley rolled to the fridge, grabbed a container of yogurt, then proceeded to the dining table. It pleased her that the mere act of standing wasn't resulting in painful throbbing anymore, and she was getting good at managing the mobility device. Just as she sat down to eat, she discovered she forgot to grab a spoon. When she looked towards the silverware drawer, there was Tom standing before her, holding out the utensil. She took it and uttered a sheepish "thanks."

They both sat down at the table, enjoying the view out the picture window into the yard. When she finished the yogurt, she watched Tom take the empty container to the sink and rinse it before tossing it into the recycle bin.

Ainsley was still watching Tom as he rinsed her spoon and stooped forward to put it in the dishwasher. With his backside angled towards her, she locked in on his flexing hamstrings. When he straightened up, his glute muscles flexed, revealing a very attractive booty under those well-fitting Wrangler jeans.

Tom didn't look at her, and she continued to watch undetected—so she thought. Staying at the sink, Tom squeezed the excess water from the sponge to wipe down the already clean counter. He glanced up with a smile and she averted her gaze, feeling embarrassed at being caught staring at his backside.

"Thank you, Tom," Ainsley blurted out.

"You're welcome?" The inflection in Tom's voice showed he needed an explanation.

"I mean for everything. Thanks for everything."

Ainsley gathered in her mind all the times she noticed how easily Tom fit into her household dynamics. He managed the domestic chores and seemed to have a bottomless pool of patience, even though she could be trying. Despite the challenges, he still took care of them while handling his affairs.

"Of course. It is my pleasure."

She studied his face while his focus drifted to the view out the big window. Wondering what he might be thinking, she wanted to know why he was there at her place, other than to look after them. How does a huge star living in the lap of luxury switch to being a capable regular guy?

Tom faced Ainsley's thoughtful stare.

"Oops, I was staring. Sorry."

"Yes, you were, but don't be sorry." He smiled from the corners and tilted his head in contemplation.

"I see you so differently than I have been picturing you for the past ten years," Ainsley blurted again without warning.

"Different in a good way?"

"In a good way, yes." She mirrored his relaxed smile.

It was his turn to stare, perhaps trying to read her mind. Then he said, "You are just as I've been picturing," and his expression smoldered.

"How can that be?" She didn't know what he saw, but she was not the girl he knew. The sum of the harshness of reality, the struggles to survive, the pressures of being an adult, added up to a very different person. There was much about her that had changed. Whether he saw it, she knew she couldn't possibly be what he had pictured.

"I'm gonna walk to the living room so you can have another look at my butt."

He turned and delivered a coltish, playful smile. "Mmhmmm, I see you. You're watching."

"Phhh." Air escaped between pursed lips and Ainsley buried her face in her hands. So distracted by her embarrassment, she hadn't heard her cell phone ringing in her pocket.

"Oh." She extricated the device and activated it. "Hi, Mom." There was silence while Rose spoke.

"I'm happy you and Daddy are enjoying the vacation."

Pause. "No. There's no reason to cut short your retreat week. Tom's taking care of Jesse. We are doing fine."

Pause. "No, I haven't returned to work, but I am learning to use the scooter to get around. I will request limited duty on Monday."

Another pause as Rose spoke, then Ainsley pressed her lips together hard. "Okay, but I assure you that is not true. That is not the arrangement."

Her jaw tightened, and her teeth ground together. "Thanks, Mom. I appreciate your concern. I will see what can be done."

"Is everything okay?" Tom asked. He had seen Ainsley at the end of the call with her head down, as if there was something interesting on the floor to look at.

"That was my mom. She was calling to check on us." She didn't elaborate beyond the simple answer. Omission was not the same as lying, was it? She knew the answer. She had learned that lesson big but had yet to apply it. Hadn't she learned from the past? Would she ever?

Tom nodded, but he seemed to know there was more to the phone call than a quick "hello." "Okay then," he said, taking her word for it for now. "It's nearly three o'clock. What time do I pick up the girls from Pete's place?"

Tom went to retrieve the kids from the barn. Before he left, he made sure she had everything she would need while he was gone.

After he left, Ainsley made a phone call to Phillip, but he didn't answer.

"Hey, Phillip." Tom jumped out and approached. "Am I mistaken? I thought Ainsley brought the children home from riding lessons on Saturdays."

"Ainsley does." Phillip's response did little to clear the confusion.

Before their conversation could go further, they could see Jesse and Emily walking towards them.

"Here they come. Hey, Em, Jess." Tom greeted the half-pints.

"Hey, girls." Phillip spoke with his mouth barely moving. "Em, get in the car."

The kids exchanged a nervous glance, finding the situation odd. Then Emily did as she was told.

"I'll call you," Jesse announced to her friend, then stood beside her dad.

Tom put his arm around Jesse protectively, waiting, but Philip had nothing more to say. He continued to glare at the musician with stone-faced agitation.

"C'mon, Jess. We best be going, too."

They didn't speak as they walked to Tom's truck for a quiet ride home.

Ainsley wheeled her scooter into the yard to capture the lengthening shadows as the sun took the lower journey across the sky. She was twirling a sweet gum leaf that had come off the tree from the neighboring yard.

"Hey, Jess." Ainsley said to her returning daughter, who grunted a quick greeting as she scurried up stairs.

"She's heading to her room to call Emily," Tom said.

"They were together all day. What more could there be to talk about?"

Tom shrugged. "I'm not sure what happened. Phillip was there when I got to the barn. He seemed angry. Jesse seemed concerned about Emily. It was quite strange."

"Strange is turning into his normal regarding Phillip," Ainsley mumbled, then said, "I'm so sorry. You shouldn't have to put up with his bizarre attitude."

"Nothing I can't handle." Tom remained calm. "It's Phillip who should be apologizing. To me and the girls."

"Phillip is not well." She wanted to explain things to Tom, but didn't know where to begin.

"So I've noticed. We all got stuff, Ains. There comes a point where you can't keep cutting him a pass."

"You are right."

"And as Jesse's parent, I am prepared to protect her from harm. I don't want her around him."

Though his statement was unexpected, she understood his perspective and respected him for it. She nodded to acknowledge the message was received.

Ainsley was done with handling this on her own. This was bigger than whether they could remain friends. Inside Phillip, there was something deeper happening. She could only envision one approach. It motivated her into action regarding the safety and well-being of Phillip's daughter as well. She knew she owed it to the memory of her departed friend, Désirée.

"Please fill me in on the drama that went down today," Tom requested, as he sat on the ottoman facing Ainsley, re-wrapping her injured limb after dinner. He had made the meal and went about the household chores while Ainsley and Jesse were both occupied with their phones.

"I am sorry for not including you."

"I'm not being nosey or trying to involve myself where I don't belong, but I am a good listener." Tom had finished wrapping the ankle and went to retrieve an ice pack.

"It's not about it being a private matter, but it is embarrassing." She felt uncomfortable dumping more on his already weighed down duty list. But this was information about something that was affecting Jesse. Tom had every right to know.

Ainsley explained her history with the Martin family and how she and Jesse drew closer to Phillip and Emily after Désirée's passing.

"When Désirée died, it was devastating." Ainsley paused as emotion got the better of her. Tom remained still and in listening mode. With the wrap securely in place, his hands still holding her foot, he let her speak, neither commenting nor moving to comfort her.

"Somewhere along the line, Phillip changed. I found his behavior annoying. He was taking liberties to involve himself in my life personally. He had this notion that we should start dating, and he concerned himself a little too much regarding who I went out with."

Tom nodded his head with a better understanding.

"I don't know when, but Phillip started drinking. He has been discreet about it and, as far as I know, has not been drunk in the presence of the children. I spoke to Jesse, and she said she never saw him drinking when she was over there. In fact," Ainsley remembered, "the first time I saw him drinking in front of the kids was when he brought his own beer and crashed here. He had had a stressful day and chose alcohol to drown his angst. At least he came over here, where Emily would be safe. That's when I noticed the alcohol consumption was affecting him negatively."

Ainsley wrestled with her fingers in her lap, organizing her thoughts, then continued. "I kept trying to stay in the friend zone, and Phillip assured me he understood, but his actions did not match his words. I thought we had ironed out the wrinkles when I went riding with him and Emily when you and Jesse were in Nashville. That was the last encounter, and he was remorseful and assured me he didn't want to lose our friendship. Then this morning Phillip showed up here to get Jesse, and… you know the rest."

"I think there is more your friend is struggling with than unrequited feelings for you." Tom was digesting the information. "Can you tell me what's been going on today?"

"Phillip's escalating whacky behavior has spilled over the boundaries of privacy. Rose called to let me know he had called her to report a rumor about me."

"A rumor?" Tom asked. "That kind of thing rarely bothers you."

"It doesn't bother me. I couldn't care less what Phillip thinks, or anyone else."

Ainsley had learned how to handle gossipers at an early age when, as a teenager, she was the subject of rumors about promiscuity. Regarding the bullying, Aunt Ruthie had been Ainsley's source of comfort and advice. Since then, Ainsley wasn't someone who succumbed to the pressures of the community's opinion.

"The problem is that what others think is important to Rose and it could spill over into Jesse's life as well as yours." Ainsley explained.

Tom sat back, placing his hands on his thighs. "For us in the music industry, having a thick skin is a requirement. But for Rose and Jesse and you, Ainsley… If there's anything I can do, please ask."

"Well," Ainsley brightened, "thanks to my Aunt Ruthie, my mother has a plan. After years of not talking, Rose and Ruthie are back on good terms, thanks to Rose's therapy and changes. They're teaming up to tackle Phillip's possible alcoholism with the help of the church clergy. Aunt Ruthie is a natural healer with experience with this kind of thing, so she's happy to help, especially since this concerns our safety. Rose thinks we should keep our distance from Phillip. Unfortunately, not seeing Emily is the toughest part. And we care about her so much."

"We have to keep connected to Emily for safety's sake. And Emily's well-being is attached to Jesse's," Tom concluded.

"Jesse will stay in touch with Emily. We can trust Jesse to come to us if Emily needs any help. I need to be there for Emily, but am caught in the conflict with her dad."

"I haven't been a dad for very long, but I believe keeping things close to what's familiar is best for them."

Ainsley appreciated Tom could see the situation without bias.

"If we are as non-confrontational as possible, the children will go to school together. All the stuff that normal preteens do. Would it help if I handle the interactions with Phillip, thus removing you as an element of discord?"

She mulled over his plan. "That would eliminate one point of contention, but I'm not sure it would ease the dissonance. There is one more thing I need to tell you..." she hesitated.

Tom waited and appeared nervous for the first time since the conversation began. "If you're pausing for dramatic effect, consider it successful."

Ainsley continued, "The rumor? About me? Phillip started it. It's about *you* and me..."

Ainsley spoke the words in a hush, then waited, but didn't get the reaction she expected. Tom seemed amused. "So, what Phillip said about us is too embarrassing to talk about?"

"Why are you laughing?"

"Ainsley, there is nothing about us that could be more embarrassing than the actual truth."

"If you won't be serious, how effective do you think you'll be?" Ainsley remained defensive.

"Oh, sweetie." The conversation had reached a point where Tom could comfort her. Moving from the footstool to sit with her on the couch, he said, "I am serious, but I'm also keeping my sense of humor. I am not making light of this. It's called coping, keeping a healthy perspective."

In his arms, she leaned closer, and with her ear pressed against his chest, she decided she liked how his voice sounded from there. "I have a tendency to over dramatize," she admitted.

"Just a smidge." Tom chuckled, and it made Ainsley's head bounce. "And Phillip runs a little hot with emotions, too."

CHAPTER 34

Finishing the Song

"Tom's here. Bye, Mom." Jesse hugged her mother as she readied herself out the door where Tom was waiting to drive her to begin the next week of school.

"Okay, sweetie," Ainsley shouted from her room, knowing the child had already closed the door behind her and couldn't hear a word. "See you this afternoon. Have a good day."

After Saturday's drama, Tom had arranged a one-day retreat for Ainsley and Jesse. A phone-free, media-free, drive to the coast for a mental reset day. Fully immersing herself in the sensory experience, Ainsley was only somewhat pouty when Tom, Jesse, and Brooke left her sitting in the truck while they romped and played on the shore. From the cab she could see the breakwaters and hear the waves crashing and the seagulls calling. The foghorn way off in the distance sounded its warning. The soothing breeze coming through the wide-open windows danced across her skin, and she laid back her head and closed her eyes. She reveled in a moment of peace.

On the drive inland, Tom had given his two cents' worth of cowboy wisdom. "Today will be the day we draw upon as an example of what to do when life gets to be too much. Get a new perspective."

"In 2 Corinthians, 4:18, it reminds us not to focus on what's seen in the physical realm, but what is unseen, spiritual, eternal. By looking beyond what is directly in front of us, we are free to live in the moment and know God's will is done. It's the beginning moment of many more to come. We will return to reality soon enough, but today with just us three, we set the foundation for our next moments together from here forward."

It was as good a theory as any, and Tom's way of wording made it seem like such a simple idea, but Ainsley had a hard time wrapping her mind around that. Phrases like "If you get lemons, make lemonade" or "The only thing you can change is your perspective," were easier said than done.

When Monday rolled around, Ainsley returned to the more pressing issue: her ankle and her inability to perform her job. She had emailed the paperwork from Dr. Davis to her supervisor and expected to hear from management soon. Feeling useless at home, she was counting on her supervisor assigning her to limited duty. She had hoped she could walk at this point, but here she was, *kick-push, kick-push*, making her way on the gravel driveway. For the scooter, it was a bumpy ride, but she was outside and moving her body. She nodded a greeting to Mrs. Dixon and chatted with the landlady, who asked about her recuperation from the ankle sprain.

"It is a slow recovery."

"Good thing for you that Tom is such a nice guy," Mrs. Dixon decided, based on how Ainsley described Tom's help.

"It has been nice having him here. Jesse is on the moon with enjoyment."

"And as for you?" Mrs. Dixon pried with curiosity. "How do you feel about having Tom West as a caregiver? Or is he maybe a little more than that?"

"Of course I am grateful for the assistance, but there will be nothing more than that between us. We have a child together and the rest is in the past."

"Well, it appears, as a nurse, he has a pretty good bedside manner, if you know what I mean."

"Mrs. Dixon!" Ainsley scolded, then added with a grin, "Actually, he does."

"Keep an open mind, dear." Mrs. Dixon addressed Ainsley as the young woman rolled away. "We never know what's in store. Keep yourself open to the future."

Back inside the cottage, she retreated to the couch to elevate her injured limb. She would be ready when her boss called to discuss her medical condition and her return to limited duty. When her cell phone rang, she slid the device out of her pocket. It was her supervisor.

"Hey Ainsley, this is Bob from USPS."

"Hi, Bob." Ainsley went right to the subject. "Did you get the documentation? The doctor gave me a release for restricted jobs. Did you see the paperwork? I filled out the forms."

"We got the forms and all the medical documents. Everything is in order. However, we won't be able to put you on light duty. There isn't enough to do around the office to fill your day, and according to the labor contract with the Union, we can't pay you less than your forty-hour shift."

"Well, alright then." Ainsley spoke calmly to herself in response to the disappointing news, though she felt tumultuous inside.

"Upon your doctor's releasing you to full duty, you can return. Until then, a temp will cover your route."

"So, that's it? No light duty?"

"I wish I could give you better news," Bob said. "Goodbye." Then he hung up.

In the quiet of her cottage, she processed the information thought-fully. *No worries*, she decided. Time would heal all wounds.

Instead of freaking out about her job or money, she became pensive. She thought about the phrase that came to her mind as she coped. It was Rose Fitzgerald Kennedy who once wrote, "It has been said, 'time heals all wounds.' I do not agree. The wounds remain. In time, the mind, protecting its sanity, covers them with scar tissue and the pain lessens. But it is never gone.'

Ainsley was so deep in thought, she failed to hear Tom arrive. "I could've robbed the joint," Tom announced from right beside her, and Ainsley jumped.

"Didn't mean to startle you. Is everything okay?"

"No," Ainsley confessed. Still feeling the emotion of her tortured thoughts, she wanted to wrap her arms around Tom and never let him go. If she held on, maybe she could squeeze out the past, wipe away the anguish.

Tom leaned down for a loose hug and gave a heavy sigh. He must have picked up on her angst but couldn't have known whence it came. "What's happening?"

Searching for an answer to the question, she created a segue to redirect her emotions that were on the brink of spilling over. "You must be so tired of the drama that is my life."

"In all honesty, I'd love to come here and find you all happy and smiling, with two functioning legs so you could jump up and give me a real welcoming hug."

"Hmmm." Ainsley smiled all the way to her tear brimmed eyes. "I would have loved that, too."

If only he knew how badly she wanted to do what he suggested. She imagined what would have happened if she could reach out physically and from the heart. Bum foot or not, it was fear that stopped her from being vulnerable. The fear in her head was disabling her heart. Shaking her line of thinking off its track, she tried to focus while Tom was speaking.

"...and if I have shown you anything over the past...almost a week, it's that nothing is as bad as it seems. Nothing bad lasts forever. Now, tell me. What's going on?" Tom stepped over the ottoman and lowered himself into the chair opposite the couch where Ainsley sat.

"Oh, you know." Ainsley found it difficult to talk about her troubles. "The post office doesn't have any limited duty to offer me. I cannot resume my job until I'm able to return to my route."

"Great. At least you can give that ankle proper rest for better healing."

Ainsley wished Tom would stop solving problems by always finding something positive on which to focus. It was annoying how he could take a bad thing and always find a favorable angle.

"Not great." Ainsley argued. "I must work. I have bills to pay, rent. We need groceries."

"You're doing it again. In moving mountains, when all you need is a chisel, you bring dynamite."

"Not the cowboy wisdom again." Ainsley groaned.

"You can't argue with what works. Cowboy wisdom, or wisdom from the Lord above. It's all good. Now, about lunch. What shall I fetch for us?"

"Well, there is nothing in the kitchen with which to make lunch. The cupboards are bare."

"We'll have to see about that, won't we?" Tom took her statement as a challenge.

Tom began rummaging around, opening and closing cabinet doors. The refrigerator. "Freshly squeezed lemon would be better." He talked to himself as he worked. He mixed a short list of ingredients in a bowl.

Within minutes, Ainsley was enjoying a tasty lunch of Ritz crackers and tuna spread. "I could have made this myself."

"Just say thank you, Ains." Tom winked.

"Jesse is doing well with her riding. Pete says she'll be ready for the horse show." Tom bragged like a proud papa and seemed grateful for the opportunity to sit in the quiet cottage and relax.

"Jesse's confidence has flourished since she started riding Casey. I remember when she was afraid to canter him. They would ride 'round and 'round the arena at the trot." Ainsley had finished eating and hobbled to the stove to make tea.

"You are getting along quite efficiently," he observed. "I am happy to see your progress."

"That is what I wanted to talk to you about."

"Oh?" Tom slid another Ritz cracker with tuna on top into his mouth.

"You have been so generous. We have appreciated your kindness. You have looked after me and made sure Jesse's life stayed on schedule." Ainsley paused when Tom's expression turned from open and listening to guarded with a hint of amusement.

"I'm being fired, aren't I?"

She acknowledged his humor. "Not so much fired," she smiled, "as being downsized."

"Wait, you are firing me?!" Tom's comment had been a joke. Her response surprised him.

"You are so busy. Time is valuable. It is too burdensome for you to divide yourself between your music and Jesse and me."

As Tom processed what she was saying, she continued with her line of logic. "I am getting better. I can move about the house and William is loaning me one of his old plumbing trucks. It's an automatic. I am not yet capable of driving a clutch."

"I guess you have this all figured out."

"Well, I have been thinking about it, yes." She realized Tom seemed neither grateful nor relieved at being released from duty. The water for tea was heating, and she readied the cups with tea bags.

Tom said nothing. He simply stared at her.

"Why are you looking at me?"

"I'm trying to see inside your head." Tom paused. "Jesse is my daughter. I will see to her needs as her parent. Not as a favor, or to be of help, but because she is my responsibility and I relish the duty. There is nothing for you to appreciate."

It shocked her to hear him say what she had thought all along. He was there to tend to his responsibility. Her biggest concern, the driving force behind her decisions, had been to relieve him of a sense of duty and he boldly confessed that is why he was there. "So, that's it then? You are fulfilling responsibilities?"

"That's what you heard? That's what you think? Your thought process is a mystery to me."

"That is what you said. Your words, no subtlety."

"What I said and what you translate it into in your head are miles apart."

"What do you mean?"

"Hasn't my being here meant anything to you? Am I mistaken? Haven't you been feeling what I've been feeling? Forget about what you think, Ainsley. What is in your heart?" He was pushing into territory that left her feeling vulnerable.

"I'm sorry. What about my heart?" The steam rose from the kettle as she poured hot water over tea bags.

"You heard me." Tom was waiting for her answer.

Her nerves compelled her to find words. "It's been wonderful having you here, not because we needed you, but because I've enjoyed your company." Her words seemed to her to come from the heart. "Let's leave it at that. It's for the best."

"It's for the best?" Tom repeated. "Just like that, you decide for everyone? Do you think you might not know what is best for us all?

And what about Jesse? Does she get to weigh in when you are deciding for her?"

Her heart lurched into a full-on forward race, leaving the trembling behind. Why did he insist on conflating Jesse with issues where she wasn't involved? "This has nothing to do with Jesse."

"The hell it does!" His voice rose. "It's not about my time, either. It's not up to you to help me manage my life, my business. I am to decide how I spend it. I'm here by choice. Let me choose to be right where I am. Right here."

"For now," she whispered.

Tom had drilled into Ainsley's deepest, most sensitive fear. How could she trust his intentions if he was only there because of extenuating circumstances? What Ainsley wanted was for him to have stayed with her all those years ago. She wanted him to have chosen her. With all these thoughts in her head, the only words that came were, "You are welcome here for Jesse. I will not stand in the way of your relationship."

"I have the relationship I want with Jesse. It's not enough. I want all three of us to be together. I want you, Ainsley. It's always been you." He tried again to get through.

She shrugged and picked up her cup to take a sip of tea. Once again, Tom was waiting for her to respond. She held the cup to her mouth and just as the brew was about to touch her lips, Tom's hand came down on the tabletop with a smack so hard it rattled the tea pot. "Damn it, Ainsley. I'm choosing you."

Ainsley's arm jiggled when Tom smacked the flat surface and the scalding brew splashed her on the lips and she dropped the cup. Jumping out of the way to avoid the spilt tea, she forgot about her ankle.

"Ahhh!" she cried out from the pain, then half reached, half fell for Tom, who was already on his feet beside her. He steadied her balance, forgetting they had been at odds moments ago.

"I've got you." Tom's arms came around her and he lifted her up.

"Let me set you down." He carried her through the kitchen. "We need to check that ankle."

He administered first aid, unwrapping the bandage and pressing. "Does this hurt?"

"No," Ainsley said as tears welled up.

"Then why are you crying?"

"I don't know…" she said through tears. She couldn't feel her ankle. Her scalded lip was numb. It frustrated her to feel so emotional and out of control.

She had been attempting to piece together what Tom said before he whipped his hand on the table. He was defining his reason to stay and care for her. He said he was right where he wanted to be. He was choosing her. She tried to articulate through sobbing breaths, realizing that with the confirmation of his feelings to her, she wished to affirm hers to him.

"Ainsley?" Tom asked, unable to decipher her babbling. "You are shaking. Is it the pain? Are you going into shock?"

"No," she shuttered. "I am not okay."

The sentiments in his eyes intensified. "What is it, Ainsley?"

Ainsley's heart was gaining confidence, pushing through the constraints. "I haven't been okay since you left."

"Since I left?" Tom asked.

Ainsley searched for the words to express the love she had suppressed for the past decade. Tom looked at her with concern.

"You left me and I was broken. So badly hurt, but I couldn't keep you here. I couldn't let a child tie you down, and I couldn't go with you." Her heart gushed. "You broke my heart, and it has remained in pieces. It has broken me for ten years."

"I am so sorry." Tom reached his hand up and thumbed her cheek, interrupting the tear flow. His caring gesture quieted her emotions. "How could I have deserted you?"

"I am sorry, too." For ten years, Ainsley had carried the unspoken apology that weighed heavily.

"If only I could reverse my decision to leave." He moved to sit beside her with comforting arms wrapping around. "I thought you would come. Part of me never stopped waiting for you to follow. I didn't know why you couldn't."

"It's history now, part of the past." Acknowledging with sympathy the overwhelmed young man Tom had been, she hugged him back. She understood his dilemma, too. His career was taking off, and he was excited, maybe a little scared, and then bewildered when his love chose not to go with him into their future. "You were chasing your dream. And you caught it."

"I did. But in doing so, I relinquished my heart." He sounded more like a heartsick boy than the proud and accomplished music man he was, and she stayed embraced to support him.

Ainsley thought about how much it must have hurt that she didn't go with him the morning he set out for a premiere tour. He, too, had been carrying that pain. "I didn't think you would want me if you knew about Jesse."

He pulled back to look at her face, and, with his hands on her arms, squeezed her intensely, then said, "I wanted you to come with me then, unconditionally. And now, I want you more."

She reached up her hand to his face and as if seeing him for the first time, their eyes connected.

"Will you go with me now?" He waited for her answer.

"Yes, I will." Ainsley then kissed Tom with sincerity and an open heart. A kiss as gentle as the energy she felt flowing between them. A kiss full of passion, full of comfort, full of happiness and contentment.

They surrendered equally to a long and sensual locking of lips, and then slowly came apart. He kissed her again, then said, "I have loved you in my dreams for so long, Ainsley. I have missed you." Ten years of longing rolled through Tom as he reunited with the piece of his life that had been missing.

Tenderly, they kissed, hungry for the love that had been there all along. She didn't need to know anything else. She was sure of how Tom felt. She knew how she felt, too, and it was liberating. From her head to her heart, there was no disconnect.

"Let's go get Jesse. I want to tell her right now." Tom pulled away from Ainsley far enough to talk, while keeping a hold of her. If he never let go again, she couldn't slip through his fingers.

"She'll be out soon. We can tell her together when we pick her up," Ainsley said. There was so much to think about. They had to get going with a plan and Ainsley wanted to start.

"While we wait for school to let out, let's talk," Ainsley added.

Out of habit, Tom stiffened at the prospect of talking. "For ten years we went according to a plan. Will you agree to spend the next ten minutes without one?"

Looking Tom squarely in the eyes, Ainsley searched for a read. Was he mad? Or was he teasing her? Squashing the signal from her brain to even question Tom's motive, Ainsley laughed. "I can live with that idea. Let me set the timer."

Tom laughed from the depths of his diaphragm. It was low and rhythmic, and it sounded like music. Ainsley loved the sound. She laughed, too, matching his timing, adding to the melody. It was time for them to finish their song.

EPILOGUE

After the Sun Sets

"C'mon, baby brother," Jesse said to William James. "We're late. They need us to be waiting off stage for our cue."

"We got plenty of time and don't call me your baby brother. I'm almost sixteen."

"You've been working on that song all day and it isn't even in our set."

"I want to be ready just in case Jacob gives me a solo."

William James, named after his two grandfathers, was tall for his age and had been told he was more mature than most boys. His musical artistry didn't give away his tender age, either. Since he was little, he confidently showed his musical prowess and vocal abilities.

At the age of fifteen, he became a valued member of his father's band, captivating audiences in stadiums and auditoriums. Sunset West could still fill every seat in the largest arenas across the country, but tonight, they played near their hometown of Sebastopol, CA, to a sold-out crowd at the Sonoma County fair.

"No matter how old you get, you'll always be younger than me, making you my baby brother." Jesse pulled her brother off the chair he'd been sitting on where he was warming up his guitar fingers. "Let's go."

Jesse was a seasoned performer herself since first taking the stage with her father, the founder of the band Sunset West, over ten years ago. After touring for a few years, Jesse transitioned to working at her father's studio, where she became a lead musician and backup singer for recording artists. Jesse had realized the results of hard work with her own successful career in country music. Now, she was passing on the family legacy of a good work ethic to her sibling.

Peeking around the side of the plywood barrier that separated the stage from the crowd, Jesse saw only a few empty chairs among the audience. The framed tent that defined the auditorium for the fair's entertainment events held no acoustical value, but nostalgically, it had its charm.

Jesse caught sight of their folks, Tom and Ainsley West, sitting in the first row. Beside them sat their grandparents: Grandma Rose and Grandpa William and Mama and Pop-pop West. Music was a family affair.

The intimate nature of playing at fairs on rickety portable stages set in front of rows of folding chairs wasn't insulting, though some musicians of her caliber might take it that way. Jesse and her musical family came from humble beginnings and never forgot their roots.

Jesse whispered a greeting to her friends and bandmates, who were waiting in the wing.

"Hey, Jacob," she gave the current lead singer a hug. "I'm glad and a little surprised to see you. How'd it go with Belle?"

"She is recovering. My dad is with her."

Jacob's father, Brian, an original member of Sunset West, had long since retired from the stage, but he supported the band behind the scenes.

Jacob continued, "The doctor said they got all the cancer and Mom will start an abbreviated chemotherapy protocol soon."

Belle, Jacob's stepmother and Jesse's godmother, underwent a lumpectomy that morning. Jesse felt surprised but grateful to have Jacob by her side on stage tonight, although she wouldn't have blamed him if he had missed the performance.

Searching her husband's eyes for the truth behind his words, Jesse could see Jacob wasn't deeply concerned. Taking Jacob's hands in hers, she said, "Let's pray."

William James and the other members all joined hands for their pre-show ritual. Standing in a circle on the grass in the small space between the make-shift venue that backed up against a line of metal portable barrier panels that separated them from the kiddie carnival rides, they bowed their heads. The machinery clanked and whirred and the laughter and squeals of delight and fear permeated the night air. In their moment of silence, the collective energy of the band gathering to pray rose above the din below, defying interference.

"Lord," Jesse started, "we pray for Auntie Belle a speedy recovery. We thank you, Lord, for guiding the surgeon's hands, as You performed the miracle we asked for. We also thank You for the audience who continue to support us, and, God, we are grateful for the gift of music through which You give joy, that people are moved by Your spirit. In Jesus's name, Amen."

"Amen," they all said in unison.

"Now, let's go out there and rock that stage." William James released his hands and his arms shot up as he pumped the air with his fists.

The band was tight tonight, playing all their latest hits and a few from the decades before. The audience full of fans and fair-goers applauded from the first song to the last, then hollered for an encore when the musicians gathered center stage for a bow.

"You stay out here, Will," Jacob said, giving permission and encouragement to the junior member as the rest of the musicians exited. "It's your turn to do a solo. Give the fans what they want."

"You are ready for this," Jesse reassured her brother, who had been preparing all afternoon on the off chance Jacob, the newest lead singer of the band, would give him the opportunity to sing and play solo.

Jesse took Jacob's hand and gave it a squeeze as they watched young William James setting a stool as close to the edge of the stage as he could.

"Thanks for this," Jesse whispered to Jacob.

"He's earned it." Jacob beamed with pride for his little brother-in-law. "He's been dropping hints for days that he wants to go out there tonight. Said he had a surprise. He is definitely ready. Soon I'll give the band over and it'll be his turn to lead."

Jesse liked the idea of her husband staying closer to home. Jacob had been touring with the band, and she missed him terribly while he was away. Brimming with joy, Jesse turned her attention to the stage where her brother was prepared to perform.

Realizing they were getting their encore, the chanting crowd quieted. Ignoring the ruckus from the fair-goers beyond the carnival tent, the only sound in the little venue under the canvas roof was the sweet melody of a lone guitar. Before he lulled them with lyrics, William James spoke, "My father, Tom West, the brilliant singer and founder of this band, told me he wrote this song for my mother just before I was born. It's called 'Sweet Innocence of Love.'"

In the front row, his parents, Tom and Ainsley, sat holding their breath, not sure what their son was about to do. Whenever they did a legacy concert and Tom played this song, William James always claimed that it embarrassed him.

William James explained to the audience how special the ballad was and how his father, after ten years of living separately, reunited with his mother, the love of his life. The audience hung on his word, sensing the youngster had something profound to say.

"Tonight, I am singing this song as a tribute to my mom and dad, and to pass it on to the next generation." Speaking so eloquently, in a manner way beyond his years, William continued to pluck the guitar.

"He has them in the palm of his hands," Ainsley whispered as she looked deep into the eyes of the man she had loved, it seemed, for all her life. She remembered a concert of his she had attended. Her son William James looked just like his father out there. "He is a chip off the old block."

Tom beamed with pride and whispered back, "Both our kids are pretty great, luv. We make a good team, don't we?"

"This one's for my sister, Jesse and her husband Jacob." William announced, then he sang. Held captive and waiting on every note, the crowd drifted along as William James wove the lyrics of his father's ballad into the night air.

> "In a small town, where memories were made,
> Two youthful hearts began a serenade.

Innocent souls, in destiny's hold,
A love story, carefree and bold."

Jesse watched from stage left and she was shocked to realize what her brother was doing.

"Through lavender fields, they would roam,
Their love growing, like wildflowers sown.
Their youthful spirit, like a wild breeze,
Exploring the depths of love's sweet seas."

William James glanced at his sister and brother-in-law to be sure they were paying attention, and winked, then went into the bridge. Jesse looked up at Jacob, wondering if he was suspicious.

"And as time went by, their love only grew,
A precious gift blessed, one heartbeat became two.
A child, the reflection of their blissful days.
A reminder of their youthful, carefree ways."

As realization took hold of Jacob's mind, he turned to his wife. "Jesse, is there something you want to tell me?"
Jesse nodded at Jacob's question, searching for courage as her brother continued the song.

"Now, as they watch their child at play,
They mirror their love in each other's gaze.
Guided by love's true light,
They cherish each moment, day and night."

"I've been wanting to tell you," tears formed in Jesse's eyes as she focused on Jacob's face, "but you've had so much going on." Jesse took a deep breath, then said, "Jacob, we are going to be parents."
William James could barely sing as he caught sight of his sister just off stage being lifted off the ground into a bear hug . He knew she told Jacob a secret she'd been keeping for a few weeks. She was pregnant. So far, William James was the only one who knew, and he

was bursting to tell the world. Being an uncle at sixteen was a pretty cool thing for a kid.

> Smiling from ear to ear, he finished;
> "They found love when they were young,
> Innocence, their guiding sun.
> Dancing through life, hand in hand,
> Two hearts destined to understand."

From their seats, Tom and Ainsley figured out the gist of William James's performance, too. Realizing they were to become grandparents, Ainsley had the strongest desire to find her daughter.

William James finished his song, and the band members joined him for the final bow. The lights came on and the band spilled into the audience and found their families for hugs and congratulations all around.

The venue continued clearing of concert-goers until it was just the band and family. As Jesse bounced from person to person, receiving good wishes, she reveled in the love that they showered over her and Jacob.

"I can't believe you did this," Jesse scolded William James, though she wasn't angry he had revealed her secret.

"I got tired of waiting for you to tell everyone."

"So you announce it on stage with a song? Well, I forgive you, baby brother," Jesse teased. "Or should I call you Uncle Will?"

Jesse was overflowing with joy. Her immediate family and all the people in her music family, too, surrounded her.

As an only child of a single parent for the first ten years of her life, all Jesse had wanted was a family. By her tenth year, she got the answer to her prayers. In a short time, God gave her a father, and then came her brother. Adding to her family were the extended members of the band, and when her and Jacob's friendship blossomed into love and marriage, Jesse felt her life was complete. Her mother always said, "God has a plan," and Jesse never doubted it.

AUTHOR BIO

Suzanne Catalano began writing fiction and non-fiction and became a published author in 1999. She recently published two books, *A Little Dog's Adventures in a Big Dog's World* (2023) and *Sun-Kissed Mountains of Home* (2024).

Drawing from her own experiences as a young, single, working mother, Suzanne brings life to the characters in her novel, *Sunset West: Love's Last Refrain*. Filled with insight and inspiration, she shares what she has learned from raising kids, horses and dogs.

In retirement, Suzanne continues writing fiction romances featuring human and animal connections that bring out the personalities of the protagonists.

A native of Sonoma County, California, where she lived her whole life, Suzanne recently moved to Tucson, Arizona.

LET'S STAY CONNECTED

If you enjoyed reading this novel, please leave a review.
Authors are rated by and through reviews. Word of mouth is the
greatest advertisement, and good or bad, a review is a useful tool for
authors to hone their craft. Thank you.

To connect with Suzanne Catalano please visit her website:
https://www.suzannecatalanoauthor.com/

Read a bio and recent interview with Suzanne on AllAuthor.com:
https://allauthor.com/author/suzannecatalano/

One of the greatest joys as an author is connecting with readers.
Please reach out. I will respond.